GREED

PAUL BYERS

www.paulbyersonline.com

ISBN-13: 978-0-9886185-2-7

Cover illustration by Andy Wenner,
www.auroraartcompany.com
Cover and interior layout by Stanley J. Tremblay,
www.findtheaxis.com
Editing by Sean Ellis
Author picture taken by Star Morris,
www.ratstarcreative.com

CHAPTER ONE

The South Pacific, 1762

"Captain! I think I see something dead astern!"

Viceroy Javier Benito Felipe Santiago gave a waving dismissal to the idea as if dismissing one of his servants. "Something? Something? Really Captain, your crew has seen 'something' every night for the past week."

With boredom and indifference he strolled to the stern railing and leaned against it, looking out over the vast dark waters. After a few moments of gazing at the empty ocean he spun around on his heels. "See, nothing there," he said as if proclaiming a great revelation.

Captain Rafael Tercero was leaning against the railing too, bracing his arm as he looked intently through his telescope, searching for any telltale signs that they were not alone on the open ocean.

"Oh really Captain," Santiago said in disapproval; "I expect such cowardice and superstition from your rabble crew, but not from an educated man and an officer in the Spanish Navy to believe in such myths as the Diablo Oscuro…"

"He is no myth Senor Viceroy," the captain replied, concentrating on the ocean and being careful not to show his irritation with the official. "He is very real."

"And just why would the great Dark Devil show up tonight of all nights?" Santiago asked mockingly. "We've all heard the stories about how this mythical pirate only shows up to attack his unwitting victims on moonless nights. I hate to disappoint you, my dear Captain, but it's a three-quarter moon tonight." Santiago spun around and pointed with the theatrics of an actor, not noticing that the moon wasn't visible.

"True," Tercero replied as he collapsed the telescope and stuck it inside his belt. "But the night sky is covered with a deep overcast from horizon to horizon, making it as dark as a moonless night. I also think he knows that this is the only night when the moon will not join us for the rest of our journey to Manila."

Viceroy Santiago was in his early twenties and was a short, high-strung man. He was wealthy and powerful and often surrounded by men who were his friends only because of his money, so he wasn't used to people not readily agreeing with him. Even though the situation was serious, Captain Tercero stifled a grin as the Viceroy walked across the deck. Wearing a white wig—a mark of his gentlemanly status—that was too big for his small stature and with his long face and hawkish nose, the Viceroy reminded him of a rooster strutting across a barnyard.

Captain Tercero, like most great officers in the Spanish fleet, had been at sea since boyhood. At twelve, he ran away from home to escape bitter poverty and a drunken father who took out his frustrations on him through almost nightly beatings. He had worked his way up from cabin boy and had achieved his first command at twenty-one. He was a hard but fair man and expected everyone in his crew to work as hard as he did. Above all, he was a cautious man and had learned to trust his instincts over the years, and tonight they were telling him that great danger was very, very near.

"But what do we have to fear from this pirate that no one has ever seen?" Santiago said. "How do we know that he even exists at all and isn't the phantom of some drunken sailor? If he supposedly kills all his victims then how do we really know he is real?" Santiago was pacing back and forth now like a lawyer presenting his case.

"True Your Excellency, but the Dark Pirate always leaves one member of the crew alive to tell his tale. Perhaps if we are attacked and overwhelmed, you can convince him that you should be the one spared to tell of his wicked deed."

The sound of muffled laughter drifted across the quarterdeck. Tercero knew it was dangerous to make fun of the Viceroy, but he had to break the men's tension and ease their spirits. Santiago ignored the jibe, not getting the joke or perhaps weighing the idea and testing its merits.

"But again, Captain, why do we have to worry? There is not a ship that can measure up to the *Victoria*. Why, her very name says it all; no pirate in his right mind would dare to even think about attacking her."

"You are correct once again, Your Excellency." Tercero replied, bowing slightly, trying to make up for his earlier comment. "The *Victoria* is not just a galleon, but a Manila Galleon." The captain's voice reflected his pride in his ship. The *Victoria's* keel was laid from the stoutest oak and her four masts were shaped from the tallest, truest pine. With gun ports up and dressed for battle, she looked like a porcupine with her three gun decks bristling with cannons, the largest being over 11 feet long and weighing over 5000 pounds.

But Tercero also knew that all this strength and power came at a price. The *Victoria* was powerful, but she was also very cumbersome, unable to outrun even the slowest of ships, and that was her greatest weakness. Still, even with her flaws, she was *his* ship. He paused for a moment as he ran his hand gently over her solid teak railing as if he were caressing a beautiful woman.

"She is the pride of the fleet and yet she is not the swiftest."

"You speak in riddles, my good Captain. We are strong and powerful; so what if we are slow?"

"I fear that it will be used against us."

"How?"

"If the enemy gets close enough to board us then they may be able to overpower us. That is why I protested so much back in Mexico about having to leave soldiers behind to take on extra cargo."

"Oh, what could a few more soldiers do?" Santiago replied, dismissing the whole idea as absurd and hardly worth his breath.

"We left over *fifty* men, Your Excellency."

"Yes, yes, and by leaving those fifty men behind we could carry an additional fifty five chests. We have 165,000 more coins to carry on the

King and Queen's business in the Far East, trading with China, Japan, and the Dutch East Indies for spices and silk."

"That may be true, but it also may cost us the ship, and your precious silver," Tercero replied, his tone sharper than it should have been.

"Oh, you are so dramatic Captain; no pirate in his right mind would dare attack us."

Suddenly off the starboard beam, a bright flash lit up the night sky followed by a muffled explosion that sounded like rolling thunder. Everyone rushed to that side of the ship, straining to see what was happening.

"There!" the lookout shouted from the topmast. "She sits about a mile out, Captain!" Two more flashes and two more thunderclaps quickly followed.

With each flash of light, the silhouette of a two-masted ship could be glimpsed before it returned to the darkness.

"He is a coward," Santiago said, seemingly unconcerned. "See, his cannon shots are landing nowhere near us."

"Yes," Tercero said quietly to himself. "Something is not right here; he is far out of effective range."

Three more cannons flashes and again the ship was not hit nor even splashed by near misses.

Santiago tucked his lace handkerchief into his sleeve and spun around, looking at the crew as if they were his audience. "See, not even close. A coward just as I said," pronouncing the matter closed and ready to move on to something else.

"Mr. Ortiz, beat to general quarters, and do it smartly!" Tercero suddenly ordered, then turned to Santiago, "and you had better have your sword at the ready, Your Excellency."

Santiago sighed and drew his rapier to appease the Capitán though he really had no idea of how to use it. Some aristocrats were trained in swordsmanship, but he had never felt the need; after all, he was gentleman, not a ruffian. In fact, it was only the third time he had ever drawn his sword from its sheath. The first time had been during a ceremony in the royal court with the King and Queen and the second time was to slice some fruit to impress a young lady when his servant had ignorantly forgotten the table knife.

"Si, Capitán." Ortiz turned to give the order, but the words never got out of his mouth because a well thrown dagger sank deep into his chest. In shock and disbelief, he stared down at the handle protruding from his chest. His eyes rolled back in his head and he slumped to the deck.

"Repel Boarders!" Tercero shouted.

Pirates suddenly appeared, swarming over the port side of the ship like locusts. Surprise now gone, the pirates let loose a volley of pistol shots that rang out like church bells on a Sunday morning, dropping the surprised crew, many of them where they stood.

Heeding the call, the crew of the *Victoria* erupted from below decks with cutlasses drawn, rushing to defend their ship. As the pirates stormed over the railing, three broke off from the main group and sprang up the stairs to the upper deck. One rushed up to attack the helmsman, the other went for the captain, while the third went for the Viceroy.

Santiago's eyes grew with fear to the size of a full moon when he saw the pirate charging at him, sword held high over his head, yelling at the top of his lungs. When he reached the Viceroy, the pirate stopped and disappointment flashed across his face as he realized there would be no challenge to this fight. Santiago straightened a bit then swished his sword through the air in a show of false bravado, which only made the pirate laugh. With a crooked, evil leer, the buccaneer brought his blade down hard, knocking the Viceroy's rapier out of his hand. Santiago let out a little yelp like a wounded puppy but stood his ground, either out of defiance or sheer fear.

Tercero heard the Viceroy's cry and quickly bloodied his blade with a deep slash to his opponent's rib cage. With his adversary crumpled on the deck, the captain turned and rushed to help the Viceroy.

The pirate turned to face his new challenger and with one hand shoved Santiago out of the way. The Viceroy landed unceremoniously in a heap on the deck, his royal pride hurt worse than his royal backside. When the pirate saw that it was the ship's captain who was challenging him, his eyes grew brighter with anticipation as he let out another high pitch yell. Now he had a real opponent to fight.

Tercero wasted no time in his attack as he continued his charge, wielding his Toledo steel more like a club than a finely crafted weapon, beating his adversary into submission. With his last blow, instead of bringing his sword straight down as he had with his last few strokes, the *Victoria's* captain dropped his shoulder and brought his blade underneath the pirate's guard to put a huge gash into his foe's upper leg. The man instantly cried out in agony and dropped down on his wounded leg. Tercero swung around in a tight circle and smashed his steel into the pirate's weakened defense. The pirate's sword went sliding across the deck and skidded to a halt in front of Santiago. Disbelief flooded the pirate's face as he looked at the Viceroy then back at the captain, but it didn't remain there for long as Tercero swung around again, and in one fluid motion, thrust his sword deep into the man's chest.

Tercero stood over his opponent, his chest heaving, feeling every ounce of blood raging through his veins, driven by a torrent of adrenaline that only battle can bring. He did not just savor the victory, but drew the very marrow out of it. At that moment, he was stronger than any oak beam in his mighty ship.

He spun around ready to dare anyone else to challenge him, but the sight before him tempered his charge and cut him deeper than any pirate's sword ever could. The deck of his once proud ship was now the center of a melee, a crowded battlefield with more than three dozen men locked in mortal combat. The clashing of steel against steel and the crackling thunder of gunfire swept across the deck like a twisted, evil symphony. Mixed in with the murderous melody was the gruesome chorus sung by dying men. Soft groans of those already wounded were accentuated by the sharp outcries of pain as blade cut flesh and powder and ball broke bone. The dirge blended with the last desperate gasps of souls departing their bodies.

Tercero's resolution wavered as he stood and gazed upon the carnage. His crew was being massacred; it was a burden he didn't think his heart could carry. Then, coming up over the railing, rising like a specter from the grave, was a figure dark as the night itself. In an instant Tercero knew it was no ghoulish apparition but the Dark Devil himself.

Looking at the butchery that lay before him, Tercero knew his ship might be lost, but at least he would have the satisfaction of sending the devil back to hell before he would meet him there. He drew his pistol and leveled it straight at the devil's heart and prayed his aim would be true.

The shot rang out and Tercero watched with great satisfaction as his bullet found its mark, hitting Diablo in the center of his chest. But his feeling of satisfaction quickly melted away like wax before the flame as Diablo staggered back a step but remained on his feet, unaffected by a shot that would have killed any other man.

Diablo Oscuro threw back his head and roared with laughter, defying death. Seeing the unnatural sight, most of the crew of the *Victoria* lost all hope and stopped fighting. They simply dropped their weapons where they stood, not knowing how to fight a man who couldn't be killed. Others panicked and hurled themselves over the railing, choosing to face the perils of the sea rather than the Devil himself.

With the fighting ended, the defeated crew of the *Victoria* was taken below decks to await their fate while Captain Tercero and the Viceroy remained topside on the quarterdeck, forced to kneel with their hands bound behind their backs, each flanked by two guards.

An eerie calm settled over the ship. Even the wind refused to pass through the rigging and the sails hung limp like curtains in a great hall. All was still and silent on the galleon, save for one sound: the methodical steps of a single pair of heavy boots moving slowly across the blood soaked deck.

Captain Tercero saw fear swirling through Santiago's eyes when he heard the sound of the boots start climbing the stairs. As each agonizing step grew closer, he could see terror shaking the Viceroy's body like a leaf being blown by a strong autumn wind. But there was something else: a stubborn, if foolish, anger rising in the Viceroy's face as he looked up, waiting for their ruthless captor to appear.

Tercero suspected the Viceroy's building fury was not for the loss of the ship or even for the treasure they carried. He was more upset at the inconvenience of it all. What a strange little man Santiago was, Tercero thought; how sad. The young Royal still didn't realize that they were all dead.

Tercero too looked up, but he was not looking for their captor to scold him for his rudeness; he was looking beyond, toward the bow of the ship. Though the galleon was now brightly lit with lanterns, it was still difficult to see all the way to the bow in the night mist. As the lights flickered, he could see the massive bowsprit with its tip disappearing into the darkness, but what he was really was looking for was just below that. He strained and could see the flowing hair on the left side of the figure-head; he could barely make it out, but it was enough.

During the construction of the *Victoria,* he had been able to have the image of his wife, Maria, used as the model for the figurehead of the mighty vessel. It had cost him dearly, both in terms of favors owed and in money paid, but it had been worth it. Maria had been duly impressed with his show of affection and was touched by the notion that she would be with him in his travels. But she was also a practical woman and was not happy when she discovered the cost.

He sighed deeply. He would miss Maria. Being a sailor's wife had not been easy for her but she had come to accept it. What would be hardest for her would be not knowing, the uncertainty of his fate. He knew that the Diablo Oscuro would leave no trace of the ship, nothing for the authorities to speculate about; nothing solid to tell the widows at home other than they had simply gone missing at sea.

Tercero strained again to get another glimpse of his beloved, but the only thing he saw was the face of the pirate captain rising above the deck as he climbed the last few stairs.

As soon as the man was standing on the deck, Santiago shrugged free of his captor's hands, and looked up at Diablo.

"I am Viceroy Javier Benito Felipe Santiago..." his voice cracking at first but becoming more sure the longer he spoke, "...and this ship belongs to King Charles III of Spain and I *demand* that you release us at once!"

Diablo smiled and raised his hand to stop the Viceroy. "Yes Viceroy," he bowed his head slightly in mock respect, "I know who you are and who Captain Tercero is, and I'm afraid you are in no position to demand anything, sir. The *Victoria* may have belonged to the King at one time, but she now belongs to me."

"Captain," one of the pirates interrupted, "the longboat is coming alongside."

"Longboat?" Santiago asked.

Diablo nodded, and the men holding Tercero and Santiago helped them to their feet then let them walk over to the starboard side of the ship. Leaning over the railing, they saw a twenty-five-foot longboat with a crew of three pulling alongside the *Victoria*. Tercero recognized immediately that this was no ordinary longboat. It had a small bowsprit and was rigged with two masts, complete with yardarms and six small boarding cannons attached to each gunwale.

"Very impressive," Tercero said.

"What is? I don't understand," Santiago said impatiently.

"Don't you see?" Tercero explained. "They disguised this longboat to look like a real ship from a distance, especially at night. And see the cannons? With a little extra powder they'd make a loud report and bright flash just like a culverin would firing from long range. We saw just what we expected to see. While this 'pirate ship' distracted us, the real one slipped alongside and boarded us." Tercero paused for moment then looked directly at Diablo. "I understand *this* deception, but the bullet?"

Diablo smiled and reached in under his coat and pulled out a steel plate and threw it on the deck. The indentation of several bullets could be clearly seen.

"Of course," Tercero said quietly, and then looked directly at Diablo, "I hate to say this, but I admire your ingenuity and cleverness, sir."

"You admire this scoundrel?" Santiago scoffed. "I shall be sure to include that in my report to the King."

Diablo roared with laughter, "and what makes you think that you will ever get to write that report?"

"You're not going to kill me." Santiago said smugly. "The ransom the King will pay for me makes me far more valuable to you alive than dead."

Diablo smiled and shook his head. "With all the treasure you've got on board this ship, I don't need the *small* ransom the King and Queen *might* pay."

The arrogance quickly drained from Santiago's face. "But, but...you always leave one person alive to tell of your great victory so the world would know who did this. Isn't that so Captain?" Santiago looked at Tercero desperately for confirmation as if his word would be enough to make it so. "And we all know that that person should be me. After all, I am a Viceroy and of royal blood."

"What do you think Captain?" Diablo said looking at Tercero. "Should I let him live or you?"

"Why this is preposterous. I should be the one to live," Santiago protested, his smugness returning.

Captain Tercero just shook his head slowly. "It doesn't matter; he won't let either of us go."

"Of course he will, he has too. I'm sorry Captain, but you do understand that I should be the one set free."

"No, Viceroy Santiago, I'm afraid the good Captain here is correct," the pirate said. "You see, with this much silver and gold at stake, His Majesty is not just going to write it off, he's going to want it back. So this time, I don't want anyone to know it was me. It's better to let them think your disappearance was just another one of the great mysteries of the sea rather than have half the Spanish fleet in the Pacific looking for me."

Just then, two pirates came struggling up the stairs, hauling a large chest between them. "Captain, I've never seen anything like it," one of the men said. "The holds are full of these chests, and I mean full."

"You should have brought more men and fewer chests." Diablo said, looking at the Viceroy. The heavy chest landed with a loud thud as they laid it at their captain's feet, presenting it to him like an offering to an angry god. Diablo glanced at Tercero and then at the Viceroy as he smiled and threw back the lid.

The chest was completely full of silver pieces-of-eight. Diablo grabbed several handfuls and threw them to his crew standing on deck. "You see Viceroy, with this much wealth I may just have to retire." He walked leisurely across the deck, turned around and leaned against the railing as if he were on summer holiday. "Maybe I'll return to Spain as a rich gentleman, perhaps buy an estate in the country. I hear yours might be for sale?"

Diablo burst out in laughter again then gestured for the chest, along with the two prisoners to be taken below decks.

Viceroy Javier Benito Felipe Santiago disappeared down the hatchway with a look of sheer terror and disbelief on his face while Diablo Oscuro's laughter rang in his ears.

CHAPTER TWO

South Pacific, present day

"Captain on the bridge!" The young crewman barked out, then snapped to attention.

Captain Hiram Yates stood in the doorway, hands clasped behind his back, arching on the balls of his feet as he surveyed his bridge. Yates was solidly built; standing six-foot-two with short neatly trimmed dark hair, deep set eyes and a firm jaw. More than just a mariner, he preferred to see himself in the vein of the great sea explorers of old, like Magellan and Cook, since his job was searching for the great mysteries that the sea was so unwilling to surrender.

Yates strode over to the helm in his neatly pressed khaki uniform. "Status!" he barked out in his best command voice to the sailor on duty.

"Holding steady on course 237 at sixteen knots, sir!" the helmsman barked back with nearly equal enthusiasm.

He nodded slightly and a smile slowly curled his lips; all was as it should be. But suddenly a dark cloud appeared on the captain's horizon as he saw his first officer sitting in the radio room. With furrowed brow, Yates walked over and bent down, addressing his second-in-command in a low voice.

"Mr. Murphy, you are not in proper bridge attire; did you not get my orders? Although your khaki pants and open collar shirt are within regulation, I believe that as officers it is our duty to set an example for the crew."

The first officer turned slowly and was careful to keep the irritation out of his voice. "Begging the captain's pardon, but this is a mineral/oil research vessel, not the bridge of a Navy cruiser. I understand that a certain amount of discipline and decorum are necessary, but I think that dress uniform for the bridge duty officer is a bit much... sir."

He kept his sigh to himself. He knew the captain meant well, but he took himself a little too seriously at times. Before Yates had a chance to retort, the navigator spoke.

"Captain, I have a blip on the radar."

With a scowl, Yates shot Murphy a "we'll finish this later look," then turned and walked over to the radar station on the other side of the bridge. "What have you got, Price?" Yates said as he leaned over the scope. "Plane, ship, or land?"

"Land sir." Sarah Price was the ship's technician, running the radar, sonar, and the computer modeling when the ship did test drills.

"What island are we close to, Mr. Crawford?"

Doug Crawford was the communications and navigation officer and technical whiz aboard the *Pacific Searcher*. He was of average height but supported more than average weight, caring a spare tire that would fit a Mack truck. He had round, gold wire rimmed glasses that made him look a little like John Lennon, and kept his blond, shoulder length hair pulled back in a ponytail most of the time. Crawford's long hair drove Yates crazy, but the captain tolerated it because Crawford was the best at what he did.

Crawford punched a few buttons on his console then pushed his swivel chair to the door of his office and stuck out his head. "We aren't near any islands, Captain. The nav-com shows nothing within two hundred miles of us. I think Sarah's equipment must be freezing up because it's so cold over there. *My* equipment, however, is working perfectly fine."

Sarah didn't miss a beat as she continued monitoring her equipment. "Better check your hard drive Doug; I heard it was a little 'floppy' after our last port call."

Murphy raised an eyebrow, the gauntlet had been thrown down and he could tell there was a battle brewing between the techno-nerds. Like his counterpart, Sarah had shoulder length blond hair, but that's where all similarities ended. Sarah was young and as beautiful as she was smart. She wore jeans and a T-shirt or sweatshirts most of the time and neither diminished her figure.

Murphy remembered the first time they had attended a formal function at corporate headquarters and all the whispered comments about how well she cleaned up.

"*Both* of you check your equipment." Murphy ordered, saving them from the wrath of the captain.

"Yes sir!" they replied in unison.

Murphy stifled his laughter at Sarah's comeback as he made his way into the chart room looking for the paper charts of the area. Yates believed in technology but he was also a firm believer in being prepared, so he maintained hard copies of all the charts that were in the computer. Murphy searched the massive wall of charts then grabbed the tube he was looking for and unrolled the chart on the table and studied it for a moment.

"Doug's right, Captain. The chart shows nothing in the area." Even before he could turn around, he felt Sarah's icy stare drilling into him as if he had betrayed her. They had been divorced for nearly a year now and yet her stare still bothered him. Though there had been no betrayal, she still blamed him…for everything.

"That's assuming that Doug's coordinates are correct," he quickly added, trying to keep peace on the bridge.

Yates slowly sat down in his chair, placing his elbow on the armrest then put his head in hand, assuming the position of Rodin's *Thinker*.

And like the statue, Yates was deep in thought. What if, just what if, this truly were an uncharted island? He, Captain Hiram Fitzgerald Yates had discovered a New World. He would be the first to walk on virgin territory, and he too would know what it was like to be in the shoes of Columbus, Magellan, and the other great voyagers of the past. His name would go down in history next to theirs as one of the last great explorers.

Yates sprang into motion as he started shouting out orders as if he were taking the *Pacific Searcher* into battle.

"Helm, give me full speed ahead! Mr. Murphy, check all the maps and crosscheck with the available computer and paper charts for whose waters this mysterious island lies in. I want to know if it's in international waters or if it falls under anyone's sovereign jurisdiction. Mr. Crawford, Ms. Price, continue to monitor the situation and your equipment. I want to know if there are any other ships or aircraft in the area and I want to know if *anyone's* equipment is malfunctioning."

Yates turned and faced his first officer. "Mr. Murphy, you will also prepare a landing party and survey team."

He turned back and addressed the entire bridge. "Okay people, let's stay focused." The usually dull and quiet bridge was now transformed into a beehive of activity as the crew began their assigned tasks.

Murphy smiled. Yates may have been a lot of things, but there was no doubt that this was *his* ship.

The *Pacific Searcher* was a two hundred and ten foot, state-of-the-art oil exploration vessel, owned and operated by WWEC-- the World Wide Energy Corporation. The ship was designed to search for new deposits of oil and natural gas but she also had the ability to drill and take samples to a depth of three thousand feet, making her one of the few ships in the world capable of that feat.

But what really set the WWEC flagship apart was her communications system. The *Pacific Searcher* maintained constant, uninterrupted contact with the corporate headquarters' mainframe computer. It had more computing power than many small countries and was constantly being updated in real time, not only with mundane information such as weather reports from around the world for any natural disaster that might affect the land base or fleet operations but also for any sudden changes in the political climate in a foreign nation that would affect supply and demand.

It not only monitored civilian traffic but military as well, keeping track of sea, land, and air operations with a closely guarded and little known program that predicted fuel usage and automatically diverted resources to anticipate how military needs would affect civilian markets.

Thirty-seven minutes later the words that all sailors long to hear came from the forward lookout: "Land ho!"

It was a squawk delivered over the ship's intercom rather than a shout from the crow's nest but the message still carried the same weight as it had for centuries.

Sarah spun around in her chair, feeling vindicated. "I told you there was nothing wrong with my equipment."

"And there's nothing wrong with mine either," Crawford quickly shot back.

"Excuse me, sir," Murphy interrupted, wanting to stop the feud before it could get started again. "But why are you so interested in this island, Captain?"

Yates was standing at the front of the bridge peering through his binoculars, trying to get a glimpse of their mysterious island.

"Just think about it Mr. Murphy. In this day and age we can put a man on the moon, pick up the phone and talk to anyone on the planet, we have satellites that can count the hairs on your head from a hundred miles up, and yet we may have an island here that man didn't know existed until now."

"Yeah, I hope we don't find the island surrounded by a mysterious fog, a fifty foot high fence and a giant ape on the other side," Sarah added, raising a chuckle from everyone on the bridge.

Yates lowered his binoculars, turned and frowned at her. "You're missing the whole point here, people. We have the chance to become true explorers; to walk were no man has walked before, to see things that man has not seen before."

"To boldly go where no man has gone before!" Crawford said, not wanting to be outdone by Sarah.

"Are we going to raise the flag and claim the island in the name of WWEC?" Murphy kidded.

"As a matter of fact, yes," Yates replied. "While it's not a slam dunk, if the island is uninhabited and not under anyone's control, then it goes a long way towards solidifying our claim. Any oil deposits that we find we could claim as property for WWEC and we could also get a healthy bonus if anything of value is found there."

"I like the sound of that," Crawford said.

"Yes, I thought you might." Yates turned his attention from Crawford to his first officer. "Who do you have lined up for the landing party, Mr. Murphy?"

"I've got you, myself, Sarah, and Doug. We can always come back later with more of the crew if we find anything."

"Very well; we should be making landfall soon." Yates raised his binoculars again and turned his attention back to the mysterious island. "All of you make whatever preparations you need and gather your equipment. We'll meet on the boat deck in precisely one hour."

CHAPTER THREE

Although Murphy knew Yates would never admit it, he could tell that his captain *was* just a little disappointed that the island wasn't surrounded by a mysterious fog or that there wasn't a massive wall left behind by an ancient race. At a glance, the island looked like one of a thousand others that dotted the vast Pacific.

Murphy was standing on the outside port bridge wing, enjoying the warm sunshine as the cool breeze caressed his face and watching as the clumps of green on the horizon slowly began to take shape as individual trees, vines, and rocks. He could feel the excitement beginning to build throughout the ship and even in himself. After all, it wasn't every day you could land on an uncharted island and claim it for King and Country, or in this case, for the economic gain of the WWEC.

Sarah's radar showed the island to be an egg-shaped mass of land about nineteen miles long and fifteen miles wide. The "yolk" was a perfectly formed harbor carved out of the coral at the northern tip. There were two large mountain peaks, one that rose a couple of miles inland from the bay and another, larger peak at the island's center.

Lush, green vegetation surrounded their bases and stretched half-way up the slopes where barren rock took over. Each was crowned with a classic rim and crater. The twin peaks were no doubt the volcanic belly buttons left over from the island's violent birth; Murphy just hoped they had mellowed in their old age and had settled down to a dormant life.

Murphy looked down and was pleased to see that a school of dolphins was out on recess to accompany the ship. None of them danced on their tails or stood up and chattered like their trained counterparts at the big marine theme parks, but some engaged in a playful game of leapfrog while others darted around the ship like a pack of children following the neighborhood ice cream truck.

Ancient mariners looked upon the company of dolphins as good luck, a favorable omen that they would have fair winds and a safe journey. Being a man of the 21ˢᵗ century, Murphy didn't believe in sailing off the face of the earth, or sea monsters waiting to devour men and ships. He believed in modern technology, in computer-guided satellite navigation, radios and the steady drone and power of the ship's engines. Yet he was still a sailor and while he might not trust "red sky at night, sailor's delight; red sky at morning, sailor take warning" as an accurate weather forecast, he decided the dolphins were a good sign.

As they approached the inlet, the dolphin escort left their charge in the shallow waters and headed back out to the open sea. The *Pacific Searcher* nudged carefully into a channel that was about a hundred yards wide and perhaps a half mile long that opened into the small bay. Murphy leaned over the railing and watched the seafloor pass slowly beneath him. The seabed was a kaleidoscope of coral of every imaginable color laced with long patches of white sand. The water in the channel was a light aqua reflecting the blue sky off the white sandy bottom, but as they entered the bay, the water turned a remarkably deep turquoise as the bottom settled out seventy-five feet below their keel.

The inlet was small but with the *Pacific Searcher's* maneuvering thrusters, it was easier to turn the ship around than to parallel park the latest SUV. The bow and stern anchors dropped, not only shattering the placid waters but also the calm air, sending up a flock of birds from the nearby trees. The startled birds squawked in protest at having been disturbed, circled once, then settled back into their penthouse homes.

Murphy left the bridge and went down to his cabin to gather his gear, anticipation growing with each step. As he went, a small smile found its way to his lips as he envisioned Yates actually carrying a flag to plant on the beach.

Ten minute later, Murphy emerged from his cabin with his pack and walked the short passageway to the boat deck where he saw Sarah and Crawford watching as the crew prepared the boat to take them ashore. Sarah was carrying a single backpack but Crawford had two packs and large shoulder bag.

"What's with all the carry-on luggage?" Murphy asked, looking at Crawford.

"He thinks its Gilligan's Island and we're going on a three hour tour." Sarah said.

"Ha ha. The *Captain* wanted me to bring all this stuff. He said he might want to take soil samples and run some preliminary tests and just wanted to be prepared."

"Yeah, that sounds like the captain all right." Murphy nodded, "Okay, I want a straight answer out of your two."

Sarah and Crawford looked at each other with puzzled looks then turned to Murphy, waiting for him to explain.

"Why didn't this island show up on any of the charts, either paper or computer? I can't believe in this day and age that this really is an uncharted island," Murphy said. "I mean for Pete's sake, you can go to Google Earth and pull up a satellite picture of your own back yard."

Sarah was the first to answer. "I can't speak for Doug's equipment," she said in a conciliatory tone, "but I can say the charts are accurate because I picked them up myself from the corporate office in Hawaii. I asked if these were the latest updates and the guy said they were less than two weeks old."

"There's nothing wrong with my computers," Crawford started to say defensively, then took a deep breath and eased his tone. "Sorry. I ran a quick diagnostic before we pulled into the bay and didn't find anything wrong. I'll run a more comprehensive check tomorrow."

"Mr. Murphy, you all want to stow your gear before we lift the longboat over the side?" Murphy smiled; he never got tired of the southern drawl that seemed so out of place on the deck of a ship in the middle of the South Pacific.

"Thanks Joe Bob, good idea." Murphy and the others tossed their bags into the boat. Joe Bob smiled as he snapped the hook from the cradle straps to the crane hook and signaled to the operator, who gently raised the launch.

Joe Bob—Robert Lee Thornbird III to be exact—was originally from Georgia, and despite having been at sea for five years and having sailed all over the world, had never lost his country accent. Murphy had jokingly called him Joe Bob three years ago when they had first sailed together and the nickname stuck. Thornbird actually enjoyed the nickname because whenever anyone heard his southern accent, they automatically deducted 15 points off his IQ. So when he had all the right answers, he exceeded everyone's expectation. But he was far from being a simple country bumpkin. Thornbird had a degree in computer sciences from the University of Atlanta and was working in an apprenticeship program under Crawford.

As they watched the boat being lifted over the side, Crawford continued. "I don't think that it's that far out of the realm of possibility that we found an island that's not on the charts. After all, if you stop and think about it, the Pacific Ocean covers nearly one-third of the earth's surface and in that 65 million squares miles there are over 25,000 islands; so yeah, I think it would be easy to miss one or two. But in any case, as I said earlier, I'll run a complete diagnostic tomorrow."

"In the spirit of détente," Sarah said, "I'll help."

Crawford nodded and tilted his head; "Thanks."

"It's good to see everyone playing nicely," Yates said as he walked up. "Now if you two have kissed and made up, I'd like to go see my island."

Yates was standing in the bow with one foot raised on the gunwale. Murphy smiled as he cut the engines when they approached shore. He was sure that the captain would have preferred to hear the sound of the water swooshing past the bow when the oars dug into the water; it would have made the experience much more genuine. But modern technology did have its advantages and the slapping of the oars was replaced by the drone of a seventy-five horsepower outboard on the back of the "longboat," which was actually an 18-foot Zodiac; a rigid hulled inflatable runabout.

The entire scene reminded him of the picture of George Washington crossing the Delaware. The only thing missing was a large, three-cornered hat and a sword hanging from Yate's side. The boat slid to a stop on the white sands and Yates jumped into the surf and waded ashore.

Murphy helped the others out of the boat then walked a few feet up the beach and stopped to stretch. They had been at sea for a little over a month and it felt good to stand on solid ground that wasn't constantly swaying. It was a cloudless day and he took a moment to let the sun bathe him, enjoying its radiant warmth on his face. He deeply inhaled air that smelled of grass, trees, and dirt seasoned by the ocean's salty presence.

Looking around, they could have been in the middle of a travel brochure for a South Pacific getaway. The white sand beaches were kissed by the sun's rays and massaged gently by the waves that wrapped around the inlet. The white strip of sand sloped up from the sea about eighty feet where it met bowing palm trees and thick, lush jungle foliage.

Murphy had spent time in the South Pacific before but he had never in his life seen such a wide or vibrant array of colors. There was every shade and variation of green imaginable, all accented by the brilliant reds, yellows and oranges of exotic jungle flowers. The scene was completed when he heard a squawk and looked up to see a bird that was more brightly colored than any six-year-old's imagination could conjure up.

Murphy turned and saw that Yates was still in his own world or in another century anyway, but the rest of the crew had spread out a little and seemed to be enjoying the island as much as he was. His eyes stopped when they fell on Sarah and he felt a familiar jab of pain. This place was so romantic, the perfect setting. He let out a sad sigh knowing they would never be together again.

Almost as if reading his mind she turned and looked at him. Suddenly he felt embarrassed, like a seventh grader caught staring at his first crush. His initial reaction was to turn away but he stopped himself; no, if she didn't want to look at him, then *she* could turn away. And unfortunately that's just what she did. She smiled briefly, the kind of smile given a stranger passing on the street, and then she picked up her bag and started walking toward the tree line. It wasn't unexpected, but it hurt nonetheless.

"Just think of it, Mr. Murphy," Yates said walking up. "We may have discovered a Brave New World here." Yates took another deep breath of discovery, slapped Murphy on the back and started walking toward the jungle.

Ten feet into the tree line, Murphy knew he was out of his element as a sailor. The bright rays of the sun were suddenly filtered out by layers of jungle foliage, creating a giant web of shadows and light set against a green background. He also noticed the saltiness was gone out of the air, replaced with the heavy fetid smell of decaying plants.

Everyone one slowed down as they gawked at surroundings so foreign to them; everyone except Yates, who marched forward as if he were strolling down to the corner store.

After ten minutes of weaving in and out of the palm trees and hacking though the thick foliage, Crawford stopped, dropped his backpack and leaned against a tree, panting to catch his breath. "Are we going anyplace in particular, sir, or just walking until we reach the other side of the island?"

Yates stopped and turned around. "In case you hadn't noticed Mr. Crawford, we've been following a trail. Someone or something has made this path, so we're going to see where it leads. Once we've establish whether anyone's living on the island or not, then we'll start doing our surveys. In a few minutes we'll rest a bit if you still feel the need."

"Someone or *something*?" Crawford whispered to Sarah. "He's kidding, right?"

"Who knows?" she said, shrugging. "I hear there used to be cannibals in these islands." She pushed past him, barely able to hide her smile. Crawford, eyes wide, looked to Murphy for reassurance but the latter just shrugged as he walked by.

Crawford picked up his pack and muttered to himself as he began walking again. "Great, now I've gone from a pack mule to meals on wheels."

They continued walking in silence for a few more minutes, Murphy and Sarah exchanging glances and laughs at their shipmate's expense, and Crawford nervously staring into the jungle and jumping at every sound he heard.

"We'll rest on the other side," Yates said as they come to the base of a small hill. He paused only long enough to make sure everyone heard him, then continued on, hiking up the hill.

As he neared the crest, Yates suddenly stopped then crouched behind a fallen log. Murphy watched in bewilderment as Yates peered over the edge then turned around and motioned for everyone to get down. Murphy looked at his two companions, who were equally mystified.

Yates quickly peeked again then signaled for Murphy to join him. Murphy felt funny, sneaking up the hill like a soldier, but he was curious to see what had commanded Yates' attention. He knelt down next to the captain and anxiously peered over the fallen tree.

He was expecting just about anything but what he saw. In the stream in front of them was a young woman, perhaps in her early twenties, washing her hair. She was kneeling in the stream, softly humming as she cupped the water in her hands and let it flow over her long, dark locks. She was wearing some sort of dress made from a combination of animal hide and cloth. Murphy chuckled to himself; she looked like one of the Flintstone's neighbors.

Mesmerized, Murphy continued watching as she washed her shoulders, the sun glistening off her rich colored, brown skin. He felt like a voyeur watching her like that, but finder her here was just so unexpected. He was about to say something to the Captain when he saw a sudden flash of movement in the jungle behind her.

"Did you see that?" Murphy whispered.

Yates nodded. "Yeah, but I couldn't tell what it was."

He caught another glimpse of movement again, only this time it was closer to the girl. Whatever it was, its motion was so fluid that it was hard to tell if it was real or the sun was playing tricks on his eyes.

Murphy watched in fascination as the shadow creature moved along the edge of the jungle, and seemingly passed in and out of reality. He raised his binoculars for a better look, but just then, the shadow stopped and slowly turned. Despite the tropical heat, Murphy felt a chill run down his spine. The shadow was looking back at him.

Slowly the mysterious figure began moving forward. The eyes were the first distinguishing feature to emerge. They were large and amber with huge dark pupils floating in their centers. Set against the murky jungle backdrop, they seemed almost to glow, but it wasn't the warm friendly light of a campfire; it was a menacing, sinister, smoldering glow.

The darkness reluctantly released its grip on the creature as it inched to the edge of the clearing revealing its true nature: a black panther.

"Look at the size of that thing," Yates whispered in awe. "It must be nearly ten feet long from nose to tail and weigh a good two hundred pounds. And look at those claws. They could tear a man to shreds with just one swipe. That would make a great center piece for my trophy room."

"That thing's about to have that girl for lunch and all you can think about is how good it will look in your trophy room?"

Yates frowned and was about to rebuke his first officer when he noticed the panther tensing its shoulders, preparing to pounce.

Yates drew his pistol and jumped over the log and fired a shot in the general direction of the panther. The shot sounded like a howitzer as it shattered the stillness of the jungle. The air came alive with the sound of rushing wings as startled birds took flight.

The big cat froze like a statue, its velvety black coat glistening in the sunlight. The only movement came from its eyes, darting back and forth looking for the source of the great noise. Suddenly they stopped and rested on Yates. The panther stared at the man and he stared back. Yates was a little surprised… and unnerved, as he looked into the animal's eyes. They held a strange intelligence in them, not the emptiness of a wild, unthinking beast as he expected. The big cat almost looked like it had a smirk on its face as it licked its mouth. Suddenly Yates' resolve began to waver.

Sensing fear, the animal made no attempt at stealth and began running full speed at Yates. Yates steadied himself and pulled up, aimed and fired at the charging beast. To his dismay, the bullet went wide, splintering a nearby branch. Undeterred, the panther continued its charge toward him. Yates fired three more rounds but all three missed because the animal was moving too fast.

Murphy watched in horror as the big animal came rushing toward his captain. He knew he had to do something, but what? He didn't have a gun. His only weapon was a machete, great against jungle vines, but he didn't think it would do much good against a beast like this. But Murphy also knew that if Yates went down, he would be the next item on the panther's ala carte menu.

The black cat was less than fifty feet away when Murphy stood and started jumping up and down, waving his arms and shouting. In a split second the animal changed targets and turned sharply toward Murphy.

Murphy gripped his machete in both hands as if it were Excalibur, and stood his ground before the raging beast. He brought the blade up but he could tell it was already too late. He had underestimated the speed of the big cat. The panther sprang and Murphy knew it would hit him in the chest.

Time seemed to stop.

He could see every detail of approaching death in vivid slow motion. The beast was so close he thought he could smell the stench of rotting flesh on the animal's breath. The panther's ears and whiskers were pushed back by its great speed; its teeth were bared in an angry snarl. The fangs looked huge, like they belonged to an ancient saber toothed tiger rather than a modern jungle cat.

Suddenly, he heard two dull pops and something seemed to snatch the animal out of the air, hurling it sideways. Instantly, everything sped up to normal time as the panther landed with a dull thud on the ground at his feet, dead. Murphy took a huge gulp of air, not realizing that he had forgotten to breathe.

"Are you all right, Mr. Murphy?" Yates said as he walked up, putting in a new magazine. "Smart thinking, distracting him like that. It made him turn, giving me a better angle." Yates slowly circled, admiring his newest trophy. "Look at the size of that thing. It'll barely fit into the longboat."

Murphy was looking, but not seeing. His heart was nearly beating out of his chest as he stared at the dead animal and realized that that could easily have been him. He had never been that close to death before, let alone being torn apart by a wild animal. He closed his eyes and took several deep breaths and released them slowly, trying to regain his composure.

As he opened his eyes, he looked over and saw that the girl was still standing in the middle of the stream, frozen with fear and surprise.

Still too shaken to speak, Murphy raised a trembling hand and pointed at the girl.

Yates saw her and holstered his gun, put on his best bar-pick-up-smile, and started toward her. That was enough to break the spell; she splashed from the stream and dashed into the jungle.

"Captain," Murphy said, after regained some composure. "Maybe we should leave before she comes back with the rest of her tribe."

Yates shook his head. "We're not going anywhere. Do you think the great explorers of old turned tail and ran at every little obstacle? No, they didn't, and neither will I. Did you forget why we came here? We came to explore this island," he said sweeping his hand before the jungle theatrically, "and that's what we're going to do.

"Besides," he continued, looking down at the panther, "I'm not going to leave this magnificent trophy here to rot in the jungle."

Murphy shook his head. "We're in over our heads here, sir. We're not set up to deal with natives. We should leave and get back to the ship."

"Did I hear somebody say leave?" Crawford puffed as he and the others came rushing up.

"What was all that shooting..." Sarah suddenly stopped in mid-sentence when she saw the dead animal. "Is that a panther?"

Crawford stepped up and peered over her shoulder. "It's dead isn't it?"

"Yes, Doug, it's dead." Murphy replied.

"I wonder how it got all the way out here," Sarah said. "I didn't know that big cats like these were native to the islands."

Crawford shook his head. "They're not, but it's not totally unheard of. Back in the old square rigger days, crews would drop off pigs on some of the islands so that when they sailed back that way they would have some meat to eat. In the case of our feline friend here, he was probably being transported and he was either lost overboard during a storm or released from the ship just to get rid of it."

"Well thank you Dr. Doolittle," Sarah said.

"Hey, I can't help it if I like reading *National Geographic*."

"No matter where it came from, we need to leave now Captain," Murphy insisted.

"Why?" Sarah asked, "What's going on here?"

"Is there another panther out there?" Crawford asked.

Murphy shook his head. "We spotted a native girl bathing in the stream over there. She was about to be lunch for kitty here when the captain shot him. I think we should go back to the ship before the other natives come back. We don't know how they'll react to outsiders."

"I think that's a good idea." Crawford added. "I mean, what if they're cannibals or something?"

Murphy frowned at Crawford and shook his head, then gave Sarah a dirty look as she started to giggle.

"They're not cannibals," Murphy insisted, with less conviction in his voice than he'd hoped for.

"Good. I'm glad you think so," Yates said, "because they're here."

At the far end of the clearing, a group of at least a dozen men emerged cautiously from the jungle with the girl tucked in behind the leader, peering round his side. The natives were dressed in loin cloths, some made of animal skins with other made of a dark colored cloth. A few of the men wore crude sandals but most were barefoot and they all were armed with spears and primitive bows. They approached hesitantly, switching their stares between the dead animal and the strangers.

"We should just leave *now* captain," Murphy urged. "Forget the animal and let's go."

"Stow it Mr. Murphy. I'm not leaving my prize, and besides, just look at them. They're carrying spears and bows; they're no match for us in a fight."

"That's what Custer said," Murphy muttered under his breath.

Yates ignored him. "Okay, everybody stay calm and we'll be just fine." Then he turned and smiled and took a few steps towards the islanders with his hands raised in a gesture of peace.

The natives continued to approach cautiously. When they were about fifteen feet away they stopped, eyes filled with a combination of wonder and fear. Then they fell prostrate on the ground.

Murphy was taken aback; he was expecting anything but this. He looked at his companions and the expression on their faces mirrored his. Even Yates seemed to be at a loss, not quite knowing how to deal with people who appeared to be worshipping him. The air was filled with an awkward silence that was finally broken as the leader spoke, his face still buried in the ground.

"I am Hoku. The *chica* said fire come from your hand and beast fall. I don't believe, but there is *pantera*, dead. You are great god. We are your servants."

Once again all four crewmembers looked at each other in stunned disbelief. Not only at the sight of people worshipping and calling them gods, but also because they were speaking in English.

"Oh, chief...oh Great Chief," Yates stammered out, still trying to wrap his head around being called a god. "We...ah...we are happy to be here." After an awkward moment he continued. "Stand, please," he said looking down at Hoku.

Slowly Hoku stood but kept his head low, not looking Yates in the eyes.

"I must say I am surprised," Yates paused and turned to his crew, "in more ways than one," then looked back at Hoku, "to hear you speaking in English."

"En-gl-i-sh?" Hoku said, tipping his head to one side.

"English, yes that is our language, the words we use."

A smile of understanding came to Hoku's face. "Yes, we know words of *blanca* men." Hoku said proudly. "Many years ago, *blanca* men wash up on shore. They teach us *mucho* before they die."

Crawford leaned over to Murphy and whispered. "It sounds like he is speaking in both English and Spanish. What gives?"

"It makes sense," Murphy said. "There was a lot of Spanish influence in this part of the Pacific so their native tongue probably was Spanish to begin with and if British sailors were shipwrecked here and taught them English, it would stand to reason that they would use a combination of the two and revert to Spanish if they didn't know the English word for it."

"Well, I am happy that they taught you the language of the gods," Yates replied.

"The language of the gods?" Murphy almost shouted out.

The chief looked confused, eyes darting back and forth between Yates and Murphy.

Yates shot Murphy a dirty look then continued. "I am not a god, but I am God's servant and He has sent me to your island on a quest."

"CAPTAIN!" Murphy shouted.

"Stow it, Mr. Murphy."

Murphy wanted to say more but a stern look from Yates kept him quiet.

Hoku immediately threw himself down on his knees. "We not worthy of such *honrar*," the chief said, his forehead pressed to the earth.

"Honrar?" Yates said, looking at Murphy.

"Honor, sir."

Yates nodded. "It is a great honor indeed. Will you help God's servants in our task?"

"We obey."

"Arise now, for we must go," Yates said, raising his hands dramatically. "Tomorrow when the sun rises we will return and talk with you again."

"Wait!" The chief shouted as he stood. "We *honrar* God's Servant with a *fiesta* tonight."

Murphy shook his head emphatically but Yates didn't even look his way.

"We must leave now, but we will return for the feast when the sun goes down. Now go and prepare!" Yates shouted, using his sternest command voice. The natives responded by scattering and fleeing back into the jungle.

As soon as they had disappeared into the thicket, Murphy spoke. "Moses, Moses, Moses, are you going to part the stream now so we can walk across on dry ground? Begging the captain's pardon sir, but what in the hell are you thinking telling them you're a servant from God?

"Stand down, Mr. Murphy," Yates ordered. Yates paused and took a deep breath to calm the situation, then continued. "Look at them. To these people we *are* gods; just think about it. If a race of space faring creatures, with all their advanced technology landed in New York tomorrow, don't you think that some people might consider them gods or at the very least having been sent by God? This is no different; we have technologies that far outweigh their ability to comprehend, so to them we must be gods, besides, I kind of like being called the Servant of God."

Murphy shook his head. "It's wrong for you to pass yourself off as God's special servant. The ramification could last long after we're gone."

"This isn't Star Trek here and the Prime Directive," Yates answered, his irritation building again. "We may have a tremendous opportunity here to make a lot of money, and I intend to take full advantage of it. If this island has any natural resources then the natives will know where they are and will make our job a lot easier. Plus, if this island is in international waters and if no nation has claims on it, then there's just that much more profit for the corporation with no negotiating fees and that means a substantially larger bonus for us!"

"What do you think?" Murphy said, turning toward Sarah.

"I think the captain has taken a potentially dangerous situation and turned it around. Now we have nothing to fear from the inhabitants and best of all, they will help us find whatever's out there."

Murphy frowned, clearly not getting the support he was hoping for. "Doug?"

"This isn't a democracy, Mr. Murphy," Yates said, before Crawford could reply. "Agree or disagree with my methods, I don't care. You will follow my orders. When you get your own ship, then you can do things your way. Until then, *I'm* the captain."

"Yes sir!" Murphy snapped back.

"Good. Now let's get my panther to the boat and back to the ship. We have a dinner party to get ready for."

The trip back to the beach was quiet as Yates led the way, while Murphy and Crawford struggled with the dead animal with Sarah bringing up the rear of the procession.

Yates personally supervised the unloading of his prize panther and ordered it stored in the ship's freezer until they got back to port. When he was satisfied that his trophy would be properly taken care of, he called over the rest of the landing party.

"Mr. Murphy, you and Mr. Crawford will wear your dress whites tonight, as will you Ms. Price. I want you all to treat this as a formal dinner, acting just as if it were with the heads of the WWEC. If we can gain their trust and cooperation then it will make our jobs a lot easier. Mr. Murphy, would you please find some trinkets that we can give to the chief that will duly impress him? Any questions?"

Yates didn't wait for an answer, but spun on his heel and headed for the bridge. Crawford shrugged and left for his cabin, leaving Murphy and Sarah on deck.

Murphy turned to Sarah, making no effort to hide his irritation. "You know you could have given me a little help back there. I think it's wrong for the captain to be leading these natives along like this. I think that..." He trailed off when he saw a familiar, angry glare on her face.

"There you go again, thinking that you're right and everybody else is wrong, thinking that everybody should agree with you."

"And there you go," Murphy said, "never letting me finish, never listening to my whole idea or and letting me complete a sentence. Once you hear something that *you* don't like or disagree with, you stop listening."

"That's because you generally don't say much of anything worth listening to," Sarah shot back.

Murphy could feel his face turning red. "That's because you only hear what you want to hear. You mean to tell me that you think it's okay for us to pretend to be servants of the Almighty and to take whatever we want from them?"

He paused, suddenly finding himself back in familiar, painful territory. He always hated it when they fought and they had been doing a lot of that the last few months when they were still married. He was almost glad they had finally split up just so the fighting would end...almost. And now here they were, fighting again, and he didn't even know why.

Murphy shook his head as he was about to say something when four crewmen walked by, carrying the dead panther.

"See that?" Sarah said. "That's us. We are like that panther. Dead! I will work with you on this ship on a professional level but not on any other level. It's over between us, Dallas. The sooner you can accept that, the better." She turned and disappeared down a hatchway.

Murphy leaned over the railing, shaking his head. He drew in a deep breath and then let out a long, heavy sigh. What had possessed him to take this assignment when he knew she would be on board?

Murphy stayed on deck for another hour, alone with his thoughts as he watched the sun slowly sink behind the island. The colors were tremendous with reds, oranges, and yellows so brilliant that when the sun settled behind the island, it looked like the trees were on fire.

Would the servants of God be allowed to stay this time or would they be kicked out of Eden again?

Murphy finally decided that he had felt sorry for himself long enough and threw his melancholy mood over the side of the ship. He held his head up high and started below decks. He still had a job to do and regardless of whether he disagreed with the captain or Sarah, he was going to do it.

CHAPTER FOUR

Yates waited to board the longboat until after the first of the evening stars could be seen, wanting to make his grand entrance in the dark. They were met at the shore by two native men, each carrying a crude torch. Both bowed low, and without looking him in the eye, nervously asked the Servant of God if he would please follow them. Yates simply nodded and gestured for them to lead the way.

Soon after leaving the open beach, the lights from the ship disappeared and the shore party was swallowed up by the darkness of the jungle. The dim light cast by the torches was barely enough to see the path, let alone keep the oppressive darkness at bay. An occasional fleeting glimpse of starlight managed to penetrate the canopy, but the jungle was jealous of its hold on the newcomers.

Even though the night air had been cool at the beach, in the jungle it was still hot and humid. They were surrounded by strange sounds, encircled by a constant humming from the insects that crawled on the ground, clung to the tree branches, and flew through the air. It reminded Murphy of the steady drone of the engines on the ship, which should have offered a sense of security. But unlike the engines, the humming of the insects had a disturbing tone to it that left him feeling uneasy.

Sometimes the light from the torches would reflect off the eyes of animals hiding in the jungle, watching the strange looking creatures intruding into their domain. Some eyes glowed with the reflection of the torches while others shone with a red glow that looked menacing, almost evil.

The members of the group started sweating as they trudged through the underbrush, partly because of the dress uniforms that Yates made them wear, partly because of the heat and humidity of the jungle, but mostly because of the anticipation of the unknown fate that lay ahead.

Crawford didn't wait long to start complaining. "Captain, why did we leave the ship so late? It's creepy out here and what if that little kitty you killed earlier has a wife who's out looking for her wayward mate? And why can't we use our flashlight? It's not like we don't have enough batteries. I can barely see my hand in front of my face."

"I hear that on these isolated islands anacondas have been documented up to thirty feet and longer," Sarah teased, talking in a low tone as if she were telling a campfire ghost story. "And did you know that once they get a hold of you and wrap their coils around you, they squeeze you so tight that they break all of your ribs? And that the only way to get one off of you is to cut its head off?"

"Captain!" Crawford protested, like a little brother telling on his big sister.

"Sarah! Why are you scaring Doug and lying to him like that?" Murphy scolded, shaking his head. "I mean, really. At least tell him the truth. Like how when it swallows you whole, you're still alive!"

Sarah laughed and Murphy smiled to himself. It was good to hear her laugh at something he said after their earlier argument.

"That's enough Mr. Murphy, Ms. Price. I do not need the two of you upsetting a member of my bridge crew right before an important meeting by scaring him with half-truths and innuendoes."

"Thank you Captain," Crawford said, a sense of justification filling his voice.

"You forgot to tell him that they eat their victim's head first and that it takes hours for them to swallow all of you."

"Captain!" Crawford shouted above the howls of Murphy and Sarah.

After the laughter died down, Yates continued. "Okay everyone, just follow my lead. Mr. Murphy, I know you don't approve of my methods but please remember that I expect you to follow orders and not to disrupt the negotiations. Are we clear on this?"

"Yes sir," Murphy said. After returning to his cabin from their earlier trip, he had thought it over and decided that if no one got hurt and that they didn't change the natives' religious beliefs, then he could go along with it.

As they approached the village, they began to catch flickers of light penetrating the dense foliage. Yates dismissed his guides just before they stepped into the clearing.

"Why are we stopping?" Murphy asked.

"Because I want to make an entrance befitting the Servant of God. I will step out first, Mr. Murphy you will be behind me, Mr. Crawford to his right, Ms. Price to his left. On my mark, Mr. Crawford, you will light the lantern in your left hand and turn on the flashlight and shine it upwards with your right. Ms. Price you will do the same thing using the opposite hands and Mr. Murphy, you will hold your lantern so it is even with my shoulders and shine your flashlight straight up. I know it's a bit theatrical and over the top but I think it will help reinforce to the natives our claim of who we are and make dealing with them a lot easier. And remember, follow my lead."

The four officers from the *Pacific Searcher* stepped silently through the jungle curtain and onto the stage of the village clearing. "Okay on my mark, three, two and one!"

"Heeeeerrrrrrre's Johnny," Murphy whispered under his breath just before they turned on their lights. The three lanterns flashed on behind Yates, bathing him in light and silhouetting him against the dark jungle, giving him an angelic appearance. The flashlight beams were the crowning touch as they reached skyward.

An audible gasp escaped from the villagers and they all quickly fell to their knees. Yates was pleased that the display was having the desired effect.

"Now that's what I like," Sarah remarked. "Men bowing down before me."

"Hush!" Yates whispered and then started walking forward. After allowing the natives to grovel for a few moments, Yates ordered them to rise.

The chief was the first to look up and slowly got to his feet. He took two steps forward then bowed low before Yates. The man wore a gold helmet that reminded Murphy of something a conquistador would wear along with matching chest armor. Underneath that, he wore a roman style leather skirt. Draped over his shoulder was a long, brightly colored cape made of layered feathers from at least half a dozen different birds.

"We happy you come, oh great Servant of God. You *honrar* us. Come please." The chief clapped his hands and eighteen warriors, nine on each side, lined up on the path that led to an area that had been prepared for them. Each warrior had breastplate armor like the chief's except it was polished silver and not gold. They didn't have the leather skirt like the chief's; each one wore an oversized loincloth that looked to Murphy like baggy gym shorts. The honor guard stood at attention with long spears and lit torches in their hands.

The chief bowed low again then gestured for them to walk down the center between the warriors. Each of the guards kept his stare straight ahead and ignored the crewmembers as they walked by. Murphy was apprehensive about walking through the forest of spears. Suddenly Sarah's earlier comment about cannibals wasn't so funny anymore. He wasn't sure if they were being shown the dinner table as the guests of honor or as the main course.

After passing through the gauntlet, the Chief led Yates to a raised table where the two of them sat. Murphy, Crawford, and Sarah were seated at a lower table to their right and three village elders were seated at another table to the Chief's left. One of the natives wore a large and very colorful ceremonial headpiece made of feathers, reminding Murphy of an Indian Chief's headdress from an old western. Murphy figured him to be the head witch doctor. The man sitting next to him looked very old and was dressed in a long cloth coat that looked like he had just stolen it from a bum on skid row. The coat looked as old as the man wearing it and he guessed he was the tribal elder or wise man.

"Did you see the chief's armor?" Crawford said to Murphy. "It looks like real gold. Where would they get something like that?

"I was wondering that myself. They certainly don't have the technology to forge it themselves."

"Maybe it was left by pirates," Sarah said, knowing Murphy's fascination with them."

Murphy smiled, not knowing if she was being serious or sarcastic.

"Arrrrr Matey," Crawford said.

"Pirates or not, I can't wait to ask Hoku about it."

Murphy took a drink then noticed the last man sitting at the table with the Medicine man and the tribe elder. He had a mean expression that somehow reminded Murphy of the way the panther had looked at them when it was charging. He could tell that the man didn't want them there and that he didn't trust these outsiders. A good head and shoulders above most of the other natives, with a powerful build, Murphy felt safe in his assumption that he was looking at the village's best warrior.

The warrior glared at them one at a time, sizing up each of them. He gave Murphy a long, steady stare that was almost a challenge in itself. Murphy took an immediately dislike to the man. He appraised Crawford but his gazed didn't rest on him too long as he clearly didn't see Crawford as much of a threat. Next his eyes fell upon Sarah and they lingered on her longer than the other two. His eyes moved up and down her and when he was done, he looked back at Murphy and threw him a small, wicked smile.

Murphy wanted to leap up and beat the arrogant S.O.B. right then and there but common sense, his commitment to the mission, and the fact that the warrior outweighed him by a good fifty pounds kept him in his seat. Murphy was fuming when he looked over and saw that Sarah had stolen a glance at the warrior.

He wanted to explode but then he didn't want to give either one of them the satisfaction. If Sarah wanted to play that game then fine, that was her business. He quickly glanced at the villagers who were sitting in front of them around the large fire like an audience, and noticed that several girls were looking at him.

The girls were standing in the back by one of the huts and he recognized one of them as being the girl they had seen earlier bathing in the stream. They were huddled together like a group of teenagers at a school dance. They were all in their mid to late twenties and were wearing short, wraparound dresses and each had a different colored flower in their hair.

Three were tall, with long, straight hair and the forth was shorter and wore her hair up. One girl in particular caught his eye. Her hair was longer than the others, almost reaching down to her hips and it framed the soft features of her beautiful face perfectly. She looked at him then quickly glanced down, then sheepishly looked back up with a tiny, shy smile. If Sarah wanted to play games, then he could too. Murphy smiled back.

Then, just like in a Hollywood movie, Hoku clapped his hands and the evening erupted into motion and sound. The floorshow began as the four women who had been standing in the back came forward and starting dancing to the steady beat of drums and a crude xylophone made from bamboo.

Their dancing reminded Murphy of the shows he'd seen the hotels in Hawaii put on for the tourists. There were a lot of similarities with the hand motions and swaying of the hips but the dances were definitely different. They danced in front of the Chief and Yates first, then moved over to the table where Murphy Crawford and Sarah were sitting.

Murphy looked over and saw a big smile on Crawford's face as one of the dancers, the shortest one of the group, seemed to pay special attention to him. Murphy also sported his own smile as the girl he'd looked at earlier kept making eye contact with him. He thought about looking over to see Sarah's reaction but decided against it. Why should he give her the satisfaction of letting her know he was thinking about her?

They danced in front of them for a few more minutes then continued swaying as they moved over to the other side and danced for their fellow tribe members.

Murphy wouldn't have been surprised to see men jumping out of the shadows with flaming torches, twirling them in rings of fire, and start dancing around. But no fire dancers appeared and the girls slowly swung and swayed their way into the background.

As the dancers left, a seemingly endless line of servers appeared and began bringing in baskets full of colorful and exotic looking fruits and placed them on each table. Next, platters of fresh seafood ranging from crab, shellfish and several kinds of white fish were brought in and served to each guest.

Murphy looked down at the food before him and was impressed with the natives' spread. He also noticed that instead of being served on crude wooden plates and wrapped in leaves, they were served on real plates. He was not an expert, but the dishes looked like they were fine China.

Another surprise was that they were given knives, forks and spoons. Murphy picked up one of the forks and marveled at its intricate design work; and judging by its look and feel, decided they were sterling silver. There was something familiar about the patterns on the plates and in the scrollwork on the silverware but he couldn't quiet place it.

Who *were* these natives? How, in the middle of nowhere, did they come up with Spanish armor that belonged in a museum and sterling silver flatware? He wanted to have a very long talk with the captain about these natives but the questions would have to wait as the ceremony continued when four men walked down the center of the camp carrying a large, roasted wild boar on their shoulders and placed it in front of Hoku and Yates.

After nearly an hour of song, dance, and eating more than he should have, Murphy couldn't contain his curiosity any longer.

"Chief Hoku, where did you get these beautiful plates? Did you make them yourselves?"

"I happy you like. They were left by our old ones in a *almacén*, hidden in jungle."

Almacén? Murphy sat there for a moment racking his brain. *Almacén?* What did it mean? His Spanish was fair, but not great. Suddenly his heart started to race as he understood the meaning: *storehouse!* "Is there anymore in the almacén?" he asked.

"I do not know. It is deep in jungle and way there is lost."

Just then they heard a grunt coming from the natives' table. "Chief Hoku, the way is not lost. I can take Great Servant of God there."

Murphy turned to see who was speaking; it was the Neanderthal that had been eyeing Sarah.

Hoku smiled and turned to Yates, "This is Kekao, our bravest warrior. If you wish, he can take you to *almacén*."

"Thank you, Chief, but that won't be necessary. However if my First Officer would like to go then he has my blessings."

Murphy gave Yates a sideways glance then looked at the chief. "Yes Chief, I would like very much to go."

Kekao frowned. "It dangerous *viaje* to *almacén,* deep in jungle; can helper live without your *proteccion,* Great Servant?"

"I'll be just fine," Murphy shot back, not failing to notice the small smile that curved around Kekao's lips.

"Captain, I would like to go too," Sarah said.

"Jungle no place for woman," Kekao said firmly.

Sarah's pleasant smile fell away. "In that case, I'm definitely going then," she said defiantly, then quickly threw in "Sir!"

Murphy shook his head. That was the wrong thing for Kekao to say. He couldn't keep her out of the jungle now even if he tried.

Yates smiled. "Yes, Sarah, I think that would be a good idea. Mr. Crawford, I think you should join the expedition as well."

Crawford nearly choked on the piece of fish he was eating. "Begging the captain's pardon sir, but I was thinking about doing some survey work around the village and mapping the coastline."

Yates shook his head. "I think you could be of greater use surveying the interior of the island and seeing if there are any indications of oil deposits. After all, we are an oil exploration vessel."

"Yes sir," Crawford replied, clearly not wanting to go.

"What is... oil?" Hoku asked.

Yates thought for a moment. "Oil is a thick, black fluid that we take and refine and use it to power our machines. In fact, we use oil to power our great vessel."

Hoku paused for a moment, thinking. "I know not of oil. There are pools of sticky mud we put on huts to keep out rain and make torches burn for long time."

Yates' eyebrow rose, "really?" He said, trying not to sound too excited. "I would like to see these pools."

"*Sí, Sí,* yes, yes," Hoku said excitedly, "I be most *honrado* to take you there."

"God will be very pleased with your help," Yates said.

"Have you been where God lives? Is it long *viaje* from here? Does it look like here?"

"Heaven is far, far away across the vast ocean." Yates said, pointing roughly westerly, "and it's a very beautiful place. It is so big that parts of it are green, like your jungle here, other parts are covered with brown desert sands as far as the eye can see and yet other parts have huge mountain ranges that reach up to the very threshold of the stars."

Hoku sat enthralled, hanging on every word Yates was saying, like a child sitting on the lap of a department store Santa Clause for the first time. "Heaven sounds *maravilloso*, can you take me there?"

Yates smiled and shook his head. "No, I'm afraid not, Chief."

"Then you show me your ship that moves across never ending waters?"

"Perhaps," Yates replied, taking a bite out of a piece of red fruit.

Murphy looked at Yates in surprise. He didn't like the idea that the captain would even consider allowing any natives on board the *Pacific Searcher*.

"Speaking of the ship, shouldn't we be going now, Captain?"

"I know you come far," Hoku interrupted. "But stay. People long to have God's Servant with them. It great *honrar* you being here."

Yates smiled, flattered by the attention, but he shook his head. "Tomorrow when we return, I would like you to show us around your island; in return, perhaps I will show you my great iron ship."

"Captain!" Murphy said sternly. "I don't think they need to see the ship. I really think we should go now!"

Hoku looked at Murphy, puzzled, then back to Yates. "Does Servant of God allow helpers to talk to him in such way? He no show you *respeto* you deserve."

Yates smiled at the chief, then turned his head and looked at his first officer with a look so hard that Murphy knew he'd better not say a thing. "He is young and has much to learn. But he is right; we must leave."

Yates stood and the others followed suit. "Oh, before we go, I have brought you gifts in appreciation for your great kindness to the Servant of God and his helpers."

Murphy approached the table and the stern look from Yates told him he had better do this right. Murphy sighed inwardly then put on his showman's face. "Oh great Chief," he started, bowing low with a sweeping motion of his left hand. "Indeed, we have brought you wondrous gifts from far across the endless waters."

Murphy reached into his satchel, and then exclaimed, "Behold!" as he pulled out a flashlight and turned it on and pointed it up toward the sky like a spotlight. "I bring you the power of light."

The natives gasped in wonder as they saw the light shining into the sky but what really got their attention occurred when Murphy brought the beam down and shined it on the chief's chest.

Hoku sat motionless as he saw the light touching his chest yet he was amazed because he didn't feel anything. He reached down and tried to touch it but Murphy moved the light. With child-like wonder and frustration, Hoku kept trying to touch the beam and Murphy kept moving it.

Fearing for his chief's safety, Kekao sprang to his feet. Murphy jumped down and stood beside the fire, wielding the flashlight like a light saber. Kekao had just taken a step forward when Murphy shined the light onto Kekao's chest. Murphy had purposely moved next to the fire so the flashlight's beam would shine through the smoke, turning it into what looked like solid beam of light. Kekao froze in place as if the beam had physical weight. Murphy, seeing a mixture of fear and anger on the warrior's face, made no attempt to hide the smirk that crossed his own.

Then, just like every child who has ever gone camping, he held his hand over the light and instantly his hand turned red and appeared to be on fire. A collective murmur swept through the village like a gust of wind. Murphy smiled at his showmanship but was even happier when the saw the mighty Kekao take a step back.

He turned off the light then walked over to the chief. "I give you the power of light. I know it will be safe in your hands, oh great Hoku."

Hesitantly, the chief reached up and took the flashlight out of the first officer's hand. He examined it closely then let out a cry as he accidently turned it on and shined it in his eyes.

Startled, he let out another shriek as instinctively he covered the light with his hand and it turned red. Fumbling frantically, Hoku managed to find the switch and turned the light off. He quickly set the flashlight on the table and glanced at all the villagers with an *I meant to do that* look, and no one dared challenge him. Murphy smiled to himself; it *was* good to be king.

Next, Murphy reached into the satchel and pulled out a cigarette lighter. He held it up for everyone to see then turned back to the chief. "You have the power of light, now I give you the power of fire!"

He held the lighter in his left hand and brought his right hand underneath it. As his hand passed in front of the lighter, blocking it from the chief's view he spun the striker and as his hand came up, a flame appeared.

Hoku's eyes grew big as this tiny stick in the Servant of God's helper's hand burned with a steady flame.

"No longer do you have to keep the hot embers lit," Murphy said, "because now oh great Chief Hoku, you can command fire anytime you wish."

He handed the lighter to the chief, only this time he showed him how to use it. Hoku greedily took the lighter and flicked it on and off a dozen times, marveling at his new found power. On the last flick, he stood and held it high for the entire village to see. Murphy almost laughed out loud as it struck him that the chief looked like the Statue of Liberty. Hoku was all smiles as he waved the lighter around to everyone's applause.

Yates stood and Crawford and Sarah followed. As Sarah walked from her table to join the Captain, Murphy noticed that Kekao was staring at her and that she cast a glance at him that lasted just a little too long in Murphy's opinion. She looked at Murphy with a coy smile. "Is there something wrong Dallas?" He gave her a disgusted look and shook his head and she replied with a small laugh which made him even angrier.

He turned away before he could give her any more satisfaction and saw that Crawford was lagging behind, talking to the native dancer who had been paying particular attention to him. The way he was fidgeting with his hands and rocking back and forth reminded him of a junior high school boy trying to get up the nerve to ask a cheerleader out.

"Doug!" Murphy barked.

Embarrassed, Crawford blushed then hurried up his goodbye. He took a few steps, turned around, and gave her a quick wave. As he did, he tripped and fell over one of the benches. Even more embarrassed, he sprang to his feet and dusted himself off. With as much pride as he could salvage, he walked over and joined Murphy and Sarah without looking back.

"Show a little professionalism." Murphy snapped angrily. "You're acting like a love-struck teenager. The only reason she's even looking at you is that she thinks you're some kind of god. She's not interested in you, Doug Crawford the man; she's interested in one of the minions of the Great Servant of God."

The joy in Crawford's face instantly drained away, his spirit crushed. He didn't even look up as he slowly turned; his shoulders slumped as he walked toward the tree line.

"That was just plain mean, Dallas," Sarah said, glaring at him. "If you want to be angry with me, that's fine, but don't take it out on Doug."

Murphy sighed. "I know, I'm sorry," he said quietly.

"Don't apologize to me." Her voice still sharp, showed him no sympathy. "He's the one you need to apologize to." She gestured with her head toward Crawford, then turned and joined the captain.

Murphy just stood there and watched as his friends, both of whom he had managed to make angry, walked away. He thought about calling out to Crawford but knew it wouldn't do any good right now. He turned around, put on a fake smile, and stood next to the captain as they said their goodbyes to their host.

It was a quiet walk back through the jungle as no one talked. When they reached the beach, Yates thanked their guides, watched the jungle swallow them again as they returned to the village then walked down to the shore and leaned against the boat, waiting silently until the others gathered around him.

When Yates was satisfied that the natives were gone, he turned to his First Officer. "You did a nice job of wowing the chief back there with your little demonstration. It also looks like you managed to tick everyone else off though."

Up to this point, the captain's voice and expression had been neutral. Now, his voice became coldly intense, his look deadly serious. "Don't you ever talk to me like that in front of the chief again. I'm trying to negotiate a deal here that can make all our jobs easier and perhaps make us a lot richer. I don't need you undermining my position."

"I'm not trying to undermine your position Captain, but you shouldn't be telling Hoku that he can see the ship. WWEC's policy is very clear about unauthorized people on board."

"I don't care about polices or regulations," Yates shot back, "I'm trying to do my job and make some money here."

Yates jumped into the boat and started the engine. Angrily, he slammed it into reverse and Crawford barely managed to tumble into the boat before it pulled away from shore. When they cleared the beach, Yates spun the wheel around like he was driving the family runabout.

"Contradict me like that again, and so help me I'll throw you in the brig."

CHAPTER FIVE

The flag hung limp at the stern of the *Pacific Searcher*, with not a breath of wind blowing. Murphy leaned against the railing, watching the new day dawn. The surface of the lagoon had a glassy sheen to it that he had rarely seen before. It had such a flat, mirror shine that he was afraid that when they lowered the boat into the water, it would break the glass and the ship would immediately fall through to the bottom.

He enjoyed the solitude of the early morning. It gave him a chance to clear his head and start anew. Looking at the tranquil scene, he only wished his mind and soul were as calm and serene as the panorama before him.

Last night he had managed to upset not only his friends but the captain as well. Maybe Sarah was right; maybe he was too hardheaded and needed to listen more. And maybe the captain was right too; after all, the natives would also benefit greatly if the island turned out to be rich with oil. It could and should be a win-win for everybody.

He let out a long sigh; he knew he would have to make things right with all three of them. If he could just keep his big mouth shut....

Murphy looked up from the placid waters to the jungle beyond. The sun's rays were just reaching the trees now, crowning them with soft, yellow light. With no breeze to stir the air, it would become stifling hot after only a few hours. He dreaded the thought of spending several days, if not a week, in the jungle and yet there was an air of adventure about the whole thing. The thrill of the hunt, of knowing that just around the next bend or buried beneath a canopy of twisted vines they would make a discovery that had been hidden for over three hundred years.

He had always enjoyed the past, exploring its mysteries and the search for hidden truths, but now maybe he was catching a little of the captain's passion for history, his desire to know what it was like to live and experience it, to be the first one there.

He did enjoy history, but he had no intention of *becoming* history, he thought as he felt the weight of the Glock in his shoulder holster. With the rising threats of terrorism and piracy on the high seas, the WWEC allowed him to carry a firearm. He knew his way around a gun and could tell the difference between a pistol and a revolver but he wouldn't classify himself as a true gun enthusiast.

"Morning."

Murphy turned around and was surprised to see Sarah standing beside him. "You're up early," she said.

"You know me, early bird gets the treasure, that sort of thing."

"Treasure, what treasure?" Crawford said as he came on deck. He looked like he was going on an African safari, wearing a khaki shirt and matching shorts along with a pith helmet; two canteens were clipped on one side of his belt and a machete hung on the other. He also wore a large canvas backpack and was carrying a smaller gym bag.

Crawford's arrival was an uncomfortable reminder of how the dinner party had ended. "Listen Doug, about last night..." Crawford held up his hand to stop Murphy. "Don't worry about it. It's water under the bridge."

Murphy looked at his friend and didn't see animosity or bitterness in his eyes, yet he still felt that he had to say something. But before he could, Crawford continued. "And let me beat you two to the punch, something like 'me Tarzan, you Jane' would be appropriate I think, or 'Dr. Livingston I presume?' Get it out of your systems now."

Murphy and Sarah looked at each other then burst out laughing.

"I know, I know," Crawford continued, "but I intend to be prepared. Now, you were saying something about treasure?"

"Yeah," Sarah said, "Exactly what do you hope to find? I've never seen you get so excited over dishes before. "

"It's not the dishes; it's where they're from."

"What do you mean?"

Murphy took a quick glance around then turned back to Sarah and Crawford, "Last night something about the plates and silverware caught my eye so when we got back to the ship, I checked the computer. The dinnerware was a special pattern created by the governor of Mexico City for the governor of Manila as a present. Last night I believe we ate off the plates that belonged to the Spanish galleon *Victoria*."

When the light of understanding didn't flash above Sarah's head, Murphy continued. "The *Victoria*? Really, Sarah? All those hours I spent on the computer, going to the library, those charts I laid out on the kitchen table, the History Channel specials and you don't remember me mentioning the *Victoria*?"

Sarah shook her head. "Sorry."

"The *Victoria* was the pride of the Spanish Manila Treasure Galleons that sailed these waters over three hundred years ago and she was carrying one of the largest cargos of silver and gold every recorded when she disappeared. Most sources think, and so do I, that the ship fell victim to the pirate known as Diablo Oscuro."

"Dark Devil?" Sarah asked.

Murphy nodded. "That's what they called him though no one knows his real name or who he really was. Some say he was English, some French, and others that he was a Spaniard robbing from his own people. One thing's for sure though, he was the most feared pirate in the South Pacific."

"Sounds as if you really like this guy," Crawford said.

Murphy shook his head. "Like? No. He was ruthless, showed no mercy, killed everyone on board the ships he attacked, except for one that he kept alive as a witness to tell the world that another ship had fallen prey to the Dark Devil. Many of the survivors reported that during battle, he would receive mortal wounds, yet he didn't die; they didn't even slow him down. It was also said that when the Dark Devil came up on deck during a fight, his head and beard would be on fire, adding all the more to the legend that he was a devil and not a man."

"On fire? Sounds like they had too much rum or something," Sarah joked.

Murphy shook his head. "It's not as farfetched as you may think. You two have heard of Blackbeard, right?"

Both nodded.

"Well, he was known to have put matches in his hair and weave hemp rope, or cannon fuses, in his beard and light them on fire. It must have been quite demoralizing to see a madman with his hair on fire charging your ship. And the amazing thing is that Blackbeard's reign of terror only lasted about two years. It sounds like Diablo probably did the same thing things. So like him, no: admire how he did things? yes."

"So what are we talking about here? A parrot on your shoulder singing 'pieces of eight, pieces of eight' and 'sixteen men on a dead man's chest'?" Sarah said.

Murphy answered her sarcasm with a smile. "Pieces of eight, yes. The *Victoria* carried nearly two million of them in over 500 chests." Depending on condition, if it's all intact, the estimated value of the treasure is anywhere from ten10 million to nearly a billion dollars, yes, that's with a "B." Murphy's smile grew even bigger as her sarcastic smirk quickly vanished.

"Rumor has it that Diablo Oscuro made such a large haul off the *Victoria* that he retired and was never seen again."

Both Sarah's and Crawford's eyes grew wide. "So you think..."

"That the treasure from the *Victoria* may be somewhere on this island," Murphy finished her sentence. "I think it could be in the great storehouse that the chief talked about last night."

"You're serious aren't you?" Sarah said.

Murphy nodded. "If the dishes from the ship are here, the rest of it should be too." Murphy smiled, he could see the wheels turning inside her head, spending her pirate booty buying new houses and new cars. "You're thinking too small," he said, reading her mind. "Stop thinking of a king's ransom and start thinking like relieving the National Debt."

"Are you going to tell the captain about this?" Crawford asked.

"Good morning, people." Yates strode onto the deck. "Yes, tell me what?" He said looking at the three of them.

"Uh, nothing sir," Murphy quickly replied.

Yates accepted the answer. "Are you three ready?"

"All set Captain," Murphy replied. "I figure we'll be gone three to four days, unless Cro-Magnon man gets us lost."

"He's offering to help us," Sarah said, "and all things considered, I'd think you'd be grateful. Besides," she added with a sly smile, "you feeling a little threatened?"

"You're right, he can be of help. After all, he was the one to point out to us that the jungle was no place for a woman."

"Very good then," Yates said, ignoring his officers' bickering. "While you three are searching in the jungle, I'll be negotiating with Hoku and checking out the pools of oil he claims they have. Do you have all your equipment Mr. Murphy?"

"We've got everything we need. Joe Bob helped me pack all the gear last night. We've got tents and cooking equipment and enough food and water for five days."

Yates nodded in approval; "Good, let's take our time to explore and make sure we don't miss anything about this potential gold mine. Check in once in the morning and once in the evening on your radio. If anything happens we can have the chopper out to get you in less than thirty minutes. "Remember, this isn't just a little camping trip here; I expect you to be keeping your eyes open for potential oil or natural gas deposits."

"Understood, sir."

"Good; let's go then."

"Can we get breakfast first?" Crawford asked.

"It's nearly 6:15 and you haven't eaten yet?" Yates said. "The day is half gone already. Fortune and glory await us out there. Fortune and glory." His eyes lingered on the island for a moment longer then he turned and headed toward the longboat.

Crawford rolled his eyes in frustration as the captain walked by. Murphy shrugged his shoulders and followed Yates while Sarah reached into her backpack and pulled out an apple and tossed it to Crawford. "Think of it as a continental breakfast," she said as she walked past, following Murphy.

Crawford sighed, looked at the apple, took a big bite out of it then trailed dutifully behind the others as the three explorers followed their captain to the longboat.

The big crane slowly lifted the boat, swung it across the deck and dangled it over the side like a carnival amusement ride. With a deep, low whine, the electric winch engaged and after an initial lurch, slowly lowered the longboat into the tranquil sea, where it settled into the water. Ripples broke the surface and raced across the glassy lagoon.

Crawford unhooked the harness cable and Murphy started the engine. Rather than push the throttle forward and speed to shore, he nudged it just past idle and slowly motored in.

"Is there a problem with the engine, Mr. Murphy?" Yates said from his usual perch in the bow.

"No sir, just enjoying the morning and the scenery." When the captain didn't say anything, Murphy took that as a sign that he too was enjoying the peaceful ride.

"Careful of that deadhead over there," Crawford said, pointing off the starboard bow. Murphy followed Crawford's finger and saw what looked like the tip of a log bobbing gentle on the surface.

As they pulled closer, Crawford leaned over the side to look at the unusual shape, then quickly sat back up, startled to see a pair of eyes staring back at him. Suddenly, there was a flurry of splashes, followed by a loud thud against the hull that set the boat rocking, almost spilling Yates into the water.

"What was that?" Crawford blurted out.

"What did you hit, Mr. Murphy?" Yates said sharply, regaining his balance.

"I didn't hit anything, sir; it hit us," Murphy replied, pointed behind them.

They saw a round, four-foot saucer rise slowly out of the water for a moment then silently slip beneath the surface again; the giant sea turtle swam leisurely away, none the worse for its run-in with the longboat.

"That thing is huge," Crawford said as he followed its shadow underwater until it faded into the depths.

"That'd make enough soup to feed the entire crew," Murphy joked

Sarah reached over and hit him. "Not funny."

"Stow it," Yates intervened. "Over there," he said pointing toward the shore, "I see our welcoming party."

Hoku was standing near the water's edge waiting for them, waving excitedly. Murphy picked up speed a bit then cut the power and let the boat slide silently up the sandy shore.

Yates had resumed his perch in the bow and his timing was perfect as he jumped off the front of the boat just as it hit the sand. With a small leap, the momentum of the boat sent him flying effortlessly through the air, giving him almost twice the distance he normally would have gotten.

Hoku, Kekao, and five other natives with them fell to their knees, seeing the Servant of God "fly" off the boat.

"A guy could get used to this." Yates whispered under his breath to Murphy and the others as they got off.

"Oh great Servant of God, again you *honrar* us."

"Rise, Chief Hoku," Yates said with an exaggerated sweep of his hands. Slowly Hoku and the others stood, but only Hoku and Kekao dared to look up.

"Kekao say it three-day's *viaje* into jungle and to *almacen*. Are your helpers ready?" Hoku asked.

"Yes we are," Murphy quickly answered, looking Kekao straight in the eye.

Kekao grunted a little and looked at Sarah, then signaled for two of the other natives to go over and retrieve their gear from of the boat.

Kekao grunted again. "Come, our *viaje* takes us to far side of mountain." And with nothing more to say, he turned and started walking into the jungle.

"Why is it always on the other side of the mountain?" Crawford asked, turning to Murphy as he picked up his pack. "Why can't it be just at the end of the block or just around the next bend?"

Murphy smiled at Crawford's "enthusiasm" but hoped the entire journey wouldn't be like this. He could just hear it now...*Are we there yet? Are we there yet?*

Yates stood on the beach and watched until his crew had disappeared into the jungle, then he turned to Hoku. "Now then, Chief how far away are those pools of oil you spoke of last night?"

"Not far, but first, you come to village. My wife has made special meal in your *honrar*. She would be very hurt if you not come."

Yates smiled at the flattery. "The oil has been there for millions of years. Another hour or two won't matter; and besides, I wouldn't want to disappoint your wife. Please, lead the way, Chief."

Hoku beamed like a little child. "Thank you oh Great Servant. She will be most happy. Come, come, we hurry."

Hoku took the lead, darting in and out of the jungle, wearing a smile from ear to ear and constantly encouraging him forward. He reminded Yates of a family dog trying to please his master.

CHAPTER SIX

Kekao reached the edge of the village then marched on through into the jungle on the other side, making it clear he was taking no prisoners when it came to setting the pace. Crawford was crushed when they reached the village and didn't stop. The smell of the morning fires and of freshly cooked food was enough to make him think of mutiny. The grumbling in his stomach was nearly as loud as the grumbling under his breath as he marched through the village.

Not being able to stop and eat was bad enough, but it was made even worse when he saw the girl who had been flirting with him the night before come out of one of the huts and eagerly smile and wave at him. The disappointed look on her face when he didn't stop to talk hurt almost as much as his hunger. He wasn't sure if Yates could really throw him into the brig like he had threatened to do to Murphy, but what he was sure of was that the captain could get him fired if he didn't go on this little Boy Scout trip.

He straightened up a bit as he walked by and put on his brave explorer face, hoping to impress her with his fearless trek into the deep, dark jungle. He gave her a friendly smile and a wink as he picked up his feet and put them into a soldier's pace instead of a complainer's shuffle. With one last look over his shoulder, he smiled and disappeared into the jungle.

Murphy wanted to stop in the village as well, but not for the same reasons as his love-struck shipmate. Although breakfast would have been nice, what he really was hoping for was to get a better look at the village in the daylight and to see if they had any more artifacts he could identify. He wanted to enjoy the sights and sound of the jungle—he wanted this to be an adventure, not army maneuvers in jungle warfare—but there was no time to waste; Kekao make it clear that they would not be taking time to stop and smell the roses.

Murphy, Sarah, and Crawford dutifully followed Kekao through the village, followed by their two native porters. For several minutes they traveled along a well-worn path that made keeping up with their guide fairly easy. The path spilled out into a large meadow carpeted with wide-bladed grass. The three-foot-high tufts of grass swayed gently in the breeze, reminding Murphy of the great wheat fields of the Midwest.

They all stopped for a quick break that allowed them to admire the postcard beauty of the tree-lined field with the towering twin mountains in the background.

"Look," Crawford said to Sarah, as he took out a bottle of water from his pack, "you can make a grass skirt and go native. I bet we can even find you a pair of coconuts to wear too." He smiled.

"You know," Murphy added with a snicker, "in the early days of grass skirts and such, the men wore loin cloths and the women were topless."

Sarah just rolled her eyes and shook her head as she pushed her way past them. "Boys. I'm surrounded by nothing but boys."

The small expedition continued across the meadow and forded a small, ankle-deep stream on the other side, then re-entered the jungle. The pace Kekao set was fast but easy as they followed a game trail through the low lying flatlands that led up to the base of one of the mountains.

In the foothills, they came to a small clearing that would have made a perfect place for them to stop and catch their breath, but Kekao never broke stride as he kept going and started to penetrate the jungle curtain on the other side of the clearing.

Suddenly Crawford shot out from behind Sarah and passed her and Murphy like a sports car passing two semis on the freeway.

"This is ridiculous," he said as he stormed passed. "I'm not quite as ignorant as you two think I am. Both of you know as well as I do that we crossed the same stream twice and that Kekao is leading us on a wild goose chase just to make his point, but you two are too stubborn to say anything, wanting to prove to him that you're both just as tough as he is, but I'm the one who's paying the price for your little pissing match!"

"Kekao!" Crawford shouted just as their guide disappeared behind a wall of green. Crawford shouted again when the big man didn't stop. He was about to shout a third time when Kekao came storming back through the jungle.

Murphy looked at the charging native then back at his friend. Crawford lost a little of his resolve but he seemed determined to hold his ground. Kekao was fifteen feet away and still in full stride when Crawford spoke: "Kekao!"

The name came out with such authority and conviction that Murphy had to do a double-take just to see if it really was Crawford talking. "I know that you really don't like us and that you think the jungle is no place for a woman but I am not an animal, able to run with leaps and bounds through the jungle while you three show each other how tough you are. Your chief sent you to help us, the servants of God, and I don't think Hoku would be too happy with the way you're 'helping' us."

Crawford promptly sat on a fallen tree. "I'm tired. But I am smarter than all you three because I'm at least willing to admit I'm tired. Now let's all sit down and take five before we push onward and upward." He reached down, grabbed one of his canteens and unscrewed the cap. "I think we..."

He stopped in midsentence with his canteen halfway to his lips, his eyes suddenly filled with fear, frozen in sheer terror.

Murphy was looking up the slopes at their next challenge when he heard Crawford stop talking in midsentence and he turned back to see why. He froze for a moment as his brain was processing what he was looking at; their native guide was pulling a knife on his friend. As if in slow motion, he reached in and started to grab for his pistol but immediately realized that Kekao had too much of a head start and that he would never get his weapon out in time to save his friend.

CHAPTER SEVEN

Even though the day was still young, it was already getting warm in the jungle. Yates smiled to himself thinking of his three crewmen traipsing in the hot jungle for three to four *days*. He knew he had made the better choice.

Rank does have its privileges, he chuckled to himself.

Following Hoku and his guide to the village, Yates looked up and saw a pack of small brown monkeys swinging through the trees. They were following them, swinging from branch to branch in the high canopy, keeping pace with the small group like a school of dolphins following a ship at sea. At sea, dolphins were a sign of good luck and so he liked the analogy of the monkeys following them and hoped it would bring him good luck here too.

The breeze failed to penetrate the dense foliage and the air was getting warmer all the time. Soon he would be breaking into a sweat, and it just wouldn't do for the natives to see the Great Servant of God sweating.

Slowly sounds of civilization began overpowering the sounds of nature as they drew closer to the village. He heard the hacking sounds of an axe chopping into trees, coconuts being smashed open against rocks, and the voices of the villagers as they went about their daily business.

When Yates stepped out of the jungle and into the village clearing, it was like a breath of fresh air. Literally. When he inhaled, it felt good to taste air that didn't feel like it had just come out of an oven.

Two men were carrying a bundle of bamboo poles on their shoulders while a third man walked beside them. Three women were coming out of the jungle, walking single file with large pots on their shoulders. Other villagers were carrying fruit and several were huddled around the open fire in the middle of the village cooking.

Suddenly a shout rang out like an alarm and the villagers started scurrying like someone had just called battle stations. Yates watched the natives running around like Keystone Cops, and then understood the reason for the confusion.

There weren't the rows of armor-clad warriors waiting to greet him like the night before; this time there were four women standing in two rows. Gone were the grass skirts, instead, each wore a simple wraparound dress and they all had on matching flower necklaces. Each woman was carrying a woven basket with flowers in it and were throwing petals at his feet as he walked between them.

Yates sat down next to Hoku at the same table he'd been at the night before. The instant they were seated, they were swarmed by women surrounding him like worker bees tending their queen, only this time it was a King, and he was it.

Some of the women set the table with dinnerware while they were closely followed by those who decorated the table with more flowers; still others began serving them food.

Mangos, bananas and other assorted sizes and colors of fruit were set on the table in woven baskets. When those were placed, another server brought him a bowl of what looked like pale purple oatmeal. He looked down at it and didn't know exactly what it was or what to do with it. Was he supposed to spread it on something or eat it like soup?

Yates looked over and saw that Hoku seemed particular excited about this dish. Hoku smiled and nodded for him to begin. Hoku didn't have a spoon in his hand so did that mean he was supposed to pick it up and drink it out of the bowl?

He looked down at the bowl then back at Hoku who continued to smile with anticipation. Hoku nodded his head again then put his index and middle fingers together and made a scooping motion with them for Yates to eat the purple oatmeal.

Suddenly it became clear, this was poi. He'd seen breadfruit trees coming into the village and this was their version of poi made from the fruit. He'd eaten poi when he was in Hawaii and the Philippines but didn't much care for the flavor or texture.

Besides taste, he now faced another problem; should the Great Servant of God use a spoon or eat it with his fingers? After a moment he decided to show his humanity and scooped some of the poi up with his fingers and ate it. Hoku grinned from ear to ear and began eating himself.

After the poi, several platters of broiled fish were placed on the table along with boiled roots and roasted nuts.

After eating far more than he should have, Yates could have easily fallen asleep right then and there but he knew he couldn't because he did have work to do. While he lingered there, dreading the thought of having to get up, a young woman came up and handed him and the chief each a cup of hot liquid. As she did, Yates did a double take; he could have sworn she winked at him. She flashed a sly, coy smile then turned and left.

"You like?" Hoku asked.

"She's very pretty."

Hoku smiled. "Her name Malana and she is pretty, but was asking about drink."

Yates smiled and took the cup and held it up to take in the aroma, it smelled like coffee. He then took a small sip, it was more bitter than coffee and had an earthy, root taste to it; still it was surprisingly good.

"This is very good, Chief."

Hoku beamed, "I happy." He drank some of his then put the cup down. "If you ready, I take you to sticky mud now."

"Yes, that sounds very good." Yates stood and stretched. So far, he had been treated like royalty, fed better than a king and all before ten in the morning! If he were to discover oil then this day just couldn't get any better.

He followed Hoku out of the village. As they were leaving he turned and saw Malana smiling seductively at him as she went into one of the huts. He smiled wickedly behind the chief's back. Maybe it *could* get better.

CHAPTER EIGHT

Kekao unsheathed his knife and drew it high over his shoulder. Like a pitcher delivering a fastball to home plate, Kekao brought his arm down and threw the knife. Somewhere in the confusion of the moment, Murphy heard Sarah scream. He started to turn his head to look at her but then his eye caught the flash of the knife as it left Kekao's hand and he locked onto it like radar.

The crystal clear image of the knife stood out against the blurry green background of the jungle as the missile flew through the air. There was no scream, no shriek of agony, only a dull, sickening thud as the knife struck and buried its blade deep into its target. Crawford dropped his canteen and, as if in slow motion, it fell to the soft jungle floor. Trapped in the moment, the water gurgling out sounded like a rushing river.

Suddenly everything fast-forwarded back to reality. The knife was true to its aim and hit its intended target, only the target wasn't Crawford as Murphy had thought, but a three-foot-long snake coiled next to Crawford. Kekao's blade had struck true, pinning the snake's head to the log Crawford was sitting on.

"This is very deadly snake," Kekao said as he calmly walked over and pulled his knife out of the snake and the log. "If snake bite him, he be dead before we could get him back to village."

Kekao wiped the blade off on the grass then put it back into its sheath. "There more snakes here. We can go safer place uphill or stay here to rest. You chose, oh Helper of the Great Servant."

Crawford stared at the dead snake that was just inches away from his hand then slowly reached down to pick up his canteen. He tried to screw the cap back on but his hands were trembling too badly. After the third try, Murphy walked over and put it on for him. Crawford stood, drew in a deep breath then slowly let it out, and without a word, gestured for Kekao to lead the way. With less smug self-righteousness than Murphy expected, Kekao bowed his head slightly and turned. His pace was a bit slower as they started up the trail, but not much.

The travelers were silent, saving their energy for more important things—like breathing—as Kekao continued to drive them up the hill at an unrelenting pace. Tree roots, stripped naked of their dirt clothing by the monsoon rains, reached out like tentacles to ensnare any careless foot or ankle. Jagged boulders lay strewn across the path like land mines, ready to finish the work of the out stretched roots.

The trail was narrow and dangerous, overgrown almost to the point that Murphy felt like he was going down the rabbit hole in *Alice in Wonderland*. Only the occasional glimpse of clear blue sky through the overhanging vines kept them from being completely swallowed up within the bowels of the humid jungle.

At last they broke free of the jungle and found themselves on a beautiful plateau. Short green grass covered a small meadow with currents of tiny, brightly colored purple flowers flowing through it.

Crawford was sucking in air like a Hoover when he reached the top and didn't say a word as he sat down on a large rock though he did take a moment to thoroughly check the area for snakes.

Murphy stopped and drank in the beauty. The whole scene reminded him of one of those fantasy golf courses he'd seen in magazines, the courses that only the richest of the rich could play. He could almost visualize it: from here, he would have to drive the ball a hundred yards out, but it would drop five hundred feet down to the next hole that lay at the base of the plateau. The green would be on a tiny island floating in the middle of a blue lagoon with a four hundred-foot waterfall cascading down in the background.

Murphy grabbed his canteen, dropped his backpack, and walked slowly over to a rock outcropping near the edge of the plateau. He sat down and dangled his feet over the edge as he admired the vista. They had climbed to about a thousand feet above the beach and from here he had a commanding view of this side of the island.

Off to the left, he could see the telltale threads of smoke rising up from the village. Almost directly in front of him was the *Pacific Searcher*, lying quietly at anchor in the turquoise bay, looking like a child's toy in the bathtub. Murphy's eyes moved from the sea of blue to the sea of green that surrounded them. Every imaginable shade of green and shape of leaf lay before him in a quilted collage of texture and color that he had never experienced before.

A soft breeze touched his face ever so gently, teasing him as it passed. It was not enough to cool him down after their hard climb. Sarah came over and sat down beside him, another painful reminder of something he would never have again.

"Beautiful isn't it?" Murphy asked, stretching his hand out over the panorama like he had just created it.

Sarah nodded as she took out a couple of energy bars and offered one to Murphy.

"So what do you think of what happened back there with Kekao and the snake?" Sarah asked.

Murphy took a long drink from his canteen then wiped off his mouth with the back of his hand. "I still don't trust him if that's what you mean."

"Don't trust who?" Crawford said, walking up to the others and cautiously peering over the edge.

"You!" Murphy said.

"Me! What'd I do?"

"Back there on the trail, several times when you were in front of me you pushed branches out of your way and then let them snap back. If I'd been close enough, those slingshots would have knocked me over. Don't you know that you're supposed to hold the branches and let them go back slowly? Weren't you ever a Boy Scout or go out and play in the woods when you were a kid?"

Crawford smiled vaguely and shook his head. "Sorry, but the closest I ever got to camping in the great outdoors was when we went to visit my aunt and uncle in New York and we went for a picnic in Central Park." Crawford paused for a moment, a curious look hanging on his round face. "So now that you know I'm not Daniel Boone you don't trust me?"

Sarah frowned then reached over and hit Murphy in the arm, hard. "We weren't talking about you. Dallas doesn't trust Kekao."

"But why? He saved my life."

Before Murphy could answer, they heard a loud roar that seemed to echo through the jungle, followed by a low, gurgling sound, almost like the purr from a cat, if the cat was on steroids. All three snapped their heads around, scanning the tree line for the phantom saber tooth tiger.

"What was that?" Crawford asked, his voice on the edge of cracking, his eyes wide with fear.

"That is mate of beast Great Servant killed." Kekao said, walking slowly up to the group who had unconsciously huddled closer together. There was no fear in his eyes, but rather an amusement because of the fear he saw in theirs.

"He searches for lost mate. He knows something wrong."

Just then another low grumbling was heard from the edge of the plateau. "He searches, but not alone," Kekao continued, his voice low and deliberate. "He hunts with others, find her... or to take revenge."

At that moment, if Kekao would have said, "boo," Crawford would have set a new world record for the 100 yard dash...in any direction. Murphy found himself fidgeting with his holster and Sarah was sitting perfectly still, her energy bar hanging out of her mouth like an unlit cigar.

Kekao savored the moment then reached into his pouch and pulled out three necklaces. "Take," he said as he handed one to each of them.

"Wha-what's this?" Crawford managed to stammer out.

"Powerful *magia* to protect from spirit of the beast you killed. If her spirit finds you, her mate will know and attack without *misericordia*."

The necklaces were made of a light leather string, looking much like a shoelace and held one larger claw dangling from the middle that was flanked by two smaller ones from a panther. Crawford snatched the charm out of Kekao's hand like a greedy child grabbing at candy and quickly put it around his neck.

Sarah took hers and held it up to examine it, then put it on as well. "Not much of a fashion statement, but at least we don't look like tourists anymore." Her statement was meant to be funny, to break the somber mood that Kekao had created, but it failed.

Murphy looked at the necklace in his hand, then at Kekao.

"Wear or not, I no care." Kekao said. "Chief Hoku said to protect you. I try." Kekao looked indifferent as he turned and walked away.

"What's the matter with you?" Sarah said looking at Murphy. "He's only trying to help."

"Is he?"

Sarah looked at Murphy then turned and got up. It was a look he'd seen too many times. It was a look of frustration, with a little of "how could you be so stubborn?" surrounded by "why do I even bother?"

Before he could say anything else, Kekao grunted, telling them the rest stop was over and that they had a long way to go before they could camp for the night. Murphy stuffed the charm in his pocket as he turned and followed the others.

CHAPTER NINE

Yates and the chief followed their two native guides as they entered the jungle. Yates attacked the vegetation with his machete. Each vine, leaf and stock that fell proved he would not be denied this treasure.

When he was a kid growing up, there was a huge blackberry patch behind his house and he would take his Dad's old machete and spend hours hacking his way through the thicket, pretending he was a great explorer, daring man or beast to keep him from his destiny. Some days he would pretend he was in the deepest, darkest part of Africa, fighting lions and tigers, searching for the fabled Lost City; others, he would be in the steaming jungles of the Amazon basin, fighting giant snakes and looking for ancient lost cites of gold.

Now, he was actually living the dream; he was on a real quest to find something more valuable than mere gold...black gold. They crested a small hill and he paused, placing his left foot up on a rock and surveyed the green carpet below. This would make a great picture in the history books, he thought, and imagined the caption to that photograph: *Hiram Yates on his way to discovering the greatest oil reserves ever known.* He was a little disappointed that a shaft of light didn't break through the trees, bathing him in glory.

Forty-five minutes into the hike the thrill of adventure was beginning to wear off. He was hot, sweaty, and his arm was getting tired of swinging the machete. He paused again, this time to sit on a small rock outcropping and took a long drink from his canteen.

"Your men look tired, Chief. I think they deserve a break," Yates said, trying to divert them from realizing that he was the one who was tired.

"You are wise, Great Servant."

Yates had another sip then took a break from his fantasy of being world conqueror to look at his surroundings. In the short time since leaving the village, he had seen more varieties of plants and animals than he ever knew existed.

They had come across several different species of monkeys. Most were small, playing in the trees, swinging back and forth and leaping from branch to branch. But there were also larger monkeys foraging on the jungle floor.

Unfortunately, Yates had also seen several varieties of snakes and he had almost walked into one hanging from a branch like a Christmas tree ornament. He tried not to look frightened or startled as he slapped it away. After all, it just wouldn't do for the Great Servant of God to show fear.

But most of all, he enjoyed the host of birds, most dressed in a kaleidoscope of colors and ranging from sizes that would fit into has hand to those with wing spans reaching several feet.

"Anything wrong, Oh Great One?" Hoku asked, seeing Yates faraway look.

"No, Chief, just taking in the moment." Hoku tipped his head to one side, not understanding. "Never mind...how long until we reach the pools?"

"Not long, we come to pools when sun is highest in sky."

Yates glanced at his watch, about an hour or so, he thought. He put his canteen away and jumped up. "Let's go then, the world is waiting."

Hoku tipped his head again, but Yates didn't see the chief's puzzled look. He was invigorated by the cool water and a little rest; visions of glory began calling him again. Yates moved out with a spring in his step and walked past Hoku, machete in hand, attacking the jungle.

CHAPTER TEN

The path that led down the other side of the plateau was much easier than their ascent: it sloped gently downward then leveled out. The going was easy as the trail was fairly open, allowing the breeze to keep them cool. The ocean was now behind them as the path wrapped itself around the hillside, curving toward the interior of the island. A sea of green now replaced the blue of the ocean as they looked down upon the canopy of the jungle.

The hill they were walking along curved into a collision course with a jagged rock outcropping that rose out of the jungle to their right, towering three hundred feet above them. The hill they were on and the outcropping closed to within fifty feet of each other, leaving a narrow gap between them.

As the small band followed the trail, the mountain on their right suddenly retreated, opening onto a small valley before them. The path continued to descend to the valley floor where it felt like the temperature had risen by ten degrees.

Standing on a small rise overlooking the valley, Murphy was transported back in time. Most of the valley floor was covered in knee-deep jungle grass. Occasionally a breeze off the ocean would manage to penetrate through the jungle barrier and the grass would roll and bend, making it look like a giant, living thing. Small groves of palm trees were scattered throughout, and the entire valley was rimmed by lush green hills. From their left came the sounds of exotic birds as they chatted, squawked, and sang their ageless melodies.

The sun was on its downward trek and had just slipped behind a thin band of clouds hovering in the afternoon sky. The filtered sunlight cast a bronze haze over the entire valley, softening its colors, and Murphy could almost believe he was standing at the dawn of creation. At that moment, he wouldn't have been surprised to see a dinosaur wander slowly out of the jungle and start nibbling on the treetops.

For a moment, a sense of newness washed over him, a sense that all the past mistakes had been removed and that life was a clean slate. He didn't want to look at Sarah, but he couldn't help himself. Would it ever be possible to really start over? It had been three years since their divorce and they had managed to stay friends but at times it had been awkward and strained. And for the life of him, he couldn't remember why they had divorced in the first place. At moments like this, it was all he could do not to reach out and take her hand.

Suddenly a flock of birds fluttered from their perches and flew to the safety of the other side of the valley when the sorrowful howl of the lonesome panther pining for its mate invaded the valley's serenity.

Crawford reached for his necklace and Murphy reached for his pistol. Sarah searched the jungle then reached down to her own charm hanging from her neck. She was not superstitious but seemed to be trapped between two worlds, taking comfort in Murphy's pistol yet hesitant to completely discount the power of the native amulet. The big cat howled again and Murphy could hear the anguish in its voice. He identified with its loss.

True to form, Kekao just grunted and said that they had to keep moving and that they would camp at the far end of the valley. Crawford quickly fell in line behind Kekao and one of the guides, followed by Sarah then Murphy, with the last native bringing up the rear.

The trail snaked its way through the middle of the grass and Murphy kept a constant vigil. The grass provided perfect cover for a stalking panther to sneak up on them. Murphy thought they should have kept to the tree line where they would at least have a chance of spotting the cat before he attacked. He also thought Kekao should know this. Was he leading them through the tall grass because it was the easiest way or did he think there was no danger? Or was it that he just didn't care?

With each wave of the windblown grass, Murphy became more anxious and uneasy. He slipped his hand to his holster and released the snap. He wanted to take out the gun, to feel the confidence that its weight in his hand would provide, but twice he saw Kekao glancing back with what Murphy could have sworn was a smirk. He refrained from drawing his weapon, not wanting to give Kekao any satisfaction.

Halfway into their march to the other side of the valley, something caught Murphy's attention. Off to one side there was a large mound of vines that seemed out of place in the middle of the flat, grassy plain. He called out to the others then headed toward it.

"What do you see?" Sarah called out as she fell into step behind him.

"I don't care," Crawford said as he caught up to them, "as long as it gives us a quick breather."

"I'm not sure," Murphy replied, "but this clump of vines seems out of place here in the middle of all this flat ground. It looks like it's covering up something."

"No waste time here." Kekao said.

"Well it's my time to waste," Murphy replied and reached up and grabbed a handful of vines. Ripping the plants away, he could see that the jungle was definitely hiding something. With both hands, he reached up and began pulling back large patches of the overgrowth.

"I got something here," Murphy said.

There was no need for further encouragement. His two friends joined in and grabbed their own handfuls and attacked the vines like angry gardeners. After a few minutes of weeding, they stepped back to see that their labor had uncovered part of a fuselage.

"What is it?" Crawford asked.

"It looks like an old Japanese plane from World War Two," Murphy answered.

"How can you tell that?" Sarah asked.

"From the meatball on the side."

"Meatball?" Crawford said. "Don't tease me with food."

Murphy chuckled. "Right here," he said as he peeled back more vines. "This big red circle was the insignia the Japanese painted on the sides of their aircraft; the Americans called them 'meatballs.' Come on; help me clear the rest of it."

"We go make camp while you *jugar*," Kekao said.

"No." Murphy replied. "You don't have to help, but I want you three to stay here with us."

"Did he say jaguar?" Crawford asked nervously as he watched Kekao leave.

"*Jugar*, not jaguar," Sarah corrected. "*Jugar* means play in Spanish."

"Oh. I wish they would stop speaking part English part Spanish."

"You remember what Dallas said?"

"Yeah, yeah, English is a second language to them so if they don't know the word, they revert to their native Spanish. Still, I wish I could just 'press one for English.'"

Murphy watched Kekao walking away fuming, followed by the two porters. Right now he didn't care what Kekao thought as they took their time to uncover the entire fuselage and the tops of the wings. The plane was a patchwork of bare aluminum, faded and chipped green paint and rust. The large red ball on the side was faded, but still distinct. The three blades of the propeller were bent and curved inward: the plane had made a wheels-up landing.

"What is it?" Crawford asked.

Murphy jumped up on the wing. "I don't believe it. It's a D3A Val, a carrier-based dive bomber. "

Murphy could see a line of bullet holes running along the wing then up the side and into the cockpit. Most of the canopy was intact but there were several large cracks from bullet holes right behind the pilot's seat. With some hesitation, he stepped over and peered into the cockpit.

"Is...is there anybody in there?" Crawford asked grimly.

Murphy knelt down. The cloth seat covers had long since rotted away and vines had started to creep up through the floorboards but had not yet covered the controls. The dials and gauges were amazingly intact except for the compass and the radio; both had been smashed by fifty-caliber rounds. Other than that, he thought the interior was in remarkable shape for being in the jungle for over seventy years.

"What do you think happened?" Crawford asked, staring at the wreckage.

Murphy stood up and gazed at the valley. "It probably came through there." Murphy pointed at the entrance between the two peaks, retracing the final flight of the Val. "I wonder what they were doing way out here...?" He could imagine that it was late 1942 or early '43 and the Val was on a reconnaissance mission, out looking for the American fleet.

"It would be a great honor for the ship and to the Emperor if we were the ones to find the American fleet," Airman Akihiro Endo reported from the rear gunner's position.

Captain Riku Yoshida smiled at his crewman's naive enthusiasm. What his young inexperienced gunner didn't realize was that it was not just a matter of honor but of survival.

"Keep your eyes open, Endo," Yoshida said, "or the only honor you will have today is meeting your ancestors."

"Yes sir!" Came the crisp reply.

Honor was one thing, Yoshida thought to himself, but revenge was another. He had survived the defeat at Midway and had seen the humiliation it had brought to the navy and the devastating blow to morale back home. Yoshida wasn't seeking honor, he was seeking revenge. He had lost many friends to American bombs and he was looking to avenge their deaths and yes, to restore honor not only to himself but to the Emperor as well.

"Sir!" Endo called out loudly.

"What is it?" Yoshida asked.

"Sir, low, behind us off our right wing. A pair of American fighters."

Yoshida twisted his neck as he looked over his shoulder and saw the planes about 3000 feet below them. The Americans were still flying straight and level which meant they hadn't been spotted. Yoshida quickly pulled his plane into a cloud bank for cover.

"Good job, Airman," Yoshida said, "it looks like the Americans did not see us. We will circle above them using the clouds as cover then follow them back to their carrier and report their position to the fleet. We will have sake tonight!"

Relieved from the past several hours of boredom, Yoshida could feel the excitement coursing through his veins. Carefully, he monitored his instruments, making notes of their speed and heading. Satisfied, he eased the nose of his plane down, descending out of the cloud, expecting to see the enemy aircraft in front of and below him.

The sky was empty.

Concern, more than panic, began to tighten around his chest. They should be right below them. "Airman, do you see them?" Yoshida asked as he quickly scanned the sky and double checked his calculations.

"They're behind us!" Endo shouted so loudly he didn't need the intercom to be heard. A split second later, Yoshida felt his plane shake as it took hits from the American guns.

Yoshida immediately swung his plane back and forth to throw off his adversary's aim. He yanked back on the stick and pulled back into the safety of the clouds, then banked hard left in an attempt to throw off his pursuers. He felt his restraining straps dig deep into his shoulders but knew that minor bruises would be the least of his worries if the enemy fighters got within range again.

A quick glance showed all his instruments were intact and his engine was running smoothly. Yoshida let out a long sigh of relief. All in all, they had been lucky. "Endo, are you all right?" he called out over the intercom. There was no reply.

"Endo?"

Yoshida felt his shoulders sag. He liked Endo and didn't want to look back and find his friend torn to pieces by the enemy's bullets. Slowly he turned his head, dreading what he might see, but to his relief, Endo was staring at him, wearing a grin and was holding up the severed cord from his head set. Yoshida returned his smile and laughed as he watched his the airman swing the frayed cord back and forth.

Yoshida shook his head then signaled that he was going to take the plane down for a look and for his subordinate to keep his eyes open.

As he eased his plane into a gentle dive, he estimated that they should be about two to three miles away from the Americans. With guidance from their ancestors they could find the Americans again and follow them back to their carrier, but after their close call, he would settle for empty skies and a safe trip home.

They emerged from the cloud and both men quickly scanned the skies, desperately searching, knowing that their very lives depended on who saw the other first.

This time it was Yoshida who spotted the enemy first. One of the fighters was a thousand feet below the bottom of the clouds on their left, flying away from them. Yoshida was happy to see that they were above and behind the Americans when suddenly he remembered that there were two of them. Where was the other fighter?

Almost immediately he heard a muffled shout from Endo over the roar of the engine and the distinct sound of their tail gun firing.

Yoshida didn't know how, but the American had somehow managed to stay with them and was now in a perfect firing position behind them, high and to their left. If he pulled up and tried to get back into the safety of the clouds, it would give the American a near perfect profile shot, almost impossible to miss. Pulling left or right was almost as fatal. He had one option left, but it too was risky.

With tracer bullets flying past his canopy, Yoshida flipped his plane on its back and dove down, reversing course. His gamble paid off as the American fighter overshot and went streaking by, not expecting a dive bomber to be so nimble.

Struggling against the g-forces pinning him to his seat and fighting to maintain consciousness, Yoshida pulled back on the stick in a desperate attempt to climb back into the safety of the clouds before the enemy fighter could reverse course.

Just before the clouds swallowed them, Yoshida saw a flash out of the corner of his eye; it was the other fighter. He felt the plane shake and heard the ping of the bullets as they slammed into his plane. He let out a yelp of pain as several rounds smashed into his instrument panel, sending shards of glass and bits of metal into his face. Had he not been wearing his goggles, he would have been blinded.

Suddenly, all was quiet as they were enveloped in the hazy mist of the cloud. Yoshida turned around. Endo was not wearing a smile this time; he looked badly shaken but was alive and replied with a weak thumbs-up.

Yoshida tested his controls and the plane responded accordingly, with no major damage to the outside of the plane, but the inside was a different story. The two most important pieces of equipment on the aircraft had been destroyed: the compass and the radio. With both gone, it would be almost impossible to find their way home or call for help.

The only thing he could do now was to get a fix from the sun and set a general heading. But to do that, he would have to leave the safety of the clouds. This time instead of going down, he decided to go up.

Breaking through the top of the cloud, Yoshida brought his plane into the sunlight. He didn't even bother looking for his foes as he concentrated on getting a fix on his position. By chance, he saw that he was flying in a southwesterly direction, which was the last know position of their fleet. If his luck held, at best they will come across one of their picket ships; at worse, they could find an island base to land at.

Yoshida held their heading and dipped back into the safety of the cloud. As he looked around, he saw a small stream of mist trailing them. He had noticed a similar stream earlier when they first emerged from the cloud, following them as if they had snagged a thread of the cloud and they were unraveling it. He had paid no attention to it then, but it should not be there now.

He scanned his instruments again and his heart sank. The needle on his fuel gage was dropping steadily; the fuel tank must have been hit by the last burst from the American fighter and that's what the trailing mist was. He estimated they had only a few more minutes of fuel left.

Twenty minutes later the engine swallowed its last gulp of fuel, sputtered once, then fell silent. They dropped down out of the cloud into an empty sky and an empty ocean, save for one tiny speck on the horizon.

They managed to glide to the speck which turned out to be a small island. Yoshida saw a large clearing and decided to try to land rather than bail out. With no power he knew he would have only one chance at this. As he lined up the plane he prayed that he would not be meeting his ancestors today.

In his mind, Murphy watched as the plane shot through the gap between the hill and the mountain then crash landed, skidding in on it belly, leaves and branches thrown into the air by this giant flying lawnmower. He saw the plane coming to a slow stop in the mud and tall grass and the crew looking at each other and then bursting out laughing, happy to be alive.

"Well?" Crawford asked, seeing Murphy's faraway gaze.

"Sorry." Murphy replied, fast forwarding back to the 21st century

"I said, are there...any bodies in there?"

Murphy shook his head, coming out of his daydream. "Nope, it looks like they survived the landing." He jumped down and walked toward the back of the plane.

Fortified by the knowledge that there were no human remains in the plane, Crawford excitedly climbed onto the wing then let himself down into the rear gunner's station, his own imagination beginning to run wild.

Just then, off in the distance, they heard the lonely howl of the panther again.

"Yeah, just let him try to get us now. Here kitty, kitty," Crawford said, then swung the gun toward the jungle and pulled the trigger.

But instead of the rat-tat-tat sound that Crawford was going to make, the machinegun woke up from its seventy-year nap. A stream of bullets ripped through the underbrush in a dancing line of flying dust, dirt, leaves, and branches straight toward Murphy.

Crawford immediately let go of the trigger, but sat there paralyzed with fear as the booming echo of the gunfire reverberated throughout the valley like rolling thunder. He didn't see Murphy standing anymore and wasn't sure if he had hit him or not, but he was afraid to get up and check.

The last of the thunder finished rolling down the valley and a deathly silence filled the void behind it. "What do you think you're doing!" Murphy exploded, springing up off the ground like a mad jack-in-the-box.

"Dallas, I'm so sorry," Crawford said, scrambling out of the plane. "I had no idea the thing was loaded. I mean who would have thought that after all this time it would still fire?"

Crawford reached Murphy and started brushing and plucking grass off him.

"It's okay Doug," Murphy said, trying to fend Crawford off.

"Dallas! Are you okay?" Sarah shouted, coming around from the front of the plane.

Murphy slapped Crawford's plucking hands away. "Yeah, I'm fine. Good thing the Red Baron here isn't a very good shot."

"I didn't mean to, okay? It was an accident. I got in the plane and was pretending to fire the gun, only when I pulled the trigger, it really fired."

"Unbelievable," she said looking at Crawford then turning to Murphy. "Are you sure you're okay?"

"I'm fine, really," Murphy nodded. "Come on Kekao, let's go." He said, then started walking at a fast pace. He didn't want them to see that he was shaking like a leaf.

CHAPTER ELEVEN

Yates' heart skipped a beat and his pulse quickened as he caught the unmistakable whiff of oil when they broke out from under the jungle canopy into a small clearing. Yates shoved his way passed the two guides to get his first glimpse of his world-changing discovery.

He had hopes of finding a huge lake, a reservoir of bubbling and boiling oil so big he could skip a stone across it. Instead, he found three small pools, each a couple of yards across. Momentarily disappointed, he quickly cheered up. These were only the tip of the iceberg; the real oil lay beneath the surface he told himself.

He slowly circled the pools, tempering his visions of wealth and fame against whether there really was enough oil here at all.

"Are there any more pools Chief?"

"I do not know. These meet our needs so we look no more." Yates nodded as he continued to circle the pools like a hungry vulture, deciding which carcass to feed on first. He settled on the largest of the three pools and knelt down beside it. He reached down and touched it with the tip of his finger to make sure it wasn't too hot, then cupped the oil in his hand like he was going to take a drink. He let the warm, black substance ooze between his fingers. He checked the consistency, the density and the general feel of the oil to give him some indication as to its value. He took out a small test tube from his backpack and filled it.

Yates stood, held the tube of oil up to the sunlight and swished it around as if he were judging a fine wine. Then, in almost silent reverence, he moved on and carefully repeated the procedure with the two other pools.

Hoku stood to the side, watching quietly like a little child waiting for his father's approval after showing him his report card. After Yates took the last sample, Hoku could remain quiet no longer. "Are you pleased, Great One?" he asked in eager anticipation.

Yates stood in silence, his arms crossed as if in deep thought, wearing his best poker face. On the outside he looked indifferent, even bored, but inside, he was doing cartwheels.

The oil looked good, *very good.* So good in fact, that refining costs could be reduced by nearly twenty percent or more he thought. The only real question now was whether these were shallow pools or a foretaste of a much larger feast. He would come back tomorrow with ground radar equipment and see just how far down the pools went. His calculating, professional mind kept his imagination in check as he analyzed the situation. Still, he did allow a small smile to cross his lips. "Yes, Chief, I think this will do just fine."

Hoku beamed from ear to ear. "I am happy you are pleased. We will feast tonight."

"Yes, yes, that will be just fine," Yates replied, his mind still on the oil

"My Master pleased. I go on your *poderoso* ship? *Mucho honrar* to see Great One's place of power. Please. Would be a story to tell my people. Songs to pass on to children's children."

Yates hadn't thought of the idea of being immortalized in song but it did have its appeal. For a brief moment, he envisioned Hoku with the tribe gathered around a huge fire as he acted as part story teller, part choir director as he told the tale of how *he* was given the *honrar* of visiting the great metal ship that the Servant of God called home.

But the vision quickly faded because he knew he really couldn't let any unauthorized people on board the flagship. Slowly he shook his head. "I'm not sure that's a good idea, Chief."

Hoku quickly bowed his head, almost cowering, and refused to look Yates in the face. "I understand, I not worthy of such *honrar.*"

"It's not that Chief," Yates replied, feeling a little remorseful. "It's just that what you ask is a difficult thing."

"Your head servant, the one called Murphy, does not want you to do this. As chief, I too know you must listen to those who serve you so as not to anger them."

A sudden flush of anger shot across Yates' face as he remembered Murphy scolding him in front of the chief. Maybe taking Hoku on the ship wasn't the greatest idea, but what was a really bad idea was for Hoku to think that he was weak and not really in command.

"You are right Chief, men such as ourselves who rule over many do have a responsibility to listen to those under us, but while it is good to listen, it is up to us, not them, to make the decisions."

"You wise," Hoku said, bowing slightly.

"In fact, now would be a good time to call *my* servant and see if he is following *my* orders," Yates said, taking out his radio.

"Mr. Murphy, do you copy?"

"Right here Captain."

"Is everything all right?"

"Other than Doug trying to shoot me, things are fine."

"I beg your pardon?"

"Sorry sir, long story. Everything is fine here. Have you checked out the oil yet?"

Yates turned from Hoku and lowered his voice a little. "I found three small pools and the oil looks very promising."

"That's good news, sir. We'll stay in touch."

"Very good, over and out."

"They *bueno*?" Hoku asked.

"Yes Chief. I must return to my ship and process these samples..." he said, slapping Hoku on the back, "...and you have a feast to prepare for."

CHAPTER TWELVE

The group walked silently through the waist high grass, following single file behind Kekao and the two porters. With no jungle canopy to protect them, the sun beat down mercilessly on the travelers. Soon their clothes were saturated with sweat and their backpacks began to feel as though they were full of bricks.

The only good thing about the heat, Murphy thought, was that it kept Crawford from complaining. As they were walking, they heard a panther's faint growl in the distance, carried by the slight breeze that did little to cool them. Crawford looked in the general direction of the sound but was too hot and drained to really show much emotion.

Murphy looked at Sarah and could tell that the heat was wearing her down too but she was showing less strain than her techno geek counterpart. He took out his canteen and drained it with three big gulps. This was the part of the adventure he could do without.

They reached the end of the valley and came to a stream that ran along the base of the foothills. They were happy to reach the refreshing water but just as happy to crawl under the shade provided by the overhanging trees on the far bank.

Crawford had dropped his pack and was just about to dive into the stream when Kekao stepped in front of him. "We cross here, spend night at top of hill. Get water and check yourselves after we cross."

That drew the attention of all of them. "What do you mean, 'check ourselves?'"

Murphy asked.

"There are *animales* in water," Kekao replied, speaking slowly and almost in a whisper, as if speaking out loud would somehow stir the creatures. "They start small, but turn *grande* when they feed."

Murphy couldn't tell if it was a shadow cast by the swaying tree branches or not, but he thought he saw small, sadistic smile curl Kekao's lips.

"Great," Murphy heard Crawford say, with much less sarcasm and annoyance than he expected. "If we don't get eaten by a huge panther then we get sucked dry by vampire leeches. I'm so hot, to hell with it, I'm going in anyway."

Crawford dropped his backpack then rummaged through it, producing a roll of duct tape.

"Duct tape?" Sarah said. "That's pretty nerdy, even for you."

"Like my Dad always said, 'there are few things in life that a bigger hammer or a roll of duct tape won't fix.'"

"I like your Dad." Murphy said.

Sarah just rolled her eyes. "Boys and their toys."

Crawford took the roll and wrapped tape around his waist like a belt. He wrapped it several times around each thigh, taping the legs of his shorts to his body. "That should do it," he said as he tore it off.

"What *are* you doing?" Sarah asked, staring at him.

"If the little devils want to feast, then let them. The tape is making a seal to keep them out and let them know that this section of the buffet is closed." He tossed the tape on the ground then ran into the water hollering like a kid jumping into the local swimming hole.

Sarah stood there shaking her head, watching Crawford as he splashed around. "Do you believe this?" she said as she turned to Murphy but stopped in mid-sentence.

"What?" Murphy said as he finished wrapping his legs. "I'm hot too." He tossed her the tape and jumped in. Five minutes later, wearing a silver duct tape bathing suit, Sarah was enjoying the cool water with the others.

After ten minutes, Kekao grunted and told everyone that it was time to go. Reluctantly, they got out and gathered their things and carried them over to the far bank. All three looked at each other with apprehension.

"Well this is it, the moment of truth," Murphy said.

"I don't care. It was worth it," Crawford said as he shook his head like a St. Bernard, throwing water everywhere. He took a deep breath then turned his back to Murphy so he could check for leaches. Murphy looked at Sarah then rubbed his hands together. He yanked his shirt up like an artist revealing his latest masterpiece, expecting dozens of the creatures to be hanging off his back like tinsel from a Christmas tree.

For a moment the only sound was that of the birds singing and the trees rustling. "What is it?" Crawford asked, his voice heavy with apprehension. Sarah looked at Murphy then she let out a small scream.

"What? What?" Crawford cried. "Is it that bad?"

After another moment, both Murphy and Sarah burst out laughing.

Crawford stood there dumbfounded, not realizing what was going on. When he looked over and saw that even Kekao was smiling, he knew the joke was on him.

"There's nothing there, is there?" Crawford said, pulling down his shirt. Still laughing, Sarah just shook her head. "Sorry Doug, Sarah made me do it."

"Liar," Sarah said, hitting Murphy on the shoulder.

"We go," Kekao said gruffly.

They quickly finished checking each other but no leeches where found anywhere. Refreshed, they quickly geared up and started up the trail after Kekao.

"There never were any leeches in the stream were there?" Murphy asked.

Kekao just smirked and turned and began walking up the path. They all fell in line behind him and began moving up the path that wound gently up between the two hills that were the backdrop for the stream. The ground foliage was much less dense, providing room for the air to move instead of being held captive by the twisting leaves and branches of the jungle. The trees reached high and spread out over the path, shading them from the tropical sun and making the walk almost pleasant.

"What do you think happened to the two guys from the plane?" Crawford asked, coming alongside Murphy.

Murphy shrugged. "It's hard to say. The romantic in me wants to think they survived the crash and were later picked up and returned home and lived long and happy lives. Chances are, since we're so far off the beaten path, they probably just died here. Or, who knows," he said looking around, "they could still be alive and be like that one solider in the Philippines who stayed hidden in the jungle for twenty years after the war ended and didn't know it was over. They could be watching us right now, thinking we are still their enemy and getting ready to ambush us."

"Very funny. I'm gullible, but not that gullible," Crawford said.

Suddenly their quiet conversation was shattered by an ear splitting scream coming from the jungle just behind them.

"Banzai!"

Crawford spun around; eyes and mouth wide open in fear that soon squinted into anger. While he and Murphy were talking, Sarah had slowly lagged behind, hid in the jungle then, shouted her war cry. She stepped out and she and Murphy instantly started laughing.

"You should have seen the look on your face," Sarah giggled, gasping air between her laughter.

"Think about it, Doug," Murphy said, holding his side, "Even if these guys were alive, they'd be over 80 years old. They'd be doing their banzai charge in a wheel chair."

Crawford just stood there, glaring at his friends. "I don't understand why you two think it's so funny to scare me. You know I didn't want to come out here... that I'm not comfortable in the great outdoors. I'm a fat geek who likes his 32-inch monitor, big office chair and a beer at hand. I'm not like you two who enjoy playing Tarzan and Jane, matching your wits against Mother Nature and Mr. Personality up there." He pointed at Kekao.

Sarah started to say something but was stopped by an upraised hand from Crawford.

"Save it," he said to Sarah then looked at Murphy, "you too. Just leave me alone."

"Doug!" Murphy protested, but Crawford turned and walked up the path, passing the two porters and falling silently into line behind Kekao.

"Wow," Murphy said as he fell in beside Sarah bringing up the rear.

"I guess we have been a little hard on him," she said quietly. Murphy nodded. "Yeah, I guess so."

The group was silent as they continued on for another hour, up out of the draw and into another small meadow, near the base of the smaller volcano.

"We stop here," Kekao said. "You sleep here," he pointed to a large grassy spot, "and we sleep over there in trees. Do not go into jungle. Many things that can kill you. You get wood for fire. We hunt."

They got their equipment from the porters and began setting up their small tents. Both Murphy and Sarah noticed that Crawford was having a little trouble setting up his tent but after what had happened, they were afraid to ask if he needed help.

After five minutes of struggling with the stakes and the poles, Crawford threw them down in frustration. "Okay, I'm a geek and a nerd and a city boy. Can one of you please help me here?"

Murphy nodded his head. "Sure Doug," he replied, by way of an apology. After a few minutes, Murphy had Crawford's tent up.

"Thanks," Crawford said, his tone less harsh but still reserved.

"And if you don't mind a little advice," Murphy said, "make sure you keep the flap zipped up at all times. It will help keep out any unwanted guests."

Just then they heard the cry of a panther echo in the distance, answered by another who was much closer.

"I don't suppose a zipped up flap will stop one of those things?" Crawford asked, tilting his head toward the jungle.

"Sorry," Murphy said, shaking his head. Murphy watched as his friend rubbed the necklaces that Kekao had given him.

"Didn't think so. I'm going to take a nap. Please wake me when Kekao and the boys return with dinner." Crawford crawled into his tent and zipped the flap shut.

"That sounds like a good idea," Sarah said, grinning. "I need to freshen up a bit then decide what I'm going to wear for dinner."

"Always the fashion diva," Murphy replied with his own smile.

As Sarah disappeared into her tent, Murphy thought about taking a snooze too. He was tired, but like a little kid, he was afraid he would miss something if he fell asleep. Instead of napping, he finished stowing his gear then went about setting up camp.

He made a fire ring away from the tents, gathered some wood, being careful not to disturb any sleeping snakes and in anticipation of Kekao's success, found some sticks to use as skewers to roast whatever beast the mighty hunters might bring back.

As he laid the last of the sticks down for the fire, he saw Kekao and the other two natives emerge from the trees halfway down the meadow. They were carrying three animals that looked like fat rabbits. He was amazed that they could kill such nimble creatures with just spears.

He recalled a time in his younger days when he'd lived in Las Vegas. He and two other guys from work went out shooting into the desert with shotguns and pistols, to have a little fun. As they were looking for something to shoot at, they spotted a rabbit. They thought it would be a great, manly thing to do to kill their dinner and cook and eat it in the wild.

The next thirty seconds sounded like the Allies storming the beaches at Normandy as all three of them blasted away with their shotguns then emptied the clips of the handguns. After the smoke cleared and the dust settled, the rabbit just hopped away untouched.

"When woman wakes, have her clean and cook," Kekao said to Murphy as he threw the animals on the ground.

Murphy laughed. "You don't know Sarah very well. You could be waiting a very long time."

"I got this," Crawford said, coming up behind Murphy. "Tell you what, Kekao, you have Thing One here," he said, nodding at one of the porters, "gut and chop these things up and send Thing Two with me to keep me safe in the jungle while I gather some herbs, and I'll fix the best tasting rabbit... or whatever you call these things, you ever had in your life. Trust me," he said, patting his large belly.

Kekao looked at the fat helper of God and considered it for a moment, then ordered his two men to do as Crawford had asked.

"Dallas, go ahead and get the fire going," Crawford said, "I'll be back in about half an hour if I can find everything I need."

"Will do," Murphy replied, "toss me your lighter please."

Crawford nodded and tossed him the lighter then turned and disappeared into the jungle with his bodyguard in tow.

By the time Crawford came back, Murphy had a good fire with hot coals going and Kekao and the other native had the meat cut and prepared. Out of the supply packs the natives had been carrying, Crawford got the pots and pans and began cooking.

Murphy watched with fascination as his friend set about making a gourmet meal in the middle of nowhere. Crawford made a stew in one pot, adding large chunks of meat then throwing in roots, herbs and vegetables. In another pan, he took smaller pieces of meat and fried them along with more vegetables and put them on skewers as appetizers.

"Where did you learn to cook like this?" Murphy asked.

Crawford smiled. "You didn't think I got this big by just eating fast food and frozen pizza did you? I learned early on that I liked food so I figured since I like eating so much I should learn how to cook."

"That smells wonderful," Sarah said as she emerged from her tent. "And I thought we were just going to have some freeze dried junk."

"I see you decided to dress casual for dinner tonight," Murphy joked.

Crawford handed her one of the skewers, "You're just in time."

Sarah took the skewer and tentatively nibbled on the roasted vegetables and meat. "This is really good. Did you do all this, Doug?" she asked, looking at the feast that was spread out before her.

"It was a group effort," Crawford replied. "Kekao and the boys brought the meat, I got the vegetables and cooked, while Dallas gathered the wood and built the fire."

"I guess the only thing left for me to do is eat," she said, taking another bite.

"Or do the dishes," Crawford said.

Murphy burst out laughing and Kekao grunted in approval which brought a scowl to Sarah's face and made Murphy laugh all the harder.

Everyone ate and relaxed, and Murphy could feel the tensions of the day and their hard journey fade away. He noticed that Kekao and the porters Crawford had dubbed "Thing One" and "Thing Two" enjoyed the meal as well. Kekao even talked a little, allowing himself to complete an entire sentence or two without his customary grunts.

Before they realized it, the sun had sunk into the deep waters of the Pacific and the night creatures had firmly secured their hold on the jungle.

"We eat too long," Kekao said as he stood. "The jungle is bad place at night. You all sleep now. We have long *viaje* to the great storeroom tomorrow. If you must pee during the night, be *rapido* and stay close."

"You'll get no argument from me," Crawford said. "Good night all." He got up and went to his tent. Kekao and his men also got up and headed for their campsite, leaving Murphy sitting alone with Sarah.

He sat there watching the firelight dance in her eyes and desperately wanted to say something clever and cute to start the conversation, but nothing came to mind. He looked up at the intense night sky, and couldn't remember the last time he had seen the brilliance and clarity of the stars without being diluted by manmade light. He wanted to talk to Sarah in this wild setting, so far away from their normal everyday lives; he wanted to ask her what had gone wrong, what he had done that was so terrible to make her leave, and how he could fix it.

There had been the occasional date here and there but he had never really gotten over her; he still loved her. It wasn't a pathetic, clingy love, but one still based on respect and admiration. He wasn't sure which hurt worse, the fact that she had left him or that he really didn't know the reason why.

There had been the usual fighting and bickering that all couples have, and she had cited only "irreconcilable differences" in the divorce papers, but he had always felt there had been something more, something hidden just below the surface that she had never told him.

Feeling like a teenager gathering his courage to ask a girl on a date, he turned to her just as she stood.

"What's that?" she said, pointing at the sky.

Murphy followed her stare and saw what looked like a falling star, only much closer. "It looks like a flare," he replied, "and it looks like it's coming from the village.

Murphy grabbed his radio to talk to Yates, but the only reply he got was static.

CHAPTER THIRTEEN

The darkness of the night sky vanished in the blink of an eye as the flare burst high over the village. Everything stopped as if the pause button had been pushed on the video player. All conversations were cut off in mid-sentence, music ceased in mid-beat and villagers froze in their tracks. The only thing moving was the flickering flames of the campfires. Then, as if on command, the entire population of the village fell prostrate where they were and silently faced the Servant of God.

Yates had come up with the idea of using the flair gun as a way of impressing Malana with his "Godhood" and he'd hoped the rest of the native would take notice as well, but he had no idea it would be this extreme. He smiled to himself looking at all the villagers lying before him like toy figures toppled by the wind.

Allowing himself a moment more to bask in his own glory, he finally spoke.

"Arise, Great Chief Hoku, and all of your people. I, the Great Servant of God, have brought down a star for you, one I picked from the very heavens themselves to show how pleased I am with you."

And pleased he was. The oil samples tested out better than he could ever have wished for. He only hoped that the oil ran deep and was not just surface pools. If the oil was drillable, then he would call headquarters and start negotiating a deal. If not, then this was just a pleasant little distraction that he could write off as R&R for the crew.

Hesitantly, Hoku looked up and was relieved to see Yates smiling. Hoku allowed himself a small smile as he slowly stood. Taking their cue from their leader, the other villagers began to rise as well.

"We know you are great," Hoku said, his voice trembling, "but thought only God that *potenta*. We are most *honrar* and *bendito* to have you with us."

As Yates looked out over his followers, his gazed stopped at Malana. She wore a strange look, a combination of fear and admiration and one other emotion that he recognized and was beginning to feel himself: lust.

Their eyes met and Yates could feel his passion beginning to rise. He held her gaze for just a moment longer, then turned to survey the rest of his people. He might be the Servant of God, but he was itching to show her a devil of a time.

Hoku led Yates to the table where they sat down and with a clap of his hands, the feast began. Yates was once again impressed with the spread laid out before him. He smiled at all the pageantry, food and music; it reminded him of a Vegas dinner and floor show. At any minute he expected to see a spotlight shine down and to have Don Ho being brought in on a giant pineapple stage singing *Tiny Bubbles*.

After eating far more than he should have, again, Yates leaned back on some grass mats and enjoyed sipping some of Hoku's coffee. After all the feasting over the past few days, he was going to have to spend more time in the ship's gym, not only to work off the few extra pounds but to stay in shape for Malana.

Throughout the evening, Yates had been stealing glances at Malana. Sometimes she would turn away, seemingly embarrassed by his attention, yet a few times she held his gaze, which made him shyly turn away. He felt like a teenager back in high school.

As he watched, Malana got up from the table where she had been sitting with the other women, then slowly walked over and stood in front of him. He expected her to say something yet she remained silent, just staring at him with her dark brown eyes. He was a little uncomfortable with the long silence and he was just about to say something when the music suddenly started up again.

Yates felt a lump in his throat as she began swaying seductively to the music. He quickly glanced to Hoku to see if she was doing anything wrong but his simple, almost child-like smile said that this was normal. Yates had to concentrate to keep his smile from turning into a leer as she moved closer. He wondered if this was some kind of mating ritual. Was he about to get married? She was very beautiful. Oh the sacrifices he would endure for the company. He smiled to himself. He would enjoy the honeymoon at least until the deal was set and they weighed anchor.

He was so focused on Malana that at first he didn't notice that the music had stopped and that everyone was looking toward the clearing. He finally realized that she wasn't dancing any longer and he peered around her to see what was so damned important to interfere with his celebration.

Three men stood at the edge of the clearing.

At first he was angry that his crew had interrupted his island lap dance but then he took a closer look; the men weren't wearing their uniforms. He would not only chastise them for interrupting, but also for being in civilian clothes. Then it struck him: these men were not part of his crew.

But who were they and how did they find the island and why were they here? Did other people know about this place? Suddenly his visions of exclusive oil rights and wealth were beginning to slip through his fingers.

Yates stood and was quickly followed by Hoku as the men approached. They looked more Asian than Pacific Islander which added all the more to his fears that his undiscovered country was not as isolated as he had hoped. Yates could tell by their clothes that they weren't from any commercial fleet; they looked more like fisherman or independent merchants in their cargo pants and T-shirts. He couldn't see any weapons, but that didn't mean anything. The men looked rough and even though the natives had spears, they'd be no match for these guys if they had guns.

"What can I do for you?" Yates asked, keeping his tone friendly.

"The question is, what can we do for you?" The tallest of the three men said. He was a little bit shorter than Yates, but younger, in his mid-twenties, and had a lean, hard face.

Yates cocked his head, waiting for an explanation.

The man smiled, but there was little warmth in it. "We were several miles out when we saw your flare and thought you might be in need of some assistance."

Yates looked at the three of them, sizing them up and not liking what he was seeing. "Yes, well thank you for your offer, but as you can see, everything is fine here and we don't need your help."

The leader nodded as he looked around at the celebration, paying particular attention to Malana and the other women. "If we can't help you, then perhaps you can help us?"

"How so?" Yates asked cautiously.

"We are simple businessmen, independent traders, trying to scratch out a living and we've been out of port for over a month. My men and I could use a little distraction from our hard days at sea."

Again, Yates could see the man's eyes wander over the women of the village but his eyes lingered on Malana. Yate recognized the lustful grin the man was trying to hide and he also knew they weren't "simple businessmen." They were smugglers at best, pirates at worst.

He wasn't worried about the safety of his ship. The *Pacific Searcher*, the flagship of the fleet, was equipped with technology that would be extremely valuable to competitor companies and even to some sovereign nations, so she also had a well-trained crew who knew how to defend the ship and enough firepower to sink the navies of many Third World countries. They even had an anti-aircraft missile on board, though he was the only one who knew about it; not exactly legal, but corporate espionage could be just as dangerous and deadly as any nation sanctioned spying.

His confident smile faded, however. The ship, with all her guns and the men to wield them, were in the harbor, while he was here alone and unarmed.

"We would be happy to supply you with all the fresh fruit and roasted boar you and your men can eat," Yates said, gesturing to the tables, "but I don't think it would be a very good idea for you to join us."

The man took a few steps forward. "My men work hard, and we like to play hard. I don't think a steak and a couple or mangos are going to satisfy them."

"Maybe not, but that's all we can offer," Yates said, his voice assuming a tone of finality.

The man paused, looking at Yates and sizing up the situation. "I think you have a lot more to offer than that," he said, looking straight at Malana this time.

Yates took a step forward. "That's all you'll get. I suggest you take it and leave."

A mean ugliness swept across the man's face as he too took a step forward, meeting Yates' challenge. "Listen Captain, Ahab, I don't think you understand. We'll take what we want, whether you want to give it to us or not."

Hoku now stepped up beside Yates. "Not dare to talk to the Great Servant of God like that," he shouted, anger radiating from his voice.

The man stopped and looked at his two companions and they all burst out laughing. "Great Servant of God?" he said, looking at Yates. "You really know how to party. I want to smoke some of whatever it is you gave those guys," He laughed again.

"Show respect," Hoku shouted out again.

"Listen to me Zulu Chief, or whatever you are," he said, all laughter gone. "You show me some respect."

He took a pistol from behind his back. "We'll take your fruit and meat, old man."

He gave Yates a hard stare. "And we'll take her too," indicating Malana, "and those three over there." He pointed to a group of women sitting at the table.

"We'll take them to our boat and bring them back in the morning when we're done." He waved his gun. "We can do this the easy way or the hard way."

Suddenly a spear pierced the sand between the man's feet. His eyes went wide in stunned disbelief and grew even wider as he saw several more natives standing with spears at the ready.

"I told you, speak with respect to Great Servant." Hoku said.

Seizing the moment, Yates spoke. "Do you really want to do this?" he said, looking directly at the man. "We can do this the easy way or the hard way. Why don't you and your men simply turn around and get back in your boat and leave. No one needs to get hurt."

"Okay, okay, you win," the man said as he held up the gun with his finger off the trigger, then slowly returned it to its hiding place behind his back. "No woman is worth getting killed over." He turned to go, then looked back at Malana, "but you were close."

Yates and Hoku stood silently and watched the three strangers disappear into the jungle. As soon as they left, Hoku turned to Yates. "Those evil men. I no trust them. They come back I fear." Hoku paused, not sure if he was pushing his bounds. "I know you not want us on your great vessel but you must take Malana and the women that evil men *deseo*. They will be safe with you."

"I don't know…" Yates started to say, but was interrupted by the chief.

"Please Great Servant of God," Hoku pleaded. "God not be angry with you for protecting your people."

Yates knew that Hoku was right. The smugglers would be back, if for nothing else than just to prove their point that they were not going to let an old man and a bunch of "Zulus" push them around. He could justify to God—in this case, corporate headquarters—that it was the right thing to do, not only morally, but as a matter of good business; it made sense to protect the rightful owners of the island… and the oil.

"I'll take the women with me to the ship and then I'll come back with some men to help protect the village."

"Thank you, thank you oh Great One." Hoku bowed low before Yates. "But do not send your men. We strong warriors," he said, pounding his fist against his chest, "and we can defend our village."

Yates smiled and shook his head. "I have no doubts about your bravery, Chief Hoku, but these men have guns."

"Have faith in your servants. We be fine."

Yates nodded reluctantly, "Very well then Chief, gather your people and escort us to the beach. I'll call my ship and have a team waiting for us there."

Several more warriors now appeared, joining the others who had held the smugglers at bay. Each man had a spear in hand and a twelve-inch long curved knife in his belt. There were no ceremonial headdresses or clothing here, these men were ready for combat. They stood guard while the villagers scattered, preparing for what would be a long and possibly dangerous night.

As the villager scurried about, Yates took out his radio. He looked down and saw he had a muted incoming message. He hoped it wasn't the ship calling saying they had trouble.

"Yates here," he answered.

"Captain, it's Dallas. Are you okay? We saw a flare go off and tried to call but you didn't answer."

"Yes, Mr. Murphy, there was a little bit of trouble here but all is fine."

"Trouble sir? What kind of trouble? Do you want us to come back? We can head back first thing in the morning if you want."

"No, that won't be necessary. Some local riffraff tried to crash our party but they've left now. Hoku is posting some men around the village tonight just in case, but I don't think there will be any problems." He didn't tell Murphy that he was bringing the women on board the ship because he didn't need to hear his First Officer's objections, and didn't want to appear weak in front of Hoku by arguing on the radio with his head minion.

"What's your situation?" Yates continued.

"Everything is good here. Kekao says we should reach the storehouse by mid-morning. I'll give you a call when we get there and let you know what we find." He paused for a moment then continued. "Are you sure you don't want us to come back, sir?"

Just then, Hoku came up and stood bedside Yates. "No, Chief Hoku and I," he said smiling at Hoku and putting his hand on his shoulder, "have everything under control. Yates out."

"Your servants *bueno*?" Hoku asked smiling, pleased that Yates was showing confidence in him.

"They're fine. Murphy says they should be at the storehouse by noon."

"This is good."

"Are the women ready yet?"

"Yes, they come now."

The four women came out of the far hut escorted by four more guards. Each woman had a shawl over her head and carried a small leather bag. Yates smiled to himself; even in the middle of nowhere, women still had to have their purses.

"Thank you for keeping women safe from evil men," Hoku told him. "I have spoken and women know their place. They sleep in open and they bring their own food and water. They will not be a *carga* to you."

"They are not a burden if that's what you mean; they are my guests and will be treated as such. You have shown me great kindness and now it is my chance to repay. They will be safe and treated well. This I promise."

"We owe you much," Hoku said.

"Yates smiled inside; just the words he wanted to hear. "Are you sure you don't want me to send any of my men?"

Hoku shook his head. "Knowing women safe, we can fight."

"I'm sorry this had to happen to spoil the magnificent feast you prepared. I wish we could erase all evil from the face of the earth," Yates said.

"To know you watch over us is *suficiente*," Hoku replied.

"Thank you Chief. I will return in the morning." Yates nodded and start toward the beach, followed by the women and the guards. When he reached the edge of the clearing he turned to see Hoku directing his people as if they were preparing for a great battle. He only hoped that it would be nothing more than a drill.

CHAPTER FOURTEEN

"What's going on?" Crawford said, hearing the concern in Murphy's voice talking on the radio.

"There's been some sort of trouble back at the village," Murphy replied.

"What kind of trouble? Are we going back?"

Murphy shook his head. "The captain said everything was under control and for us to keep going to the storehouse tomorrow. It looks like business as usual."

"All right then," Crawford said as he turned back to his tent. "I'll see you all in the morning."

"Goodnight Doug," Sarah said.

Murphy hoped she would want to sit and enjoy the fire and talk, but just as he was about to ask her, she spoke first.

"I think I'm going to call it a night too. It's been a long day and even though I took that nap, I'm still exhausted."

Murphy managed to keep the disappointment from showing as he spoke. "I understand. It has been quite a day. Goodnight, sleep tight, and don't let the bedbugs bite, or whatever else is out here."

"Very funny. Goodnight, Dallas."

He sighed as he watched her walk away. Even though he was tired too, he didn't want to go to bed. He threw a couple of logs on the fire and daydreamed about what they might find tomorrow.

After an hour and a half of bouncing back and forth between feeling sorry for himself and spending the millions from the treasure they were going to find, he decided it was time to go to bed. He threw three more pieces of wood on the fire to help keep kitty-kitty away, and then went to his tent.

Just as he was getting ready to open the flap, Murphy heard a noise, like someone whispering his name. He looked around, but didn't see anyone, and decided it must have been the wind rustling through the trees. He unzipped the tent and was just about to crawl in when he heard it again, only this time he was sure it was his name.

"Dallas."

"Who's out there?" He whispered loudly, not wanting to wake anyone just in case it was the wind and his imagination.

"Over here," the voice whispered back, barely audible. "It's me, Doug."

"Doug? What are you doing?" Murphy asked as he stepped over to Crawford's tent and started to open the flap.

"Stop, stop, stop," Crawford whispered as loud as he dared.

"What is it Doug, what's wrong?"

"Something is in here with me." Murphy could hear the panic in his voice.

"What is it?"

"I don't know."

"What do you mean, you don't know?"

"I crawled into my sleeping bag and left it unzipped because it was hot. I was almost asleep when I felt something brush up against my leg. When I started to move to see what it was, I heard this hissing sound so I froze. I think it's a snake."

"How did it get in there?"

"I must have left the flap open when I came out to see what was going on with the captain and the radio."

"What's going on?" Sarah said as she stuck her head out her own tent.

"Doug has company in there and it isn't your bedbugs."

"Can you get him out of there?" Concern rising in her voice.

"Every time I try to unzip the flap, whatever's in there starts getting nervous," Murphy replied. "We'll have to cut out the side of the tent and go from there." Murphy took out his knife and inserted it into the side of the tent near the top.

"Hang on a second," Sarah said as she ducked back into her tent, then reappeared a moment later. She flipped open her own knife then stood beside Murphy and started cutting downward as he cut across the top. The sharp blades cut easily through the thin fabric walls, but they moved slowly and carefully to avoid upsetting Crawford's guest.

"Almost got it," Murphy said. He had made a horizontal cut across the top of the tent while Sarah had cut vertically down the side. Murphy moved to get behind Sarah to cut down along the other corner of the tent to peel it down and open up the entire side, but as he moved, he tripped over Sarah's foot and his arm hit the fabric as he stumbled to catch himself.

"Stop!" Crawford said as loud as he dared. "It's moving, it's moving! It just crawled over my leg. It's between them now." Murphy and Sarah froze, not moving a muscle, waiting for Crawford to tell them what was happening.

"Okay, the thing has stopped moving." Crawford said, barley able to control his trembling voice.

"Hang in there Doug," Sarah whispered, "we're almost there."

Murphy made the last cut and they peeled back the entire side of the tent. They turned on their flashlights, revealing Crawford lying in his sleeping bag, his hair matted from sweat and his arms stiff at his sides, lying outside of the bag. With agonizing slowness, he turned his head to face his friends. "Hurry please; I don't know how much longer I can stand this," he pleaded.

"Hand on Doug; we're going to get you out of there," Murphy said. He tilted his head back for Sarah to follow him. "Got any ideas?" he asked Sarah once they were out of Crawford's hearing.

"Maybe we can slowly pull back the sleeping bag to see what we're dealing with."

"We can try, but I don't think it'll work. If that thing gets twitchy from us just touching the zipper on the flap then I don't think it will like the idea of us taking the roof off its new home."

"Got any better ideas?"

"I'm thinking. Snake removal wasn't one of my merit badges in the Boy Scouts."

"What wrong?" Kekao asked as he came up behind the pair.

Both Murphy and Sarah were startled by Kekao's silent approach and Sarah let out an involuntary cry of surprise.

"Something crawled into Doug's sleeping bag with him," Murphy said: "we think it's a snake."

Kekao just grunted and stood there thinking.

"Well?" Sarah said impatiently after a few minutes of silence from their guide.

"Wait," was all he said as he turned and walked back to where he and his friends were camped.

Sarah looked at Murphy in disbelief as he left. Murphy just shrugged, not understanding either. After a few moments, Kekao and the other two natives returning.

"Where is it?" Kekao asked Crawford.

Crawford gasped several times then answered. "It's curled up between my legs."

"Can you feel the head?"

"N-n-noo. I think it's in the middle of its coil."

Kekao stood over Crawford, his head tilted to one side, examining the situation and thinking. "I cannot see *animale*. Show me where your body ends and legs start."

Crawford had a puzzled look on his face. "What?"

"He wants to know where your crotch is, Doug," Murphy said. "For Pete sake, be accurate."

Crawford didn't understand but he did as he was told. He slowly moved his hand on the outside of the sleeping bag and cupped his finger. "Here." He said, his fingers trembling.

"What are you going to do?" Sarah whispered.

Kekao ignored her questioned. "Close eyes," he told Crawford, who quickly obeyed.

Sarah started to speak again but Murphy pulled her back as they watched all three men move quietly and carefully into the tent. Suddenly all three raised their spears and with lightning fast movement, began plunging their spears over and over again into the sleeping bag between Crawford's legs.

Crawford screamed then fell silent. With spear raised, Kekao threw back the sleeping bag. The snake was dead, cut into a dozen pieces. He bent down and picked up a large section of the body with the head still attached and examined it. "Very bad. It bites you, you dead," Kekao said as he threw it into the fire.

"Is he all right?" Sarah asked as she rushed over and knelt beside Crawford's unmoving form.

Murphy looked at his friend. "I think he just passed out," he said as he unscrewed the cap off his canteen. "I always wanted to see if this works in real life."

He poured water onto Crawford's face. Crawford spit the water out then sat straight up, wide eyed and dazed. He looked at his friends, not really seeing them, then looked down and saw all the blood between his legs, turned white as the proverbial ghost, and passed out again.

Murphy couldn't help but chuckle as he poured out a little more water then gently slapped his face.

"It's okay Doug," Murphy said. "It's not your blood."

Crawford slowly propped himself up on his elbows and looked down at the chopped remains of the snake. "What happened?" he finally managed to ask.

"Kekao and the boys here sliced and diced your bunk buddy," Murphy told him.

"Thank you." Crawford managed in a weak voice.

Kekao just grunted as usual then spoke. "We move when sun comes up. Check beds, go sleep."

He turned and the three of them went back to their camp.

Crawford slowly stood and steadied himself with Murphy's help. He took a long drink from the canteen. "I always wanted a house with a skylight," he said looking at the ruins of his tent. "Obviously I can't sleep in there. Can I bunk with you tonight?" he said looking at Murphy.

"No offense, Doug, but have you seen yourself? You're filthy and, well, you stink." Crawford looked a little hurt at first but then he caught of whiff of himself and understood.

"Don't look at me," Sarah threw in quickly.

"Tell you what," Murphy said," I'll let you sleep in my tent tonight and I'll go hang out in the trees with Kekao and the boys."

"Thanks Dallas, I really appreciate it."

"But you use your own sleeping bag. Just wipe it down and then turn it inside out and you should be fine."

Murphy grabbed his sleeping bag and gun and started walking toward the trees where Kekao and the other were sleeping. As he passed by Sarah, he hoped she would ask him to stay with her but she only smiled at him as he walked by.

As he walked up, Kekao pointed to a small tree. "You sleep there."

"Thanks for letting me use the guest bedroom." Murphy said as he started climbing.

Kekao just gave him a strange look. "Wrap vines around you so you no fall. The fall not kill you, but things that crawl on ground might."

"Thanks for the info, and I'll try and not leave the toilet seat up either." Murphy crawled in the sleeping bag and wrapped himself up.

Kekao frowned and didn't respond with his customary grunt which drew an even bigger smile from Murphy. Despite the excitement, he soon fell asleep, staring up at the moon shining through the rustling leaves.

Even though sleep came quickly, it was a fitful rest, as he dozed off and on. He was comfortable in his cocoon, yet even in sleep, his subconscious mind was uneasy, knowing he was suspended six feet above the ground. Glancing over, he saw the embers of the fire, the flames long since gone but the coals still glowing a deep red. He saw the familiar peaked outlines of the tents.

He was just about to close his eyes and drift off to sleep again when he noticed a dark shape at the edge of the field. Thinking it was just shadows of tree branches cast by the moonlight, he felt his eyelids grow heavy. He was ready to surrender to sleep's call.

Then it moved.

Suddenly his eyes popped back open again, his brain overriding the need for sleep, as he realized that the shadow was moving in the open, away from the trees! He sat up so quickly he nearly spilled out of his tree bed, rocking back and forth like a dinghy in rough water.

Steadying himself, he concentrated on the shadow, trying to see if it was real or just his imagination. He stared at it for so long he was just about to credit it to his imagination when he saw it move again. It glided forward a few feet then stopped, then glided a few more. Then it got smaller, like it was crouching down.

Crouching down? It was the panther!

He looked at the shadow then looked to see where it was going; the panther was heading straight for the tents. Murphy hurriedly tried to kick out of his sleeping bag, lost his balance and flipped over his bed. He crashed through the branches and landed with a loud thud on the ground, knocking the wind out of himself.

He tried to shout a warning but his lungs were empty. Staggering to his feet, he could only manage a loud whispered warning as he charged toward the tents. Fumbling with the holster, he drew his pistol and fired a shot in the general direction of the shadow.

The blast shattered the night, sounding like a battleship's gun firing. Murphy heard Kekao and the others jumping out of their beds but he continued on, not waiting for them. He lost sight of the panther in the darkness as he ran forward and reached the camp. Catching his breath, he looked around and saw the tents, but no panther. He hoped the gun shot had scared it off.

Then silently the big cat appeared from behind Crawford's tent and stepped into the open. Murphy was more stunned than frightened at its boldness, and marveled at its beauty and strength. He locked stares with the beast and was mesmerized; its eyes were a deep, glowing red, reflecting the embers of the fire but also shining with an intense and strange combination of both intelligence and primal savagery.

Almost in unison, Sarah and Crawford stuck their heads out of their tents to see what was going on, and both froze the instant they saw the panther.

It didn't seem to be afraid as it stood its ground, staring intently at the three humans. It let out a low, rumbling growl then cautiously took a step toward Crawford. Crawford's eyes grew as big as the moon itself then he ducked back into his tent and zipped up the flap.

Suddenly a spear appeared out of nowhere, landing two feet in front of the panther. It crouched down, setting its ears back and hissing, baring all its teeth.

"Shoot it!" Sarah shouted.

Sarah's voice shook Murphy out of his trance. He started to bring the gun up but it was too late; the panther had already disappeared back into the darkness.

"Why didn't you shoot it when you had the chance?" Sarah asked, climbing out of her tent.

"I-I don't know," Murphy replied, not really sure himself. "It was really weird being that close to it, staring it in the eye."

"Maybe you have no cojones ," Kekao said, walking up and pulling the spear out of the ground.

Murphy spun around and faced his native guide. "I didn't lose my nerve," he replied, anger filling his voice.

"Dallas," Sarah said, putting her hands on his chest, trying to defuse the situation. She leaned closer so Kekao couldn't hear. "Let it go...please."

"What is it with Mother Nature and me?" Crawford said, crawling out of his tent. "Did I do something to tick her off?"

That seemed to break the tension and they all relaxed a little.

"That does it, I'm not sleeping anymore tonight," Crawford said as he grabbed a couple of pieces of wood and threw them on the fire. "May I?" he said as he took a spear from Thing One and sat down on a rock in front of the fire. "I'm just going to sit here and wait for the sun to come up."

He said it so matter-of-factly that Murphy and Sarah just looked at each other and burst out laughing. Murphy glanced at his watch. "I think I'll join you. I was getting seasick in that swaying birdhouse anyway," he said, throwing another log on the fire and sitting down beside his friend.

"Well you boys have fun with your male bonding," Sarah said. "I'm going back to bed and grab a couple more hours of sleep. And if I hear just one verse of *Kumbaya,* you'll wish the panther had got a hold of you instead of me."

Murphy held up his hands in surrender. He made some coffee, and then he and Crawford sat under the stars and solved all the world's problems.

CHAPTER FIFTEEN

"Good morn'in Cap'n," Joe Bob said.

"Good morning Mr. Thornbird," Yates replied, stepping onto the bridge. He smiled at Thornbird's smooth twang; it was a welcome relief from the natives' choppy monotone. He sat quietly in his chair, sipping his coffee and began reviewing the reams of paperwork associated with running the flagship of one of the world's largest energy companies.

He had just signed the last form when he heard a giggle behind him. He turned around and saw Malana standing in the doorway.

"Malana, you shouldn't be up here." His tone was a little sharper than he intended; he was taking out his irritation at the paperwork, not her. Instantly her smile faded and she fell to her knees.

"Forgive me, Great Servant," she said, her voice trembling in fear. "I wanted to see the *trono* of your kingdom. I go from ship now."

"I'm sorry Malana," Yates said as he went over and helped her to her feet. "You and your friends must stay. It may not be safe yet for you back on the island. Besides, I would be hurt if you left before I had a chance to personally show you the ship."

Malana's smile quickly returned and she even blushed.

"But until then," he said, holding her hands, "I must ask you and your friends to stay in your rooms for your own protection. Can you do that for me?"

"Oh yes! I tell others and they will obey."

"Thank you. Now please go back to your room as I have very important things to look after. I will come for you when I have finished."

Malana smiled and nodded eagerly, then turned and left. Yates watched her skip down the passageway. When she disappeared around the corner he looked back at Thornbird.

"I'm taking an armed party ashore. While I'm gone, please ensure that the crew stays on full alert and that all sentry posts are manned until we know what the smugglers intentions are. And as much as possible," he added smiling, "please keep our guests in their rooms."

"Yes sir," Thornbird replied.

With the longboat brimming with an armed landing party, Yates felt more like he was taking Iwo Jima instead of Columbus discovering the New World.

When the boat nudged up on the beach, there were no native guides to greet them and Yates didn't know whether to take that as a good sign or not. Cautiously, he and his four men entered the jungle and began following the trail to the village. They paused every once in a while, stopping to listen for any sounds of trouble. As they drew nearer to the village, Yates smelled smoke. He looked up through the canopy and saw several small spirals of smoke rising where the village should be.

Was it just smoke from their cook fires or the smoldering remains of a burned village? He quickened his pace.

Coming out of the jungle and into the clearing, Yates was relieved at what he saw. Hoku was seated at the table with several other tribesmen. The fires were going and the women were fixing breakfast: life as usual.

He was glad to see that things looked normal in the village, yet he was a little puzzled. After their encounter with the smugglers last night, he would have thought that at the very least he would have seen a few warriors standing guard.

Hoku saw Yates and immediately jumped up from the table. "Oh Great Servant," he said as he came running up, "I not know you were coming. Forgive me, no food ready."

"There's nothing to forgive," Yates said looking around. "Do you have any guards posted, Chief?"

"No," Hoku smiled, showing Yates to the table. "Come sit, I have food brought. Your servants may stay or go. We safe now."

"Safe now?"

"Yes, bad men gone." Hoku replied matter-of-factly.

Yates looked puzzled. "You saw them leave?"

"We followed your orders," Hoku smiled broadly.

"My orders?"

"Yes, you said evil should be removed from the earth. We did what you say. You like fish? It good with fruit."

Yates felt his stomach begin to tighten. He hoped Hoku hadn't done what he was thinking. He had to ask the question but wasn't sure if he really wanted to hear the answer. If his fears were true, he didn't want any witnesses to the chief's admission.

"Parker, take the men back to the ship. I'll be fine."

Parker acknowledged and Yates waited until they had disappeared into the jungle before he spoke again.

"Tell me Chief, what exactly did you think my orders were, and what exactly did you do?"

Hoku looked surprised then became worried when he saw the stern look on Yates' face.

"I sorry," Hoku began pleading, "has Hoku done wrong? You punish me?"

"No!" Yates said, his voice on the verge of anger. "Just tell me what you did, please."

"You said men evil and evil should be *eliminado*, so we do what you say, we *eliminado*."

"Removed them? How?" Frustration and concern clearly filled Yates' voice.

Hoku cowered. "We follow them back to their boat. You said they evil," he threw in, defending himself.

"Hoku!"

"We killed them, Oh Great One. You not pleased? Why? We only do what you say. You say *eliminado* evil so we did."

"I didn't mean for you to kill them," Yates blurted out.

"But you said…"

"I know what I said, but that wasn't what I meant." Yates got up shaking his head. "What have you done?" he groaned to himself and started pacing back and forth.

By now all the other villagers had left, not wanting to be anywhere near the angry Servant of God. Yates stopped pacing and abruptly sat down, burying his head in his hands, his mind working in high gear, muttering out loud.

"This can't be happening." Yates muttered to himself. "I don't need the authorities involved with any of this. All the bureaucracy will do is nothing but tie everything up in the courts for years to come. And once the world knows that oil has been discovered, there'll be half a dozen countries trying to claim sovereignty over the island...and my new found riches." Suddenly he had a headache.

"Okay, where are their bodies?" He asked Hoku.

"We leave them on their boat."

"Where is the boat then?"

"Far at sea. We sink it beyond the reef. Evil if far from us now. We know you only wanted to protect us by telling us to kill them," Hoku added sheepishly.

"I didn't tell you..." Yates started to say, but then stopped. "What did you just say, Chief?"

"I said we took the boat..."

"No, I got that part. What did you say after that?"

Hoku looked confused and was slow to speak, afraid of saying the wrong thing. "That we know you only protecting us?"

"That's it!" Yates burst out laughing but could tell by the look on Hoku's face that he didn't understand. "Don't you see Chief? You were only protecting yourself. It was self-defense. No jury in the world would convict you for defending your homes. And besides, if they can't find the bodies or the boat, who's to say anything happened at all?"

Hoku was puzzled and confused but happy that at least the Great Servant was smiling again. "Everything good then?" he managed to say.

"Yes, yes, everything *is* good, Chief." Yates replied, slapping Hoku on the back.

"Now, as you were saying earlier, something about the breakfast?"

CHAPTER SIXTEEN

Sarah stepped out of her tent into the morning light, yawned and stretched. The morning sun felt good on her skin though she knew she'd be cursing it later in the day. She looked over to the campfire where she had left her two friends the night before, expecting them to be slouched on the ground sleeping, but they weren't there. She looked at the tree line to where Kekao and the others had slept but they were nowhere to be seen either.

She picked up a stick and poked at the fire, stirring the sleeping embers, then threw another piece of wood onto it. She thought it a little odd that no one was around but she enjoyed the solitude just the same. She was not a loner in any sense of the word but working on a crowded ship left her very little truly private time.

She was mindlessly poking at the fire, enjoying the songs of the birds when she had an uneasy thought. When they had talked to the captain last night he said there had been some trouble; could the trouble have found them all the way out here? A deep frown crossed her face. Had something happened to Dallas and Doug, and the others? She heard a noise behind her and instantly spun around.

"Good morning Sunshine," Murphy said as he and Crawford came out of the jungle, their arms full of exotic looking fruits. "I see by your look that you missed us."

"Very funny. What have you got there?" she asked as they piled the fruit in a heap.

"Breakfast, Sheena, Queen of the Jungle," Crawford said.

"Thank you, how thoughtful," she said, smiling at Crawford, then turning to Murphy and slugging him hard on the arm.

"Ouch! What'd you do that for?" Murphy said, holding his arm.

"I told you not to sing *Kumbaya* last night didn't I?"

Crawford laughed. "I told you humming it was just as bad."

"Hurry and eat," Kekao said as he walked up. "Rain comes. We must reach shelter of storehouse before it comes." Before anyone could reply, he grunted and walked away.

"What? He's afraid of a few spring showers?" Crawford said as he peeled a banana.

"Does the word monsoon mean anything to you?" Sarah asked.

"A lot of rain; so what." Crawford replied.

"In these latitudes it can rain pretty heavily but the storms usually last for less than an hour when it's not monsoon season, but we're at the tail end of the season. The record rainfall during a monsoon was 37.1 inches in a 24-hour period in India in 2005. That's over three feet of water!" Sarah said. "That's gather the animals up two by two and get them in the ark rain. Now I don't think we'll see anything like that, but it's not unusual to get nearly 2 inches of rain in an hour during a typical monsoon, and I for one really don't want to be caught out in the open if it does rain."

"Hurry up and eat," Murphy said, "I'm with her. I want to leave in twenty minutes."

Twenty-five minutes later the expedition was on its way. For over an hour they skirted the base of the shorter mountain, climbing and descending, as Kekao led them on. During that hour, the pristine blue sky was marred and wrinkled by a steadily increasing number of clouds.

They stopped in a small clearing about a quarter of the way up the side of the smaller of the two mountain peaks. In front of them was an unobstructed view of the ocean and their backs were against the side of the mountain.

Murphy stopped and looked out over the ocean. Being a sailor, he knew how to read the skies and the sea to predict the weather, but one didn't need to be an experienced sailor to know they were about to get very wet.

The dark clouds formed a moving wall that spread across the ocean as it approached. The streaks of falling rain seemed to pull the cloud across the surface of the water like the stubby legs of a giant millipede.

"We're not going to make it to cover are we?" Crawford said.

Murphy shook his head. "Nope." He turned around and looked at the mountain. "But we might be able to find some overhanging rocks to hide under or better yet, a nice cozy cave to wait out the storm in."

Just then they heard a low, steady roar. Not the roar of a passing freight train, but quieter and with a steady pounding rhythm. It was continuous in strength but constantly changing in pitch.

The falling sheets of rain advanced like a slow juggernaut, moving from the water up onto the sandy beaches then devouring the jungle like a biblical swarm of locusts.

"Here it comes," Murphy yelled as they all started running toward the mountain.

"Still think that's just a spring shower?" Sarah yelled above the roar, dashing toward the hoped-for sanctuary of the mountain.

They reached the base of the mountain and were confronted by a sheer rock wall rising 500 feet above them. "No help here," Murphy shouted, "Which way"

Kekao just grunted and pointed toward the base of the cliff.

They weaved in and out of the trees and vines and boulders along the rock wall, seeking any crack or crevice they could find shelter in. Their search grew more feverish the closer the storm came. The pelting sound of the downpour on the plants sounded like the marching boots of a thousand soldiers trampling down the jungle.

Murphy knew it was just rain but still, the apprehension and near panic was just as real. Frantically searching, he found a small grove of large-leaf plants and decided that that was where they would make their "stand." They could cut the leaves and use them as makeshift umbrellas. They would still get soaked, but it would help keep most of the heavy rain off.

By now they were enveloped in a heavy mist, like one sees at the bottom of a raging waterfall, only this mist was moving, rolling in front of the rain itself, soaking them instantly. They could no longer see the rain coming but they could hear it chewing up the jungle, drawing closer and closer.

"Over here," he shouted as he took out his machete and started hacking at the stems.

Quickly the others gathered around. Kekao and the two natives saw what Murphy was doing and began cutting the leaves too. Murphy raised the machete… and nearly took Crawford's head off.

"Watch where you're standing," Murphy yelled at his friend. "I could have killed you." He took a steadying breath. "You and Sarah go over there out of the way, and we'll hand the leaves to you."

Crawford took a step back and tripped over a vine, stumbling backward into Sarah, and then hit the ground.

"Sorry Sarah…" he started to say but stopped in midsentence. She was gone.

"Sarah?" His eyes darted back and forth but she was nowhere to be seen.

"Dallas!" he shouted above the roar. "Sarah's gone."

"What do you mean she's gone?" Murphy shouted. "Where did she go?"

"I don't know," Crawford said frantically. "One minute she was standing right behind me and the next she was gone. All I was doing was…."

"Hush," Murphy held up his hand to stop Crawford. "I think I hear something."

He heard what sounded like moaning and turned around to see the branches and vines behind them start to move. Then, like something from a zombie horror film, an arm shot out of the vines. Crawford let out a cry when another arm shot out, fingers twisting, reaching, grabbing.

Murphy just stood there, not knowing what to do, then he noticed the wristwatch on one of the arms. "That's Sarah!" he cried, and reached out and grabbed her arm.

Prying away the leaves and branches, Murphy almost felt like he was delivering a baby as her body, then finally her head, emerged from the vines.

"Are you okay?" Murphy asked, "What happened?"

"I'm fine," she said brushing herself off. "When Doug tripped, he knocked me into these vines."

Then she grabbed Murphy's hand. "There's a cave in here. I can't see much, but I think it's big enough for all us to ride out the storm in."

With the rain just starting to fall in stinging drops, no one needed extra encouragement. With Sarah leading the way, they squeezed through the vines and entered the cave. Once inside, the roaring sound of the deluge became muffled.

Murphy set down his pack and grabbed his flashlight. By its light, he could see they were in a cave about ten feet by ten feet, with a tunnel at the back. The air was cool but dry with no musty or stale odor to it.

"Not exactly the Ritz, but it'll do," Sarah said, looking around.

"Everyone might as well get comfortable," Murphy said. "I think we're going to be here awhile." As Sarah and Crawford sat down and began digging through their packs for their lights, Murphy went to the back of the cave and disappeared into the tunnel. After a few minutes, Sarah noticed that Murphy hadn't come back yet.

"Dallas?" she called out, her voice falling dead, swallowed up by the cave. When he didn't respond, she called out again even louder, but still no answer.

"Come on," Sarah grabbed Crawford by the arm. "Hansel there probably got himself lost with no bread crumbs to follow or Gretel here to tell him what to do."

Sarah had just stared down the tunnel when she let out a small yelp of surprise when Murphy suddenly emerged from the darkness.

"Don't do that," she said, catching her breath.

"Sorry. Look what I found."

"What is it?" Crawford asked. "It looks like a stick."

"It's a torch."

"You made a torch?"

"No, I found it, and it looks pretty old."

"Found it?"

"Then that means…"

"It means that someone else has been here before us," Murphy said.

Murphy turned to Kekao, "is this the storehouse?"

Kekao shook his head, "no."

"This just got more interesting," Sarah said.

"Give me your lighter," Murphy said to Crawford.

"You really don't think that thing will light after all these years do you?" Sarah asked.

"Only one way to find out." Murphy took the lighter and put the flame to it. It smoldered at first then slowly caught fire and the flames soon spread and engulfed the entire head of the torch.

"Cool," Crawford said, watching it burn.

"What now, Indiana Jones?" Sarah asked.

"I saw a couple more torches on the floor back there. I say we grab them and go exploring."

"I'm in," Crawford said eagerly.

"You coming Kekao?"

The big islander just grunted.

"I'll take that as a no. Let's go then."

CHAPTER SEVENTEEN

Yates stepped out of the stream and shook himself off like a dog. The water was cool and refreshing and it was nice to take a swim in fresh water. He sat on a rock and let the warmth of the sun dry him off but knew the sunshine wouldn't last long, seeing clouds gathering off in the distance. As he relaxed, Hoku walked up and gave him a piece of fruit.

"Thank you," Yates said. "It feels good to just relax and forget about everything for a while, you know?"

Hoku smiled and nodded as he sat down and took a bite of mango. "Leading my people is heavy burden. I lead only a few, but your burden is much greater. That is why I bring you here. This is where I come to rest."

"Very true Chief, very true, and thank you by the way." Yates tipped his head and took another bite while watching a strange looking red and green bird hop along a branch. "We can be just ordinary men for a few more minutes, but then I need to get back to the ship."

Suddenly, just to their right, a flock of birds rose from the tree tops, startled by something coming their way. A moment later they heard the rustling and breaking of leaves, branches and vines. Something was running toward them...fast.

Yates quickly reached down to grab his pistol but his hands fell on his empty hip. He had left it on the far side of the bank after stripping down to go swimming. Looking up, he saw a young native woman burst out of the jungle and freeze, her head darting back and forth, deciding which way to run. As soon as she saw Yates and the chief, she fainted.

Yates ran over, picked her up and carried her back to the stream. He recognized her as one of the women he had taken onboard the ship last night. He held her while Hoku wiped her face with the water. As he was holding her, her eyes flew open and she started to struggle.

"Sefina!" Hoku grasped the girl's head in his hands. "Sefina, calm down. You safe now."

Wide eyed, she looked back and forth at the two men. Her struggling stopped and the fear slowly drained away as she realized who they were.

"Sefina, tell us what happened." Hoku said in a gentler tone.

She took a deep breath then began to speak. "He took them, he took them!"

"Who took who?" Hoku asked.

"He took us all!"

"Slow down and start from the beginning," Yates said.

She took a deep breath then began. "We had just left the Servant of God's ship. We walking back to village when man jumped out and grabbed us."

"Who? What man?" Yates asked.

"One of the bad men who came to village last night."

"That not possible," Hoku said in disbelief.

"He very angry. He say you killed his friends and took their boat. He say he was on shore when you came in night and killed everyone. He make us go with him."

"Is Malana with him?" Yates asked.

Sefina nodded. "Yes, he has her and Ailani."

"What of Hanakahi?" Hoku asked.

Sefina shook her head. "I don't know. She ran into jungle."

"Do you know where they are now?" Yates asked.

"They are by waterfall, near where mountain starts."

"Do you know where that is?" Yates asked, looking at Hoku.

Hoku nodded. "Yes, it not far from here."

"Good." Yates turned his attention to the girl. "Now listen to me very carefully, Sefina. I left my radio back at the village so you have to go get help. I also need you to go to the ship and tell them what has happened and for them to send a team. Do you understand?"

She nodded. "Yes, Great Servant."

"Good. Now hurry!" He helped her to her feet and sent her down the path toward the village. As soon as she disappeared, he turned to Hoku. "We've got to get up there. We don't have time to wait for the others."

Hoku nodded. "Come, I lead."

After nearly an hour of making their way through the jungle, Yates knew they were close because he could hear the waterfall. Hoku crouched down and they edged their way through the last wall of foliage.

Peering through the leaves, Yates saw the stream in front of them, and off to the right was the waterfall that Sefina had talked about. They were about sixty yards downstream from the falls and had their purpose not been so dark, it would have been a beautiful sight. Tall trees framed the water that dropped about forty feet into a wide, mist covered pool surrounded by ferns and a variety of wide leafed plants.

Both men studied the surrounding area and after a few minutes, Yates nudged Hoku with his elbow and pointed to a spot near the top of the falls.

"He's there, to the left of the trees. And I think I see the women, just to the side of those boulders."

Yates and Hoku watched as the man paced back and forth. He was clearly agitated and threatened the women several times by waving a gun at them.

"We can't afford to wait for the others," Yates said.

"I agree. What we do?"

"I think if we split up we will have a better chance of catching him by surprise. See that rock outcropping behind him? I'll circle around and come at him from above while you cross downstream and come at him through the trees behind the girls. That way if he spots one of us, the other one will still have a chance of getting him."

"That is wise."

"Good; give me a few minutes to work my way around before you cross the stream and move up."

Both men nodded then Yates turned and disappeared into the jungle. Though he was hurrying as fast as he could, the going was still extremely slow. The jungle was dense and he didn't have his machete though he probably wouldn't have risked using it for fear of the noise.

After nearly twenty minutes of plowing his way through the jungle to get upstream of the kidnapper, he finally reached the stream and was ready to cross. He was halfway across in knee-deep water when movement caught his eye. At first he thought it was just a branch floating in the water then realized that it was floating *sideways* to the current. A four-foot snake was coming right for him.

Instantly he froze, not knowing if it was poisonous or not. Despite standing in the middle of a cool stream he was sweating bullets as it came closer. He held his breath as it drew nearer; he wanted to run, to slosh his way to the other side as fast as he could but he dared not agitate the snake. His eyes grew bigger and his body more rigid as it brushed up against the side of one leg then continued on, swimming between both.

The panic subsided as it disappeared downstream. Taking a deep breath, he continued to the other side. He hated snakes as a kid, and it was one of the few childhood phobias that carried over into his adult life.

Safely on the other side, he started moving toward the rocks above the man. He glanced at his watch. It had taken him way too long to get into position. He only hoped Hoku had been patient and waited for him.

He crept to the edge and surveyed the area downstream, looking for Hoku, in order to signal that he was in position and ready to go, but the chief was nowhere to be seen. Had the chief run into trouble himself, or did he get impatient and charge in on his own?

Yates inched his way forward to get a better view of the area just below him. As he neared the edge he could see Malana and Ailani. Malana was sitting with her head bowed but occasionally looking up. Ailani lay in a crumpled heap on the ground, not moving. He hoped she was unconscious and not dead.

Just them, Malana looked up and saw him. For a moment her eyes lit up and she began to smile. Yates quickly shook his head and put his finger up to his lips, signaling for her to be quiet. She understood and turned away. After a moment, she glanced up again, then frowned and tilted her head forward.

As Yates slowly lifted himself for a better view of the scene below, his heart began to sink. He saw a body: first the legs, then the torso, the arms and finally the head. It was Chief Hoku, lying face down on the ground.

Yates ducked down. The element of surprise was gone. What was he going to do now? He looked over the edge again and saw that Malana was looking at him. She tipped her head again, then stood.

What was she doing?

"You no need them." Malana said, her voice on the edge of submission with just a touch of seduction in it.

"Shut up," the man snarled at her, "I'm trying to think here. I had everything under control until your chief showed up."

"I can help," she replied softly, then moved over in front of Hoku so that the man's back was toward Yates.

Good girl, Yates he thought. She was creating a distraction. She was as smart as she was beautiful.

"You can, huh?" the man said, walking over to her.

Malana nodded. "Yes, I know this island and where boat is you can use to get away."

"And why would you want to help me?"

"I no want any more of my people hurt," Malana replied, moving slightly to the left, making sure he didn't see the captain out of the corner of his eye.

He looked at her for a moment, "You mean..." he said as he began twirling her long hair with his left hand... "like your friend up there."

He backhanded her hard, and sent her sprawling. At the same time, he spun around, aimed and fired at the small knoll behind him.

His aim was true.

Only there was nothing there for the bullet to hit. The man stood there puzzled and confused. He could have sworn that he saw the girl looking up at the rise behind him.

Yates had the limb cocked back like the Might Casey at the Bat. While Malana had distracted the man, he had climbed down and made his way around to the front of the clearing. He had crept forward and was just about to swing for the fence when he stepped on a loose stone and his foot skidded.

The limb came down quickly, but the man was quicker and managed to get his arm up, partially blocking the branch. Yates had hoped to avoid a fight altogether by taking him out with one blow, but not now. At least he had managed to knock the gun out of his hand.

Yates was no stranger to a good fight. He'd been in plenty of barroom brawls and had even done a little boxing when he was in the navy, but that was a long time ago. His opponent looked to be in good shape and was at least twenty years younger, but Yates pegged him for a rough, undisciplined street brawler.

Yates could use that to his advantage.

He didn't give his opponent time to think, but quickly threw several jabs. The man wiped the blood from a split lip and looked at Yates with a crooked smile. "My turn."

With unexpected speed, the man threw a flurry of punches, only about half of which Yates was able to block. Several smashed into Yates' rib cage and several more landed squarely on his jaw, staggering him back a few steps.

Yates realized the fight was going to be a lot harder than he'd first thought. He charged forward, swinging and jabbing. He was hoping to get the man on the ground, where he could use his weight to pin him down and beat him into submission.

It was a good plan but the man was too quick to be tied down; he kept dodging, weaving, sidestepping Yates' charges. Yates was beginning to tire. In his prime he could go all twelve rounds and then some, but he was *way* past his prime now. It was time to pull out all the stops.

Yates moved in and with power he didn't think he had left, threw punch after punch, driving the man back. When he sensed the time was right, he cocked his right hand back to deliver a knockout. But as he pulled back, he was vulnerable, his guard was slightly down. Normally if his adversary tried to counter he would have been able to block the punch and set up again. But age and fatigue had slowed his reflexes and a fist got through.

Yates staggered then dropped to his knees. There were a galaxy of stars spinning around his head and his vision was blurry. In a daze, he watched helplessly as the man picked up the fallen gun then went over to Malana and yanked her to her feet by her hair. She yelped in pain as he dragged her over in front of Yates.

"I'm going to do her and her friend in front of you, then make you watch as I kill your friend there. Then I'm going to get off this rock and come back with a few friends of mine and kill everyone else. What do you think about that?" he laughed, bending down and poking the gun into Yates' chest.

Yates swayed back and forth slightly then managed to raise his head. "I can't allow that."

The man reared back in laughter. He leaned over the bruised and blood-ied Yates and was about to poke him in the chest again, but as he tried, Yates grabbed the gun with his left hand and yanked down on it, then thrust his entire body upwards, driving his right fist with all his strength into the man's jaw. The man flew off his feet and landed with a thud.

Yates shook his hand, reeling from the pain in his fist then slouched to the ground, exhausted. He managed to grab the gun and drag himself over and to lean against the rocks. The man was stirring, and Yates was disappointed to see that his best punch had not been enough to knock him out. The man sat up and rubbed his jaw, looking at Yates with ha-tred in his eyes.

"You must kill him," Hoku urged weakly, as he managed to sit up. "If he lives, he will bring more evil men, they kill our people. You must protect us. You must protect Malana."

Seething with rage, the man stared at Yates. Yates had no doubt that if allowed, he would tell others about this place and would return. He looked at Malana. He hadn't risked his life to save her; he did it to keep the secret about the oil safe, to protect *his* profit. The first smuggler had been right, though: no woman was worth dying for, but she was close.

He looked back at her and smiled weakly, then pulled the trigger.

CHAPTER EIGHTEEN

"There are at least half a dozen offshoots here," Sarah said following closely behind Murphy. "What made you choose this particular passage in this rat's maze?"

"If you look closely, there are markings, scribbled every so often on the walls."

"So you followed them like a road map, then?"

Murphy shook his head. "No, I followed this tunnel because there were no markings. Diablo wouldn't leave clues along the way like a treasure map. He would use disinformation to lead anyone off the track."

"So what do you think?" Crawford asked. "Do you think this cave was used by your pirate buddy?"

Murphy shook his head. "I doubt it, but who knows? I wouldn't be counting all my red Ferraris just yet, though."

"If it is his cave, do you think it's booby-trapped?"

"You watch way too many movies," Sarah answered.

"Booby traps or not, we still need to be careful," Murphy cautioned.

"Look!" Crawford shouted, excitedly pointing in front of them. "It looks like it opens up into another room. Come on." He turned, and darted off down the passageway.

"Doug, wait!" Murphy called out, but Crawford ignored his shipmate and kept going.

"Doug!"

"Come on slowpokes. Maybe we'll find the Lost Ark in there," he joked.

"Doug wait!" Murphy shouted with such authority that Crawford immediately stopped.

"What's wrong? Crawford asked. "I'm usually the one who gets cold feet and doesn't want to do anything." He stopped and looked at his friend's expression. "Wait a minute," he said slowly, thinking as he talked, "You really don't think this place could be booby-trapped, do you? I mean, what are the odds that this is the treasure room where the great Diablo or whoever stashed all his booty?"

Murphy looked a little embarrassed, "I just think we should be careful, that's all."

Crawford laughed. "Sarah, make a note. This must be Freaky Friday because Dallas and I just switched bodies. Follow me. Adventure awaits!"

Crawford took another couple of steps when suddenly they heard a deep rumble and a big puff of dust shoot up from the floor as a large section of it dropped from sight. Crawford's eyes flew open wide as he teetered on the edge with one foot raised in mid-step. After awkwardly swinging his arms back and forth trying to regain his balance, he began to fall forward. Murphy reached out and grabbed his backpack and for a moment held him, but Crawford's weight and momentum were too great and Murphy could feel himself starting to slip.

He threw his free hand back in the air like a bronco rider trying to gain some balance, but it was a losing battle as his feet started sliding forward in the volcanic cinder.

Suddenly Murphy felt a pair of hands grab his free arm and yank hard. He gritted his teeth in pain as he felt his shoulder pop from the strain of Crawford's weight and the pull on his arm. He looked back and saw that it was Sarah holding onto him.

She was squatting down like an anchor man in a tug-of-war game, her face twisted in painful concentration as she pulled with all her strength. With one big yank, the tug-of-war was won: Crawford got both feet planted firmly on the ground. His face was porcelain white as he stood at the precipice and looked down.

"I will never, *ever* doubt you again," Crawford stammered. "Thank you."

"Yeah, thanks," Murphy gasped, turning around and looking at Sarah. He held the torch and all three leaned forward, looking over the edge. "The bottom of the pit looks about ten feet deep," Murphy said. "The fall probably wouldn't have killed you but it sure would have ruined your day."

"Oh *that's* comforting," Crawford shot back sarcastically.

"Move the torch to the left there," Sarah said as they were looking down. Suddenly she gasped. "Is that what I think it is?"

They were staring at a pair of skeletons. They were leaning against the side of the pit with tattered remnants of rotted clothing hanging from their bones.

"Poor guys," Murphy said.

"Do you think they fell into the trap and it reset on them?" Crawford asked.

Murphy shook his head. "I doubt it. Diablo probably killed them because they helped build this place and knew its secrets. It's what the Egyptian Pharaohs did to keep their secrets safe when they built the great pyramids."

"It's looking more and more like this could be the place," Crawford said excitedly.

"Don't get your hopes up," Murphy said. "I mean, think about it; what are the odds that this is Diablo Oscuro's cave and that his treasure is here?"

"True, but why else would there be a couple of dead guys here, in a pit, in a cave, buried beneath a stone slab, if there wasn't anything here to hide or protect?"

"You could be right. I just don't want to build up anyone's hopes."

"Hey, it's just like the lottery," Crawford said undeterred. "Somebody has to win."

"All the same," Murphy said, "maybe I should lead."

Crawford looked down at the two skeletons. "Please, be my guest."

Murphy held up his torch and examined the right wall, running his hand over its surface. After a few minutes he shifted his attention to the left wall.

Crawford turned to Sarah. "What's he doing?"

"He's becoming one with the rock," Sarah said sarcastically. "He's always been a little hard headed."

Murphy ran his hand along the base of the wall, digging under the sand. "Very funny," Murphy said looking up, "I'm trying to find..." he stopped in mid-sentence as they heard a clunk. Everyone jumped back a step and nervously looked down as they heard the grinding of stone on stone, the floor sliding back into place over the pit. "...the reset button."

"Cool," Crawford said as he took a step forward. Before he could take another step, Murphy grabbed his collar and yanked him back. "Let's not go through that again, okay?" he said, shaking his head. "Step along the left side here, just in case. Here, follow me."

"Sorry," Crawford replied sheepishly.

With tentative steps, Murphy worked his way around the edge until he was standing safely on the other side. One by one, he helped Crawford, Sarah, and then the natives who had now joined them, to walk along the wall and past the booby-trap.

Beyond the passageway, they could immediately sense that they had entered a vast cavern. The air was cooler and the beams of their flashlights and the flicker of their torches were swallowed up by the darkness.

"It's like the blind leading the blind," Sarah complained as she stumbled on a rock. "I can't make out anything in here. Everything looks like a giant charcoal painting: all grey with dark, fuzzy edges."

Murphy turned and shined his light against the walls. "Let me see the torch," he said to Crawford. He took the torch, held it up and lit another one he found hanging on the wall. He grabbed that one and handed the other one back to his friend. "Here, go check that side."

There were other torches mounted on the walls and soon they were surrounded by a ring of light that revealed they were indeed in a much larger cavern. It also revealed something else.

"Take a look at this," Crawford said, calling the others over. "At first I thought it was just a big boulder but once we turned on the lights, so to speak, I could see that it wasn't. It's a chest."

Quickly they all gathered around the chest like campers around a fire on a cold night. "Do you think it's booby-trapped too?" Crawford asked, apprehension heavy in his voice.

"Who knows?" Murphy said, shrugging his shoulders as he leaned over and examined it. "But I wouldn't put it past our dear friend, Mr.

Diablo Oscuro." He slowly reached around to the back of the chest. As he did, he let out a loud scream.

Everyone jumped and Murphy fell over on the ground laughing. "I'm sorry," he said between laughs, looking at their panic stricken faces, "I just couldn't resist it."

"Not funny, Dallas," Sarah snapped, glaring down at him.

"Okay, okay." When he stood back up he opened the chest and everyone gasped. "Maybe you'll forgive me now."

It was full of silver coins.

"There must be thousands of them." Crawford whispered, entranced. He dipped his hands into the chest like he was scooping water from a flowing stream then let the coins slip through his fingers. They made a very satisfying ring as they fell back into the chest.

Sarah picked up one of the coins and examined it. "Is this what they call a piece of eight?"

Murphy nodded. "Yes, the Spanish piece of eight was the money standard back in its day. The eight meant that it was worth eight *reales*, or eight coins. A little history lesson here," he said, picking up several coins. "Our monetary system is still affected by this little coin here. When bartering, to make change, they would cut the coin into eighths, hence another reason for its name. You don't hear it much anymore today, but the term 'four bits' or fifty cents and 'two bits', a quarter, all came from this coin. In fact, if you've noticed, the stock market still deals in eighths of a dollar."

"I don't care what you call it." Crawford said, now scooping up coins with both hands. "All I know is that all of this is ours."

Just then they heard a familiar grunt and turned around to find Kekao and the boys standing behind them.

"Did you know this was here?" Murphy asked, looking at Kekao.

The big native slowly shook his head. "No," was his simple reply.

Murphy noticed that Kekao and his two companions were as enamored with the treasure chest as Crawford. Murphy flipped the coin back into the chest then began walking around, looking at the others in the chamber.

After a few minutes, Sarah came over to Murphy who was sitting on one of the chests. "What's wrong Dallas? You don't seem very happy. Isn't this what you were hoping for?"

Murphy shone his light around the room. "There are forty-three treasure chests here the size of that one and another thirty or so of various sizes."

"And?"

"And, that's not enough."

"Not enough?" Crawford said, popping his head up from another chest he had opened.

"Now who's the one being greedy?" Sarah snickered.

Murphy shook his head. "No, you don't understand. I've checked, and while some of these chests are from ships I don't recognize, the majority of them are indeed from the Spanish galleon *Victoria*."

"So that's a good thing, right?" Crawford said, standing up now and joining his friends.

"Yes and no."

"For a man who just realized his lifelong dream–and who just became a millionaire, I might add–you sure seem confused," Sarah observed.

"I'm happy. Don't get me wrong," he said, shaking his head, "I'm not explaining myself very well here."

Murphy took a deep breath then continued. "It's not that I want more money. It's that there were far more chests on the *Victoria* than we see here."

"More?" Crawford said.

"More?" Kekao echoed, almost in a whisper.

"Maybe the pirates spent it all," Sarah said.

"Yeah, wine, women and song. You know, pirate stuff," Crawford added.

"There should be several *hundred* chests just from the *Victoria* alone, not to mention any other plunder they might have gotten."

"Did you say several *hundred*?" Crawford asked in astonishment, not quite sure he heard his friend right.

"Yeah, that's why this doesn't look right. That's why I said this wasn't enough."

"So you think there must be another treasure hideout somewhere then," Sarah said.

"It's possible, but then he'd have to worry about protecting two places at once and trusting someone to guard the other location for him. As you can see from our two friends out front there, trust is not real big with pirates."

"Then he and his crew either spent the rest of it or it all didn't make it back here," Sarah said.

"Or..." Murphy began, his voice trailing off as he stood and started slowly walking around the cavern.

"Dallas?" Sarah said, but was ignored as he remained silent, diligently looking around.

"What's he doing now?" Crawford asked, "Becoming one with the cave?"

"There," he shouted, pointing to the back of the cave. On the back wall, there was a pile of chests stacked four high along with several barrels and a few crates. "Come on!"

"What are we doing?" Crawford asked as he stepped around a chest, following Murphy.

"It's what Sarah said," Murphy replied, "about having another place to hide the treasure. The Dark Devil was a careful man and knew what the thought of all that money could do and how tempting it would be for someone to try to take it. So, rather than have to guard two locations, he'd put it all here, in one location."

"Okay," Sarah said, "what am I missing here? You just said that there wasn't enough stuff here for this to be his main stash."

"The man was a master." Murphy said. "Think about it. We stumbled on the place totally by accident and look what happened when we did. Doug here was more than happy to settle for what he saw and I'm betting Diablo was willing to make that same bet. Happy with what they had here, why would anybody bother to look for more?"

"You think there's a hidden room!" Sarah exclaimed.

"So it's the old hidden in plain sight thing," Crawford nodded. "It makes sense. You hide all your goodies in two places, but only have to guard one."

"I may be wrong, but I don't think so. Come on, help me move this stuff. Doug, grab that barrel there. Kekao, you and your boys bring these chests down after we get these barrels off."

After some straining, grunts and groans, the wall was clear.

"Now what, boss?" Crawford asked. "Another secret lever to open the wall?"

"That's what I'm thinking. All this stuff piled along the wall is the only logical place to hide a door big enough to fit all the treasure chests through."

Murphy walked to the wall and held up a torch. The lighted flickered off the solid rock as he slowly moved up and down the cavern, examining it closely.

"Okay, everybody help me look for some sort of lever or catch or seam in the wall," Murphy said, disappointed that he couldn't find the entrance right away. "But be careful! Pardon the pun, but as we've already seen, Diablo Oscuro can be a sneaky devil."

Sarah just groaned and shook her head at Murphy's joke as she and the others converged on the wall. However, the joy and expectations of finding the secret lever and more wealth untold soon diminished as no shouts of discovery were forthcoming.

After ten minutes of fruitless searching, a frustrated Murphy sat down on the cinder floor with his back against the wall. Kekao and the other natives had abandoned the search as well and had wandered off and were looking in the different chests when Sarah sat down beside him.

"What are you doing?" Murphy asked, looking up at Crawford. He was examining one of the brackets that held the torches.

Crawford shrugged his shoulders. "It always works on TV," he said, pushing, pulling, and twisting on the bracket. "You know, the hero enters a deserted hallway in his mansion, twists the candleholder on the wall and *voila*, a secret passage opens and he either escapes the villains chasing him or goes into this secret room like the Bat Cave or something."

"You got the Bat Cave part right," Murphy said, waving his hand around the room.

"Wait a minute." Sarah said, her head cocked to one side, an amused look on her face. "Hero? You think you're the hero here in our little island adventure?"

"Why not?' Crawford replied defensively.

"If anything, I should be the heroine here," Sarah said, "especially since I have to put up with you two."

"Hold on," Murphy protested. "It was my idea to come out here looking for this stuff. That makes me the leader, therefore the hero."

"So what am I, the trusty sidekick?" Crawford shook his head. "No, no, that's not going to happen; the sidekick always gets killed in the end."

"You're right," Sarah said, "I don't think of you as the sidekick. I think of you more as the comic relief."

Murphy and Sarah both burst out laughing.

"Very funny," Crawford said. He sat down hard on one of the chests and folded his arms and pouted, which brought even more stifled laughter from his companions. He huffed then turned his back on them.

Murphy and Sarah looked at each other and sighed, realizing they had gone too far again.

"Listen Doug…" Murphy began in an apologetic tone but was cut off as Crawford turned back around and faced them with his own stifled grin that soon grew into a full-fledged smile. "Gotcha!"

Both Murphy and Sarah nodded in agreement. "Yes you did," Murphy said.

"I thought you two said you were going to be nicer to me?"

"Sorry," Sarah said. "You know, old habits." She looked over at Murphy, whose smile had vanished. "What's wrong?"

"I don't know, I guess I could be wrong, but I was so sure that there was another treasure room here," Murphy answered.

"What, you're more upset at what we didn't find than happy at what we did?" she asked.

Murphy shook his head. "It's not that. I guess I'm just disappointed that I'm not as good a Sherlock Holmes as I thought I was."

"Hey guys?"

Something about the tone in Crawford's voice made them stop instantly and look at him. He was seated on one of the chests staring at his feet. When he looked up, even in the dark flickering shadows they could see the worry and concern in his face. "Is there quicksand in here?"

CHAPTER NINETEEN

Malana rushed over to Yates' side and began crying as she hugged and kissed him.

"I'm okay." he said between smothering kisses. "Really, I'm fine. Go check on Ailani."

Malana nodded between sobs and went to check on her friend.

"Are you okay, Chief?" Yates asked.

Hoku nodded slowly. "I think so," he replied bringing his hand from the back of his head, looking at the dried blood on his fingers.

"What happened? Why didn't you wait for me?"

"I was hiding in trees, waiting, when he started to beat Ailani. I was too far away but had to do something. I ran at him but he saw me."

"She won't wake up." Malana cried.

Yates and Hoku went over and kneeled beside her. "She may have a concussion; we need to get her to the ship as quickly as possible." Yates scooped her up in his arms and they headed down the path to a spot where they could cross the stream.

As Yates was picking his way across the stream, being careful not to stumble on the slippery rocks, he noticed that it seemed to be darker all of a sudden. He stopped and looked up; gone was the pristine blue sky that had started the day. Instead, it was now covered with dark, menacing clouds. It was also noticeably cooler and the wind had picked up. Yates didn't need his years at sea to tell that a storm was coming.

He took a few more steps and stopped again. Above the noise of the rushing waters, he could hear another sound, loud and growing louder. It was a roar, like the sound of storm waves pounding the beach but in one continuous crash.

Hoku and Malana were nearly across and they too stopped, all looking at each other, wondering what was happening.

Yates felt it before he saw or heard it. When he had first stopped, the water had been just below his knees. Now, he could feel it swirling around his lower thighs. It was as if the tide had suddenly risen, which he knew was impossible.

He looked up at the waterfall and watched in disbelief as a wall of water about a foot high came surging over the top. Then came a tremendous, deafening roar and he looked back over his shoulder to see the jungle behind him being inundated. Horrified, he understood what was happening and started pushing through the water to the other side as fast as he could. Desperately, he struggled with Ailani's weight, trying to maintain his balance on the slippery rocks and push his weary legs against the rushing current. He was moving as fast as he could, but he knew he wouldn't make it in time.

Yates knew that a monsoon had struck on the other side of the island and was making its way toward them. He'd heard about monsoons before and seen them on TV but had never really experienced their destructive power.

Until now.

The overflow of the torrential rains was pouring down from the mountains and was swelling the stream into a flash flood. With a thunderous roar, the wall of water crested at the top of the falls and crashed to the bottom.

He turned his back to the approaching wall of water and braced himself in the now waist high stream the best he could. The wave hit with such force that it immediately swept him off his feet, sending him and Ailani tumbling.

Bobbing up and down, coughing and choking, he struggled to keep his and Ailani's heads above water as they were carried along like so much driftwood. Between the frenzied wave tops he caught a fleeting glimpse of a fallen tree trunk jutting out from the shore. If he could get close enough to grab it, he might be able to save them both.

With all his remaining strength he shoved himself toward it, his feet now barely scraping the stream bottom. The current was carrying him at breakneck speed and he slammed into the downed tree so hard it knocked the wind out of him and broke his grip on Ailani.

The swirling current grabbed her and started pulling her away. He tried to reach for her but didn't have the strength. Worse, he didn't know how long he could hold on himself.

He watched helplessly as Ailani was dragged out of reach to the end of the log, ready to be swept away forever when he saw a hand reach down and grab her, and at the same time, felt a hand grasp his collar. Looking up, he saw that Hoku had crawled out on the tree and grabbed Ailani while Malana had swam out and was dragging him to shore.

Yates staggered to shore and was ready to collapse when he heard Malana screaming that Ailani wasn't breathing. With great effort he managed to crawl over to her still body.

Wearily, he reached over, checked her pulse and found none. Immediately, he got to his knees and started doing chest compressions. Then he bent over her, pinched her nose and blew two quick breaths into her lungs, then he started the whole thing all over again. He was just about to give up, too exhausted to continue, when Ailani coughed.

Water gushed out of her mouth and nose and she coughed again as she struggled to breathe. He helped her sit up as Hoku and Malana watched, marveling that the Servant of God had just brought their friend back from the dead.

Yates rolled over and collapsed right where he was while Hoku and Malana tended to Ailani, which was just fine with him. He closed his eyes and took a deep breath; nothing was going to move him from this spot.

Suddenly the jungle seemed to explode in sound. He had been so busy trying to save Ailani's life and his own that he had forgotten about the storm. It arrived with hardly any warning; one second the sky was empty, the next they were hit with sheets of pouring water.

The big, heavy drops hit with such force they stung his skin. He immediately rolled onto his hands and knees and tried to get up but it was a struggle as the heavy rains literally beat him down.

He tried to shout to the others but even though they were only a few feet away, they couldn't hear him above the din. He motioned to Hoku and together they picked up Aitani and ran for the cover of the jungle. Yates found some plants that had huge, broad leaves, about the size of a garbage can lid and quickly ripped them off their stalks. They wouldn't provide much cover but at least they would break the sting of the driving rain.

They huddled together next to a tree trunk, holding their leaf-shields over their heads. The rain pounding on the leaves reminded Yates of the sound the rain made on the roof of an old camping trailer his parents had when he was a kid. He had a rollup bunk, kind of like a hammock, above his parents' bed in the trailer and he liked to listen to the rhythm of the pounding rain on the roof. What he wouldn't give to have that trailer right now.

He was holding Ailani with his left arm around her waist, pulling her close and holding the leaf above their heads with his right hand. He knew the storm would pass quickly, but just as it had in the trailer when he was a kid, the pounding rain and his own exhaustion soon made him drowsy.

He didn't know how long he had been asleep when he was awakened by a scream from Malana. He knew he should have been more concerned but he was so tired that his first thought was, now what?

Because he wasn't fully awake yet and still groggy, when he felt the water swirling around his feet he immediately thought he was on his ship and that it was sinking.

Instantly he was fully awake and realized they weren't sinking, but they were in just as much danger. The river had overflowed its banks.

CHAPTER TWENTY

"Quicksand?" Murphy asked. "What are you talking about?"

"Look." Crawford tilted his head down but kept his body frozen in place. Between his feet, the cinder dust was moving, swirling away like water going down a bathtub drain.

Murphy studied the vanishing sand for a moment; then his eyes lit up in epiphany. "That's it!"

"What's it? Sarah asked.

"What's the first rule of real estate?" he asked excitedly.

"What are you talking about?" she said again, looking at Murphy like he had lost his mind.

"What's the first rule of real estate?" Murphy repeated.

"Location, location, location?" Crawford said hesitantly.

Murphy, still excited, shook his head. "Okay, what's the second rule?" When no one answered, he continued. "If you can't build out, you build up...or in this case down."

"If you don't tell us what you're talking about right now you're going to be six feet down," Sarah snapped.

"More like eight."

Sarah scowled, but before she could answer, Crawford shouted. "Hey! A little help over here if you don't mind."

"Sorry." Murphy reached out and grabbed his friend's hand, then pulled him off the chest.

"Now would you mind telling us what that was all about?" Sarah asked, staring hard at Murphy.

"I was right. It makes perfect sense now. I should have thought of this sooner. Diablo *does* have a second treasure room hidden. Since we're surrounded by solid rock the only way to go is up..." he paused as they all looked toward the ceiling, "or down."

"It's underneath us!" Crawford shouted.

Murphy nodded in satisfaction. "Your 'quicksand' is sand that's leaking through the cracks in the floor, or ceiling, depending on how you want to look at it. Come on." he said, starting to dig at the cinder. "I still think this is the best place for a trap door."

A few minutes later Crawford cried out, but it wasn't the hallelujah of discovery all were hoping for.

"Ouch!" he shouted, holding up his hand. "I think I just got a sliver."

The three friends all looked at each other and realized at the same moment that a sliver could only have come from a piece of wood, and that that piece of wood meant Diablo Oscuro had built something here. Frantically they dug even quicker and soon cleared the sand away until they had revealed the outline of a trap door.

"I've got a handle here," Sarah said.

Excitedly, Murphy reached for the handle, looked at his friends and smiled, "here goes nothing," and then pulled.

The door didn't budge.

"Nothing is right," Sarah laughed.

Murphy smiled nervously, tightened his grip and jerked again.

"What's the matter oh great and fearless *leader*? Too heavy for you?" Sarah snickered again. Crawford laughed and reached over and gave her a high-five.

"Cute," Murphy said. "Now, if you two are done, maybe we can have a little *teamwork* here and lift the door together."

"Anything you say, *boss*," Sarah couldn't resist.

Three sets of hands grabbed the handle and with a nod from Murphy, they lifted together with one big pull. The large wooden door creaked, but for all their efforts, it opened but a meager inch. While Sarah and Crawford held it open, Murphy squatted in front of it, slipped his fingers into the crack, and lifted with his legs. With a continual groan of protest, from both the hinges and Murphy's back, they managed to raise the door all the way and shoved it over, making a loud thud as it hit the wall.

The open door revealed a set of stairs that descended into the darkness, reminding Murphy of an entrance to a storm cellar. He studied the door for a moment. It looked like a cargo hatch cover from an old sailing ship, another good sign that they were on the right track.

"Would you like to go first?" Murphy asked Crawford, pointing into the void.

"No, that's all right, you can lead if you want too." Crawford's voice was steady, but there was no masking his uneasiness.

"Give me that," Sarah said, reaching for Murphy's torch. In the glow of the flame, he could see the apprehension in his ex-wife's face but he also saw the stubborn pride that wouldn't let her back down, one of the things he loved and hated so much about her.

When he wouldn't let go, she stared at him and tugged at it again. She expected to see resentment and defiance in his eyes for her questioning his authority earlier but instead she saw compassion and understanding. She used to love it and hate it... when he looked at her like that. She relinquished the torch.

With flaming torch in one hand and flashlight in the other, Murphy began walking down into the depths, tentatively testing each step as he went. At the bottom of the stairs, the flashlight's beam was devoured by the pitch blackness, penetrating only a few feet into the cavern, but it was enough for Murphy to find several more wall mounted torches which he quickly lit.

The darkness grudgingly withdrew, but only after leaving long dark shadows to cover its retreat. In triumph, the light revealed a room about the same size as the one above, plus it revealed something more. Lining the walls and in three neat columns in the center of the floor were row after row of chests, neatly stacked three high. The ceiling was braced by a row of support columns running down the center of the room.

Murphy walked over to one of the pillars and studied it. The supports were round and appeared to be made from the masts of a ship, and the ceiling was heavy deck planking. Murphy nodded thoughtfully; it made sense. Diablo Oscuro, after capturing the *Victoria*, couldn't just go sailing around in her; she was too well known a ship. But instead of simply scuttling her, he had found a better use for her massive timbers.

"Oooh, this is the good stuff," Sarah said. She had gone over and opened one of the chests. Murphy and Crawford walked over and were joined by Kekao and the others. Murphy held his torch over the chest and it burst into light as the flames flickered and danced off the polished gold coins. Kekao reached down and grabbed a handful of coins. He smiled as he held them then gave each of his companions a couple of them.

"Pretty nice huh?" Crawford asked.

Kekao blinked as if in a trance, then his smile quickly vanished and was replaced with his usual scowl. He just grunted and tossed them back into the chest, but Murphy noticed that he hadn't thrown all of them back, but had secretly kept a few in his other hand. He thought it a little odd that the big native would keep them, but then again, the tribesmen did have gold covered breastplates for their ceremonial armor.

"It looks like all the chests down here are filled with gold," Sarah said, calling from halfway down the room. "I've checked five so far and each one has gold coins instead of silver."

"It makes sense again," Murphy said. "If his hideaway was discovered, Diablo would be content to let anyone steal the cheaper silver, knowing all the while that the more valuable gold was safe and sound down here."

"Hey," Crawford shouted from the back of the room, "look at this; it looks like Indiana Jones was here after all."

Murphy and Sarah looked at each other, puzzled, then headed toward Crawford. Even though he was just forty feet away, Crawford, surrounded by the oppressive darkness, looked instead like he was a hundred miles away, holding a match instead of a burning torch.

As the others stood beside him, Crawford pointed, using the beam of the flashlight. "I guess he forgot to put that one away."

The beam came to rest, shining like a spotlight on a gold jewel-encrusted cross that stood about eighteen inches tall.

"Wow!" Murphy exclaimed.

"It's beautiful," Sarah whispered in awe.

Murphy stared at the cross, its beauty and brilliance accented by the pure black background. He couldn't get over how out of place it was. Was Diablo so proud of it that he wanted all to see it, to show it off even when he wasn't there? Maybe, but a nagging feeling deep down inside told him that that wasn't the reason.

"I can't wait to see the look on the captain's face when I pull that thing out of my backpack and wave it in front of him," Crawford said.

The cross was resting on top of several crates that lined the wall. To reach it Crawford would have to climb on the smaller crates that were stacked in front of it, leading up to it like stair steps. Crawford was on the first step and was in mid-stride when Murphy cried out.

"Stop! It's a trap!"

Crawford's full weight came to rest on the second step when he heard Murphy's cry. He stopped and turned slowly around and looked at his friend, fear and anxiety etched in his face. Everyone stood frozen like statues.

"What do I do?" Crawford whispered, as if talking in a normal tone would somehow spring the trap.

"Just stay where you are for the moment," Murphy replied, "I think the cross is booby trapped like the door was upstairs."

Before anyone could say anything else, the box Crawford was standing on suddenly collapsed and he fell through the step like he was falling through a trapdoor. Everyone jumped as if they too had fallen and Murphy found himself crouched with his hands outstretched to keep Crawford from falling. He looked over and saw that Sarah was bent in much the same way, willing Crawford from toppling.

Crawford remained on his feet with one leg buried up to his knee in the collapsed crate. After what seemed like a lifetime, he allowed himself to take a breath. "Maybe it was a dud, you know being over three hundred years old and all." He said it almost as a plea rather than a statement, smiling nervously.

Suddenly they heard a loud crack, like a tree trunk being snapped in a windstorm. The noise was quickly followed by a crashing sound and all heads turned toward the far end of the room. They watched in horror as the support columns began smashing into each other in a giant game of dominos. Each crashing timber was followed by sections of the roof collapsing, with an avalanche of falling debris.

Murphy grabbed Sarah by the arm and spun her around, throwing her into Crawford, knocking them both out of the path of destruction. Out of the corner of his eye he glimpsed one of the beams swinging down from the ceiling like a battering ram. He thought that it was odd, falling in the opposite direction of the other beams, but he didn't have time to dwell on it as he saw one of the support beams crashing down, ready to crush Kekao. Murphy took three steps, then dove and shoved him out of the way.

Then everything went dark and quiet.

His eyes were open; at least he thought they were. Everything was black, the darkest black he had ever experienced. He remembered once as a kid, going on a tour of the Oregon Caves and being impressed and a little freaked out as the tour guide turned out the lights so everyone could see what total darkness looked like. This was worse. Much worse.

Maybe blackness was not the right term; it was blankness, a void... the absence of everything.

A sudden chill ran down his spine, was he even still alive?

He'd heard Hell described as the absence of light but thought it was meant more spiritually as being separated from God, the Light of the World. But now, as he lay there peering into the endless emptiness, it seemed much more literal.

He tried to move, but a sharp pain in his left leg stopped him. He was both relieved and worried at the same time. Relieved because at least he was pretty sure he was alive now, but the other side of the coin was that he now knew he was hurt, but not how badly.

His mind flashed to Sarah and Doug; he hoped they were okay. He took a deep breath and called out to them, but his words fell dead, trapped, just like he was. He had to take stock of the situation and get himself out of there to be able to help his friends. He was lying face down on the floor and as he had already discovered, his legs were trapped and moving them hurt. His hands were pinned to his sides so he couldn't push or pull himself along.

First order of business was to get his hands free.

Just as he tried to move his right arm, he felt something trickling down the side of his cheek. At first, panic struck as he thought he was bleeding from a head wound but then some of the liquid dribbled into his mouth and instead of the warm, coppery taste of blood, he tasted the cool refreshment of water. He wondered where the water had come from but right now he wasn't going to look a gift horse in the mouth.

At first, he enjoyed its coolness, but then the trickle turned into a small, steady stream. Where was the water coming from? Had the cave-in ruptured some underwater spring? Was this part of Diablo Oscuro's trap? To drown whoever tried to steal his gold?

Being a sailor, drowning was always in the back of his mind but he somehow thought it would be during a storm or some catastrophe at sea. The thought of drowning on land had never occurred to him,

He began rocking back and forth frantically, struggling to get his arms free. The pain in his leg was tremendous but he ignored it. He had to get free.

His mind flashed back to Sarah. Was she okay? Was she pinned down in some deep, dark hole like he was? Was she drowning too? Suddenly his heart hurt. It had been his idea to go on this treasure hunt and he could not, would not be responsible for her death.

With new determination, he screamed even louder as he rocked back and forth like a madman. He twisted and turned, squirming like a worm being put on a hook, but to no avail. He tried to relax his neck muscles because he was getting tired of holding his head up. Even though the water had stopped flowing for the moment, he couldn't rest his head because of the large puddle in front of his face.

With a desperate burst of energy, he let out a tremendous yell and arched his back, pushing with all his strength against the planks. He felt them give way slightly. Encouraged, he used his last ounce of strength for one more massive push. The planks gave an inch then slammed back down so hard the force of the impact slapped him to the ground, driving the air out of his lungs. Too tired to lift his head, he could only roll it to the side, gasping like a freshly hooked fish.

CHAPTER TWENTY ONE

Yates looked at the surging water swirling around their feet and thought how odd it was to see a flood on an island; the two just didn't seem to go together. For a brief moment he wondered if those on Atlantis had the same thought as their island was sinking.

The rain was still coming down in buckets and when he looked over to the riverbank, there was none. The water had long since climbed free of the confines of its boundaries and was transforming the jungle floor into a marshy lake.

Exhausted, Yates struggled to his feet. He helped Hoku up and together they got Malana to her feet. He then he picked up Ailani and unceremoniously threw her over his shoulder in a fireman's carry.

Logically, they should head for higher ground, but the water was cascading down the hillside, eroding it away, carrying with it rocks and chunks of debris that were as deadly as the water they were trying to escape.

"Come on!" Yates shouted. The water was now up to their knees as they headed in the direction of the trail that had led them to the waterfall.

They had taken only a few steps when Yates heard Malana scream.

"Now what?" Yates muttered under his breath. He was tired, hungry, and every muscle he had was screaming in pain.

This oil had better be worth all this trouble, he thought.

He stopped and had just started to turn around and see what was wrong when a large log slammed into his legs. The force of the impact sent him sprawling forward, headlong, into the water. As he fell, Ailani slipped from his arms. He felt the log steamrolling up his legs... his back... slamming into his head, pushing him deeper into the water.

Under the dark, swirling waters, Yates saw a galaxy of bright stars. He felt his body go limp as he teetered on the edge of unconsciousness. Then his forehead slammed into a rock and the sudden jolt of pain brought him back to reality.

His head breached the surface and he gasped for air. He quickly looked around and spotted Hoku and Malana clinging to a nearby tree. Frantically he looked for Ailani, but she was nowhere in sight. Then he caught a glimpse of her limp body wedged between two trees in a pile of twisted and broken branches.

He made his way toward her as fast as he could through the torrent. With some hesitation, he reached down to her. Fortunately she was still breathing and Yates let out a sigh of relief. He was too exhausted to carry her, so he grabbed her under her arms and towed her floating body behind him.

With his head down, trudging along like a caveman from the cartoons, dragging his woman behind him, he noticed that the sky was getting brighter and the rain was letting up, and then, just as suddenly as it had started, it stopped.

Shafts of sunlight sliced through the dark clouds, and all of a sudden, everything was green again. Almost immediately, small wisps of steam began rising from the rain soaked plants. Yates knew that it wouldn't be long before the humidity became unbearable.

The water was beginning to recede. With Ailani's feet dragging on the bottom, he managed to pull her over to a large tree. Exhausted and with the danger past, Yates plopped down into the ankle-deep water, leaned with his back against the tree and pulled her between his legs, resting her head on his chest. The warmth of the sun felt good on his face and before he even knew what was happening, sleep overcame him.

CHAPTER TWENTY TWO

Murphy felt like he should still be struggling, hanging on to life and not just lying down to die, but part of him knew that his body was spent; there was nothing physically more he could do.

As he lay there, he thought he heard his name being called. It was so soft and muffled, it sounded like it was coming from the far side of the moon. He lay as quietly as he could, holding his breath, listening, straining to hear. Nothing… wait, there it was again, only it sounded just a little closer. Was he losing his mind? Was he hallucinating already? How long had he actually been there?

He heard his name called out one more time, then, without warning, his world exploded. Suddenly he was free, the weight of that world was pulled from his shoulders and he was staring into a bright light.

Had he died?

He heard his name again - it was the voice of an angel - then he felt two sets of powerful hands reach down and grab him, pulling him up toward the light, toward heaven he presumed….he hoped.

Suddenly he felt the shooting pain in his leg again. Why was he feeling pain? There wasn't supposed to be pain in heaven was there…unless he wasn't…

"Okay, put him over here." Sarah said as Kekao and one of the other natives picked Murphy up from the rubble and laid him on the cavern floor. "Give him some water." She ordered.

Crawford took a bottle of water out of his pack and put it up to his friend's lips. In a daze, he thought the water was flowing again and that he was going to drown. He sprang up like a jack-in-the-box and started flailing his arms wildly, knocking Crawford down and nearly punching Kekao in the face.

"Dallas!" Sarah grabbed his swinging arms. "Dallas, it's okay, you're safe now. It's us."

Confused, Murphy just sat there, looking around as his mind slowly began piecing things together. He looked up and could see they were sitting in the middle of a crater, rubble piled all around them where the roof had collapsed. He glanced over and saw that the cross, the thing that had triggered all this was still standing on the crate, untouched by the cave-in.

Murphy looked at Sarah and managed a weak but grateful smile.

"Nice to have you back," she said.

"Thanks," he replied then looked at Crawford who was picking himself up off the ground. "Sorry Doug."

Murphy started to get up but was stopped by a sharp pain in his left leg. "Maybe I'll just sit here for a while," he said as he eased back down.

"Here, let me take a look at that," Sarah said.

"How long was I under there?" Murphy asked.

"About ten minutes."

Ten minutes? His brain screamed. Only ten minutes? It had seemed like an eternity.

"Is something wrong?" she replied, seeing the confused look on his face.

"Just wondering what took you guys so long, that's all," he stammered, trying his best not to let on that he was on the verge of losing it back there.

"Hey! Easy there Florence Nightingale," Murphy said as Sarah worked on his leg.

"You'll be okay," she said as she helped him to his feet. "It's just a bad bruise with a little sprain. I can either put it into a makeshift splint or you can find something to use as a cane to help support it."

He gingerly took a step and nearly fell. He picked up a broken plank and leaned against it. "It still hurts like hell but I think I'll take the cane."

Murphy felt like Captain Ahab, leaning against his wooden leg, surveying his damaged ship. "Is everyone all right?"

"We're fine," Crawford replied. "I was out of the line of fire so to speak and you saved Sarah and Kekao by shoving them out of the way too. Thing One and Thing Two were over by the stairs and missed the whole thing."

"Good, let's get out of here; I've had enough excitement for one day. Grab that cargo hold cover and lean it against the wall. We can use it to climb out of here," Murphy said.

Kekao nodded, then as he and the other two natives pick up the cover and dragged it over and leaned it against the wall. Sarah moved toward the ladder and Murphy started hobbling after her when he noticed that Crawford was standing in front of the cross.

"Don't even think about it," Murphy warned.

"If you think that after all this I'm going to just leave this thing behind, then those boards hit you harder in the head than I thought."

"Doug, don't..." Murphy cried out, but it was too late. Crawford leaned against the crates and reached up and grabbed the golden cross. Everyone held their breath and their eyes darted around the room again, waiting to see if the rest of the room would collapse. A collective sigh of relief filled the cave when the ceiling didn't fall and crush them all.

"See, what do they say about lightning striking in the same place twice?" Crawford smirked as he shoved the cross into his pack.

Murphy shook his head and took a step then stopped and tilted his head. "Shhh," he said. "Did you hear that?"

"Hear what?" Sarah said.

"It sounded like ice crackling?"

"Ice crackling?" Crawford said. "Ice? I was only kidding earlier about the beams hitting you too hard in the head, but are you sure you're all right?"

Murphy didn't respond, but he stood still, listening intently. Sarah started to say something but before she could, Murphy held up his hand to stop her. "There!" he almost shouted. "Did you hear that?"

She started to speak again and was met with the same upheld hand. She was about to tell Murphy where he could put that hand when she heard it too. "It sounds like its coming from over there," she said, point-ing at the wall.

"Oh great, now you've both…" Crawford started to say, then slowed down, "…lost it," as he too heard the sound.

Slowly they began moving toward the wall, following the sound. With flashlights and torches blazing, they carefully picked their way through the fallen debris and traced the sound to the crossbeam that Murphy had seen earlier during the cave-in; it was sticking out of the wall like a harpoon from the side of a whale.

"I don't get it." Crawford said. "Why is this thing sticking out of the side of the wall, and in the direction opposite from the falling beams?"

"Maybe the falling pillars threw it out of alignment," Sarah offered.

Murphy shook his head. "I don't think so. This thing is in the middle of the row and swung through *before* all the beams collapsed."

"Yeah, but why?" Crawford asked.

As if in answer to his question, there was a loud pop, followed by a series of long crackles. They held the beams of their flashlights up to the wall and could see small trails of water, seeping out from where the beam was stuck in the wall.

All three were looking at the strange sight when Murphy suddenly spoke. "We need to get out of here now!"

Sarah turned and looked at Murphy, her face filled with apprehension at the urgent tone in his voice. "What's wrong Dallas?"

"Come on, let's go," he said as he grabbed her tightly by the arm and swung her around.

"Dallas!"

"I've already almost drowned once today, I don't want to do it a second time."

"What are you talking about?"

"Never mind; just climb over the debris. Hurry."

Without warning, the beam shot out of the wall like a cork from a champagne bottle. Water burst through the hole with the force of a fire hose. The beam grazed Crawford's backpack, spun him around and threw him crashing into the pile of rubble. Crawford let out a scream then fell silent.

Sarah was already on the other side of the rubble and safe from the initial flow, but Murphy was still picking his way through the wreckage. The jet stream missed him but hit his board-crutch. It shot out of his hand and nearly took Sarah's head off, shattering into splinters when it hit the opposite side wall.

Murphy teetered on the edge, balancing like a tightrope walker, knowing that if he fell into the water blast, he wouldn't fare much better than his crutch did. In an instant he knew he was going to fall.

Time slowed down but his mind raced at full speed. He'd heard the phrase, desperate times calls for desperate measures; now he knew exactly what that meant. He would have one chance at this and one only; timing would be everything.

Murphy felt himself starting to fall toward the rushing water. As he fell, he shrugged off his backpack and twisted his body to grab one of the straps with his left hand. As he continued to fall, the backpack fell into the water. The force of the jet stream grabbed the pack and yanked Murphy with it, spinning him around. At precisely the right moment, he let go of the pack and the momentum was just enough to tip his balance so he landed on the debris pile instead of being torn to pieces by the water.

He heard Sarah scream as she dodged yet another missile. Murphy almost laughed in relief, but the joy was short lived as he looked over and saw that he had landed a few feet from Crawford.

He couldn't see clearly because he had lost his flashlight, but what he did see broke his heart. He saw a jagged splinter, about the size of a baseball bat, silhouetted through the shadows jutting out from Crawford's shoulder.

"DOUG!" He cried out as he crawled to his friend's side. He looked up and saw Sarah scrambling over to help him.

"Here, quick, give me the light," Murphy barked. He took the flashlight from Sarah and shone it on Crawford, dreading what he would see. He expected to see blood oozing from the spike, protruding from his chest like a slain vampire. Shining the light down, Murphy felt his body go numb at the sight.

Seeing Murphy slump, Sarah gasped at Murphy's reaction and then quietly asked, "Is he gone."

Then she saw that he was laughing.

"Dallas?"

Murphy rolled onto his back in laughter.

"Dallas? Why are you laughing?" she said again, annoyed and puzzled.

"Sorry. He's fine. The spike went through his backpack, not him. Doug, can you hear me?" Murphy shouted and shook him. His smile grew even bigger when his friend started to moan.

"Help me get this thing off him; we've got to get out of here." Murphy and Sarah struggled to roll Crawford over and slip his arms out of the pack but moving him was difficult not only because of his size but also because he was wedged in by the spike.

As they began moving him, Crawford began to wake up. "What happened?"

"The cavern is flooding and we've got to get you out of this backpack. Now roll to your left," Murphy said. Though still groggy, Crawford obeyed as he rolled over and slipped his arm out.

As soon as Crawford was free, Murphy shouted to Kekao. "Get that ladder up. We don't have much time."

Crawford stood on wobbly legs then reached over and pulled the stake out of his harpooned backpack and threw it over his shoulder, then began moving through the wreckage with the help of Sarah and Murphy. Halfway to his goal, Crawford stopped and turned around.

"Wait, I've got to get the cross." he protested.

By now, the water was up to their knees and rising at an alarming rate.

"No way!" Murphy shouted back. "We don't have time."

"But it's worth a fortune. I'm not leaving without it. It's mine!" Crawford shouted.

For a moment, Murphy didn't recognize his friend. Gone was the familiar smile and easygoing nature that made Crawford who he was. Instead, there were cold angry eyes looking back at him, no warmth or friendship but something much more sinister: greed. Crawford's chest was heaving in and out, and for a second, Murphy thought that Doug was going to hit him.

"That thing has almost cost you your life twice. Is it really worth it?"

"I'm going to take it!" Crawford said coldly.

"Oh for Pete sake," Sarah said as she grabbed Crawford by the shirt, yanked him close and kissed him hard on the lips. When she was done, she slapped him in the face. "Now snap out of it and let's get out of here."

Crawford stared at her for a moment then blinked. "Sorry guys, I-I don't know what came over me."

"Just don't let it happen again," Sarah said as she jumped into the water and headed toward Kekao and the other two natives.

"She kissed me," Crawford said showing a schoolboy's smile to Murphy as he moved passed him.

Murphy just shook his head. "Come on, we don't have much time."

"You keep saying that, why? And where did all this water come from?"

Murphy stepped over a fallen beam but scraped his leg on a rock that was lying beneath the still rising waters. He bit his lip in pain but continued moving. "You saw all the tunnel offshoots as we came down here; that's probably why Diablo chose this place because it's honeycombed with chambers and passages and he chose this particular cavern as a failsafe to be flooded."

"Isn't flooding this place just a bit of an overkill? I mean a worst case scenario is that we simply float our way to the top of the entrance then climb out of here."

Murphy shook his head. "He would have thought of that. I don't trust him. The sooner we get out of here the better. Old Diablo Oscuro has something up his sleeve and I don't want to be around to find out what it is."

"Come on you two," Sarah shouted from the other side.

Like two battered soldiers, Murphy and Crawford leaned against each other as they struggled over the debris toward the entrance. Both natives had already climbed up the makeshift ladder while Kekao was halfway up and Sarah was standing at the bottom. She held her hand out shouting and urging them on while Kekao and the other natives just stood there.

With no warning, no snapping of timber or crumbling of rock, the entire floor simply vanished beneath their feet. Murphy felt himself being sucked down into a dark abyss.

CHAPTER TWENTY THREE

Murphy still held onto his flashlight as they slid down the dark tunnel. The light bouncing off the walls mixed with the screams and yells from Sarah, Doug, and himself, all combining to make it feel like they were on a thrill ride to hell.

Murphy could only guess that they were sliding down an old lava tube that had been worn smooth by hundreds, even thousands of years of water flowing through it.

Then, just as suddenly as they had been flushed down the chute, they reached the bottom, splashing down in a huge pool.

"Is everyone okay?" Murphy shouted, spitting out a mouthful of water. "Sarah, Doug!"

"Over here." Murphy shone his light and illuminated Sarah's head bobbing in the water just a few feet behind him. He swam over to her. "Are you okay?"

"I'd be better if you'd get that light out of my eyes."

He pointed his light to the other side of the pool and saw Crawford hanging onto one of the support beams that had washed down with them. Crawford gave him a weak thumbs-up, then laid his head back down on the beam.

Murphy took his light and shone it around the room. The cavern was at least twice the size of the treasure room above. There were a few stalactites hanging down from the twenty-foot-high ceiling, but otherwise the rest of the ceiling and walls were smooth.

"Here, hold this." Murphy said as he handed his flashlight to Sarah and took off his backpack.

"What are you doing?" she asked.

"Calling the cavalry."

"Good idea," Crawford agreed.

"A good idea," he said as he reached into the backpack, "but unfortunately, one that won't work," he continued as he pulled the radio out, or what was left of it. The casing was shattered and the insides were spilling out like candy from a broken piñata.

"Back to square one," Murphy said as he shouldered his pack.

"Look, there's a light over there." Sarah called out. "Maybe we can get out that way."

At the far end of the cavern was a vertical slit in the wall about a foot wide and five feet in length. Murphy and Sarah sloshed through the nearly chest high water while Crawford half waded, half floated toward the light.

"Sarah, can you stick your head out the hole and see what's out there?" Murphy asked.

"Why me?"

"Because you're the smallest and the only one who will fit through the slot."

"Fine! Just don't let me slip," she replied, clearly not happy to be poking her head out the side of a mountain.

Sarah grabbed the edges of the rock and wiggled her way into the hole. It was a strange sight to see just her legs dangling from the wall, making it look like she was being eaten by the cave. After a few moments, the cave monster spit her back out.

"Well?" Murphy asked.

She shook her head. "We're not getting out that way."

"Why?" Crawford asked.

"Because this cave comes out about half way up the side of the mountain, that's why. It's a good one hundred feet down to the bottom and another hundred feet to the top."

"We can't go back up the way we came, that's for sure," Murphy said, looking at the tunnel entrance. "It's too steep to climb, and more water is beginning to come down."

"Where is all this water coming from?" Crawford asked. "I don't care how smart you think your pirate friend was, he couldn't have done all this."

Murphy nodded. "Yeah, you're right; he couldn't have planned this intricate a trap. This mountain is an old volcano so it's bound to be laced with lava tubes and pockets from when it was formed. As for the water, you saw how hard it was raining. An awful lot of water came pouring down and when the cave-in happened, it opened up new paths for it to follow. We've got to get out of here," he said as he shined his light around the cave.

Sarah picked up on the slight urgency in his voice. "I agree, but what has you so worried, other than the obvious?"

"What makes you think I'm worried?" he replied, trying to sound nonchalant.

"You forget who you're talking to here."

Murphy smiled. "I never could get one by you could I?"

"Nope. Now what gives?"

"We're at the bottom of the well here and there is no other way out and it's filling up fast. Even with the crack to act as a drain, all it will take to plug it up is a few boards floating down and jamming against this hole and we'll all drown. Heck," he said as he patted the side of the cave, "this wall could give way under pressure like the floor did above and we'd be swept out in a major waterfall."

Murphy suddenly realized he was leaning against the wall and slowly pulled his hand back, deciding it wasn't such a good idea to be pressing his weight against it.

The water was nearly up to their shoulders and the cavern was continuing to fill.

"The rock face looked pretty sheer," Sarah said, "but I think I saw a ledge. Maybe we could climb out on that. Hold onto my legs, I'm going to take another look."

Murphy helped her up, and once again she was half-swallowed by the cave monster with her legs dangling loose. After a few minutes, Sarah signaled she was ready to come back in.

Murphy grabbed her legs and started to pull, but she wouldn't budge. A flash of panic swept over him when he pulled a second time. Again, she didn't move. He felt Sarah's leg tighten up and she started kicking wildly. She was starting to panic.

He wrestled against the raging torrent and finally won as he got her back inside.

She coughed out several mouthfuls of water, then spoke through chattering teeth. "There is a ledge off to the right and it looks wide enough for us to stand on but it's down below us, five, maybe six feet. I couldn't really tell."

"Hypothermia is starting to set in," Murphy said as he wrapped his arms around her, his own teeth starting to chatter. "This water is way colder than I thought it would be."

"We're in the tropics," Crawford complained. "I thought all the water was supposed to be warm."

"We're deep inside a mountain; it's going to be naturally cold."

"But it's a volcano."

"A dormant volcano. Would you rather it be active and cook us in boiling water?" Murphy's tone was more sarcastic than he intended.

Crawford sighed. "No, but it looks like we'll be dead either way."

Murphy knew Doug was right; they had to do something or they would be dead. Looking around the cave, he felt desperate, and looking down at Sarah shivering in his arms, he began to feel hopeless.

Think, Murphy, think! He shouted to himself. Drown or hypothermia, drown or hypothermia, what could he do?

THINK!

What to do, what to do? Both forms of death involve water. Get rid of the water was the obvious choice. He paused and shook his head. No kidding Einstein, he laughed to himself. Easier said than done.

There was no place to get out of the water, which was pouring in faster than it was going out. The hole was simply too small to drain all the water. As he was thinking, the wooden beam that Crawford was using to float on hit him in the chest, throwing him off balance.

"That's it!" He shouted, startling both of his companions.

"Doug, bring that beam over here."

Crawford nodded, partly out of acknowledgement, part out of shaking from the cold. Murphy grabbed the front end of the beam and pointed for Crawford to grab the other end.

"Sarah, you need to stand over there to the side," Murphy shouted, "and hold onto anything that you can. Doug and I are going to use the beam as a battering ram and try to punch a hole through the wall. If we make it too big you could get swept out with the water."

"Her!" Crawford shouted. "What about us? We're the ones standing right in front of the hole, pounding at it with a log."

"I need your strength to help me break open the wall. Besides, I'm standing in front of you; I'll be washed out first."

"And that's supposed to make me feel better?"

Just then they heard a deep rumbling and everyone looked expectantly at each other. "What was that?" Crawford said. "Don't tell me that the volcano is erupting."

"Hurry!" Murphy shouted as he grabbed the beam. "We don't have much time."

"What is it?" Sarah asked.

"I think the dam just broke so to speak. I think these cave-ins weakened the catacombs and the weight of all the water trapped in the mountain is about to come crashing down on us."

"Well, what are we waiting for?" Crawford asked.

Murphy looked over his shoulder and gave his friend a nod, they grabbed the beam, pulled it back then slammed it into the rock beside the lip of the hole. Nothing happened, other than Crawford yelping because he got another splinter. He shook his hand from the pain then nodded to Murphy and they hit the wall again.

They heard a loud whoosh and turned just in time to see water surging down the shaft, creating a wave as it hit the pool. This miniature tsunami slammed Crawford into Murphy who in turn smashed against the side of the wall. Murphy cried out in pain as a protruding rock tore a gash in his forehead.

"Are you all right?" Sarah asked, holding Murphy's head in her hands.

Murphy felt the warmth of blood trickling down his cheek. He reached up and flinched when he touched the open wound.

"I guess it's a good thing there are no sharks in these here waters," he said weakly, talking in a pirate's voice. "I'll be fine," he lied. His head was beginning to throb and he was starting to feel slightly dizzy. "Come on, we've got to try it again."

They had to tread water to keep afloat as the drain hole they were working on was now completely under the water. Sarah swam around and got in behind Crawford and together, the three of them slammed the beam against the wall.

"This isn't working." Sarah gasped as her head popped above the water.

"We've got to keep trying." Murphy shouted above the roar. "I'm not going to drown in a cave. I'm going to grow old sitting on the front porch watching our grandchildren running around our feet. Now come on and let's do this again."

They drew the beam back like they were loading a crossbow, then with all their might, they fired it, slamming the beam against the wall.

Nothing.

"I'm sorry guys," Murphy said slowly, his voice filled with defeat and resignation.

"Dallas," Sarah began to say but didn't get the chance to finish as she suddenly disappeared underwater.

"Sarah!" Murphy shouted, then dove down after her.

To his horror, Murphy saw her dark figure swirling around, silhouetted against the light from the hole. Combined with their battering ram and the pressure of the added water, the rock around the slit had given way, tripling its width. Sarah, being the smallest and lightest, was caught in the undertow and was being sucked down in a whirlpool.

Frantically, he reached for her and just managed to grab the carrying handle on her backpack. She went sweeping by and nearly pulled his shoulder from its socket when he tried to stop her. It was like trying to stop a runaway freight train; Murphy suddenly found himself being dragged toward the hole by Sarah's momentum. He could see the light at the end of the tunnel, but instead of leading heavenward, this light was leading him to a one hundred foot plunge.

Murphy saw and felt Sarah pull him as she tumbled out the hole, the entire weight of her body straining his shoulder and fingers as he struggled to hang on. He desperately reached out for anything that would stop his fall and he somehow managed grabbed hold of a rock just on the inside of the hole. Even through the rushing water, he could still hear Sarah's muffled screams. She was suspended in mid-air, hanging halfway in the flow of the waterfall, and dangling halfway out. He was happy that Sarah was able to breath, but he couldn't. He was still submerged inside the cave with thousands of gallons of icy water washing over him. His shoulder felt like it was going to be ripped out of its socket and his lungs were beginning to burn. He could feel his strength draining away like the flowing water; it wouldn't be long now.

His grip failed and he felt himself being swept out the hole. The water had receded just enough that there was now a small gap of air between the water and the top of the hole. Instinctively, he shoved hard against the floor with his legs and managed to grab one last gulp of air before he went over the edge.

Despite the numbing cold he suddenly realized that he hadn't plummeted to his death. He also realized that his other shoulder was now screaming with pain.

Looking up, he could now see that he, like Sarah, was suspended in the waterfall. He could also see why his other arm and shoulder were hurting so badly and why he was still alive.

The beam they had used as a battering ram was crossways again the opening and Crawford was leaning against it with his arms over the top, holding on to his right arm with both hands.

"Do something!" Crawford shouted. "I can't hold on much longer."

Do something? Do something? He wanted to shout. He was the one literally stuck in the middle, what was he supposed to do? Use his super powers and fly them all to the top of the mountain?

He looked at Sarah. The fear in her eyes was almost more than he could stand and yet he also saw a glimmer of hope, of trust that he could somehow save her. But, as he looked down at her, he saw something else: ledge that she had told them about earlier.

"Sarah, how far below you is that ledge?" He shouted above the roar of the rushing water.

She hesitated for a moment then looked down but quickly looked back up again, her eyes shut tight. But before he could say anything, he saw her take a deep breath then look down again.

"It's about four feet below me," she stammered out, then quickly looked away again. Murphy could see her body shaking, not only from the frigid water but from fear and anxiety. He was about to say something when she drew a deep breath and looked back down. "It looks to be about two feet wide, it's hard to tell though. It's off to the side about four feet."

"Doug!" Murphy shouted. "We have to swing Sarah off to the side, there's a ledge just below her and I'm going to drop her onto it. Can you do it?"

Crawford just gritted his teeth and nodded. Murphy smiled then looked down at Sarah. "Sarah, we're going to swing you to your right and then I'm going to drop you onto that ledge below you."

Murphy didn't think it possible, but her face turned even paler when he told her what he was going to do. She was so scared she couldn't even speak, she only shook her head in a violent, no way motion, then squeezed her eyes tightly closed again.

"Sarah, I know you are scared, but there's no other way, we have to do this." She just shook her head again.

"Sarah, we've got to do this, I can't hold you much longer. You've got to trust me."

Slowly she looked up and gave the faintest nod. He gave her a reassuring smile then looked back up to Crawford and nodded. Murphy could see the pain and agony on his friend's face as he summoned his remaining strength to start swinging them. Murphy's arm was burning with pain at just holding onto Sarah. He couldn't imagine what Crawford's felt like having to hold onto *both* of them. But along with the pain, he also saw a look of determination he had never seen before.

"Hurry!" Crawford shouted, "I'm losing my grip."

"Get ready!" Murphy yelled to Sarah as he slowly started swinging her in time with Crawford's pulls. "Almost there."

With one last pull, he flung Sarah toward the rock shelf. She landed hard on her feet then collapsed to her knees. The momentum carried her forward and she ended up face first, sprawled out on the ledge.

Her left leg started to slip over the edge but she quickly pulled it back and rolled over on her side with her back leaning against the side of the mountain. She opened her eyes and screamed when she realized she was facing open air. She instantly rolled back over, burying her face against the side of the mountain.

Murphy looked up and smiled at Crawford but instead of joy at having swung Sarah to the ledge and safety, he saw sheer terror and he realized that his friend could no longer hang him.

Before he fell, Murphy had just enough time to spin around and reach out toward the cliff. Fortunately, when Crawford let go, Murphy was swinging toward the ledge. He didn't have enough momentum to carry him all the way; instead, he landed hard against the edge and just managed to shove his hand into a crevice in the ledge before his feet went sailing over the edge.

Hanging on for dear life, Murphy managed to get one foot braced against the side of the mountain, relieving some of the strain on his arms and especially his fingers, but he knew he couldn't hang on for long. He looked over to Sarah for help but she wasn't moving, either frozen in fear or passed out.

He was on his own. He succeeded in getting his other foot planted against the rock face, and after resting for a moment, used the last of his strength to pull himself up and swing one leg up onto the ledge.

He lay there for what seemed like hours in utter exhaustion, his arms aching beyond belief and his body quivering from the cold water. He managed to turn and lift his head up just enough to see Sarah and was relieved to see her back slowly rise and fall from her breathing.

Then he suddenly realized that Crawford was still up above. Carefully he rolled over onto his back and looked up. Crawford was slumped against the beam, exhausted, possibly unconscious. The water level had fallen and was no longer pushing him against the timber and he was now in danger of slipping off and falling into the waterfall.

"Doug!" Murphy shouted. There was no response and he had to yell three more times before his friend finally stirred. Crawford slowly opened his eyes as if waking from a long night's sleep. His eyes few open wide when he saw where he was. In his start, he pulled down on the beam and it shifted and fell out of the entrance. Murphy watched as it seemed to fall in slow motion. He followed it as it plummeted down the waterfall, twisting and turning end over end then smashing into splinters when it hit the rocks below.

Crawford yelled as he slipped, but managed to grab hold of the side of the cave entrance with his right hand. The momentum of the water swung him around and he grasped the rocks with his left hand, clutching the face of the mountain.

"Hang on Doug!" Murphy shouted. "There's a small hollow just to your left, only a few feet away, you can make it."

"No I can't. I can't move," Crawford whimpered back.

"Yes you can, you can do it!"

Crawford's only reply was to violently shake his head.

"One step at a time, just move your left hand ten inches over, just ten inches."

Crawford hesitated then slowly moved his hand, feeling the wall until he found a solid place he could grip.

"That's great Doug, now move your foot over, just a little to the left, there's a hole you can put your toe in."

Again, but with a little more confidence, Crawford slowly dragged it across the face of the cliff until his foot slid into the hole.

After five minutes of coaching, coaxing and occasionally cajoling, Murphy helped Crawford cross the six feet of open cliff to slip into the hollow. It was like a country club estate compared to the narrow ledge Murphy and Sarah were on. Crawford could actually stand up and turn around without fear of tumbling over the edge, a luxury Murphy could only dream about.

By now, the rain had stopped and the sun had pushed its way through the clouds. Murphy could see the dark storm clouds passing over the rest of the island and retreating out to sea. The warm rays felt good, driving the cold from his body. Wisps of steam were rising up from the broad jungle leaves and he could see a rainbow coloring the mist at the base of the falls. All in all a very beautiful sight if not for their being stranded on the side of a mountain with no apparent way down.

Murphy's travelogue moment was suddenly interrupted by a low rumbling that echoed from deep inside the mountain. A second later, Crawford's head appeared over the ledge looking down at him.

"What was that?" Crawford asked, more wariness than panic in his voice.

Before Murphy could answer, the mountain answered for itself. The rumbling grew increasingly loud, and climaxed with a deafening roar as a massive column of water burst through the hole.

The water continued to flow at a tremendous rate but began to slow after a few minutes. Murphy looked up and could see that debris that had washed through the tunnels was beginning to clog the entrance.

"Wow," Crawford said, looking down at Murphy.

Murphy smiled. "You have such a way with words."

"Guess it's a good thing we got out when we did."

"You can say that again."

"Any bright ideas on how to get us down?"

Murphy shook his head. "No, but at least we are safe for the moment."

"Great, just great."

"What's wrong?" Murphy muttered, desperately wanting to get some rest.

Crawford's head popped out over the ledge again. "The cliff is leaking."

"Leaking?"

"Yeah, water is oozing through the cracks in the rock."

Murphy thought that was odd, but then again, the entire mountain was a catacomb of tunnels. "It's probably just water leaking out of the hole and running down the side of the mountain, I wouldn't worry about."

"It's not runoff, Dallas, it's leaking through cracks in the rock."

"It's fine, Doug. Just move over to one side out of the water."

"But the entire rock face is leaking."

"Doug, it'll be..." Murphy stopped in midsentence when he realized what was happening. "Doug, you've got to get out of there, you've got to get down here, NOW!"

"Climb down there? No way. I'm not a mountain climber. I barely made it to this ledge; I'm not going anywhere. I'm sitting right here until Kekao and the others lower a rope down to us."

"You don't have time; you've got to get down here."

"Why? What's the big rush?"

"The main exit for the water is blocked so the pressure is building up. If water is seeping through the rock right there it means it's weak and the pressure could blow out that entire section of the mountain."

Slowly Crawford turned around and looked at the wall as if it were a two-headed monster. The water was now escaping in long, steady streams. He wanted to reach out and touch the wall but was afraid, thinking that even the slightest touch would cause the dam to burst.

"What do I do? I can't climb down," Crawford said, pleading. "I'm a fat computer geek, not some cliff crawler who gets his kicks climbing up sheer rock faces."

"If you don't move you'll be a dead fat computer geek."

As if to confirm his words, there was a crackling sound like the one they had heard in the cavern earlier, and water was now bubbling out of one of the larger cracks at an alarming rate.

Crawford disappeared at the sound as he turned to look and when his head popped back over the edge, Murphy could see the terror that filling his eyes.

"I don't know if I can do this, Dallas."

"Yes you can you big baby." Both men turned in surprised to see Sarah standing and looked up at her friend. "If I can play paratrooper and *drop* down on the ledge then you can haul your second rate hacker's butt down here."

"I just love it when you talk tough." Murphy winked at Sarah then turned back to Crawford. "Drop your pack first."

Water was beginning to seep out of a fissure that ran all the way up to the ledge Crawford was standing on. Murphy knew that not only where Crawford was standing would go, but also this entire section of the mountain would be torn away.

"And hurry up," he quickly added.

Crawford hesitated, but suddenly changed his mind as a chunk of rock about the size of a golf ball shot out from the rock wall, propelled by a stream of water. Terrified, he looked down at Murphy then quickly threw his backpack him.

Murphy had expected Crawford to simply drop his backpack instead of throwing it down. It hit him on his shoulder and he managed to hang on to it but was thrown off balance by its speed and weight. With his free hand, Murphy spun it around like a windmill trying to maintain his balance. He teetered on the edge when he felt a hand on his shoulder holding him down.

"Sorry," Crawford called.

"Just hurry up and get down here." Murphy replied. Just then they heard another deep rumbling from within the mountain, punctuating Murphy's words.

Crawford peered over the edge, looking past his friend to the swirling mist of the waterfall far below, then turned around and got down on his hands and knees and backed toward the edge. He lay down on his stomach and slowly slid his legs over the precipice.

Water was beginning to flow over the ledge Crawford was on and ran down the side of the rock face, creating its own miniature waterfall.

"Hurry up." Murphy yelled.

"I'm trying, I'm trying."

Murphy reached up but he couldn't quite grasp his friends flailing legs. "Stop kicking, and put your feet against the wall."

"I-I can't, I'm slipping," Crawford shrieked, and then fell…

He dropped onto the ledge in front of Murphy with a thud. He landed on both feet and stuck the landing like an Olympic gymnast scoring a perfect 10. The amazement on his face was matched by Murphy's as the two stared at each other, then burst out laughing. But the wonder didn't even have time to fade as they heard a loud crack and Crawford dropped straight down.

One moment Murphy was looking at Crawford and laughing with him, the next he and Sarah were staring at where their friend had just been standing. Their eyes locked in disbelief and neither wanted to be the first to look down and see their friend lying on the canyon floor.

The section of the ledge that Crawford had landed on held for a few seconds then gave way and crumbled under his weight and the force of the impact. The jagged section of the outcropping looked like some great beast had taken a bite out of it, and there, in the middle of the giant teeth marks, was Doug Crawford, hanging by his fingertips.

Murphy dropped to his knees and reached down and grabbed his friend's arm. "Hang on Doug; we'll get you out of there."

Sarah also bent down and firmly gripped Crawford's other arm.

"Pull him your way," Murphy said to Sarah, "and hurry."

Water was now flowing through the cracks and crevices of the mountainside like water through a screen door. The narrow ledge was precarious enough to stand on but the flowing water was making their footing even more treacherous.

With a great deal of effort they managed to drag, push, and pull Crawford onto Sarah's side of the ledge where they both collapsed, exhausted.

"Come on," Murphy said, between gasps, "this ledge looks like it cuts across the face of the mountain and may lead us out of here but for now, we've got to get over to the far side there. This whole side of the mountain is about to go."

Without uttering a word or even acknowledging him, Sarah and Crawford wearily stood and started inching their way along the slippery, narrow ledge. Murphy jumped over the three foot gap but nearly didn't make it, teetering on the edge for a moment. He knew he was tired but hadn't realized just how much of his strength fatigue had taken.

They had only gone a few feet when the side of the mountain exploded. A huge geyser of water erupted from the cliff face, spewing rocks and debris like a volcano exploding sideways.

"Quick, get into that hollow!" Murphy shouted, as he shoved Crawford and Sarah off the trail. The hollow was a small indentation scooped out of the side of the mountain, sloping back about eight feet and measured five feet high.

It started with just a single rock or two tumbling down the side of the mountain, but quickly turned into a full scale avalanche. Rocks and boulders of all sizes clamored down the mountainside with a thunderous roar.

All three huddled in their shallow dugout and watched with a mixed horror and fascination as huge patches of earth flowed down the mountainside. Several large chunks of earth plopped on the ledge and spread out like pancake batter. The thick mud continued to pour down and more and more of it was catching on the ledge and began oozing into their cramped sanctuary.

"This is not good," Crawford said as he watched the gathering blob move toward them like something from a bad 1950's horror movie.

"Don't worry," Murphy said, "we can push it back."

Sarah frowned. "Ever try pushing pudding around on your plate with a fork? It doesn't work too well."

"I didn't say we wouldn't get dirty or that it would be easy, but we'll be able to shove enough of it out so we won't be buried in it. Just relax, we'll be fine."

Just then, as if to mock him, two huge boulders crashed onto the ledge, quickly followed by a gathering of accompanying rocks and debris, which piled up in front of them. There was a gap at the top that was large enough to let light in but too small for then to escape through. They were trapped!

"Not good," Crawford said as he watched the last of the rocks fall on the entrance. A smaller rock rolled off the pile and hit his foot. The words had no sooner left his lips when a sheet of mud and debris came slushing through the opening, nearly knocking them off their feet.

"This is *really* not good," Crawford said again, concern and near-panic flooding his voice.

"The rocks must be sticking farther out than the ledge, catching all the falling debris and acting like a giant funnel to channel it in here," Murphy said. "Come on, we've got to clear the entrance."

Both men immediately began pushing against the heavy rocks and both men immediately ended up on the floor, their feet slipping out from under them because of the thick, slippery mud. Despite the urgency of their situation, Sarah could not help but giggle; the pair looked like a Vaudeville act continually slipping and sliding and falling over each other as they tried to brace themselves to shove the boulders out of the entrance.

"Very funny," Murphy said, his frustration beginning to show. "Would you care to join us and help us move these things?"

Sarah stepped forward and shook her head, keeping her face down as she tried to hide her huge smile. She moved in between Murphy and Crawford and they had all just started to push when a huge glob of mud flowed in through the entrance again, knocking all three to the floor and covering them from head to toe.

Sarah sat on the ground and wiped the mud from her face.

"Guess it's not quite as easy as it looks, huh?" Murphy said. "What we need is better leverage."

"What we need is to get out of here," Crawford added as the soupy mixture was nearly up to their waists with more flowing in.

"Okay, I've got an idea," Murphy said. "Doug, I want you to sit with your back against the wall and with your legs straight out in front of you. Sarah, I want you to sit facing Doug. You two need to sit with your feet touching then extend your arms and interlink your fingers. I'm going to sit with my back against Sarah, using you two as a brace then use my legs to push against the rocks."

"You'd better hurry," Sarah said as they were getting into position. "This gunk is nearly up to my chest."

"Everyone ready?" Murphy asked as he sat down and leaned against Sarah. When they both answered yes, he began pushing.

Murphy began pushing slowly at first, when the rocks didn't budge, he shove harder. He could feel Sarah's back bend under the pressure but she didn't complain. "Okay, I'm going to push harder; brace yourselves."

Murphy repositioned his legs and shoved with all his strength. At first, nothing happened and he felt the hope of escaping their tomb draining away along with his strength, but then he felt a slight nudge and the boulder shifted about three inches. His joy was short lived as the gap he created didn't help them escape, but instead allowed more mud to flow in.

"Hurry Dallas," Sarah shouted, "I can't sit here much longer, the mud is nearly up to my chin."

Murphy pushed again but since the boulder had moved several inched he didn't have the same leverage and the boulder remained stubbornly still; he needed to get closer. He took a deep breath then with some hesitation, scooted down so his head was under the mud flow, placing his shoulders in the middle of Sarah's back for support.

With his knees curled up to his chest, Murphy pushed. Murphy's legs were beginning to quiver under the strain, when he suddenly felt it started to budge. He needed to surface to get a breath of air but he dared not stop pushing and lose his momentum. He could feel himself becoming a little lightheaded but he had to keep going, he had to keep the rock moving.

The stone was moving at a snail's pace, but it *was* moving. But as determined as he was, he couldn't hold his breath forever. He stopped pushing and popped up for air.

"You guys okay?" Murphy asked as he broke the surface.

"Just hurry," was Sarah's reply.

With new determination not to let her down, he took another quick breath and repositioned himself to push again. Placing his feet against the rock once more, he shoved with all his strength.

The rock moved an inch, two... then disappeared altogether, falling off the ledge. Murphy should have been elated, happy that he had moved the rock and saved them all from drowning; instead, he was fighting for his life. With nothing to hold it, the mud and debris poured out the entrance, taking everything with it, including him.

CHAPTER TWENTY FOUR

Murphy felt himself being dragged out the entrance and there was nothing he could do. He flipped over on his stomach and reached out desperately for something to hold onto to stop his fall, but everything was slick and slippery from the mud.

Just as his feet reached the edge, he felt a hand grab his wrist. Murphy threw his head up above the escaping mud, and saw a desperate Sarah holding on to his wrist. She squealed as his weight and the flow of mud began dragging her along as well.

His legs were now dangling over the edge as he continued to slide, pulling Sarah with him. "Let go!" he shouted to her, "I don't want to drag you down with me."

"Shut up, I'm trying to save you!" She shouted back as she grabbed hold with her other hand. As she did, her body twisted and she suddenly slid forward. She screamed as Murphy went over the edge and she started to follow.

"Both of you shut up," Crawford growled, holding onto Sarah's foot. He had managed to brace himself against the outflowing tide and was now holding onto both of his friends.

Crawford waited until most of the mud had flowed out before he started to pull on Sarah. As soon as Murphy was safely lying on the cave floor, Crawford spoke. "What is it with you two, you're always hanging around together and I have to keep saving your butts."

Murphy just lay on the floor. "Thanks, Doug, that's two I owe you."

"Yes it is, and I intend to collect, next time the duty roster comes around and you're assigning crew for the midnight watch, I want the day shift."

Murphy chuckled. "Done!"

"Hey, what about me?" Sarah chimed in. "If you remember, I had hold of you too."

"Okay, okay, I'll give you the mid-shift."

"Mid-shift?"

"Fine. Next thing you know, you two will want me to bring you coffee and donuts while you're on the bridge too."

Crawford and Sarah looked at each other and nodded.

"Coffee and donuts sounds good to me." Crawford said.

"I think I'd prefer tea, with a twist of lemon," Sarah said.

"Here's your twist of lemon," Murphy said as he grabbed a handful of mud and threw it on Sarah. Murphy laughed at the indignant look on her face, but his laughter was short lived as she quickly scooped up a handful of mud and flung it at him.

Now it was Crawford's turn to laugh as he watched his two friends throw mud at each other.

"Oh you think this is funny do you?" Sarah said, staring hard at Crawford. "Well here." She scooped up another handful of mud, "here's some cream for your coffee." She hit him in the chest with the glob and Crawford looked down at it as if he had been shot. He looked up to see Murphy smiling broadly at him.

"I save your lives and this is how you repay me? Fine."

Sarah started to laugh but her laughter was drowned out by mud thrown in her face.

All three looked at each other and mud was soon flying everywhere as in a kindergarten's playground. After a few minutes, Murphy held up his hand. "I surrender."

"Me too," Sarah joined in as she let the mud in her had run through her fingers.

"What do we do now?" Crawford asked as he wiped mud off his face.

"Let's take a look," Murphy said with a weary sigh. As he started to stand, he slipped and fell again. This time there were no hidden giggles or muffled laughter; they were all too tired to laugh and the seriousness of their situation was beginning to catch up to them.

"You two stay put," Murphy said as he slowly stood again. "No use having all of us sliding around."

Once on his feet he took small, measured steps and inched his way to the entrance. He looked to his left, then right, taking it all in. His surveying done, he returned and managed to sit down without slipping or falling.

"Well?" Sarah asked.

"There's nothing left of the way we came. There's a huge jagged hole hollowed out of the mountain—where the cave used to be—and the ledge we used to get this far has been wiped clean by all the debris, so we're definitely not getting back that way."

"What about the other side?" Crawford asked. "Is there a ledge still there on that side?"

Murphy nodded. "For about twenty feet, I think."

"You think?" Sarah asked, looking at him, deeply puzzled.

"It's hard to tell if it's all there or not. Everything is covered in mud and goo but I think it's intact. Beyond that, the trail is clear and it looks like it leads to the side of the mountain and the jungle where we can climb out. Come one, we can do this. Follow me."

The trio slowly made their way out of the hollow and inched their way along the mud filled ledge. Rather than take steps, Murphy shuffled along as though he were walking in deep snow, keeping his feet in constant contact with the ledge rather than picking them up to step.

"Just take it slow and easy," Murphy said as he slowly trudged along, feeling like

a snowplow leading a group of cars through a mountain pass. Progress was slow and tedious and very quiet as everyone concentrated on their footing, knowing that one slip could send them plummeting down the embankment.

After ten minutes of painstaking walking, they cleared the mudslide. Murphy stopped and let out a huge sigh of relief. "Wow, we made it."

Sarah shook her head. "What, that surprises you? You almost sound disappointed."

Murphy smiled and shook his head. "No, what I meant was that after everything we have just been through, we made it here without anyone slipping off the edge, any giant boulders smashing us or Doug's panther waiting for us on the other side. It's kind of nice when things go the way they're supposed to."

"In other words, don't look a gift horse in the mouth," Crawford said. "Trust me, I'll take it."

"Come on, we still have a ways to go," Murphy urged.

CHAPTER TWENTY FIVE

Like battle weary soldiers, the three stepped off the mountain ledge and trudged up the steep hillside, back to the plateau near the base of the mountain where their journey had begun. Reaching the clearing, they collapsed from sheer exhaustion. Murphy rolled over and lay on his back and stared up at the sky. The sky was once again a deep, clear blue and cloudless. All the colors seemed more vibrant and the air had a new freshness to it. The world looked new, with no signs that there had ever been a storm.

After a few moments, he sat up and looked over the ocean then drew in a long, deep breath and looked at the others. "Nothing like being in the belly of the beast to make you appreciate the simple things in life like fresh air, warm sun on your face, and the sight of old friends."

Sarah propped herself up on her elbows and look at Murphy then at Crawford. "I think you're right Doug, those boards and rocks must have hit Dallas in the head harder than we thought. He thinks he's a poet laureate now. I think we need to get back to the ship and have your head examined."

Murphy smiled sarcastically. "Very funny, but we can't go to the ship, we have to go back to the cave and look for Kekao and Things One and Two."

"You're hurt for Pete's sake. You can hardly walk on straight and level ground. You won't be able to handle climbing over rocks and piles of rubble in a dark cave. Besides, we can send help back and they can be here in no time with the chopper."

"We just can't leave them there; we've got to at least try to look for them. And I'm fine." To prove it he tried to jump to his feet but as he did, his leg buckled and his face twisted in pain. He barely managed to catch himself before falling flat on his face.

Sarah rushed over and grabbed him. "I'm not so much worried about those beams
that fell on your head. I can see that you're still as stubborn as ever," she said in a harsh voice, then softened her tone. "I'm worried about you, Dallas. Your leg could get infected. Besides, I think the best way to help Kekao and the others it to go and get help."

"She's got a point old buddy," Crawford threw in.

Murphy knew they were both right so reluctantly he nodded.

Crawford shot straight up. "Did you hear that?"

"Hear what?" Sarah asked.

"I thought I heard growling."

"Growling?"

Sarah cocked her head to one side listening. "I don't hear anything."

"I know I heard something," Crawford insisted. Just then, they heard twigs snapping and leaves rustling behind them. Despite their fatigue, all three jumped to their feet. Murphy grabbed a nearby branch; Crawford grabbed a rock and held it ready. Sarah reached into her pocket and flipped open her knife. Both Murphy and Crawford looked at her out of surprise.

"What?" she asked, looking back at them.

Murphy just smiled at her. "That's my girl."

He gripped the branch like a baseball bat, nervously wrapping and constantly adjusting his fingers around it. In high school, he was a better fielder that a hitter but with a target the size of a panther, he knew he'd get in some hits today.

With a loud crash, the vines and branches were thrown back and a familiar voice barked: "Not waste time here. We go village, Aata hurt."

A collective sigh of relief rose from the group. "Nice to see you too, Kekao," Murphy said, suddenly feeling foolish standing there with a stick in his hand.

"What happened to you guys?" Sarah asked, "how did you escape?"

Kekao grunted. "I trapped in chamber when floor drop but not fall like you. Rapata get vines, pull me out of pit. Aata hurt by falling rocks."

"Well, our trip was a little more involved than that," Sarah said as she folded her knife and returned it to her pocket.

"Come, we go," Kekao ordered.

Murphy shook his head, "I'm sorry Aata is hurt but we're hurt too. Like Sarah said, our trip covered a little more ground than yours did; we need to rest a bit more before we leave."

"I say go now," Kekao said sternly.

Murphy walked over to Kekao and stared him straight in the eye. "I am in charge of this expedition and we will go when *I* say so. I know your man is hurt but so are we. We will rest for a few more minutes and then go. Do you have a problem with that?"

For a moment the two men stood toe to toe, neither one moving. Kekao was the first to blink as he grunted and stepped back. "We over there when you ready."

Murphy's shoulders remained taut and ready and he relaxed his stance only when Kekao and the others disappeared back into the jungle. Murphy turned to the others. "Grab something to eat and patch yourselves up the best you can. We still have a long way to go to get back to the village. We'll leave in half an hour."

CHAPTER TWENTY SIX

Walking through the wide clearing at the base of the mountain, the group headed toward the jungle and the trail that would lead them home. The expedition traveled in two separate groups, Kekao and the natives in the lead, Murphy and the others a few yards behind. Both groups traveled in silence as they moved slowly through the meadow, tending to their walking wounded. At the edge of the clearing, Murphy stopped and turned around, marking the cave entrance in his mind and taking a last look at the panoramic view of the clear blue sky and the sun blazing down on the mountain.

He turned and stepped into the jungle and was immediately swallowed up by the giant green beast again. Murphy had long since lost his sense of adventure; each step shot bolts of pain through his leg as the party descended along the narrow and increasingly steep trail.

"This isn't the same trail we took to get to the mountain," Murphy said.

"This shorter way," was all that Kekao volunteered.

The footpath they were on turned into a trail that was barely more than a thin line pressed out against the side of the hill. The trail cut deeper into the hillside as its slope increased. The angle was becoming so extreme that all Murphy had to do was extend his arm and barely lean and he'd be touching the side of the hill. On the other side of the trail, the hillside fell away just as quickly with a snarl of vines, branches, and thick undergrowth ready to swallow anyone or anything that fell.

The group remained quiet, as they concentrated on picking their way along, trying to keep up with Kekao who seemed to be trying to set a new jungle speed record.

Suddenly Murphy stopped.

"Are you okay?" Sarah asked.

"What is it?" Crawford said, looking at his two friends.

"Don't you hear it?" Murphy said.

"Hear what?" Crawford replied with a concerned look. "Very funny. I wish you guys would stop all ready."

"No," Murphy said shaking his head, "I'm serious. Don't you hear it?"

"Hear what?" Crawford replied again sarcastically as if he were playing a game.

"That's just it, I don't hear anything."

Crawford paused and listened, then frowned. "That's not good," he said nervously looking around, "something bad always happens in the movies when everything goes quiet." Just then, as if on cue from a movie script, they heard a low growl coming from high above them near the top of the hill.

"How does that thing keep finding us?" Crawford said, his eye darting along the ridge line.

"Bagheera sure is persistent." Sarah said, trying to ease the tension a little. "Maybe it thinks you're Mowgli."

"What's a Bagheera and a Mowgli?" Crawford asked.

"Mowgli is the main character from the Disney movie, *The Jungle Book*, and Bagheera is the panther in the story," Murphy answered.

"Funny, I always pictured you as a *Pirates of the Caribbean* type guy."

"Ha ha, *Jungle Book* is one of Sarah's favorite movies," Murphy answered.

"Come, we keep moving," Kekao said. "We safe. Great cat not attack on mountain side."

"Great," Crawford muttered to himself, "now if we can only figure out a way to stay on the hillside and get back to the ship at the same time."

Crawford took out his necklace and began playing with it like it was a lucky rabbit's foot, rubbing it, as if he hoped it would create a force field around him and drive the panther away.

Murphy smiled at his friend and watched as Sarah took out her necklace too, but she soon lost interest in her voodoo fashion accessory. He reached up and took his own lucky charm out of his pocket and looked at it. Even though sailors were a superstitious lot at times, he didn't believe for one moment that this or anything other than his pistol would protect him from the vengeful panther. Unfortunately, he had lost somewhere between the water slide and mud baths they'd been in.

They had been hiking on the steep trail for a solid thirty minutes when they came to a wide spot on the hillside.

"We stop here and rest," Kekao grunted out.

Murphy and the others all looked at each other in surprise; it was usually they, not Kekao, who were the ones calling for a break. Nevertheless, they all happily agreed.

Murphy looked over the steep edge, and like everything else, the jungle quickly swallowed up the view. He grabbed a bottle of water then gingerly sat down, nursing his leg. He took a large swallow and even though it was far from being cold, it was the sweetest thing he had tasted in a long time. He looked at Crawford who had hold of his good luck charm. "You rub that thing any harder, Doug, and you may turn into a panther yourself."

"Very funny."

"I see you don't have your necklace," Sarah said to Dallas.

"Me? Nah, you know I don't believe in that stuff. Besides, after Doug here turns into a panther from rubbing all that magic out of his charm there, he can help protect me."

Sarah giggled lightly and Doug gave them both a hard look. He took out his own bottle of water and a snack bar, and then did a double take looking for snakes before sitting the rest of the way down on a rock.

"So what are you going to do with all your money?" Crawford asked.

Murphy took another drink of water then set his bottle down. "I don't know yet. I don't even know if there will be anything left to salvage. I guess I really haven't thought about it too much."

"You're kidding, right? I haven't *stopped* thinking about it ever since we got out of the Bat Cave."

"So what? The usual cars, boats, and planes and a house big enough you have to leave a trail of bread crumbs so you don't get lost?" Murphy asked.

Crawford shrugged. "I suppose, but I hadn't thought about those things much. You'll love this Sarah," he grinned and turned to Sarah. "I'm going to have the biggest, geekiest man cave ever invented. There'll be so much hi-tech stuff in there that I'll be throwing half of it away before I can even open it because the newest thing to replace it will have just come out."

Sarah just shook her head and rolled her eyes.

"What about you Sarah? What are going to spend your pirate booty on?"

"I want a castle."

"A castle?"

"Yup, an honest to goodness castle with a moat, tall towers, fireplaces in every room and a dining hall big as Grand Central Station. And if I could swing it, I'd even throw in a fire breathing dragon or two."

Murphy smiled to himself. He knew that that was exactly what she was going to say. In their better days, they would sit on the beach and talk and daydream for hours. She was going to be the beautiful princess and he was going to be her knight in shining armor, but somewhere along the line, the castle had crumbled and his armor had rusted.

Crawford nodded. "Come on Dallas, I know you must have thought a little about it."

Murphy shook his head. "Really, I haven't thought that much about it. I mean sure, I'd like the fancy new car, the bigger house and some of your man-cave toys, but I hadn't really thought about it. I guess I'm just too practical and would wait to see how much I had before I started spending it." He paused for a moment then continued. "What I think would be really cool though would be to order your coffee from the local espresso stand then leave the girl a $100 tip, or the next time you're in the grocery store, just randomly pay for the groceries of the person in line behind you."

"Wow," Crawford said quietly, "here we are, selfish, self-center people thinking only of ourselves with our castles and tech toys and you're out there saving the world." He looked solemnly at Murphy and Sarah then mockingly hung his head.

"Okay, okay, I'll tip the barista from my red Lamborghini smoking my $500 Cuban cigar. Satisfied?" he laughed.

"That's better!" Crawford said laughing.

"But what I don't get," Murphy continued, after taking another drink of water, "is the way that Kekao and his two buddies were looking at the treasure."

"What do you mean?" Sarah asked.

"They were looking it at it like they knew exactly what it was and what it was worth."

"They were probably just excited about all the shiny baubles."

"I don't think so," Murphy replied, shaking his head. "There's just something about this whole thing that doesn't seem quite right me."

"Really Dallas, sometimes..." Sarah shook her head then shouted at Kekao. "Kekao, would you please come here?"

The big native grunted as he stood, then came over and stood in front of her.

"Can you tell me what this is?" Sarah asked as she took a gold coin out of her pocket. Kekao looked at her with a blank look on his face. "Nothing to me; much to you, I see."

"See, he doesn't know or care what it is," Sarah said looking at Murphy. "Satisfied?"

Murphy scowled at Sarah, then locked eyes with Kekao, trying to read him.

"Well, I am," Crawford said. "That means we don't have to share any of it with them since they don't have a clue." Smiling as he reached down to finish off his energy bar, he suddenly noticed that it was looking back at him.

Crawford picked up the bar to examine the insects that were now scurrying about on the snack. They were a type of ant that he had never seen before. They had oval-shaped heads with large mandibles and unusually long legs and antennae, making them look more like spiders than ants. In the short time the three of them had had their conversation; legions of the creatures had swarmed over the food and had invaded the entire area.

Crawford yelped in pain and threw the bar down as several of the ants decided he was better tasting. He didn't know much about ants but these looked huge compared to the everyday backyard variety. Small in the scale of jungle life, they were nearly twice the size of other ants.

Before he could shake them off, he had half a dozen bites on his hand; large circular welts were already swelling up. A moment later, Crawford realized that the tingly feeling he had wasn't from the prospect of getting rich but from the rest of the ant colony moving on him like Grant on Richmond.

Frantically, he started peeling off his clothes.

Sarah started to laugh, thinking he was putting on some sort of crazy show, but then she saw the ants. She sprang to her feet but slipped on the steep bank and went down hard on her right knee. She cried out in pain but struggled back to her feet and tried to help Doug.

She grabbed Crawford's shirtsleeve, almost yanking it off. In his frenzy, Crawford kept throwing his arm around wildly and her grip slipped. She teetered on the thin edge of the narrow trail, circling her arms, struggling to maintain her balance, but Crawford twirled around again and hit her with his backpack, sending her over the edge.

Murphy sprang to his feet when he saw that Sarah was in serious trouble. He yelled at Crawford to stop but by this time he was in a total panic. Murphy charged forward and ducked under Crawford's twirling backpack and just missed Sarah's hand by inches. For a moment their eyes locked as she toppled over the edge. Her eyes were filled with shock and disbelief as she fell.

Sarah flipped once and landed hard on her stomach, facing uphill. Fortunately, her foot caught a root sticking out of the hill so that she was practically standing on it; it was the only thing that kept her from disappeared down the hillside. She desperately clawed at the vines and branches as if trying to swim up the side of the hill, but her legs were already getting tangled.

Crawford was completely out of control now as the ants crawled up the back of his neck and he felt several of them burrow into his ears. Fired by blind panic, he whirled around with his backpack like some mad turnstile.

Murphy was kneeling down, hanging onto the base of a tree, trying to reach Sarah. She was screaming for him to help her which made it all the worse. He leaned over, stretching as far as he could but she was still a good eighteen inches away. He stretched again, but no matter what he did, he still couldn't reach her.

Panic and frustration swept over. He knew that if he didn't do something quick, she would be gone forever. Then as quickly and as brilliantly as a bolt of lightning streaking across the sky, he had a flash of inspiration.

Inspired by Crawford's strip tease act, he quickly took off his belt and wrapped it around the tree, then put the end through the buckle and pulled it tight. He could now hang onto the belt and be able to reach her.

He wrapped the belt around his left hand then lowered himself over the edge, reaching down with his right. Out of the corner of his eye he saw Kekao approaching and he called out to him. "Come over here and help me. I've almost got her."

Straining against the leather of the belt cutting into his wrist and the pain in his leg, he repositioned himself above her and reached down again. Their hands were now just inches apart. He smiled reassuringly into her eyes. She smiled weakly back, but in an instant the reassurance he saw in her eyes was replaced by sheer terror as the root she was standing on broke and she went sliding down the hill. He lunged for her but missed, just brushing her fingertips as she slipped out of reach.

Suddenly he felt himself falling through the air. It was surreal to watch Sarah as she tumbled end over end. His eyes told him that she was the one moving, the one falling down the hill, but his body told the truth as *he* hit hard on the bank beside her. He bounced once, then flipped over and plummeted down the side of the steep embankment.

Murphy's world was now a chaotic spinning tumbling blur of greens, browns and patches of light, as he ricocheted off tree trunks, bounced off rocks, and slammed into fallen logs in the dense jungle foliage.

He thought the vines would have slowed him down, but instead, they seemed to be dragging him down faster and faster. He tried desperately to reach out and grab anything to slow his fall, but he was bouncing down the hill too fast to get a solid grip on anything. The last thing he remembered was an intense pain, a bright flash of light...then nothing.

CHAPTER TWENTY SEVEN

Murphy slowly opened his eyes. At first, all he could see was darkness. Then his eyes slowly focused and he could see that he was lying face down on the jungle floor. It felt good just to lie still, not to have his head and body flipping and spinning through the air.

He felt a weight on his back, probably a branch from one of the many trees he'd hit on the way down. He was surprised he wasn't buried under an entire brush pile. He could have stayed there longer; just enjoying the chance to lie still and relax but the branch on top of him was weighing him down, making it difficult to breathe. Summoning his strength, he started to move, but as he did, whatever was on top of him started to move too, only it didn't feel like a log or rock sliding off; it felt alive. He froze.

He had stopped moving, but whatever was on his back didn't. He felt it slowly continue to travel across his back. From the corner of his eye, he saw a snake the size of a tree trunk slither off his back and disappear into the jungle

When his breathing and heart rate returned to normal, he finished rolling over onto his back. The pain was not nearly as bad as he had expected, though he thought it must have been offset by the snake induced adrenalin.

He found himself staring up through the jungle canopy at a tiny patch of the early evening sky. The canopy had already choked out most of the last remnants of light, turning the lush, multi-shades of green into dull greys, and casting shadows that across the jungle floor.

With great effort, Murphy propped himself up on his elbows and took in his surroundings. He was lying in a clearing at the base of the hill he had just fallen down. He looked back up the hill and expected to find a wide swatch cut in the jungle where he had fallen, but the vines, leaves and branches had already closed over it.

Physically, other than having a violent headache and having every inch of his body covered in one giant combination scrape-cut-bruise, he didn't appear to have suffered any serious injury.

Suddenly, he realized that the long shadows meant it was nearly dark now; and that he had been unconscious for nearly six hours. Where were Sarah and the others? Why hadn't they come looking for him? Had something happened to them?

With great effort, he fought back the pain and struggled to his feet only to double over as a wave of nausea washed over him.

He tried again, slower and with more deliberation, rising first to his knees, then finally to his unstable feet. He swayed back and forth feeling more like he was on the deck of the *Pacific Searcher* than standing on solid ground.

He was amazed to see his backpack lying on the ground only a few feet away. He managed to walk to it without falling down. Not wanting to push his luck, he quickly sank down beside it before another wave of nausea hit him.

Everything in the backpack looked like it had been thrown in to a giant Mixmaster and blended into an undrinkable cocktail. Most of the food was smashed in its wrappers. To his joy, one bottle of water had managed to survive and he quickly unscrewed the cap and took a long drink. Rummaging through the remains, he also found one other item that had survived: the panther good luck charm that Kekao had given him. Murphy just shook his head and threw it back in the pack.

After taking another gulp of water, Murphy saw his belt, coiled up like a snake on the ground beside where he had landed.

"Never buy a cheap belt again," he told himself as he reached over and picked it up. "Good quality leather would never have broken like this."

But as he ran his fingers over the edge of the belt, he saw that it wasn't torn and frayed as he had expected. It had been cut. Cut! How could that be?

He could vividly picture Sarah, lying on the hillside, screaming for help. He couldn't reach her so had taken off his belt and wrapped it around the tree. As he was leaning down to help her, out of the corner of his eye he remembered seeing Doug spinning wildly out of control. He remembered seeing Kekao walking toward him. He had called out to him for help then turned back to Sarah. He was reaching down for her when he slipped.

He remembered vividly the expression on her face as he went flipping end over end down the hillside but there was something else, some vague memory lurking in the back of his mind like a shadowy figure in the fog.

Kekao!

Kekao had been standing beside the tree. Murphy hadn't seen a knife, the tree blocked his view, but he didn't need to because he could remember seeing Kekao's face with a big, self-satisfied grin.

Why?

Why would Kekao cut the belt? There was no love-lost between them but he didn't think there was enough animosity for Kekao to want to kill him.

Murphy shook his head. The why would have to wait: what mattered now was that Sarah and Doug were in danger and he had to warn them. He wanted to charge up the hillside and grab Kekao by the throat and beat the truth out of him but he had to save himself before he could save them.

Night was falling fast and he had no idea where he was. It was too dangerous to travel in the jungle at night especially in his condition, so he would have to stay here.

He took another deep breath and looked more closely at his surroundings. He had always enjoyed camping and roughing it, but this was extreme. He felt like he was on an episode of *Man vs. Wild*. He had to move fast before the last rays of light were completely swallowed by the unforgiving jungle.

He quickly gathered some vines and twisted them into a useable rope and then began braiding them together to make a hammock. A good hammock would take a couple of hours to make, time which he didn't have, so this would be just big enough and strong enough to keep him off the ground. As he braided, he smiled at a memory of braiding his wife's with long hair.

The smile faded. Ex-wife.

He found a nearby tree that had a large Y shaped branch about eight feet off the ground. He climbed the tree and lashed the vines between the two branches and hung his crude hammock. He wanted to build a fire but didn't want anybody to see the smoke. It was best to stay dead, so to speak, until he could figure things out. With the last of the light fading, he finished tying the last knot. He broke off a couple of large leaves to cover himself then gently lowered himself down, testing his handy work.

With dusk, the sounds of the night creatures emerging from their day-time hiding places began to fill the air. The sounds of insects were always present in the jungle, both day and night, but somehow the night bugs sounded louder, more menacing.

Now that he was quiet and began to relax a little, he noticed a different sound. It reminded him of rustling leaves, blown by a gentle breeze. But the sound wasn't coming from the branches above him, it was lower. At first there was just a few telltale sounds but the sound continued to build.

As he starred into the night, he thought he was losing his mind; it looked like the carpet floor of the jungle was moving, rippling with tiny waves like those when you throw a pebble into a pond. Suddenly he realized what was moving; it was all the night insects coming out of their burrows and scavenging on the jungle floor for food. Thousands, if not hundreds of thousands of tiny legs scurrying about in their nightly quest for food.

He heard more than saw the swirling mass of insects as they formed ranks and seemed to march in his direction. But why were they coming toward him? Could they smell him and take him as a giant smorgasbord?

Then it dawned on him: his backpack!

First rule of camping, never take any food with you to bed. His pack was full of smashed food mingled with the water from his broken bottles, now that truly was a bug's smorgasbord! He quickly grabbed it and threw it as far as he could. It landed about twenty feet in front of him in the middle of the clearing.

The sounds of the traveling insects still furnished an underlying rhythm to the other jungle sounds, but at least they weren't flowing in his direction anymore. Finally, only half-convinced that he was safe in the bosom of the tree, Murphy drifted off into a fitful sleep, tossing and turning, worrying about his friends…about Sarah.

He awoke with the changing of the guard when the daylight creatures reclaimed their domain. He glanced at his watch; even though the crystal was shattered, it was still running and read 8:00. Slices of sunlight managed to penetrate the jungle canopy, creating brilliant contrasts of bright and dull greens.

The morning dew was quickly evaporating away as wisps of stream rose from the leaves; Murphy knew it was going to be another long, hot day. Finding out where he was and finding water would be his first priorities. Food would have to be a secondary concern, though his grumbling stomach disagreed.

He looked over and saw his backpack, which he had expected to be a mangled piece of cloth torn apart by the ravaging insects, but it wasn't. It was sitting on the ground just where he had tossed it, looking none the worse for wear.

Feeling like a hermit crab coming out of its shell, Murphy pried himself stiffly out of his hammock, unfolded his arms and legs, then plopped unceremoniously onto the ground. Every muscle in his body was stiff and sore and protested as he stretched.

He gazed up the slope and was amazed that he was alive at all; there would be no climbing back that way.

Figuring that the village was somewhere west of his location, he decided he would follow the hillside since it looked like it descended into a small valley that led to the ocean.

He grabbed his backpack and as expected, the insides had been picked clean by the ravenous insects. The only things left were a nearly empty water bottle and his good luck charm. Seems the insects didn't like it any more that he did.

Greedily he drained the last few drops from the bottle. The sun was growing in intensity the higher it climbed into the sky. In this heat, he knew he would have to find water soon.

He was practically surrounded by food—fruits and nuts—but he knew that not everything on the menu was edible. Like the forbidden fruit in the Garden of Eden, something that looked lovely and appealing on the outside might be deadly. He wished he had paid more attention to those *Survivor* episodes or *National Geographic* Specials.

Before he started his jungle trek, he found a tree branch about six feet long that he could use as a walking stick. It seemed sturdy enough to support his weight, to slash through the jungle with and long enough to fend off anything that might need fending off.   It just needed one little modification. He dug into a pocket, and got out his knife.

His first pocket knife had been an old Schrade he had bought at the local hardware store when he was eight years old. He had saved up all summer for it and spent his own money, all $7.95. It wasn't that expensive, but to him it was a small fortune. His mother didn't think he should be carrying a knife, but his dad said it would teach him responsibility and that he was becoming a man. His little head had never swelled so big as when his dad had said that.

He lost that knife during the summer he was twelve, but the habit had been forged. Now he felt almost naked if he went anywhere without his trusty knife. And that in itself had gotten him in trouble on several occasions as he had forgotten to leave it at home when he went to the airport. Airport security took a very dim view of people carrying knives, even if they had only a two-inch blade.

Four years ago when he had gotten his the job with World Wide, he decided he could afford to upgrade to a Swiss Army Knife. When he went into the store, what he thought would be a fifteen-minute trip turned into an ordeal that lasted nearly an hour. He thought he would just walk in, look at several in the case and then pick one out and leave. But he was as wrong as he was amazed at what he saw.

He found one that had a built in 2 GB memory stick and MP3 player. Another one had more gadgets on it than James Bond could use— a fish scaler and hook disgorger, ruler, reamer, wood saw, pliers and wire strippers, a magnifying glass and more. Oh, and it had a blade too. He couldn't help but laugh out loud when he looked at it.

He finally settled on one that was a little more simple with a bottle opener, a couple of screwdrivers and a good blade, along with a couple of other little things he would probably never use. Gone were the days of his simple little Schrade.

He carved the end of his stick to a sharp point and started off with his walking stick/spear in hand. He heard it said that if you had just a knife, you could survive in the wilderness; he was about to put that to the test.

Even with the roundabout way he now thought Kekao had taken, Murphy figured it was a good, solid day's march back to the beach. Walking became easier as his muscles loosened up. The terrain was easy and pleasant and he was making good time.

Along the trail, he found some green fruit and picked it, staying away from the red fruit, leaning on the old adage that red was for danger and it might be poisonous. He tentatively took a bite out of one. It resembled the taste and texture of a pear and was sweet, but more importantly it was juicy, helping to stave off thirst. After about an hour of not getting sick or keeling over dead, he ate the other two.

CHAPTER TWENTY EIGHT

After several hours of hiking, Murphy came across a small stream and immediately walked straight into it, clothes and all. The cool water was refreshing, not only washing away his heat and fatigue but two days' worth of filth and grime. As he filled his empty water bottle, he thought this must be the same stream they had all stopped at two days earlier on their journey to the cave.

Had it really only been just two days ago? With all that had happened, it seemed like two *months*.

He was out of the higher mountain plains and now on the main floor of the island itself. He'd seen smoke off in the distance earlier in the morning and assumed it was from the village. It was hard to get a fix on the village since the wind carried most of the smoke away but at least he knew he was heading in the right direction.

He had lost sight of the smoke once he'd hit the lowlands where the jungle became thicker, and unfortunately, hotter. Despite his aches and pains, like a weary old plow horse heading back to the barn after a hard day in the field, Murphy kept plodding down the path toward home.

During the last couple of days, he'd had a lot of time to think, to reflect about his life, where he had been, where he was going and... Sarah. But ever since last night, all his thoughts had been consumed by Kekao. He hadn't trusted the man the first day they had met and now he had tried to kill him; why?

The more he thought about it, the more things just didn't seem right about the entire situation with the natives and the village. He couldn't quite put his finger on it but everything seemed just a little too neat and orderly, as if Hoku and the rest were just waiting for them. It was as if they were seeing everything they *expected* to see. Peaceful, cooperative natives, the promise of huge, unclaimed oil reserves... even his own favorite passion for buried pirate treasure.

It didn't make any sense though. Even if it were all an elaborate charade, what would be the purpose? Why go through all the trouble just to get them there?

Thinking about ulterior motives and hidden conspiracies was making him hungry. There wasn't a McDonald's drive thru but he spotted the next best thing. A few yards off the path he spied a clump of the green fruit he had eaten earlier.

He hacked a path with his walking stick and reached the tree. He was just about to reach up to pluck one of the fruits when a small yellow snake slithered by on the branch above. Murphy waited for the snake to go on by then grabbed the fruit.

He was just about to take a bite when he stopped; he thought he heard a voice. He waited several seconds, but heard nothing more.

Maybe it was the heat, maybe it was all the thoughts of conspiracies and Kekao trying to kill him...maybe he was losing his mind.

"Get a grip," Murphy said to himself out loud. He shook his head as if that would shake away the voice.

He had just finished the first piece of fruit and was grabbing a second when he heard a faint voice again, only this time it was answered by a second. Then, as if mocking him, there was laughter.

Knowing he wasn't crazy, he listened carefully again. This time he picked out several words and set off cautiously and quietly in the direction of the voices.

Slowly he made his way down the path and stopped at the edge of a small clearing where he ducked into the jungle and attempted to blend in. At the far edge of the clearing, Murphy could see the entrance to a cave. Someone had stacked rocks to narrow the entrance, and in the middle was a sturdy looking wooden door. Vines, branches and leaves had been hastily thrown over the rock embankment in an attempt to camouflage the entrance.

There were two natives standing outside the entrance, each holding a spear and acting like bored guards. He thought it odd that they would try and camouflage the cave entrance and even stranger that it would need guards, but the strangest thing of all was the fact that the two men were smoking cigarettes!

Cigarettes?

Where did they get those? He didn't remember seeing any 7-11s on the corner of Jungle and Vine. Yates or another member of the crew could have given them the cigarettes, yet the way these two acted it was as if they had been smoking for years.

He heard a commotion and eight more natives emerged from the path and came walking toward the cave. Three were women, each carrying a large clay pot. Two younger men, boys really, were carrying large wooden crates, and an old man, struggling under the weight of his crate followed them. They were all followed by two more men, each dangling a machete at his waist and carrying a spear.

The old man stumbled at the entrance and dropped his crate. The closest guard grabbed his arm roughly and yanked him to his feet then shoved him down again, ordering him to pick up the crate. Murphy could see that the two younger men were angry and wanted to help the old man, but a spear thrust from one of the guards kept them in their place.

The guards unlocked the door, then roughly shoved the women, boys and the old man into the cave, then slammed it shut. Murphy watched for a few more minutes but nothing else happened except for the guards smoking another cigarette and looking around like a bunch of high schoolers who'd ditched class and were smoking behind the bleachers, hiding from the PE coach. Things were getting more bizarre by the minute, Murphy thought.

Working under the assumption that the prisoners had come from the village with supplies, Murphy decided he would follow the path in hope it would lead him back there. He carefully backtracked then skirted through the jungle around the guards until he rejoined the path about a hundred yards further away.

After a few minutes he smelled the familiar aroma of wood smoke and looked up and saw a plume rising above the trees. He smiled and relaxed at the thought that he was almost home free.

His joy was short lived as he suddenly heard voices coming from behind him. He had been so caught up in trying to figure out what was going on and watching the trail in front of him that he hadn't even consider that someone would walk up behind him.

He jumped off the trail and dove into the vegetation, just as Sarah and Doug rounded the corner of the trail.

They both looked exhausted. Doug, in his khaki jungle adventure out-fit, no longer looked like the intrepid explorer out to discover the deepest darkest secrets of the jungle, but rather like a beaten, weary trail guide who had lost his entire expedition. His shoulders were stooped and there was none of the laughter or joy that always danced in his eyes. Doug looked rough but Sarah looked much worse.

She had been through the ringer. Her steps were measured and labored, like someone on a death march. Her eyes were swollen and red, betraying that she had been crying.

He wanted to reach out to her, to hold and comfort her. It tore at his heart to think that he was the cause of such grief. He wanted to relieve her pain, he was so close to her now, but he couldn't. Kekao swaggered beside them, like a man without a care in the world. In fact, he looked a little annoyed at having to slow his step so the others could keep pace with him.

Murphy didn't trust Kekao, or Hoku for that matter, and was afraid that he would cause more harm than good if he revealed that he was alive right now. He just hoped Sarah would understand.

Murphy followed them as best he could, trailing behind along the edge of the path and darting in and out of the jungle to avoid being seen. After a few minutes they stopped and he caught a glimpse of Captain Yates coming up the path. Sarah ran up to him, threw her arms around him and burst into tears. Doug joined them and they all hugged each other for a long time.

Murphy skirted through the jungle until he was close enough to hear what was being said. Between sobs he could hear Sarah say that she couldn't believe he was gone, while Doug kept blaming himself. Murphy felt good that his friends really cared about him, yet his heart ached because he knew he was the reason for their grief. He felt like an outsider, that he was violating their privacy by listening in on their grief.

After a few minutes, Kekao spoke, sounding almost impatient. "Where is Chief Hoku...oh great Servant of God?" Kekao threw the title in almost as an afterthought.

"I left him and a few others on the ship," Yates answered flatly.

WHAT! On the ship? Murphy wanted to shout out loud.

What was the captain thinking? It was against every regulation in the book to allow the chief or any of the natives onboard the *Pacific Searcher*. Yates knew this.

Under other circumstances, Murphy would have found the irony amusing; Yates had always been a by-the-book man, while he had always been the one to bend the rules when it suited him.

But this was way beyond letting someone pull a double shift because they needed money or not crossing all the T's and dotting all the I's on the daily report. The *Pacific Searcher* was the flagship and carried some of the most sophisticated technology in the business. Letting these people onto the ship would be equivalent to having an open house at the Pentagon. Murphy hoped that the Great Servant of God had not just left the front door open so the devil could come back into heaven.

Kekao did not hide his pleasure at the news that Hoku was on the ship. His grin grew wide then he pulled one of his companions aside, whispered something in his ear, and then sent him on his way.

Murphy watched as his three shipmates turned around and headed back down the trail toward the beach, and home. Kekao followed Yates and the others but slowly began to fall behind. Murphy trailed from a distance and soon became frustrated as he lost sight of the main group until the only person he could see was Kekao. The big native walked as if he were taking a leisurely Sunday afternoon stroll.

Murphy watched as Kekao entered a clearing, and then at the far edge disappeared around a corner. Murphy stayed hidden, studying the jungle, staring into the green foliage like Superman using his x-ray vision to look through a steel door. With no sign of him, Murphy was just about to enter the clearing when Kekao stepped out.

"Hello Dallas," Kekao said in a very casual and conversational tone.

Murphy quickly ducked back down into the cover of the jungle. Did Kekao really know he was there? Had he been that clumsy at following?

Kekao stood patiently for a few more moment. Then, Murphy heard a low menacing purr-growl. He snapped his head left and right; Bagheera sounded close, very close.

"See, even our feline friend knows you're here. Come out so we can talk face to face and clear up any misunderstand." The cat repeated the gargling sound as if agreeing with Kekao.

Reluctantly, Murphy stepped out of the jungle and onto the path, keeping his eyes locked on Kekao. Kekao smiled broadly, revealing his white teeth. Murphy had never noticed Kekao's teeth before; they really were white, far too white and polished to be those of a savage living in the wild without proper dental care.

"Misunderstanding? Oh you mean the part about how you tried to kill me?" Murphy said with a cold look of defiance. "By the way, your vocabulary seems to have improved quite a bit over the last couple of days. So let's just dispense with the charade that you're helping us."

Kekao burst out laughing, his roar rivaling Bagheera's. "No, I am not here to help the *Servant of God*," he sneered. "Although I image he is the one who will be needing help about now."

"What do you mean? What are you going to do to the captain? *Who* are you?

"Who I am is not important right now. What is important is that I'm going to finish the 'misunderstanding' I started with you yesterday."

"Why? Why do you want to kill me? Don't I have a right to know what I am dying for?"

"This isn't the movies where the bad guy tells you everything and then you somehow manage to escape and save the day. Real life doesn't work that way." Kekao started walking toward Murphy with strong, determined strides. Murphy thought about running but where would he go? He still had a slight limp from the fall and Kekao could easily catch him.

Just then, the panther emerged silently from the jungle, appearing like a shadow. There was no growling snarl, no low menacing gargle, no sound at all as he took three steps then stopped and looked at each man. Murphy had a strange feeling, not like the animal was trying to decide if he should be the main course or dessert, but more like he was being judged.

He always believed he would stand before the Judgment Throne of God, but never in his wildest imagination did he think he would stand before of the mighty jungle king, Bagheera.

Kekao looked on with a confident smile, as though he knew he was in good standing with the jungle king or at the very least like he had a handful of catnip. The panther now slowly paced back and forth, first in front of one man, and then the other, keeping his distance, deciding.

Murphy's heart was pounding so hard he thought his chest would explode and kill him before either the panther or Kekao could. But the decision was made as the cat suddenly charged and leaped. The big cat moved so fast Murphy didn't even have time to raise his hands to protect himself as both paws hit him full force in the chest and shoved him back into the jungle.

The last thing Murphy saw before darkness fell on him were razor sharp teeth, clean and white as if they had just been brushed; clean and white, just like Kekao's.

CHAPTER TWENTY NINE

"Dallas...Dallas."

Murphy thought he heard his name. Was he dreaming?

No, it couldn't be a dream; he was dead. Blurry images of the panther flashed through his mind. He felt the impact of its powerful paws on his chest, its incredible white teeth and the stench of its breath.

"Dallas, Dallas."

There it was again, someone calling his name. The voice was sweet and melodic, it sounded like the voice of an angel... he had to be in heaven!

Slowly he opened his eyes. He was having trouble focusing. All he could see was a vast darkness, but gradually shapes and colors began to appear. Out of the corner of the eye he saw a figure move, coming closer, leaning over him. The cherub had long flowing hair and must be the same angel that called his name earlier. He tried to reach out but something was wrong. As he moved, a twinge of pain shot through his arm and he suddenly realized that his head was starting to hurt too.

"Dallas, can you hear me?" There it was again, a voice calling out his name, only this voice was different from the first one, strangely familiar, yet different. The first voice was more feminine, this one was more masculine. The voice called out again and then he felt a pair of hands reach under him and pull him up to a sitting position.

He felt another hand gently touch his cheek, it was warm and soft and had a faint fragrance that he recognized, by couldn't place it at the moment in his blurred reality. Then the hand tilted his head back and he felt the taste of cool water pouring across his lips.

"Dallas...Dallas, wake up."

His eyelids fluttered as he opened his eyes again and this time the world was in focus as he looked into the face of the angel, his angel... Sarah. He wasn't disappointed when he saw it was her and realized that he was still alive.

However, he would have been disappointed if Crawford's was the first face he would have seen instead of Sarah's. "Hey old buddy."

"Welcome back," Sarah said gently as she cradled his face in her hands. He smiled as he stared into her eyes; he hadn't seen that look in a long time.

His joy and contentment were short lived as his vision improved and he saw who was standing behind Sarah. He immediately tensed up when he saw Kekao and suddenly realized he was on the bridge of the *Pacific Searcher* with Yates, Hoku and three other natives.

What he didn't understand was why there was none of the ship's crew there on the bridge with them and why Kekao and the other natives were dressed in regular street clothes and, even more puzzling and disturbing, they were armed, not with spears and knives, but with automatic weapons. Murphy struggled to sit up, ignoring the pain from his bruised ribs.

"Welcome back Dallas," Kekao said. "You should spend a weekend in Vegas. You are a very lucky man."

"What happened? I remember the panther attacking me and pinning me to the ground. How come I'm not dead?"

"The captain heard Bagheera's growl so we came running back and must have scared it away," Sarah answered.

Looking around the bridge, seeing the grim expressions on his friend's faces, Murphy didn't feel very lucky. He also noticed another very ominous sign: Hoku was sitting in the captain's chair.

"What's going on here?" Murphy asked. "And how did you get on the ship?"

"How we got on the ship was actually an unforeseen act of pure luck," Hoku said. "Oh we had plans to get on board but this just made it so much simpler. Remember the flair you saw and how the good Captain here said not to worry about it? Well, some unwanted guests showed and threat-ened the village, so our protector, the Great Servant of God graciously took some of the women aboard to protect them. Once on board, it was easy to set thing in motion to take over the ship. You'd be surprised how disarming and distracting a smile from a pretty girl can be. That is the how, now as to the what we are doing here is we are negotiating."

"Negotiating? Negotiating what?" Murphy asked, looking around the room. "Who are you, really? What is this all about?"

"Well, Mr. Murphy," Hoku said as he leaned back in Yates' chair and crossed his legs. "We're with a consortium that thinks that organizations such as World Wide are not good, responsible corporate citizens. Your employers are corrupt, woefully lacking in their commitment to the wellbeing of this planet, and put greed above the needs of humanity and Mother Nature herself."

"You're eco-terrorists?" He shook his head in disbelief. "No, this is way too elaborate a scheme for even the best financed Mother Earthers."

Hoku laughed. "You'd be surprise, Mr. Murphy at how many peo-ple buy that speech, and what they will do or say or how much feel good money they'll give, all in the name of being green and fighting the evil empire."

"I think green is the key word here and it's not about leaving a smaller carbon foot print is it, Oh Great Chief Hoku?" Murphy didn't hide the sarcasm in his tone. "What's your real name anyway?"

Hoku smiled. "Actually, Hoku is my real name, Alex Hoku."

He gestured to Thing One. "Aata is Adam, and Rapata—Thing Two— is Randy. Now, with the pleasantries out of the way, we need to get back to business."

"Which is?" Murphy asked.

"The good captain here was just about to give me the access codes to the ship's computer, and more importantly, the security passwords to the L.E.M. file."

Now it was Yate's turn to laugh. "The Logistical Emergency Man-agement file? You're out of your mind. There's no way in hell I'm going to give you the codes to that or any other files."

Hoku looked disappointed. "Are you sure Captain? Is there no way I can persuade you to give me the codes?"

"Go to hell."

Hoku let out a heavy sigh, "Very well. I will see you there." Hoku casually drew out his pistol, aimed it at Yates, and fired.

Yates' head snapped back from the impact of the bullet. Murphy, Crawford and Sarah all jumped at the unexpected blast, but now no one moved, no one even breathed, too stunned and in shock to do anything but stare in horror as Yates' lifeless body crumpled to the floor.

Sarah finally tore her eyes away from the grisly scene and looked at Hoku. "What are you doing?" she screamed. "You said no one was going to get hurt. You promised. Why do you need the passwords to the L.E.M. file? That's not what you came for; it won't do you any good."

She stood with her fists clenched at her sides, staring at him through tear filled eyes, and then suddenly she launched herself at Hoku. She was so quick that she managed to reach him and land a solid punch to his jaw before Kekao grabbed her by the arms and backhanded her to the ground. Murphy immediately lunged forward and grabbed her.

Hoku sat calmly in his chair, looking down at Murphy as if nothing had happened. Then he looked at Sarah and smirked. "I told you people would pay anything and do anything, all in the name of being green."

Murphy's eyes flashed with rage as he picked Sarah up and gently wiped the hair from her face, holding her as her body heaved with uncontrollable sobs.

Hoku seemed to read Murphy's mind. "Calm yourself, Mr. Murphy, and don't try any misguided heroics or else you will end up just like your captain there."

Murphy fought to control the anger that was threatening to explode. He clenched his teeth together so hard his jaw hurt and it was all he could do not to curl his fingers into fists, because he knew if he did, he would use them.

"What's this really all about? Why do you need access to the ship's computer?"

Hoku laughed. "Why don't you ask our little Mata Hari?" He nodded at Sarah.

"Mata Hari?" Murphy put his hand to her face and tried to lift her chin but she just pulled away and hid her face in shame. "What's he talking about?"

Hoku laughed. "Very well then, I'll tell you myself. You know that your company, World Wide Energy, has a less than a stellar environmental reputation for being a green, earth-friendly corporation. And as you also know, your ex-wife is very passionate about the environment but also dedicated to her job, which sometimes left her with, shall we say, conflicting loyalties?

"Such conflicts make people very susceptible to suggestion. In Ms. Price's case, we gave her the opportunity to ease her guilt at working for an eco-unfriendly company by giving her a chance to swing the pendulum in favor of Mother Earth, as it were."

"Is this true Sarah?" Murphy asked, pulling away from her a little.

"Of course it is," Hoku continued. "Who do you think reprogramed your navigational computers so you wouldn't know exactly where you were and so you could *discover* this uncharted island?"

"Hah! I knew it wasn't my equipment," Crawford said triumphantly, and then suddenly realized how stupid his comment was considering all that had just happened.

Murphy grabbed Sarah by the shoulders and held her at arm's length. "Is this true, Sarah? Did you help them?"

She turned her head and tried to pull away, but Murphy held his grip, his anger rising. She struggled to get away but Murphy held her. "Did you help them, Sarah?"

More tears came, and Murphy felt her body go limp. He let her sink to the floor and staggered back and collapsed into the empty chair at the radio console. He felt hollow inside, numb. He didn't know what to do or say. As he looked around the room, it was like he wasn't seeing things through his eyes, like he was watching a movie, his life unfolding on a theater screen.

Crawford was standing still, his arms hanging limp at his side, looking like a child who had been left at school by a forgetful parent. Yates was lying on the floor, a small halo of blood surrounding his head. Hoku was sitting in the captain's chair. Kekao and Thing One and Thing Two were standing quietly beside him.

Murphy's eyes came back to rest on Sarah. She lay on the floor in a heap, sobbing quietly. How could this woman he loved and knew, or thought he knew, be involved in all this... in helping the man who had just shot Captain Yates? He wanted to ask her but just couldn't; he felt drained, empty.... betrayed.

"Back to business," Hoku said loudly, snapping them out of their own private worlds. "We're on a schedule here."

Murphy slowly stood and walked over to confront Hoku. "What is really going on here? No more crap about helping Mother Earth? Why such an elaborate ruse to take the ship? If you wanted control of the computer, why not just hack it or use some sort of Flame or Stuxnet virus like they used against Iran? Sarah could have left the door open for you."

He stopped, remembering what Hoku had asked for. "The L.E.M. file? What could you possibly want with a program that basically just tracks what supplies the company sends where?"

Hoku laughed then waved Thing One over and whispered in his ear, after which the latter left.

Hoku turned back to Murphy. "Ms. Price could have helped us by-pass some of the security systems, true. But that would have only gotten us so far.

"Tell me, Mr. Murphy, if you knew that the *Pacific Searcher* was going to be attacked, what do you suppose would happen? I'll tell you what, in a matter of moments this ship would look more like a battleship than a research vessel. Every member of the crew would be armed, all stations manned and in the event that the ship was boarded and security com-promised, the self-destruct would be activated."

"Self-destruct? Really?" Thing Two asked.

Murphy shook his head. "Not as in blow the ship to kingdom come self-destruct, but everything with a circuit board would be fried beyond use or repair, protecting the data stored in the computers."

"Exactly," Hoku said. "So rather than storm the gates, it was easier to be invited in and walk in through the front door."

"Okay, I understand that," Murphy replied. "You don't want to destroy the very thing you're trying to capture. So I get the whole island native thing to gain access to the ship. You have it; now what? You could have hacked into World Wide's system and accomplished all this with a couple of guys in the basement of their mom's house somewhere in Detroit."

"Because you won't open the door in the middle of the night for a stranger but you would for a friend." Crawford pitched in.

"Yes!" Hoku said.

Murphy looked at his friend, still not understanding.

Crawford continued. "Any probe or attack from an outside source would trigger an alert, raising security levels. Once the alarm was sounded, it would be impossible for anyone to get in. But, if you know and recognize the person, or in this case the terminal, where the request came from, it wouldn't raise any alarms or cause any suspicions, thus rendering that person able to walk in through the front door. Such persons would have to be here, physically on the ship."

"Right again!" Hoku said with the flair of a game show host.

"Okay, it still seems a little excessive to go through all of this just to get in the front door so to speak, but what's so important about the L.E.M. program file? It's just a simple logistics tracking program."

"A simple logistics program?" Hoku roared with laughter. When Murphy didn't seem to get the joke, Hoku stopped and studied him for a moment. "You really believe that don't you?"

"Believe what?"

"Getting control of the ship and its resources was a major step, but gaining access to the L.E.M. program is the key."

"The key to what?"

"To everything!" Hoku studied Murphy again, wondering if he was stalling, or if he truly didn't understand. "This is a big picture event here so let me start at the beginning so it will all fall into perspective."

Thing One returned to the bridge carrying a tray of pastries and coffee. "Ah, perfect timing, Adam," Hoku said. "This is going to take a while and I'm getting a little tired of fruit as you can well imagine, although I have lost 15 pounds."

Thing One offered the tray to Murphy. He thought about refusing it out of defiance but he was hungry and starving wouldn't prove anything, so he took some coffee and a maple bar. Crawford also accepted but Sarah wouldn't even look up from the floor when the tray came around.

"As I said earlier," Hoku began, "we had to gain control of the *Pacific Searcher* in such a way so as not to raise any red flags or trigger any alarms. Many different scenarios were considered but none seemed workable until I caught a glimpse of Ms. Price on a news story about protesters being arrested during the World Environmental Concerns meeting in New York last year. I recognized her from her file folder."

"File folder?" Crawford asked. "You mean you have a file on Sarah? Like in name, rank, what high school she went to, favorite movie and old boyfriends type file?"

Hoku smiled. "We have files on all of you."

"You do?" Crawford's eyes flew open wide.

"Of course. We have files on all of World Wide's top people." Hoku paused and then a mischievous smile curled his lips. He leaned slightly forward toward Crawford. "But don't worry, I won't tell them about your little secret." He said, almost in a whisper and then winked.

Crawford immediately turned red with embarrassment then looked to Murphy and Sarah. "I don't have a secret. Dallas, Sarah, I don't know what he's talking about."

Hoku burst out in laughing as did the other two men.

Murphy shook his head, "Don't worry about it Doug, he's just messing with your head."

"Anyway," Hoku said after a few more chuckles, "when I saw Sarah on the news as a protester, I saw the perfect opportunity, and after many, many months of planning, here we are." He took another sip of his coffee then leaned back in his chair.

"Outside of a naval warship, the *Pacific Searcher* has the most powerful mobile computing system in the world and to have access to that is a major coup in itself. We now have access to nearly every file and folder in World Wide's system. Though there are still many programs that are protected, we're in the front door now, making snooping and hacking a lot less noticeable and obtrusive.

"We have meeting notes, emails, hotel reservation, all the little things that point to big decisions in business, giving us an insider's look and an advantage we will exploit to its fullest later. But all of that is just the tip of the iceberg."

"Later? Murphy asked.

Hoku smiled, "As I said earlier, this has all been leading up to gaining access to the L.E.M. program. As you already pointed out, if simple hacking were our only goal, then none of this elaborate scheme would be worth the effort. This goes way beyond protecting Mother Earth from simple corporate greed, way beyond. I am talking about power, total and complete power."

Murphy looked at Hoku. "Is this the part where you laugh diabolically and make claims to world domination and then I defiantly say you'll never get away with it?"

Hoku looked at Murphy for a moment then burst out in laughter again. "I'll skip the theatrics and you can save your breath about the warning, but world domination? Yes. Let me explain how this works."

Hoku took another sip of coffee then continued. "As I said, the L.E.M. program is the key to everything. Yes, it tracks the production and product flow of not only oil and natural gas but also of the other products that World Wide sells and distributes. But that in itself is not unique. Many large companies use similar tracking systems in their everyday business and even have programs built in to divert supplies such as food and water in cases of emergencies, such as hurricanes Katrina or Sandy, or the Japanese tsunami.

"But to compare the L.E.M. program to other tracking software would be like comparing a Ford Pinto to a Lamborghini Gallardo Superleggera. As you know, the L.E.M. program not only tracks production and shipments of its civilian entities, it also tracks the military's use of oil, making sure the armed forces always have a ready supply for fuel.

"But what you perhaps didn't know is that it has a subroutine to monitor political situations around the world. If there is political unrest in the Middle East, you know that's going to affect oil prices so the program makes suggestion to keep the oil flowing. If there's a coup going on in a Third World nation that may affect other nations or natural resources, again, the L.E.M. can track and make the necessary notations and recommendations.

"And what makes this wonder of technology work so well you ask? Integration, that's what. Instant communication from one system to another, alerting and moving who, what and when to where they are needed in one fluid motion. The L.E.M. command and control system is second only to the Pentagon's. One giant system controlling transportation, communication, production, navigation for the fleet and payroll for the employees, all together under one roof. Integration is the L.E.M.'s greatest strength, but it is also its greatest weakness.

"Earlier you mentioned hacking and the Stuxnet virus. As you know, the Stuxnet virus was used against the Iranians to thwart their ability to refine uranium-233 to get the bomb grade U-235. In Iran, the Stuxnet seized control of the machines running the centrifuges. It was able to desynchronize the machines, causing them either to seize up or to self-destruct. And that is what we are going to do, only on a much grander scale.

"We have developed a new strain of Stuxnet, designed specifically to attack the L.E.M. programing. Stuxnet simply desynchronized machinery to cause failures in the refinement system. Imagine what would happen when our super-bug is turned loose not to simply desynchronized machinery but to attack and destroy entire networks?

"Now imagine if computer controlled safety protocols were turned off at all of World Wide's oil and natural gas refineries. The resulting leaks and explosions and loss of life would be catastrophic and the environmental effects would be staggering. The price of oil would skyrocket, doubling or tripling overnight. The pandemonium and chaos would be devastating, not to mention the public outcry and the political backlash as they try to find someone to blame.

"That's just the oil and natural gas side of the equation. Now, factor in all the other systems that the L.E.M. program controls and you will have utter and complete bedlam. Communications would be misdirected or shut down completely, all transportation, gridlocked, adding all the more to the confusion. And, final insult to injury, not one of the over three million employees of the World Wide Energy

Corporation or its subsidiaries will be getting paid because the computer just erased everyone's salaries and pensions. How's that for a trickle down economic effect?"

"Isn't all this just a little overkill to take down a rival corporation?" Murphy asked."

Hoku shook his head. "You're still thinking too small, Mr. Murphy, way too small; after all, this is the *World Wide* Energy Corporation we are talking about. The end is as ambitious and staggering in its scope and magnitude as the means by which it will be achieved. This entire operation is not meant to bring down a single corporation; it's the prelude to gaining total control... and yes," Hoku smiled, "world domination."

CHAPTER THIRTY

Hoku paused to let Murphy digest all the information he had just given him. After a few moments, he continued. "Well Mr. Murphy, now you know why the L.E.M. is so vital, you can save us all a great deal of time and unnecessary pain and hardship by just giving me the access code right now."

Murphy shook his head. "Why? Why on earth would I give you any information now after all that? You're just going to kill us anyway like you did the captain. I know how this works: after you get the information you want, you have to kill us so we can't go to the authorities and tell them who did this."

"Well, as you have seen, I am quite capable of killing, but despite what you might think, I am not a monster. I kill only when I need to and when it is necessary. And as for the authorities," Hoku laughed, "by the time you're rescued, the damage will already be done and the waters so muddied that there will be no clear direction for them to look in, even assuming of course that they believe you and don't arrest you on the spot."

"Why would they arrest us?" Murphy asked.

Hoku continued, "We've already documented how Ms. Price helped us and have left evidence of your and Mr. Crawford's involvement as well."

"But we haven't done anything," Crawford protested.

"True, but the paper trail we have created and the large sums of money deposited in your bank accounts will say otherwise. It's amazing what you can do with computers these days. "But enough small talk. We do have a schedule to keep. Well Mr. Murphy, it's up to you, the proverbial easy way or the hard way?"

"I'd love to be defiant like the captain and tell you to go to hell," Murphy replied flatly. "But the simple truth is, I really don't have the code. I was aware of the L.E.M. program but not to the extent that you claim and I don't have any secret password."

Hoku shrugged. "As you wish."

He gave a nod to Kekao, who nodded back with a slight smile and casually moved to stand in front of Murphy. Without preamble, Kekao struck out with his left fist, driving it deep into Murphy's stomach, instantly doubling him over.

Murphy tried to gasp for air but none came; his lungs had been completely deflated by Kekao's powerful blow. He felt himself growing lightheaded as he struggled to breathe. But just as the first wisps of air got through, he caught a flash of movement and a tremendous burst of pain shot through his jaw. Agony filled his head as he slammed onto the deck. Kekao had knocked him down with a vicious blow from his right hand.

Warm, salty blood oozed out of the corner of his mouth as he lay on the deck. Instinctively he curled up into a ball and tried to shield his head as best he could from the savage kicks he knew were coming next.

"No!" Sarah shrieked. She lunged forward but was held back by Thing One and Thing Two. "You bastard, you said no one would get hurt. You said this was all about holding World Wide accountable for their environmental policies. You never said anything about gaining computer access, stealing data and planting viruses or...murder." Her voice trailed off as her eyes drifted to Yates' body on the floor.

Hoku laughed. "Of course not! If I had, you would never have agreed to help us. You were looking for a quick fix, a feel-good-about-myself moment and, yes, I took advantage of that. It's not my fault you were so naïve as to believe everything I said."

Kekao reached down and pulled Murphy to his feet. Murphy swayed for a moment, still a little dizzy then defiantly yanked his arm away from Kekao.

"Well Mr. Murphy?" Hoku said, "What's it going to be?"

Murphy wiped the blood from his mouth and stood as tall as he could. "Go to hell."

Hoku sighed. "I wish it didn't have to come to this, but remember, Dallas, this is all your doing now." He said as he nodded again to Kekao.

Murphy tensed up as Kekao raised his arm but was puzzled, more than relieved, when the man pushed him aside and grabbed Sarah roughly by the arm.

"What are you doing?" Murphy said, panicking. "Sarah doesn't know anything."

"I have no doubt that, despite your evident resolve, we could eventually break you, but I simply don't have the time," Hoku said. "Think of your pain, how your head and jaw hurt right now, how sore and tender your ribs are, how every breath is a struggle against the pain just to breathe. Now, think of Sarah with that same pain only ten times worse, because that's exactly what going to happen if you don't tell me what I want to know."

He leaned back in his chair, letting that thought weigh on Murphy. "Some people, shall we say, *persuade* other people because that's their job. Kekao here does it because he enjoys it. It's what makes him so good at what he does."

"But I don't know any password," Murphy pleaded.

"Very well then, if you must continue with this false bravado, so be it. But again, just remember, you had the power to stop this. She will be the one to pay for your stubbornness." Hoku leaned to one side in his chair as if getting comfortable for the show, then casually signaled Kekao to begin.

Kekao gave Murphy a cruel, sadistic smile.

"I told you, I don't have any password," Murphy begged.

"We'll see," Hoku said.

Kekao raised his hand to strike Sarah.

"Stop! I have the codes."

All heads turned to Crawford.

"Nice try Mr. Crawford, "Hoku replied. "But you are only delaying the inevitable."

"No. I really have them. Dallas doesn't."

"This is interesting," Hoku replied. "Why would you, a support tech, have the access codes to the company's most sophisticated and important system, and not the second-in-command?"

"That's the point exactly. Who would expect that?" Crawford replied. "World Wide's security goes beyond just its digital fortress. The first officer is the logical choice as the next one in line to have the codes, so that's exactly why he doesn't. In the event that anything like this ever happened, you wouldn't think to look beyond the two obvious choices to have control of the system."

Hoku studied Crawford intently. "I've read at your file. While you're a good programmer, I don't see the education needed to reach this level of sophistication."

"I didn't design the thing; I just have limited access and special training, per the captain's orders, whenever he needed to get into the system."

"Why should I believe you?"

"Why shouldn't you? You've studied my file. I'm no hero. I don't want to get killed or see my friends hurt either. I give you what you want, we go free and you go away."

"Don't do it, Doug," Murphy said "He'll kill us as soon as he gets the codes. You know that."

"He'll get what he wants anyway. I can't stand by and let you or Sarah get hurt when I have the power to stop it."

"Don't Doug, you can't trust him," Sarah said, staring at Hoku, her eyes filled with hatred and rage.

"Let's get this over with," Crawford pointed to the chair at his work station. "May I?"

Hoku gestured for Crawford to sit. "No tricks. Just remember what I am capable of." He nodded toward Yates.

Crawford hesitated as he moved past the captain's body, then sat down. As he began typing, Hoku got up and walked over and stood behind him.

The home page of the World Wide Energy Corporation came up. Crawford typed in a few more commands and the home page was replaced with Crawford's personal page. When the page came up, Crawford stopped typing and turned around.

"Why did you stop?" Hoku asked.

"In cyber-terms, I have gotten you into the building and with my home page gotten you onto the right floor so to speak, which is something you could probably have done yourselves, but I have put you on the top floor using the elevator instead of you having to take the stairs, and bypassed a lot of security levels along the way.

"See this desktop folder?" he said pointing to the screen. "That's the first step to the entrance to the LE.M. Program. And that's as far as you get. I may be dumb, but I am not stupid. I need more than just your word that you won't kill us."

"And what make you think that I won't just kill you now and take over from here?" Hoku slowly moved his hand toward his holster, making sure Crawford saw what he was doing.

"Because as you said yourself, you are on a schedule. I'm guessing you're going to need to uplink to Mercury One, World Wide's communications satellite, to receive and transmit any data. I also know that in order to get a clear signal for transmission, from this latitude, you're going to need to move north. And I am also guessing that you picked this week to attack because of the scheduled maintenance cycles and wanted to take advantage of the holes in security.

"You could take it from here as you said, but like I said, you're just at the beginning and you still have a long way to go. Time is money and right now you don't have the time without my help."

"So what are you proposing?" Hoku asked.

"You put Dallas and Sarah ashore with a radio. As soon as I know they're safe, I'll get you in as far as I can. The system is more complicated than you think and I don't have complete passwords. It was designed as a fail-safe system requiring two sets of codes and unfortunately you killed the captain and his set. I can't get you in all the way, but it will be a heck of a lot closer than you could have done on your own.

"Once I've gotten you as far as I can, you'll put me ashore and I'll radio the final sequence. After that you can leave and steam north and by the time you get to within optimal satellite range, you and your team will have gotten the rest of the way in yourselves."

"Done!"

"Just like that," Murphy asked in astonishment. "No negotiating or threating, just a simple 'done'?"

Hoku shrugged. "Like I said earlier, I kill only when it's necessary, and if I can get what I want without bloodshed, then so be it."

He turned from Murphy and looked directly at Crawford. "Don't misunderstand my acceptance of your offer as a sign of weakness or complacency, Mr. Crawford. If you cross me, I will hunt you and your friends down, and if you thought what I was going to do to you earlier was frightening… well, I know this will sound a bit like a cliché, but the phrase praying for death will take on a whole new meaning for you and your friends."

Hoku continued to stare at Crawford, letting his words take effect. "Do I make myself clear?"

Crawford swallowed hard then simply nodded.

Hoku held his gaze a moment longer then turned around and sat back down in the chair. "Kekao—sorry, I mean Kevin, would you take Mr. Murphy and Ms. Price ashore? Get them a radio and please make sure it has fresh batteries. I'd hate to have our little arrangement ruined because of a bad set of batteries."

Kekao and Thing One led Murphy and Sarah out the door then Hoku turned to Crawford. "I've done my part, Mr. Crawford. Time for you to do yours."

Crawford nodded and then turned around and started typing.

CHAPTER THIRTY ONE

The boat slid up onto the sandy shore and Murphy and Sarah each got out without saying a word. "I suppose you two have a lot to talk about," Kekao laughed; "I'd love to stay and see how this all turns out, but I've got a boat to catch. Here." He tossed them their backpacks.

Kekao's laughter was drowned out by the roar of the outboard as the boat sped away, leaving them stranded on the beach. Murphy simply grabbed his pack and started walking. Sarah picked up hers and walked silently behind.

The luscious greens of the foliage and the vibrant sounds of life were now just a dull gray and monotonous droning to Murphy as he walked through the jungle toward the village. He thought he heard Sarah call his name a couple of times but he was in no mood to talk. He needed time to sort everything out, from the death of the captain, to Sarah's betrayal, to the reality that the ship had been taken over by men who wanted to rule the world. He desperately wanted to wake up from this nightmare.

They came into the clearing and Murphy saw the village. It was deserted now, no "natives" going about their daily lives, no gathering and chopping, cooking fish, mending nets. When they had first arrived, a part of him had envied the natives and their simple lives, no computers or emails or phones. No appointments to keep or deadlines to beat, only the simple joy of living. But now it was as empty as he felt inside, even the ashes were cold, not offering up any of the familiar wisps of smoke or cheery, dancing flames.

He sat down at the table where he and Captain Yates had sat and drank and laughed only a few short days ago. He took out the radio and called Crawford to let him know they were safe then he shoved it back into his pack. He took out a bottle of water, closed his eyes against the bright sun and took a long drink, wishing it was something stronger than just water.

When he opened his eyes, Sarah was standing in front of him.

"We need to talk."

He just looked at her then took another drink.

"I mean it Dallas."

He screwed the lid back on the bottle then shoved it back into his pack. "Sure, Sarah, what would you like to talk about? The quarterly fitness reports for the crew? What's the best R&R port in the South Pacific, Hong Kong, or Sydney? Or maybe you'd like to talk about how you betrayed us all, and how Captain Yates is dead. Yes, I think I would definitely like to talk about that. I'd like to find out what you were thinking when you sold us all out."

"I-I didn't know any of this would happen. I never planned for this. They said nobody would get hurt."

"They told you they wanted to take over the ship and that no one would get hurt, and you believed them? Come on Sarah, really?"

"It's not like that."

"Then what's it like? Tell me so that I can understand. Help me to understand how, when Hoku told you that he wanted your help in diverting the ship to a deserted island in the middle of the Pacific and that he said no one would get hurt, you believed him?"

"He told me that all he wanted was just to gain access to the ship's computers, nothing more. He said that by setting up the diversion of the natives in a tropical paradise and the promise of easy oil that it would lower everyone's defenses. With everyone's guard down, he said he could sneak onboard, get the information he needed and no one would be the wiser. No one would get hurt and nothing on the ship would be damaged."

"And why did he say he wanted to get into the ship's computers?"

"He wanted to access the corporate files, to get the secret emails of the back room meets that would expose World Wide's greed and their total disregard for corporate responsibility in the environmental travesties they have committed and force them to confess the errors of their ways and to transform them into good, earth friendly corporate citizens."

"Wow!" Murphy said as he shook his head. "If that isn't a canned speech I don't know what is. Did they brain wash you, Sarah, or did you just lose it? Did the thought ever occur to you that the very reason they wanted you to steer us into the middle of nowhere *was* to take over the ship?"

Sarah let out a long, deep sigh. "It's complicated."

"Really?" Murphy lashed out. "Betraying the ones you love usually is."

"There you go again, judging before you even hear me all the way out," she snapped back.

Murphy was standing in front of her with his arms down at his sides. His fists were clenched so tightly that his fingernails were beginning to dig into his palms and he could feel his entire body shaking with rage.

"Judging? Judging?" he exploded, getting right up in her face. "Don't you dare try to put this on me. I'm not the one who sold out, I'm not the one who was the spy and I'm not the one who got the captain killed. Don't you even think to try and blame this on me!" He brought his right hand up and jabbed his finger in her face so quickly she flinched, thinking he was going to hit her.

"In a way, it is your fault," she said quietly, looking away.

Murphy was about to explode again, but there was just something about the way she said it that made him keep quiet.

She hung her head low and refused to look Murphy in the eye as she spoke. Her words were slow and labored and were barely louder than a whisper. "After we got the divorce, I was happy for a while, or at least I thought I was. But as time went on, I began to realize that something was missing, that I was hollow inside. After about a year, I came to discover that what I was missing was *you*."

Sarah shifted on her feet uncomfortably but continued on, still refusing to look at him. "I began to try and fill the void with different things. I tried throwing myself into my work and when that didn't work I took up the crusades. I thought that fighting for a righteous and noble cause would make me feel better.

"My stubbornness and pride wouldn't even let me talk to you, so I kept pushing you away, becoming angry and bitter. I discovered that there were times that I hated you more but that I didn't love you any less. But by then, it was too late. Hoku approached me like he said after the protest and it was my last attempt to free myself. In my warped thinking I thought that if I hurt World Wide, the company that you loved to work for so much, that I could make myself feel better by hurting them, thus hurting you.

"They told me a little about their plans, not everything obviously, but it sounded good. My part was simple, just reconfigure the navigation system to throw off our courses so it looked like we had discovered an uncharted island full of peaceful, harmless natives. They did a psych profile on the captain and knew he couldn't resist the thought of a big oil score and the fact that the natives would treat him like a god."

"What about the pirate treasure? How did you fake that? We were almost killed."

"The plates and silverware were all part of the scheme, meant to whet your appetite, and the trip into the jungle was meant to be a diversion to keep you out of the picture long enough for them to gain control of the ship. Hoku knew that you were the voice of reason and that if you were around, they might not get onboard. But believe it or not, the treasure we found was real. Hoku had nothing to do with that. None of us had any idea that we would find real treasure."

Murphy stopped and looked at Sarah. He wanted to hate her, to stay mad at her, to punish her for what she had done, but he couldn't. He could feel his resolve and righteous anger slipping away as he began to realize what she had gone through. He put his hand under her chin and lifted her face up. She tried to pull away but he gently held her until she finally looked into his eyes.

"What are we going to do now?" she said in a trembling voice.

"I don't know, but we have about a day to figure it out," Crawford said, standing at the edge of the clearing.

"Doug!" Murphy and Sarah shouted in unison as they turned to see their friend.

"What are you talking about, a day for what? Didn't you give him all the access codes?" Murphy asked.

"I gave him exactly what I said I would. I got him as far into the L.E.M. program as I could."

"But?" Murphy said, seeing the look on his friend's face.

"But, I just couldn't give Hoku everything, not after what he did to the captain."

"What did you do?"

"It's not what I did, it's what I didn't do. They'll be able to link up to the satellite and upload their virus but it won't be in the mainframe yet. During the maintenance cycle, all incoming information is held in storage until the system is back up again and run through filters. From Hoku's end it will look like it's has been downloaded but it hasn't. Once the system is back online, it will ask for a verification code before it will allow it to move from storage into the mainframe."

"And you didn't give them that code did you?" Murphy asked.

Crawford shook his head. "Nope. It'll take them three to four hours and several passes of the satellite to realize that they aren't in the mainframe and turn around and head back to us."

"Okay," Murphy said, as he turned and started pacing, "assuming they'll be steaming at full speed, twenty knots, it'll take them about fifteen to sixteen hours or so to reach their destination, another couple of hours to figure out you tricked them and another fifteen or sixteen hours back. About thirty-five hours, a day and a half, give or take a little, which would put them back here shortly after dark tomorrow night. Not a lot of time."

"Maybe a little more than you think," Crawford said with a rueful smile. "While Hoku was at my console drooling over the keyboard waiting for a download, I slipped over to the navigation controls and accessed the maintenance program and recalibrated the digital readouts for the helm. I reduced the power setting by twenty percent so when they push the throttles full forward, the readouts with display full power but in reality they'll really only be doing sixteen knots instead of twenty."

"Nice." Murphy said, nodding his head in approval. "That'll buy us another six or seven hours to get ready."

"Ready? Ready for what?" Sarah asked.

"To take back the ship."

"You want to retake the ship? What, with just the three of us?"

"We've got to do something."

"Hey, how about we hide until they get fed up and leave?" Crawford said.

Murphy shook his head. "After all the work they've gone through in setting up this elaborate ruse and killing the captain, you think they're just going to give up and go home after a few days of searching for us? Not on your life."

"Yeah, there's the key word 'life' and I'd like to keep mine. I don't think Hoku is going to be too fond of me next time we meet. I remember the look on his face when he threatened me and I have no doubt he will carry it out with a vengeance. I say we run to the hills, find some deep dark cave, crawl in and wait it out."

"Cave!" Murphy blurted out.

"Cave?" Sarah asked. "What are you talking about?"

"We may not be as alone as you think."

"What are you talking about?" she asked again.

"What Doug said about the cave, it reminded me."

"Of what?"

"After I fell down the mountain side, I came across this path and started following it back to the coast. I came across a cave where two of Hoku's men were holding prisoners and I bet they are the natives, the *real* natives that live here."

"I hope they're not head hunters." Crawford said.

Murphy just shook his head. "You've seen too many episodes of Gilligan's Island. Come on."

The three of them took off down the path toward the cave.

The entrance to the cave had stout, bamboo logs cemented into place as door jambs that were supporting a solid wood plank door. It was sealed shut with a heavy steel chain and padlock.

"How are we going to get through that?" Crawford asked, "I left my bolt cutters in my other pants."

Murphy examined the door then started looking around.

"What have you got?" Sarah asked; "I've seen that look before."

"Yeah, me too," Crawford joined in.

"Look for any sharp edged rocks or something we can use as a chisel. This is not the best construction job in the world and I think we can chip out the cement holding the door jambs and rip out the entire door, frame and all."

After a few minutes of looking, Murphy was on the right side of the door chipping away at the cement with a rock while Crawford was on the other side, pounding away with a crude rock hammer and chisel.

"I've almost got it." Crawford said as a large chunk came out.

"Here, move." Sarah said as she stepped up behind him with a long bamboo pole.

"Good idea." Murphy joined in as he grabbed the pole and inserted it into the crack. On the count of three, we'll pull. Ready, one, two, three, heave ho!"

Before they started to pull, Sarah suddenly let go and started laughing.

"'Heave ho'? Are you kidding me? Arrggh Matey, be ye a pirate or a landlubber?"

Crawford tried to stifle his amusement at Sarah's joke, but he too, soon broke out in laughter. "Sorry Dallas, but you've got to admit that was funny. Yo, ho, ho and a bottle of rum?"

Murphy smiled as he shook his head. "Okay, okay, everyone's a comedian. Sorry, let's try this again. On three. Ready, one, two, three, *pull*."

With a collective groan, the three of them strained on the pole. They continued to struggle with the stubborn door when they heard a loud crack and they found themselves lying on the ground because the pole had snapped in two.

"Shiver me timbers, we broke it," Crawford said. They looked at each other then burst out laughing again.

"Look!" Sarah said excitedly, pointing up to the door. It was torn free and was hanging by only a few stands of rope that were caught in the rocks.

Quickly they got up and Murphy and Crawford grabbed the door and ripped it down the rest of the way. Tentatively, the three of them stood around the entrance, peering onto the darkness. Murphy took a step forward and stuck his head in the entrance. "Hello!" He shouted. "Is anybody in there?"

They waited and listened but didn't hear anything. "It's okay," Murphy shouted again, "you can come out now, you're safe."

Suddenly they heard faint movement coming from inside and they stepped back.

An older man was the first to step out. His skin was tanned and leathery, wrinkled by years of being in the tropical sun. Murphy recognized him as the old man he'd seen earlier being beaten by the guards. Murphy could tell by his proud walk that he was the chief. He could also see that as the chief, he had taken the brunt of Hoku's wrath. His face had several deep bruises with a cut over his eye and a swollen lip.

Next, a young warrior stepped out, looking like the real life counterpart of Kekao. There was fire in his eyes and he was looking to strike out, to take revenge, but right now he wasn't sure who to vent his wrath on. One by one, the real natives emerged from the cave, squinting and covering their eyes, protecting them from the bright sunlight. Murphy could only guess at how long it had been since some of them had seen the daylight.

In all, forty-seven natives, men, women, and children walked about the clearing, looking like ex-POWs milling around a prison yard, not yet convinced that they were free.

Murphy went to approach the chief, but the warrior stepped in between them with an angry look. Murphy stopped and held his hands up and took a step back, but the chief gently placed his hand on his young protector and guided him away.

"You and your people are free now; we're not with those others." Murphy said.

"Are you from the *White Albatross*?" The chief asked in a quiet tone.

Crawford chucked softly. "He thinks a great mythical sea bird brought us here."

"No," the chief responded, "the *White Albatross* is a research ship from the University of Sidney that stops by here every six to seven months."

Murphy and Sarah looked at each other and then burst out laughing. Murphy then introduced himself and the others.

"I am Chief Tanaki and to answer your friend's question, we do know of the outside world. The people from the university have been coming to our island for several years now and some of our people have even gone back to Sydney with them, though most of us prefer to stay here. They are usually the only ones who come out this far. That is until the others showed up.

"About a month after the last visit from the university, a ship arrived. They said they were a film crew from Sydney and were doing a documentary about island natives and how we live our lives. They were very kind so we allowed them to stay. They set up their cameras and followed us from daybreak to the setting of the sun. They did this for a long time.

"Then one day, they gathered us all together in the center of the village. Their leader, a man named Hoku, said that they had gotten all they needed. We thought they were going to leave. Instead, they took us all prisoner and put us in this cave."

Murphy nodded. "Very clever. Hoku and his crew did on the job training in the guise of filming them. By living with the natives and following their every move on film, they could be sure to depict island life authentically to easily fool us."

"They are very bad people," the chief said, "I hope they do not return."

"I'm afraid I have bad news Chief Tanaki," Murphy said. "They are returning and should arrive back here late tomorrow night. Did the people from the *Albatross* happen to leave you any guns?"

Tanaki shook his head. "No, they gave us a few metal knives, pots and pans, things to fish with and a few tools to make life easier around the village, but no guns."

"A rifle or two sure would have been nice." Crawford said.

"Hey Mister."

Murphy turned to see a young boy about twelve standing beside him. He recognized him as one of the boys he'd seen outside the cave entrance with Hoku's men.

"I know of..." The boy began to speak excitedly but was cut off by the chief. "Ruru, do not bother us now, we have important thing to discuss." "I know sir but, I..."

"Enough! Now go."

The boy looked part angry, part crestfallen, but didn't say another word as he turned and left.

"You will have to forgive the boy," Tanaki, said. "He is young and eager.

The warrior spoke for the first time. "We have no need of guns, our people are brave and we know our island."

"This is Kai, our bravest and proudest warrior," Tanaki said.

Crawford chuckled. "He sounds just like Kekao. Now we know where he got it from."

"Only I like this real life version of Kekao," Murphy added.

"Spears and knives against assault rifles, we haven't got a chance," Crawford said shaking his head.

"Oh I don't know," Murphy said. "People have been fighting with knives and spears a lot longer than they have with guns."

"Still, a nice machine gun or grenade launcher would come in handy."

"We may not be totally defenseless," Murphy said, snapping his fingers. "Remember the Japanese bomber we found, we can strip whatever armament we can find from the plane and go from there."

Murphy turned back to Tanaki. "Chief Tanaki, Hoku killed our captain and took our ship so this is our fight, not yours. I just want you to understand that."

Tanaki nodded. "It may be as you say, but we will not run and hide. This is our home and they took it from us. We will send the young and the women into the jungle to hide, but the men will stay and fight. Will your woman go with ours as well?"

"Not on your life," Sarah spoke up.

Tanaki studied Sarah for a moment. "She has fire in her eyes," he said, then moved closer to Murphy. "I have learned long ago not to argue with my woman when she has that look in her eye."

Murphy laughed. "You are a very wise man, Chief."

"She will stay and fight," Tanaki announced.

Sarah leaned into Murphy. "And you *are* wise to listen to him."

Murphy just smiled.

"Doug, I want you to go with the chief and see what kind of weapons they have. Sarah and I will go back to the plane and salvage what we can there. We'll meet back at the village at four o'clock and compare notes."

The chief walked over to an older woman and started talking to her. Murphy watched them, and for a minute, thought they were arguing as the conversation was getting intense, but then he realized what was going on. The woman was about the same age as the chief but her long hair was still as dark as it was in her youth. She had the same fire in her eyes as Sarah; she could only be the chief's wife. He was asking her to take the villagers to safety but she wanted to stay and fight too.

Murphy stole a quick glance to Sarah and wondered if they would have arguments like that when they were old and gray...if they survived. He turned back to the chief and saw that apparently all had been settled. The two leaned together, their foreheads touching and then the chief whispered something and she smiled.

When the two parted, she started barking out orders like a drill sergeant and the women and children quickly began to fall in line and followed her back to the village.

"We will follow the women back to the village and gather our weapons," Tanaki said, walking up with Kai beside him.

"I guess that's my cue," Crawford said. "I'll see you guys back at the village."

"Okay, we'll see you at four," Murphy replied. He and Sarah watched the procession of natives as they slowly marched back toward the village. A few children gathered around Crawford as he walked; two little girls had grabbed hold of his hands and were leading him down the path while others were playing about him, all wanting to be around the big stranger who had rescued them. Murphy and Sarah just smiled and waved at their friend as he glanced back, clearly uncomfortable with his new role as hero. They both gave him a thumbs-up and watched as the last of the villagers disappeared down the path.

"Before we go to the plane, I want to climb back up to that rise above the harbor." Murphy said to Sarah as they started off. "I want to see how the harbor lies and how we can use it to our advantage."

"Yes sir, general sir!" Sarah said with a mock salute.

"That's admiral; we're sailors not ground pounders."

"Aye aye, sir!" Sarah corrected herself and gave him another salute.

Murphy just shook his head. "Come on, we've got work to do."

It was a quiet hike with little conversation as they made their way swiftly through the jungle and up to the plateau that overlooked the harbor. Once they emerged from the jungle and crested the hill, Murphy slowed down and walked to the edge of the cliff. He let the breeze wash over him as he looked over the tiny harbor below.

"What are you looking for?" Sarah asked as she came up beside him.

"We've got to retake the ship, so I'm looking at the lay of the land so to speak and for anything that will give us an advantage. We've got to get to Hoku first, before he can prepare and come after us. We've got to hit him right after he comes into the bay here."

"If Doug's calculations are right, won't they be here sometime around three or four in the morning? It would be pretty risky even for an experienced seaman to bring the ship in here at night, and I don't think Hoku is a sailor. Wouldn't they just wait until daylight when it's safer to bring the ship in or just send in a landing party?"

Murphy shook his head. "I don't think so. Time is not on his side and the few hours he'd use waiting for daylight are too valuable to burn. Besides, I don't think he would send a landing party. He'd want the concentrated firepower of the ship to back him up."

Sarah nodded her head. "What do you see down there?"

"Well, from here I can see that on the far side of the lagoon there is a small outcropping of rocks that will provide good cover and also a place to attack from. The beach rings the bay with about eighty feet of sand before the jungle starts and then it gets dense pretty quickly. We can cut down logs for cover and set up ambushes if they get ashore."

Murphy paused for moment then moved over to a small hollow in the hillside. "If we can get the machine gun out of the plane, this would be the perfect place to mount it. From here, we can target any area of the bay."

"Target any area of the bay?" Sarah said. "It sounds like you're going to war."

Murphy looked at her and gently grabbed her shoulders and held her in front of him. "We *are* going to war, Sarah. Hoku didn't go through this elaborate set up then gun down the captain just to say 'oh well, we tried,' and then sail home. Far too much is at stake for him to do that. He will stop at nothing, I repeat, nothing, until he gets what he wants. Unless we stop him first."

As he was talking, he could see fear growing in her eyes. He didn't want to scare her, only make her aware of just what was at stake. He could see what she was thinking and that the fear was about to take over but then it stopped. Fear began to fade from her eyes and he couldn't help but smile as he saw it replaced by another emotion: determination.

"Well then," she said as she turned and started walking back down the hill. "We'd better get to that plane then; daylight's a burning."

CHAPTER THIRTY TWO

"I think I've almost got it." Murphy was in the fuselage of the Japanese navy dive bomber, struggling to remove the rear machine gun. "How are you doing up there?"

Sarah was sitting in the front cockpit. "There's not much here. I found a flare gun and three flares but that's about it."

"Yes!" Murphy yelled as he freed the gun from the mounting brackets, and then he grunted. "This thing is heavy."

"What's the matter, Rambo, haven't had your Wheaties today?"

Murphy chuckled as he set the gun down and started gathering the ammunition. "We've got about 600 rounds here. I'd like to take the two guns mounted in the nose but without the proper tools, we'd never get them out. But we should be able to grab the ammo. Pop open the access panels around the engine compartment there and see if you can find where it's stowed."

"So what's the plan here, after we get the gun and all the ammo?"

Murphy jumped down to the ground then grabbed the gun and set it on the wing, then moved to the front and started taking off the panels on his side of the plane.

"I don't know yet, I'm making this up as I go."

"That'll be sure to inspire the troops once we get back."

"Yeah, well, a General Patton I'm not."

"I know, we're in the navy, you're Admiral "Bull" Murphy, right?"

Murphy chuckled. "Wow, you were awake when I was watching the History Channel."

"Or should I say, 'Bull Headed' Murphy?"

"You know me all too well."

"Okay, I found it," Sarah said.

Murphy came around from the other side and began helping her take out the ammo belts. "Let's hurry up and get this stuff back to the village and see what Doug has come up with on his end. We're on the clock here."

"Yeah, let's hurry up and get this stuff that we don't know what we're going to do with yet back to the village."

"I'm working on it, I'm working on it." He smiled as he took out the belts of ammunition and draped them over Sarah's shoulders. "You carry the ammo and I'll get the gun."

Sarah arranged the ammo belts around her shoulders like they were scarves. "Just what all the chic commandos are wearing in Paris this spring I'm sure."

Murphy heard her joke but there was little laughter in it as he knew it was just nervous tension. She knew what the stakes were but carrying the ammo gave it a physical presence to the situation and brought home the reality of it all.

"Come on," Murphy said quietly, "we need to get to the village before dark."

By the time they walked into the village, Sarah was stooped over from the weight of the shells and her feet were dragging in the sand with slow, measured steps. Murphy's arms felt like lead, having carried the forty pound gun several miles through the hot sweltering jungle. He could barely uncurl his fingers from around the barrel when several villagers rushed up to take over.

Sarah and Murphy collapsed at the table and they were quickly brought some food and water. Murphy was starving but could barely lift his arm to put the food in his mouth. Still, the fish smelled delicious and after downing a bottle of water, his strength returned enough to eat four large pieces.

"Okay Doug," Murphy said wearily, "we have a flare gun with three flares and a 7.7 mm machine gun with about a thousand rounds or so. What have you got?"

"The chief and I were able to come up with twelve spears, an assortment of knives, lots of fishing gear, nets, ropes, and two spear guns with four spears each, compliments of the University of Sydney."

"Not exactly the report I was hoping for," Murphy said, grabbing a piece of fruit.

"So what's the plan?" Crawford asked.

"Plan?" Sarah snickered.

"What?" Crawford asked.

"Nothing, Sarah is just *trying* to be funny. And yes, I do have a plan." He said, looking directly at her. "It was a long walk back here and it gave me time to think. Chief, you and Kai come over here please."

When everyone was seated around the table, Murphy began. "Hoku has the technology and the weapons; we have the element of surprise and the home field advantage."

"Go team," Crawford said mockingly. "A lot of good spears will do against a loaded M-16."

Murphy shook his head. "Yes, a gun is a powerful weapon, but don't discount our advantages. These people are fighting for their homes and their way of life; that kind of motivation should not be taken lightly. Hoku and his people were here for a few weeks. Chief Tanaki and his people have lived their entire lives here and they *know* the island."

Murphy stood up and walked over and picked up one of the spears and held it like a rifle and pointed it at Crawford. "What do suppose would happen if this was a gun and I pulled the trigger?"

"I suppose I'd be dead."

Murphy moved a little and pointed it directly at his friend. "And what do you suppose would happen if I shoved this spear into your chest?"

Crawford smiled nervously. "It would kill me."

"That's right. You'd be dead either way. Both are just as deadly, so they have as much to fear from us as we do from them, only they aren't expecting it."

Murphy returned the spear then sat back down. "We may have the element of surprise, but I am not going to underestimate Hoku."

"So what are we going to do?" Crawford asked.

Just then there was a loud blast that sounded like an out of tune French horn.

"What was that?" Murphy said, springing to his feet and spinning around to face the unknown noise. He turned to find a woman holding up a larger sea shell and blowing into it like a trumpet. She froze in fear when she saw the expression on Murphy's face.

"We are sorry to alarm you," Chief Tanaki said, standing and putting his hand on Murphy's shoulder. "We use them to call the children in from play. Much easier than yelling."

Murphy stared thoughtfully for a moment. "Do you have more of these shells?"

"Oh yes. We have many such shells. We not only use the shells to call our children but we use them to make music, would you like to hear?"

"No thank you chief, that won't be necessary."

"What are you thinking?" Sarah asked.

"I'm not sure yet, just tucking it away to maybe use later."

"Okay, you were about to tell us your plan," Crawford joined in.

Murphy shook his head. "It's been a long day for everyone and what we all need is some rest and I need a little more time to finish putting all the pieces together."

"Far be it from me to turn down a little sack time, especially after what we've been through," Crawford said, "but do we have the time to sleep?"

"People make mistakes when they are overly tired, and we can't afford to make any mistakes. Besides, it'll be dark soon and we need the light to see what we're doing."

Crawford stood and stretched. "You'll get no argument out of me. I just realized, where are we going to sleep? Our bunks are steaming north at sixteen knots."

"You and Mr. Murphy can sleep with the warriors, and your friend," Tanaki pointed to Sarah, "can sleep with the maidens."

As the villagers began to prepare for sleep, Sarah walked over and Murphy and drew close, putting her hands on his chest. "You know, I would rather spend the night with you than with a bunch of girls."

"I wouldn't," Crawford smiled as he walked by, overhearing their conversation. "Good night," he said as he went into the hut.

Sarah giggled like an embarrassed teenager.

"You don't know how long I have waited to hear you say that," Murphy began, then hesitated.

"But?"

"But, as much as I want to, I need to concentrate, to bring the plan together."

"And I would be a distraction?" She replied with a little bite in her voice.

"No, no, it's not that." Murphy began to stammer out but was silenced as Sarah put her fingers to his lips.

"I was teasing."

Murphy blew out a breath in relief then drew her closer. "Thank you for understanding."

She leaned forward and gave him a small kiss on the lips, then turned and headed toward her hut. "Good night," she said, then disappeared inside.

He just stood there a moment, alone in his thoughts. Despite what they were about to go through, he had never felt happier in his life. He shook his head at the absurdity of it all as he took a short walk to clear his head and prepare for the day ahead.

CHAPTER THIRTY THREE

After a light breakfast of fish and fruit, Murphy gathered everyone around.

"Okay everyone; we have a very long day ahead of us. I'm no 'Blood and Guts' Patton... or 'Bull' Halsey," he said smiling at Sarah, "so jump in here any time if you have any ideas. This is the way I figure it. Hoku should arrive back here during the early morning hours. He will do one of two things: he'll either wait outside the harbor until daylight, and then come in, or he will bring the *Pacific Searcher* right into the bay and immediately launch a landing party.

"The prudent thing to do would be to wait until light, then charge in, but after how Doug tricked him and with time running against him, I don't think that Hoku will have the inclination or the time to be prudent."

Crawford nodded. "I agree. He has a limited window for linking up to the satellite during the scheduled maintenance of the mainframe. Once that window is gone, all the firewalls and security protocols will be at full strength. So no, he can't afford to wait even those few hours until sunrise."

"Good," Murphy nodded, "that's what I'm betting on too. I'm also betting that he's going to feel the same way Doug here feels and that spears are no match for his guns. While Hoku is no fool, I'm counting on the pressures of time and his overconfidence in technology to give us the advantage."

"What do you have in mind?" Sarah asked.

"We have to get on board the ship, so I intend to let him capture me."

"What!" Sarah almost shouted.

Murphy held up his hands and was about to explain when he was interrupted by shouting. All eyes were drawn to the end of the village where Ruru was running toward them with his arms full.

Crawford sprang up as soon as he saw what the boy was carrying and ran toward him as if he were being reunited with a long lost love. Surprised, Murphy and Sarah looked at each other and shrugged their shoulders at Crawford's reaction, then got up and followed.

Crawford reached the boy then removed the bundles from his arms and gently brought them over and placed them on the table. Crawford picked one up and began examining it like a father checking his newborn for ten toes and fingers.

"Great," Sarah said, "Hoku has automatic rifles and we have fire sticks."

Crawford shot her a hard, disapproving look. "These are *not* fire sticks, as you so rudely put it. These are finely crafted Spanish muskets. Just look at this," he said as he held it up to the light, "beautiful walnut stock, nearly six feet in length, forty-three inch barrel and .75 caliber bore. By looking at these, you can easily see how they were influenced by German and French design."

Murphy and Sarah looked at each other in amazement at Doug's until now unknown passion for antique firearms.

"Of course." Sarah said, as both she and Murphy just shrugged their shoulders and humored Crawford with a look as if everyone should know this as he continued speaking.

"This is the M1752, an earlier model, distinguished by what is sometimes referred to as the French lock with the lock spring on the inside, but this one," he said as he put the first one down and picked up another musket, "was the Spanish Miguelet lock with the outside lock spring.

"Did you know that muskets like these were used by the colonists against the British in the War for Independence? Benjamin Franklin personally wrote a letter to the Spanish, thanking them for sending muskets to Boston."

Murphy held up his hands as he walked up to Crawford. "What are you talking about Doug?"

"Yeah," Sarah said, joining Murphy, "and when did you become an international arms dealer? I thought you hated the great outdoors."

"I've always loved these old guns ever since I first saw them on old TV shows and movies." He unconsciously drew the gun a little closer to his chest. "I was never an outside kid as you know, but there was just something about seeing those guns go off that got my imagination going. You shoot a modern gun and all that happens is the barrel kicks and there's a loud noise, but with one of these babies…. First there's the flash of fire and puff of smoke as the primer powder ignites, then the big KA-BOOM and flames spew out the barrel like a fire breathing dragon. When this baby goes off, there's enough smoke to make your own cloud.

"To me, that's real power. For just a moment, while I was pretending to fire these big guns, I wasn't that fat kid any more, the one that everyone made fun of. I was a burly mountain man or great adventurer exploring strange and faraway places."

"Wow, Doug, I had no idea," Sarah said, then added with a wry smile, "did you have a coonskin hat too?"

There was a moment of awkward silence as Crawford glared at her, then he broke out in laughter. "Yes!"

Murphy and Sarah joined in. After the laughter died, Murphy turned to the boy.

"Where did you get these?"

"These were in the cave where we were being held captive. I tried to tell you yesterday, but no one listened."

"These were probably left by your pirate friend. This was his island stronghold," Crawford said.

"Are there any more?"

Ruru shook his head. "No sir, I could only find these six."

"I am sorry," "Chief Tanaki said. "I forgot all about those. They were buried in the back of the cave. As I said, we have no use for guns and seldom go into the cave." Then he turned to the boy. "And I am sorry to you too. Ruru, I should have listened."

"Will these rifles fire?" Sarah asked. "I mean really, after all these years they can't be any good, can they?"

"These are muskets, not rifles," Crawford said. "Musket's barrels are smoothbore while a rifle's barrel has grooves cut into it to spin the bullet when it's fired."

"Excuse me, Daniel Boone," Sarah shot back.

"I prefer Davy Crocket, and you're excused. Now to answer your question, yes, they can be. I'll examine the guns and unless there is any major rust or other damage, they should fire just fine. But any powder we may find in the cave will be way too old, and without powder, they won't do us any good, except maybe as finely crafted clubs."

"Will the powder from the machine gun cartridges work?" Murphy asked.

Crawford paused in his examination of the musket and thought. "It's not black powder and modern powder is much more powerful. I'd have to experiment to find just the right measure without blowing up myself or the guns." He paused again then slowly nodded. "But I think I can do it. Unless we can find any balls, we can use the 30 caliber bullets from the shells we take apart but you won't be able to hit the broadside of a barn with them."

"That's okay; they don't have to be accurate for what I'm thinking."

"Which is?" Sarah asked.

Murphy smiled, "You'll see."

"I hate it when you do that."

"I know." He smiled back then continued. "Doug, take your rifles, ah sorry, your muskets and get to work on right away. We'll continue with the planning and I'll fill you in later."

Crawford barely acknowledged him as he set about examining his new toys.

"Now as you were saying," Sarah said, "your brilliant plan was to let yourself get captured?"

Murphy smiled. "Yup, but first..." he turned to Ruru, "I have a very important job for you. Are you up to it?"

Ruru's face beamed. "Yes sir!"

"I want you to gather all the large sea shells and clay pots that you can and bring them here. Can you do that for me?"

Curiosity replaced a little of the excitement in the boy's eyes but he was eager to help nonetheless and his smile never dimmed as he turned and ran off, ready to fulfill his task.

"Shells and pots?" Sarah asked. "Are you kidding? Is this your great plan?"

Murphy smiled, "patience, Grasshopper."

Sarah just shook her head and rolled her eyes.

"Okay, we're only going to get one shot at this. The plan is part Swiss Family Robinson, part Bible story and part inspired by our friend, Diablo Oscuro." Murphy bent down and drew the outline of the bay and the surrounding hills in the sand then outlined the ship in the middle of the harbor.

"Sarah, I want you to man the machine gun here," he said, making a small X to indicate the bluff where the two of them had been the day before. "But here, here is the key," he said pointing directly in front of the ship on the sand map.

For the next two hours, Murphy explained his plan. More than once, Sarah told him he was crazy but she continued to listen and give her input as did Chief Tanaki and Kai. During the meeting, they would occasionally hear the loud bang of exploding gunpowder, followed by a string of profanity as Crawford worked on perfecting his formula. When Murphy had finished detailing his plan and Sarah had shaken her head for the last time, everyone left and hurriedly went about their assigned tasks.

"What have you come up with?" Murphy asked as he walked up to Crawford.

Crawford pulled a couple of small pieces of cloth out of his ears. "From your earlier comments, I am working on the premise that you would rather have 'shock and awe' with these guns, than start your own sniper school."

"You know me too well."

"I've come up with two charges. Even out here, the Marlboro Man has found his way into their homes and one of the natives was kind enough to give me his stash of rolling papers. With the papers I was able to make 'cartridges' if you will, making it quicker and easier to load." He held up what looked like a hand-rolled cigarette.

"Real simple." Crawford took the packet, tore it open with his mouth and poured the powder down the barrel. Next, he took a small piece of cloth, and put it in the barrel, then took the ramrod and shoved it all the way down. Finally, he took a small amount of powder from a leather pouch that Ruru had found in the cave and filled the pan and cocked the hammer and aimed the musket in the air and pulled the trigger. There was a bright flash when the hammer came down then a split-second later came a loud *ka-boom* as the powder in the barrel ignited.

Murphy shook his head as his ears rang from the explosion.

Crawford just smiled. "Is that what you had in mind?"

Murphy nodded, "yeah, that will do."

"I thought so. Five of the six muskets are fine but the firing mechanism on the last one is broken and bent. With a little training, I can teach these guys to fire four, maybe as many as six shots a minute."

"That's perfect. After you've trained everyone, make ten cartridges apiece per gun. Then scout out your firing positions and escape routes. Make sure they understand to shoot and then move, shoot then move. I don't want anyone getting pinned down."

Murphy nodded and started to walk away. "If you need me, I'm going to the beach to see how the chief and Kai are coming with the traps, then up to the ridge to see how Sarah is doing with the machine gun."

"You got it boss."

As Murphy reached the outskirts of the village he saw that Ruru had organized the other children and was barking out orders like he was the chief. He could see that they had already gathered a small pile of shells and Ruru was having the boys gather more while he assigned the girls to collecting pots. Ruru saw Murphy and waved enthusiastically. Murphy smiled and waved back. Ruru would make a good leader someday.

Despite the pressures of the day, Murphy enjoyed the short walk down to the beach. The birds' melodies seemed just a bit cheerier and the colors of the flowers seemed just a tad brighter than they had last time he was there. Was he finally coming to really appreciate the beauty of Mother Nature or was he looking at it all through the eyes of a condemned man, knowing that he might not see these or anything else ever again?

When he reached the clearing at the edge of the beach, Murphy could see Chief Tanaki and Kai along with nearly all the other men from the villages working hard. They were busy felling trees and digging concealed bunkers. He stood back a bit and watched them work.

This was a key element of his plan and how they were going to get back on the ship to recapture it. Once Hoku's men landed on the beach, the idea was to funnel them from the beach, through the gaps in the terrain with carefully placed logs, rocks and other natural barriers.

Once inside, the natives—the real natives—would spring from hidden bunkers and ambush the intruders, capturing them, and more importantly, their uniforms. Hoku had chosen men who looked like the islanders; Murphy was going to use that to his advantage, replacing the fake natives with the real ones.

As he had explained it in the meeting, after that it would be a simple matter of taking the uniforms, disguising themselves as Hoku's men, enough to at least pass at a glance, and return to the *Pacific Searcher*, board her, and retake the ship. Simple.

This had been one of those times when Sarah had shook her head and called him crazy. The plan was not without risk and he knew it, but no one had a better idea so they were going through with it, flaws and all.

Murphy talked to Tanaki, making sure that all the details were being seen to. Even though Hoku's men would be landing at night, the camouflage had to be perfect. The *Pacific Searcher* carried night vision goggles and he felt it best to assume that Hoku would find and use them.

All during the conversation with the chief, he heard the sporadic firing of the muskets as Doug trained his crew. Then, he heard the unmistakable rat-tat-tat of the machine gun firing. He looked out over the bay and saw geysers of water shooting up as Sarah found the range with the gun. He also smiled as he heard distant hoots and hollers from her; she was enjoying her new toy.

Murphy finished up with the chief and then headed up the hill to see Sarah. When he arrived, he found her and two other women kneeling down, laying out the ammo belts and inspecting the rounds.

"Well, what do you think?" Murphy said as he walked up to her.

Sarah turned to look at Murphy, her face beaming. "We've got to get one of these."

"I'm sure you'd have no trouble convincing the captain of that." Instantly Murphy regretted his words. How could he have forgotten that the captain was dead? It had only been a day. He felt guilty, not only for his clumsy insensitivity but for Sarah as well. She had taken it especially hard, blaming herself.

"Sarah...I..."

"It's all right, don't worry about it."

Murphy took a step toward her, to comfort her, but she quickly got up.

"Come on," she said, weakly, trying to keep her emotions in check. "Come see what we've done here." She led Murphy over to the side of the cliff where they had dug a pillbox into the side of the hill.

"Pretty cool, huh? When we're finished, we'll cover the top so you would have to literally be on top of it to see it. Plus, if worse comes to worse and we get attack from behind us on the plateau, we've got some ropes we can throw over the edged and slip down the side to escape. Check this out." Sarah jumped down in the hole. She got behind the gun, pulled back the bolt then fired a short burst into the middle of the bay. "Is this great or what?"

Murphy laughed at her enthusiasm. "Easy there, Rambo. Don't be wasting all our ammo on trying to sink coconuts out there."

"Kill joy," Sarah frowned.

"Listen, I'm going back down to see how Doug is doing and to go over some firing sites with him. Do you need anything else?"

Sarah shook her head. "No, we've pretty much got it all under control here."

"Good. Finish covering your pillbox, then come back to the village. We'll all have dinner and make final plans then try to get some rest. It's going to be a long night."

CHAPTER THIRTY FOUR

The sun was settling between the twin volcanic peaks, casting long shadows over the island by the time everyone was able to come together. The mood in the village was quiet yet busy as last minute preparations were still being made.

Murphy walked up to the table and sat down wearily, joining Chief Tanaki, Kai, Crawford, and Sarah.

"I know you are all tired and don't feel like eating, but everyone must keep up their strength." Murphy picked up a piece of fish and forced it down with a smile. "I want to thank each and every one of you and your teams for your hard work today. This is a situation that none of us could have ever imagined, and yet here we are." Murphy looked into the faces of everyone there, conveying his gratitude. "Okay, where do we stand? Doug?"

"I've got four shooters, two positioned on either side of the bay with ten cartridges each. I'll lead the team on this side of the bay and Ruru will lead the other. "I'd watch out if I were you Chief, the kid's a natural leader. He could be after your job someday."

Tanaki's chest swelled with pride. "I hope so; he is my son."

Crawford continued. "At my signal, each team will fire five shots each as fast as they can, then move on to their secondary position and fire five more. After that, we'll run like hell back to the village."

"Good. Sarah?"

"We're all set, too. The gun emplacement is totally concealed and we have two guards hidden on the plateau watching our backsides in case anyone tries to sneak up on us. After finding the range, and sinking some coconuts," Sarah smiled, "we've got 473 rounds left."

Murphy smiled, "Very good. Your primary job will be to keep Hoku from landing more troops. I expect him to land one or two boats initially on the beach which is what I've planned for. If, after the fighting starts, he tries to land reinforcements, it's your job to see to it that they don't make it to the beach. But remember, you have tracer rounds and they work both ways. They help you aim but also give away your position so don't get trigger happy."

Murphy expected some smart answer or fake salute from her; instead, all he got was a somber nod. He wasn't sure if that was a good sign or not.

"Kai?"

"My warriors and I are ready!" he barked out. "We have placed the logs and debris along the path that will lead them directly into our trap. I have twelve strong warriors hidden and ready to attack."

"Your role is the most important, and most dangerous," Murphy said. "While I appreciate your enthusiasm, I want you to understand the danger. If you fail, then the entire plan is in danger."

"We will not fail," Kai said, defiance and anger in his voice.

Murphy shook his head. "I don't doubt your bravery, Kai, but you and all your warriors must be ready to kill. Despite the surroundings, you are not savages and killing may not be as easy as you think."

Kai's anger subsided as he spoke. "The men who are coming here are not savages, yet they are capable of killing are they not? They come here out of greed, to take what they want. We defend what is ours, our homes and families. We are not savages as you have said, but who do you think has the greater motivation to win?"

"Well said, sir, well said." Murphy turned to the chief.

"Those with the horns and pots will be in place. Since most of those are young, as soon as they have finished, my wife will lead them through the jungle and to the safety of the caves."

"Thank you, Chief. I don't like using children but we simply don't have enough people."

"Nor do I, but it is their village too, and their parents know what is at stake."

Murphy looked at his watch. "We got about five hours before they arrive. Take up your positions, post guards and try to get a little rest." He stood, then raised his glass. "'Tis impossible to know the end of this day's business before it comes. But it's enough that the day will end, and then the end be known. And if we meet again, then we'll smile. And if not, then this parting was well made.'"

They all stood and clinked their glass together, drank, then went their separate ways.

"That was very nice," Sarah said as she came up to Murphy, "Shakespeare?"

"Gene Hackman, from *Uncommon Valor*."

Sarah smiled and shook her head. "I'm going to go down to the beach and get some fresh air before I go climb into my perch. Wanna come?"

Murphy shook his head. "I'd love to but there are still a few details I need to take care of here."

"I'll join you if you don't mind," Crawford said. "I could use a little fresh air myself after inhaling all that gunpowder."

"Sure, not at all."

"Just don't take too long," Murphy said. "We don't know when they'll show up so we have to be ready."

Do you think this crazy scheme of Dallas' is really going to work?" Crawford said as they made their way along the path toward the beach. They had left the lights of the village and were walking along the trail in the dark. The moon was only just now beginning to cast its light, but while that was of little use in the dense jungle, Crawford and Sarah had been down the path a hundred times before and knew where they were going.

"I mean this isn't the movies you know. We don't have Rambo or the Terminator on our side. These guys have guns and we all know that Hoku isn't playing any games. He didn't hesitate to kill the captain, and he won't hesitate to do the same to us."

"You're right, this isn't the movies," Sarah answered as she stepped over a log and continued on. "But you heard Dallas; we can't just run and hide, which probably wouldn't do us any good anyway. With all that's at stake here, I just couldn't live with myself knowing that I had a chance to stop all this and didn't do anything about it."

"I suppose you're right," Crawford agreed reluctantly. "After we defeat Hoku and save the world, do you think they'll make action figures out of us?"

"What?"

"Yeah, you know. They can take a little.... a lot actually, of this from around my middle and move it up to my chest and give me rippling muscles so I'll look like Schwarzenegger. Then I could have this really big gun and a bunch of cool, world saving accessories."

Sarah chuckled. "No, you wouldn't look like a superhero; you'd look like a geek on steroids. You'd have an oversized pocket protector and on your utility belt you'd have a slide rule and protractor and wear glasses."

"Yeah, whatever, but I bet they'd be x-ray glasses, though."

"Okay, now you're starting to worry me."

"I think you'd look pretty good as an action figure."

"No way! All the girl action figures I've ever seen look like they have a life time membership to Plastic Surgeons-are-Us. There's no plastic in this body and I don't need any in the little version of me either."

"For what it's worth, I think you look just fine without it.... and I know someone else who'd agree."

"Dallas?"

"Yup. You know, he's never stopped...." Crawford stopped in mid-sentence, "Did you hear anything?"

Sarah cocked her head to one side, listening intently. She was shaking her head no, and was about to speak when they both heard the distant, faint voice of Murphy calling Doug's name.

"Now what?" Crawford muttered. He shook his head and looked at Sarah. "You go on ahead; I'll go back and see what Dallas wants, then join you in a minute."

Sarah nodded. "Okay, see you in a few."

Crawford headed back along the trail, wondering what could be so important that it couldn't wait until he got back. He was tired and needed a little time to recharge but knew that if Dallas was calling that it must be important.

He heard his name called again and he yelled that he was on his way. Crawford saw glimpses of light from Murphy's torch as he weaved his way along the path then came into view. Crawford held up his hand to shield his eyes from the brightness.

"Sorry Doug," Murphy began, "but Ruru insisted that I find you.'

"Sure; what's up?"

"Ruru said he saw you make some extra powder cartridges and that he can't find them. He wanted everything to be in perfect order for you when you came back. I told him that it could wait and that you wouldn't be upset, but he is very persistent and persuasive."

Crawford smiled. "I wasn't joking when I told the chief that he had better watch out for his job and that Ruru will make a great leader some-day. Anyway, tell him thanks, but not to worry about it. Those cartridges are a special load that I'm keeping for myself."

Murphy nodded. "Okay, I'll tell him, and again, sorry to bother you. You guys clear the cobwebs but don't stay too long, okay?"

"Sure thing, boss."

Crawford watched as Murphy left. He remained there until his eyes adjusted to the darkness again, then headed back to the beach. The path seemed like it led on forever, but that was probably only because he was anxious to get to there. Murphy was right, they couldn't stay long which made him all the more eager to get there.

Finally the jungle began to thin and he could clearly hear the waves crashing against the shore. When he broke out into the open he expected to see Sarah, but she was nowhere in sight. He scanned up and down the beach in both directions but couldn't find her anywhere.

"Sarah?" He called out.

"S-a-r-a-h!" He shouted louder this time, waiting for an answer.

Had she gone back to the village already? Had he somehow missed her on the trail? He walked down to the water's edge and looked out over the ocean for a few moments. Should he stay here by himself and relax or go back to the village? He let out a long sigh; he really didn't want to be out there by himself.

He had just started walking back up the beach when he looked down in the sand and noticed something. At first, he couldn't figure out what it was, then his eyes snapped open wide with understanding... and fear. He quickly looked around then started running.

CHAPTER THIRTY FIVE

Sarah watched as Crawford headed back to rendezvous with Murphy, then she turned and continued on toward the beach. After a few minutes of walking, she emerged into the open. The cool breeze was a welcome changes from running back and forth from the hilltop, through the hot, steamy jungle to the village, and back. She drew in several deep breaths as she stood and watched the waves sweep along the shoreline. Feeling the tension beginning to fade, she walked down near the water and sat on a log.

"That didn't take long," she said as she heard a noise behind her. She turned, expecting to see Crawford, but instead, she saw a dark shadow, and it wasn't her friend. Suddenly she felt a gloved hand clasp her mouth. An arm reached across her chest and pulled her back. Immediately she drove her right elbow back as hard as she could into her attacker's stomach. She spun around and threw her fist at him, landing a solid punch to his jaw. Her assailant stumbled back and she was about to land another punch when she felt a crushing blow at the back of her head.

Sarah fell to her knees, her head spinning. She felt like vomiting. Before she could cry for help, a piece of duct tape was placed across her mouth. Her hands were yanked behind her, and she felt her wrists and ankles being wrapped in tape. Dazed, she lay in the sand and watched as the man she had hit came charging over. Sarah braced herself, expecting retribution in the form of a kick to the stomach or head, but at the last second he was shoved out of the way by another man who told him to back off.

She lay there and watched as four more men, all clad in black with hoods, came out of the jungle dragging a semi-rigid inflatable Zodiac toward the water. At the same time, Sarah was picked up by her arms and feet and carried toward the boat. As soon as it was in the water, she was tossed in like so much fishing gear. The outboard started, and soon they were skimming across the waves at high speed.

She was on the floor of the Zodiac in a crumpled heap with no way to support herself. She felt every pounding wave through the cold aluminum hull as they sped across the water. She tried to sit up, but a boot to her shoulder shoved her hard back down

"Enough, I said!"

The leader shoved the other man back. He reached down and helped Sarah up to a seat. "You will leave her alone," Kekao said as he took off his mask. The man muttered something under his breath then took off his mask and threw it on the floor. Sarah recognized him as Thing One and the other men in the boat as "natives" from the village.

Sarah lifted her head, motioning for Kekao to remove the tape. "Why have you kidnapped me?" she asked after he took it off.

"Let's just say that you're a little insurance so that Murphy will cooperate in a timely manner."

"We gave you everything you wanted. You have your code, why don't you just go and leave us alone."

Kekao shook his head. "Don't make this harder than it has to be."

"I don't know what you're talking about."

Kekao shrugged. "Have it your way."

Clouds drifted across the moon, shrouding its glow, so very little of its light illuminated the sky. Time seemed to stand still as they passed in silence, plunging headlong into the darkness. Sarah looked around into the vast, murky darkness, the island long since gone behind them and nothing but void in front of them. It was difficult to see the horizon, to tell where the sky ended and the ocean began.

Yet, as time did pass, a light appeared in the distance. At first, Sarah thought it was just a bright star or planet rising above the horizon, but it didn't take long for her to realize that it was the lights of a ship, the *Pacific Searcher*.

The ship drifted to a stop and the Zodiac pulled alongside. Sarah looked up and saw the ship's crane swing overhead, and watched as the men climbed aboard the ship then hooked the lines to lift the boat out of the water. She also noticed that Joe Bob was operating the crane; at least some of the crew was all right. He gave her a quick smile, though there was no joy it, as he lifted the boat out of the water and swung it over and onto the ship.

"Hello Sarah, it's nice to see you again," Hoku said. "Though you do look like a drowned rat."

Kekao lifted Sarah up out of the boat and set her on the deck in front of him. She stood there and stared, still not used to seeing him in street clothes instead of island garb. Her teeth began to chatter and she started shivering; her clothes were soaked from being in the bottom of the Zodiac.

"Why have you brought me here?" She demanded.

Hoku just smiled. "Would you like to talk out here in the wind and cold or on the bridge where it's warm and dry?"

Sarah stared defiantly at him for a moment, and then held out her hands for Kekao to cut the tape.

"Very good," Hoku said. "I'll see you on the bridge."

A few minutes later, Sarah was standing on the bridge, wearing work overalls. "Same question, why have you kidnapped me?" she demanded. "We gave you everything you wanted."

Hoku got up from the captain's chair, casually walked over and back-handed her hard, sending her sprawling on the deck.

"Why do you try my patience?" Hoku said in a calm, yet very intense voice. "I would think that after you saw what I did to Yates, you would take me more seriously."

Sarah lay on the floor and touched her mouth with the back of her hand. She wasn't surprised to find blood. She cringed a little, not because of the pain, but because Hoku had reminded her of Yates' death, something she felt responsible for. She had promised herself that when she walked onto the bridge again that she wouldn't look at the spot where Yates had fallen. Now, as she struggled to get up, she realized that she was lying in the exact spot where he had died. She quickly got up, ignoring the pain in her head, and stepped aside.

"I offered to let all of you live if you cooperated, something, I might add, a lot of men in my position wouldn't have done. This operation is worth more money than you could ever image. This isn't just about simple greed; this is about controlling world markets, world governments!"

Hoku returned to his chair and casually sat down and crossed his legs. "We can do this the easy way or the hard way, I really don't much care which, but you will tell me what I need to know."

Sarah held up her hand to stop him. "Spare me," she said, wiping more blood from her lip. "I get it, you're a *bad* man, and will stop at nothing."

She moved over to her work station and sat down and opened the drawer. Immediately two guards rushed forward but stopped when she showed them that she was getting a bottle of aspirin. She took two and washed them down with some bottled water, then turned back to Hoku.

"Why did you recruit me in the first place?" She asked, then continued before he could answer. "I'll tell you why; you recruited me because you thought I would be sympathetic to your cause, that that would be my motivation. Well, you were right. Under the guise of environmental responsibility, I was willing to help you with what I thought was the right thing to do.

"Now that I know what's really at stake, you are still trying to recruit me in a way, to try to get my help. Only you're using the wrong kind of motivation here. If you want my help, you shouldn't use threats and intimidation. You should use enticements."

Hoku learned back, placing one elbow on an armrest and resting his chin in his hand, studying her. "So, what you're saying," he said slowly and carefully, "is that the correct form of motivation is money? I'm to believe that you would sell out your friends if the price is right? Greed over principals?"

"Greed is such an ugly word. I prefer to think of it as investing in the future, my future. Listen, I can get you everything you want a lot easier, and more importantly, a lot quicker than if you try to take it."

Hoku shook his head. "Why should I believe you?"

"Back to motivation again. It's simple, I want to be rich."

"It's never that simple," Hoku scoffed.

"Really? Then why are you doing this? There is no lofty goal here, no great cause to further, no ideological message to preach. You are in it for one reason, and one reason only, just like me, for the money."

She paused for a moment to let that sink in, and then continued. "I'll even prove my good intentions." She started typing on the computer but was stopped by a firm grip on her wrist by one of the guards. "Okay, I understand, we have some trust issues here. Have your men run a diagnostic on the helm and navigation systems. I think you'll find that they have been recalibrated, and that instead of travelling at twenty knots like the instruments show, in reality, you're traveling at only sixteen knots."

Hoku nodded to the man at the navigation console and he began running the diagnostic program. After several minutes he turned to Hoku with a surprised look. "She's right sir, the settings have been changed and we are only making sixteen knots."

"Recalibrate it and bring us up to the real full speed," he said to the man, then turned back to Sarah. "Let's see what other things you can tell me, shall we."

"Let's talk about my *motivation* first," she smiled. "Shall we?"

CHAPTER THIRTY SIX

Crawford nearly collapsed as he stumbled out of the jungle into the village clearing. He bent over, resting his hands on his knees, and tried to shout but couldn't because all he could do was gasp for air. He felt like the Greek runner who ran from the plains of Marathon to Athens with news of a great victory, then fell over dead. Only he wasn't bringing good news.

Murphy rushed over to him.

"Doug, what's wrong?"

The only words Crawford could get out between gasps were "Sarah" and "gone."

"What happened? Are you okay?"

Crawford wheezed, then nodded and managed to wave him on with a feeble "go."

Murphy took off into the jungle, not waiting for Crawford to recover his breath. He was quickly followed by Kai and two other natives. His mind was racing as fast as his legs were carrying him, wondering what had happened to Sarah.

Gone? Did Crawford mean she was dead? Had there been a terrible accident? Had she drowned? Or had Hoku returned ahead of schedule? Murphy tried to shove the dire thoughts out of his head.

He ran onto the beach and immediately started calling her name. He didn't see a body lying in the sand, which he thought was a good thing, but given the circumstances he wasn't sure. Then he saw what Crawford must have seen; running from the tree line down to the shoreline was a shallow trail in the sand. The only thing that could have made that was the hull of a boat being dragged to the water.

He followed the trail and found several sets of footprints. They looked like they were from some sort of boot, all except one, which was smaller than the others and smooth-soled, like the tennis shoes that Sarah had been wearing. The tracks disappeared into the water along with that of the boat.

Murphy's knees went weak and his legs start to quiver. He felt like he was about to collapse, but he refused to give in to grief. There was no blood and no body, so that meant that she was still alive, and where there was life, there was hope. Murphy grabbed onto that hope with both hands and stood up a little straighter. Hope brought more with it than just a little strength; it also brought a new determination. He would beat Hoku and get Sarah back, no matter what.

Just then, Kai and the other natives arrived, followed a few moments later by a much winded Crawford.

"You were right, Doug," Murphy said as he walked up to his friend and put his hand on his shoulder. "They took Sarah. Come on, we've got to get back to the village right away. We've a lot to talk about now."

"What? I just got here. Can't we talk here?" Crawford wheezed, drawing in deep breaths.

"I'm sorry Doug, Sarah being taken prisoner changes everything. Come on," Murphy said, then disappeared down the jungle path.

Crawford heaved a heavy sigh as he turned and started walking back toward the village.

Everyone was gathered around the fire by the time Crawford stumbled out of the jungle. He made his way over to the others then collapsed on one of the benches. He immediately gulped down some water and grabbed some fruit to chew on. He waved for Murphy to begin as he reached for more water.

"Okay, in case everyone hasn't heard, Hoku sent a boat and kidnapped Sarah."

"Are Hoku and his men on the island now?" Chief Tanaki asked.

Murphy shook his head. "I don't think so. If it were a full scale invasion we would have known it by now. I think it was just a scouting party and they got lucky and found Sarah."

"I never should have left her," Crawford said.

"No Doug, don't play the blame game with yourself. If you had been with her then you would have been kidnapped too, or worse. You couldn't have known and besides, I was the one who called you back, remember?"

"If they have the woman," Kai said, "then all is lost. They will know our plans and know what to expect. All surprise will be gone."

Murphy shook his head. "I wouldn't count on it, Sarah's pretty tough. Besides, we don't have time to formulate another plan. Since they've sent a boat, we have to assume that they're closer than we thought. So from here on out, we go to battle stations. Send everyone to their posts."

He turned to Tanaki. "Chief, with Sarah gone, we need someone to man the machine gun; can you spare an extra warrior?"

"You don't need to." A young woman spoke up and then stood, joined by another girl of the same age. "We have been working with Sarah, setting up the gun and building the bunker. We know all about the plan and what to do."

Tanaki frowned, not liking the idea very much.

The girl read his expression and continued. "She even let me fire the gun once."

"We can do this Chief Tanaki," the other girl added.

Murphy looked at the two girls closely. They were young, maybe not even twenty, but he saw determination in their eyes; Sarah had put that there. "Chief, these are your people and I won't interfere, but I believe that Sarah has taught them well and that they can do this."

Tanaki nodded. "You have faith in your friend, so I will have faith in these two." He turned to the girls. "Go, and make us all proud."

The girls smiled and giggled slightly, and for a moment Murphy thought they were going to give him and the chief thank you hugs, but instead they put on their game faces and left.

"Okay, it's settled then. Doug, take your shooters and get into position and keep your eyes open. Kai, take your men and get the trap ready and post your lookouts. Chief, get the trumpeters ready."

Murphy stood to address the entire village. "I know you are all scared, but together we can do this. You all know what to do, you all know what you are fighting for, you all know that we will not let them win. "Our opponent is strong, but all they fight for is money and power. Now, look to the person on your left, then to the person on your right. That is what and *who* you are fighting for, not for money, not me, not even for the chief, but for them."

It wasn't a rousing speech met with thunderous applause and great battle cries, but it was the best he could come up with and it got the point across.

Murphy watched as everyone started moving and gathering what they needed and going to where they needed to be. Everybody was moving and doing something, everyone but him. And then, in a blink of an eye, the village was empty and quiet and he was alone.

For a moment he felt empty and abandoned like the village; he felt like a failure, then he remembered that the village wasn't abandoned; everyone had left, not to run and hide, but to go and fight. These people hadn't left because of despair, but because of hope, hope that *he* had given them. Standing just a bit taller, he nodded in approval then headed into the jungle.

Murphy wanted to inspect the troops one last time, making sure everyone and everything was in place for the big battle. His first stop would be the machine gun emplacement atop the hill.

Even though he had his flashlight and he knew that the chances were very small that any of Hoku's men were on the island, he kept it turned off, preferring to move on the trails by moonlight. He had turned it on once, right after leaving the village and immediately he felt exposed, almost naked before the world, so he quickly shut it off. He was tempted to use it twice while climbing the hill, having fallen down and bruised his leg and gotten several scratches his face on a low branch. But in the end, he would rather be bruised and scratched rather than feel naked and exposed, so he left the light off.

Reaching the top of the plateau, he was glad he hadn't used the flashlight and ruined his night vision. Despite the darkness, it was amazing how much more he could see at night when there were no lights around. Just then he heard the lonely howl of

Bagheera. Even though it meant that danger might be near, the cat's cry just seemed to fit the moment.

He thought he could easily go straight to the gun emplacement, but he hesitated the closer he got to the edge of the cliff. Sarah had done a good job of concealing it. He took two more steps then heard a loud snap underfoot. He took one more step then stopped. This was a grassy meadow and he didn't remember any dry underbrush.

Then it hit him: the dry branches were not just dead undergrowth, but an early warning system. He looked around for a minute and didn't see anything and was beginning to think that he was just being paranoid when he caught a slight flash of movement.

He turned to see two bushes to his left and behind him begin to move, then to grow. It was like a scene from a horror movie as he watched these two shrubs grow from a height of about two feet and rise to where they were nearly as tall as he was... and look him in the eye.

Wait! It's me, Murphy!" he called out. It took him a moment, especially considering all the camouflage, to recognize one of the bush people as the girl from the village who had begged to come here.

"If I had any doubts about whether you and your friends could handle this job, they're gone now," Murphy said.

The flash of her smile, set against her dark camouflage, made her look like the Cheshire Cat. "Thank you, Mr. Murphy, we will not let you or Miss Sarah down."

Murphy nodded in appreciation. "Thank you, I'm sure of that. Good job, and stay alert!"

"We will."

Satisfied that all was well here, Murphy left. At the edge of the clearing, he turned to wave goodbye but there was nothing there, only an empty meadow. He smiled then headed back down the trail. He wanted to check in with Doug and his firing teams next, then with the chief and the trumpeters, and make his final stop with Kai at the hidden bunkers.

He came down off the plateau and was cutting across the jungle to find Doug on the other side of the bay. The jungle was less dense here and he was making good time, when all of a sudden, something hit him on his left side and sent him sprawling.

Another overactive guard Murphy thought as he started to get up, better safe than sorry. "Don't worry, it's me, Murphy." As he stood and brushed himself off, he peered at the shadowy figure and something didn't look right.

"Yes, I know it's you."

Murphy's eyes flew open wide with surprise, it was Kekao!

"Where's Sarah?" Murphy demanded. "If you've hurt her in any way, so help me I'll kill you."

Kekao laughed. "Relax, when I left, she and Hoku were in his cabin chatting away, at least I think they were talking." He smiled wickedly.

"You liar!"

Kekao laughed even harder. "I'm taking you back to the ship. Whether you volunteer willingly doesn't matter. I'm going to beat you here and I'm going to beat you on the ship. It's all the same to me."

Just then a single gunshot split the night.

Kekao smiled. "Ah, that would be Adam. He's found your friend."

CHAPTER THIRTY SEVEN

"Doug? What have you done to him?"

"You seem to worry about other people an awful lot when you have enough troubles of your own," Kekao answered smugly.

He took a quick step forward and before Murphy could do anything, Kekao reached out and slapped Murphy hard across the face.

Murphy could feel himself being consumed with anger. He wanted to charge wildly at Kekao, like a raging bull with its horns down to tear an opponent apart. But he remembered the old wisdom, lose your temper in a fight, you lose the fight. Murphy used every last ounce of will power to control his emotions. He was about to put the adage to the test and wondered if Kekao could do the same.

"Really, a slap?" Murphy said, managing a smile of his own. "Are you challenging me to a duel, or is that how you fight? Do you call names and bite and pull hair too?"

Murphy saw Kekao's eyes flash with anger, uncontrollable anger, as he let out a bellow and charged. Murphy was not an experienced fighter but he wasn't a complete novice either. He had been young and foolish once and wanted to prove he was a man to his friends and to himself, so he had gotten into his share of bar brawls.

He sidestepped Kekao's reckless charge and drove his elbow hard into the other man's back as he went by. Kekao howled in pain and arched his back as he spun around to face Murphy.

Kekao smiled with clenched teeth. "Not bad, sailor boy. Let's see what else you got."

Kekao lunged forward and threw two quick jabs, Murphy was able to partially block one, but the other landed squarely on his chin, snapping his head back.

He wiped the blood from his cut lip. "I think you slap harder than you hit," he said as he threw a couple of jabs of his own in, both connecting with Kekao's jaw.

Kekao charged again, only this time Murphy was not able to get out of the way. Kekao hit him in the center of the chest, picking him up and driving him to the ground. Murphy saw the gleam of Kekao's white teeth then nearly passed out from the force of the impact. He also saw something else.

Around Kekao's neck was the good luck charm that he had worn while playing the part of island warrior, just like the ones he had given all of them. Why would he still be wearing it now? The charade was over. Kekao didn't seem like the type who would wear jewelry.

Suddenly, Murphy had a strange thought, and his mind quickly ran with it. Images began flashing in his head, fast forwarding, then moving in slow motion...The moment they had met the natives,... the grand banquet... their jungle trek... the cave... his fall... being captured.... The one thing in common with every one of those memories was the good luck pendants. He hadn't really paid much attention before but everyone in the entire village had one and he had never seen a native without one.

A sharp pain to his face brought his mind back to reality as Kekao pummeled him. Murphy threw up his hands to block the blows, then grabbed Kekao by the collar and pushed him over. As he did, he yanked the pendant from around Kekao's neck and shoved him away. Murphy rolled over on his hands and knees with his back to Kekao so he wouldn't see him shove the pendant into his pocket.

Murphy charged and Kekao easily sidestepped him and returned the favor of an elbow hard into Murphy's back as he went by. Murphy gasped in pain, then slowly stood, placed his hand on the small of his back and started rubbing the muscles. He was doing more than just trying to ease the pain. The charge had been a diversion—a very painful diversion—so that he could position his hand at his back without raising suspicions. As he was rubbing his back, he reached into his back pocket and slipped out his charm, the one that Kekao had originally given him. He was about to play a hunch.

Murphy rushed Kekao again and tried to grab him in a bear hug so he could slip his pendant into Kekao's pocket. He managed to wrap one arm around Kekao's shoulders but the big man was too quick and strong. He grabbed Murphy's arms, spun him around and threw him like the hammer in a track and field event.

Murphy hit the ground at an awkward angle and rolled over several times, ending up face first in the dirt. He lay there for a moment, letting his head clear, wondering if his hunch was worth all this abuse.

As he started to get up, he noticed that both charms were on the ground underneath him, so he quickly fell back to the ground so Kekao wouldn't see them.

Which one was his and which was Kekao's?

If his hunch was right, it could mean the difference between life and death. With no way to tell them apart, he simply grabbed one as he got up and slipped it into his shirt and clenched the other one in his fist as he wearily stood and faced Kekao.

Murphy summoned his resolve and charged Kekao again. This time he was able to put the charm in Kekao's pocket before being batted away like a fly.

"You just never learn, do you?" Kekao said as he stared down at Murphy.

Murphy started to get up but Kekao kicked him in the ribs, sending him sprawling back into the dirt. This time, the pain kept him down.

"I've really enjoyed this, but play time is over." Kekao said with a sadistic leer.

"Bring it," Murphy replied defiantly, trying not to show that each breath sent pain stabbing through his side. Just as Kekao was taking a step forward, they heard a low, menacing growl.

A pair of yellow eyes was staring at them from the jungle.

Kekao smiled broadly. "I was supposed to bring you back alive, but Hoku will understand when I tell him that the cat got to you first."

"Humor me here," Murphy said as he struggled to his feet. "What's with the panther? How does he always manage to show up at just the right time? Is he on the company payroll too?"

"Not really, but I guess you could consider him an outside contractor," Kekao laughed. "He's not really trained. If you noticed, we all wear good luck charms to ward off the evil spirits of the cat. Each of our pendants has a tiny transmitter in it sending off a signal only detectable by the cat's sensitive ears, creating a sense of confusion and a headache. Basically a cat repellant. The three you wore were just the opposite. The electronic version of a wounded animal, sex hormones and catnip on steroids, all rolled into one. The cat is drawn to you and repelled by us."

"But why?

"To create chaos and confusion, to keep you off guard and hopefully to kill you."

The panther let out another low growl and inched forward, eyeing both men threateningly. Murphy could tell that the big cat was getting ready to attack; that one of them was going to be dead shortly and the other would get away, but who?

Suddenly the panther's eyes flew open wide and sprang.

CHAPTER THIRTY EIGHT

Crawford was walking on the trail with Ruru close behind. "Does every-one have the cartridges we loaded, Ruru?"

"Yes, sir," the boy answered, hesitated for a moment then continued. "Could you please just call me Ru, sir? Ruru sounds like a child and I am a man," he said proudly.

"Okay, *Ru*," Crawford said with a smile "Does everyone know where they are supposed to be?"

"Yes, sir."

"Even Eloni? He's a nice enough guy, but he just doesn't seem to get it sometimes."

Ru giggled.

Crawford stopped and turned around and looked at the boy. "What? What's so funny?"

"You sound like an old woman, do this, do that," the boy replied, still giggling.

Crawford gave him a hard stare and instantly the boy's mirth died. Crawford held his gaze for as long as he could, then burst out laughing.

"An old woman, huh?"

"Yes, sir," Ru replied sheepishly.

"Come on, it's okay," Crawford said as he put his arm around the boy's shoulders. They walked on in silence for a few minutes then came to a wide spot in the path where it split.

Crawford checked a nearby fallen log then sat down. "This is where you told the others to meet us, right?"

Ru nodded. "They should be here very soon."

"Good. Well, we have a few minutes then. Tell me Ruru...ah, Ru," he corrected himself, "do you want to stay on the island or go to the mainland when you grow up?"

"I wish to go to Australia someday with the crew of the *Albatross*. They talk of many wonderful and strange things that I would like to see."

"What does your father think about all this?"

Ru shrugged. "He does not like the idea very much but I don't think he would try to stop me. He says we have everything we need right here, but I want to see what's outside of this tiny island. I want to see more and do more than just fish and make baskets."

Crawford smiled. "Nothing wrong with that. Kids all over the world are just like you, wanting to see more than just the same old four walls that they grew up in."

"Father says that there is a lot of evil out there."

"He's right, but there are also a lot of good and wonderful things, too. You're a bright kid; I think you'll do just fine out there. Now where are those guys?" Crawford stood, getting impatient.

Ru picked up a bug and flicked it into the jungle. "I will go check. Eloni has probably gotten lost."

Crawford smiled. "Okay, but hurry up...and be careful."

He watched the boy disappear down the trail then sat down again. He had just started double checking his equipment when he heard a noise behind him. "Well that was quick, I didn't..." He stopped in mid-sentence as he turned around.

Standing in the shadows at the edge of the trail was a man dressed in black.

He was carrying what looked like a large sack over his shoulder and a bundle of sticks in the other. He threw the sticks in front of him and immediately Crawford could see that they weren't sticks but three of their muskets.

The man grunted, then heaved the sack and threw it down next to the rifles. It landed with a thud and a small cloud of dust. Crawford felt sick when he saw what the sack was: the limp body of Ru.

"For a kid, he put up quite a fight."

Crawford immediately recognized the voice— Aata, Thing One—and raised his musket. "What did you do to him? Is he okay? I'll kill you if you've hurt him in any way."

"Why do people always say that? It's so cliché," Thing One said. "Of course I hurt him you idiot, it's what I do. And you won't kill me. I checked your antique rifles here—"

"They're muskets."

"What?"

"I said they are muskets, not rifles. They have a smooth bore."

"Well, excuse me, Alexandre Dumas, I checked your *muskets*, and you don't have any bullets. You're shooting blanks! What are you going to do, scare me to death with a loud bang? "And even if you did have bullets," he continued, "you wouldn't shoot me. It's not in your nature. I've read your psych report, you can't kill anyone in cold blood, you're a lover, not a fighter, and not much of that either." He snickered. "You're a computer nerd, a geek who doesn't have the guts to shoot anyone. Now put down your glorified walking stick and let's go peaceably back to the ship."

Crawford could feel the weight of the gun in his hands; suddenly it felt like it weighed five hundred pounds. He could feel his resolve—and his aim—start to waver.

The man was right; he couldn't kill anyone in cold blood.

Thing One looked at him and smiled, seeing the gun slowly lowering. "That's better."

He started to take a step toward Crawford, but as he did, Crawford quickly raised the gun again, aiming straight at his chest.

"You're starting to piss me off," Thing One said. "Hoku said I had to bring you back alive, but he didn't say how alive you had to be."

Crawford maintained his aim and glanced down at Ru. He couldn't tell if the boy was breathing or not.

He looked Thing One straight in the eyes. "Are you wearing a bullet proof vest?" Thing One just rolled his eyes. "Of course I am. Duh, I'm a mercenary."

"Too bad." Crawford simply said, then pulled the trigger. In the calm and stillness of the night, the musket's report sounded like a howitzer. Thing One was thrown back several feet by the impact of the lead ball that hit him square in the chest. He hit the ground hard.

Crawford quickly knelt beside Ru and felt for his wrist. He was relieved to find a strong, steady pulse. He was just about to help the boy up when he heard something crashing through the jungle.

He stood and hastily started to reload his musket. The sound was distant, but growing closer by the second. Whoever or whatever it was, was making no attempt at hiding its presence and was rushing headlong straight toward him.

He was fighting to keep from panicking as he fumbled with the shot and ball, trying to get the musket loaded. Just as he thought the jungle was about to explode, he yanked the ramrod out, threw it on the ground, and raised the gun.

A figure broke through the foliage, then stopped, staring at the scene before him: a man and boy lying on the ground with another man aiming a three hundred year old musket at him.

"Don't shoot, don't shoot. It's me, Dallas!"

"Dallas?" Crawford replied, his voice filled with relief.

"Did…did you kill him?" Murphy asked, pointing at Thing One.

Crawford shook his head, "No, but the thought did cross my mind. He's wearing a bulletproof vest. I was very tempted to aim a little higher but you said we needed him, so I aimed lower. This baby may not have the muzzle velocity of a modern firearm, but the sheer mass of a three-quarter inch lead ball fired at point-blank range will still do the trick.

"He's not dead, but he'll be sore as hell when he wakes up. I aimed at his left side, hitting him in the ribs. He probably has a cracked rib or two," Crawford finished, a note of satisfaction in his voice.

"Well I'm glad you didn't kill him," Murphy paused for a moment as he looked at Hoku's man lying on the ground. "I thought you didn't have any bullets."

"I had Ru take me back to the cave and I found a small bag of shot. The others don't have any of these," he said as he reached into his pocket and pulled out a handful of .75 caliber lead balls, "but I do."

"How's the boy?"

"Thing One here slapped him around a bit but I think he's going to be okay. By the way, what are you doing here? Are you okay? I heard Bagheera earlier. I thought it might have been him coming down the trail at me."

"I ran into Kekao a few minutes ago. I think he and Thing One here were an advanced scouting party so the ship has to be close. We've got to hurry."

"Kekao? What happened?"

Murphy tossed him the good luck charm. "I also ran into Bagheera. Seems the good luck pendants that Kekao gave us were only good luck for them. Theirs had some kind of repellent in them, but the ones they gave us are full of catnip. I switched charms with Kekao so Bagheera attacked and killed him, not me."

"Wow."

"You're telling me. Come on, let's see if Rambo here has anything we can use."

"This guy travels light," Crawford said, as he went through his vest pockets. "I've got a 9 mil and two extra clips."

"I've got a radio, which will come in handy, and a knife. That's it."

"Too bad he doesn't have a complete set of Hoku's battle plans," Crawford laughed nervously.

"Would be nice. Okay, I don't think that anyone else came with Kekao or your friend here, otherwise we'd have seen them by now. Hoku will be here any minute so we stick to the plan. It would have been much more effective to have gunfire coming from both sides of the bay, but we'll just have to make do."

"I can stay and shoot from here."

Murphy and Crawford quickly turned to see Ru sitting up. Crawford wiped the matted hair from the boy's face, revealing a cut on his forehead and a swollen eye.

"That's a pretty nasty cut, Ru. Maybe you should go back to the village," Crawford said.

Ru shook his head emphatically. "No, I will stay and fight with every-one else. I can load the guns faster than anyone, you have seen me do this. I can take the three guns here and load and fire them just as fast as the three men on the other side."

Ru turned to Murphy, pleading. "Please, Mr. Murphy, please let me do this."

Murphy held up his hands. "Don't look at me kid; this is Doug's call, not mine."

"Oh please Mr. Doug, don't treat me like an old woman and make me stay in the village."

Crawford looked at Murphy. "How do you say no to that?" He turned back to the boy, "Okay, you're in. Gather the muskets and take up your position. You know what to do so wait for the signal and stay out of sight."

"Thank you Mr. Doug, thank you." Ru snapped to attention and gave Crawford a salute, then gathered the muskets and quickly disappeared down the trail.

Both men smiled at the boy's enthusiasm. "Come on," Murphy said, "let's take sleeping beauty here back to the village. Then you'd better find the rest of your shooters."

CHAPTER THIRTY NINE

After dropping Thing One off at the village, bound and gagged, Murphy checked in with the chief and told him everything that had happened. Then he made his way to the beach and the bunkers to update Kai.

After finding everything ready to go, Murphy sat down to wait. Suddenly he felt tired, exhausted beyond words.

Were they really doing this? Did they really think that they had a chance against heavily armed, trained mercenaries? The past few days had been surreal; nothing seemed to make sense anymore.

Just a few short days ago life was normal. Every night after shift, they would gather on deck and talk and laugh, complain...complain about...who knows what? It didn't really matter. They had even posted an embarrassing video on YouTube of Joe Bob sleeping in the Zodiac on deck. He was sprawled out in the bottom of the boat like a passed out drunk, and a sea gull had landed next to him and was picking away at his half-eaten sandwich.

Murphy sighed heavily. Now?

Now life had changed forever. The captain was dead, ex-wife had betrayed them. He'd nearly been killed while finding hidden pirate treasure, nearly been killed by a trained panther, tossed down a two-hundred-foot embankment and left for dead, and now he was leading a band of islanders against trained killers who had seized his ship and were hell bent on taking over the world.

Murphy smiled sadly to himself; it reminded him of the old joke: "Other than that Mrs. Lincoln, what did you think of the play?"

He was, thankfully, shaken out of his melancholy by shouts coming from the beach.

"They are coming, they are coming." A winded teenaged boy stopped in front of Murphy and Kai. "I can see the lights of the ship just on the horizon."

"You have done well," Kai told the boy. "Now go join the others."

Murphy grabbed a pair of binoculars that the chief had given him, a gift from the crew of the *Albatross,* and headed toward the beach.

Reaching the edge of the bay, Murphy looked through the binoculars. It was the *Pacific Searcher*, all right, and by the white spray from her bow, she was making full speed.

"They'll be here in less than thirty minutes," Murphy said to Kai who had joined him.

"We are ready."

Murphy smiled. He appreciated Kai's, simple almost child-like faith that they would win. Murphy tried to grab a hold of that because right now, he needed some of that faith.

Murphy moved into the tree line and hid, waiting. It didn't take long for him to see the *Pacific Searcher* enter the narrow channel. He could see the bridge and was pleased to note see that Joe Bob was at the helm; they would have some help on the ship when the fighting started. He also saw Hoku sitting smugly in the captain's chair. He had hoped to get a glimpse of Sarah, but she was nowhere to be seen.

The *Pacific Searcher* looked like a cruise ship coming into port with every light blazing. Murphy wasn't sure if this was to help navigate the narrow passageway, or if Hoku was making a statement. A moment later that question was answered as the ship dropped anchor and the ship's horn sounded in a long, deep bellow.

"Awful sure of yourself there aren't you, Mr. Hoku?" Murphy whispered to himself. "Pride goeth before destruction."

As if to answer, the radio Murphy had taken from Thing One came to life.

"Adam report, what's your status? Have you found Murphy or Crawford yet?" It was Hoku's voice.

Murphy's heart began pounding; he didn't know what to do. Should he ignore it completely and hope Hoku wouldn't get suspicious? Should he reply and taunt him or would that put Sarah in more danger?

He decided to give Hoku what he expected... sort of. He felt a little silly doing it, but it was all he could think of.

He pushed the button to talk, ran the radio over his sleeve to simulate static, then he spoke in short, half words, simulating a poor connection and that something was wrong with the radio.

He tried to remember what Thing One sounded like. As a kid in junior high, he was pretty good at doing voice impersonations and had a lot of fun making announcements over the school's PA system for dances and things like that. In fact, one of his teachers had signed in his year book "To the man with a 1000 voices." Right now he only needed one. "I----wh----t----be---found----d---that---Mur-- ---- - so--on---."

There was silence on the other end. Was Hoku buying it?

The radio cracked again. "Are you okay?"

"Ro---, -- ev---- th--- i- o--y."

Another pause.

"Roger that, I'm sending a boat in now."

Murphy let out a huge sigh of relief; Hoku had bought it.

He watched from his hidden position as four men got into one of the Zodiacs and were lowered over the side. He didn't see anyone with night vision goggles, which was a relief, but he couldn't rule them out as they wouldn't need them until they reached the beach. Murphy fell back to his position with Kai and the others, and waited for the boat to land.

Murphy quickly wrapped himself with vines for camouflage and mentally prepared himself for combat. He knew all too well the old adage that no battle plan, no matter how well thought out survived first contact with the enemy; he only hoped that his plan held together long enough to get on board the ship.

CHAPTER FORTY

The boat glided to the shore and crunched softly against the sand. The four men got out and cautiously walked from the beach into the low lying foliage. Murphy's hopes for success began to wane as he watched them; each carried an assault rifle and wore body armor.

The men looked more like Special Forces than mercenaries, Murphy thought. What chance did he have? He shook his head; he was not going to allow himself to go down the road of self-pity and doubt. You fight your battles with what you have, he told himself, not what you wish you had. Their planning was sound and they had the element of surprise. They had to win, and he had to believe that, otherwise what was the point in fighting?

And so far, everything was going according to plan. The mercenaries were spread out at first but slowly began to come together into a single line as the trees, brush and other obstacles the natives had put along the way began to funnel them together.

The powerful searchlight from the ship had been following them, cutting wide swatches through the darkness with each pass of the beam, seeking any hidden dangers on the tropical island. But soon the sweeping beam steadied and narrowed its focus as it shone on the men with a steady shaft of light, a lifeline ready to snatch them back at the first sign of danger.

The lead man in the team had just crested a small knoll on the trail and was descending the downward side where he would have to take a sharp right turn where the trail was heavily overgrown. Once on the other side and in the thicket, the team would be out of sight of the ship; and that was where the trap would be sprung.

They were close now.

Murphy felt his muscles tensing as he watched the last man in line step into the thicket. Just a few more steps and he would leap out of the undergrowth, signaling the beginning of the attack.

Murphy had taken several deep breaths and was just starting to move when his radio came to life, Hoku's voice sounding like it was being broadcast over a loud speaker instead of the tinny sound of a small radio.

He froze in terror; how could he have been so stupid as to not turn off the radio?

The team stopped and turned around.

"Adam? Is that you man? Don't sneak up on us like that," the team leader said. Murphy was about ten feet behind the last man in line and even though they were not in the direct beam of the searchlight, the light was behind him and still bright enough to back light him, blotting out his features.

Brass it out. Murphy told himself as he forced himself to relax and began walking calmly toward the team.

"Adam?" The leader asked again, this time with more suspicion in his voice. Murphy could see that his stance had tightened and that his gun was raised a little higher.

Murphy was now only a few feet away; he had to get just a little closer. He raised his hand in a wave and grunted, hoping that would be enough to buy him three feet of ground.

Two more steps.

"Adam, answer me!" It was more of a demand now than a request. The rifle moved to firing position.

Murphy raised his other hand in a 'what are you doing?' gesture.

One step.

Murphy took the last step and continued moving, bringing his right hand down hard against the last man's face.

It felt good, real good.

Murphy took out days of frustration on the man as he struck him. But it was more than that; he had finally taken the first step in getting the ship back and getting justice for the captain.

Murphy never stopped moving. He grabbed the next man in line by his collar with his left hand, and using his right fist like a pile-driver, pounded him into the sand.

The team leader was about to fire when he simply disappeared. Two natives had jumped out from their hiding places and tackled and quickly subdued him. Kai put the last man down with a single blow, his determination and anger equal to Murphy's. Murphy gave Kai a nod of approval and appreciation, one warrior to another.

Murphy wanted to pound his chest and yell; to let out a primeval battle cry. He had vanquished his foes and now stood victorious. But he also knew that they had been very lucky, and that adrenaline was doing all the talking now. Still, he savored the moment a bit longer, then sent two men back to the village to get Thing One.

Murphy and the others quickly stripped the uniforms off the mercenaries. The plan was for Murphy and three other natives to put them on, and then bring three more "captured" natives back to the ship.

Murphy had just snapped on his vest when the natives brought Thing One back.

"What is this, trick or treat?" Thing One said, seeing Murphy in uniform.

"Yup, and you're going to help with the trick. Get on the radio and tell Hoku that you're on the way back with some captured natives."

Thing One laughed, "And what makes you think I would help you?"

"Motivation."

"What? Motivation, what are you talking about?"

"You want to live," Murphy answered flatly.

The mercenary studied him for a moment. "You don't have the guts to kill me in cold blood." He said smugly.

"Murphy looked at him and shrugged. "Maybe, maybe not. But I think Kai here can, and will. You see, you have no cause; you're simply fighting for money. Kai, on the other hand, is fighting for his family, his village, his very way of life. I'd say his motivation to win is a lot greater than yours to keep quiet."

Thing One stared at the island warrior and saw a determination in his eyes that he didn't feel. "Okay," he replied, the defiance in his voice all but gone. "Tell me what you want me to do."

"Stop!"

"Grab him!"

Murphy heard a shout, and turned to see what was happening, then suddenly found himself on the ground where someone had shoved him as he went running past.

One of the captured mercenaries had managed to free himself from the ropes and was running back toward the ship. Before anyone could stop him, he had cleared the thicket, crested the knoll and was nearly to the open beach, shouting and waving his arms all the while.

Murphy and Kai took off after him; Murphy only hoped they could catch him before the ship spotted him. But it was too late, just as they crested the hill, he saw the spotlight reach out and capture the man in its beam. They froze as the light washed over them, momentarily blinding them. The man continued running toward the beach, shouting as he went.

Suddenly a single shot rang out.

Murphy had never been shot before and somehow he thought it would hurt more. He looked down, expecting to see blood oozing out of his vest but found none. Suddenly it dawned on him that he was not the target. He looked over at Kai and saw that he was still standing too.

Shielding his eyes from the glare of the searchlight, he saw the mercenary sprawled on the sand.

When they had captured them, they had stripped the men of their uniforms so the only thing the mercenary had on when he escaped was his boxer shorts. From two hundred yards away and in the middle of the night, he must have looked like a running native, so his fellow soldiers of fortune on the ship had shot him.

Murphy quickly turned to Kai. "Go get the others and bring them here. We've got to move *now*. Where's Thing One?"

"He's gone."

"What?"

Kai looked crestfallen. "He knocked out his guard and slipped away during the confusion."

Murphy sighed, "Well we can't worry about that now. We got to get to the ship before he does. Okay, everyone line up, you know what to do."

He grabbed the radio and in his best approximation of Thing One, growled. "Thanks for the assist. We have more prisoners, bringing them in shortly."

Hoku immediately replied, asking what was going on.

Murphy moved back into the spotlight and waved, then held up the radio and pointed to it shaking his head, pretending he couldn't hear him. He pointed and shook his head several more times then turned and went back down the trail.

"Hurry up!" Murphy shouted.

The four natives masquerading as prisoners lined up and Murphy tied their hands behind their backs using a taut-line hitch knot. At a glance the ropes looked secure but with one simple tug they could free themselves.

Murphy picked up an assault rifle and handed one to Kai. "You and your men can handle these?"

Kai grunted. "Point this end at bad guy and pull trigger."

Murphy couldn't help but laugh at how much Kekao had really sounded like him. He nodded to the big man, "Let's go."

Murphy took the lead, followed by one of the guards, who led the four prisoners with the other man and Kai bringing up the rear. They crested the knoll and immediately the radio sounded again, Hoku demanding information. Murphy ignored it as they continued to the boat. They had to hurry; Murphy could see another boat being prepped to come ashore. They could not afford to get caught on the beach when the other boat landed.

They had just got the Zodiac in the water and were starting the engine as the boat on the *Pacific Searcher* was lifted off the deck by the crane. They had made it to the water in time, but Murphy couldn't breathe a sigh of relief yet. They had been incredibly lucky so far. He hoped their luck held out.

It was up to Doug now to give the signal, or else this was going to be a very short ride.

CHAPTER FORTY ONE

"Why does a tropical paradise have to have so much jungle?" Crawford muttered to himself as another low-hanging vine he didn't see in the dark slapped him in the face. "It was never like this in the Jungle Adventure at Disneyland. Nice, easy to walk on trails, no annoying insects, no pirate mercenaries stealing your ship and trying to take over the world."

Crawford had seen the ship's searchlight and knew, as one of his favorite literary characters might say, that the game was afoot. He'd made sure the men on the far side of the bay were ready to go, but he wanted to get a better view of the ship to give the signal so he rushed back over to the other side. He was also a little worried about Ru and didn't want to leave him by himself when everything started.

Crawford pushed aside a huge leaf and saw Ru standing at the end of the small clearing. Even in the dark he could see that the boy looked scared, but it was more: he looked almost sad. Crawford couldn't blame him. After all, he was a twelve-year-boy growing up in an isolated, tropical paradise one day, and the next thrust into a world where death and deceit were common occurrences.

"Hey Ru, it's okay; everything is going to be all right."

"Oh, I don't think so."

Crawford heard the words, but they didn't come from the lips of his young friend. Thing One stepped out of the shadows, holding onto the boy's arm. Crawford immediately raised his musket.

The mercenary stepped behind the boy and squeezed his arm hard, forcing him to squeal from pain. "I wouldn't do that if I were you. Now throw down the gun or I'll snap his neck."

For a moment, Crawford was tempted to take the shot, but only for a moment. He knew that even at this close range he wouldn't trust the accuracy of the musket, especially at night. Crawford reluctantly threw the musket down.

"I'm sorry Mr. Doug, I..."

"Shut up." Thing One said, then spun the boy around and backhanded him hard, knocking him unconscious to the ground.

"Why you son of a..."

"Oh don't worry; you'll get your chance to get a piece of me," Thing One laughed loudly. "You and I have some unfinished business."

In three quick strides he was in front of Crawford and shoved him hard to the ground. "You shot me, you little weasel! That hurt like hell."

He reached down with his left hand and grabbed Crawford by the collar, then lifted him up, only to pound him back to the ground with a strong right fist. He did this several times and then kicked the helpless Crawford in the ribs.

Crawford tried to protect himself but the mercenary was just too strong. With the last kick, Crawford felt a rib crack and let out a cry of pain.

"Oh did that hurt?" the man taunted, "You haven't even begun to feel real pain yet."

"Leave him alone."

Thing One turned around to see Ru standing, aiming a musket at him. "Why is everyone trying to shoot me?" He didn't sound very worried.

"Run!" Crawford yelled.

"Stay where you are," Thing One snapped back, "or I'll kill your friend right now." He then delivered another kick to the ribs to show his intentions. Crawford tried to stifle a cry of pain but wasn't very successful.

"Give me the gun," the mercenary said, reaching out his hand. Ru hesitated and the man shouted, "I said, give me the gun!"

Then he kicked Crawford again, only much harder this time. "I can do this all day, you know. Now give me the gun!"

Ru still hesitated, which made the mercenary even angrier. "You're going to pay for that," he said as he stepped over Crawford and lunged for the boy.

CHAPTER FORTY TWO

Murphy was in the bow of the boat as Kai shoved them off the beach and started the engine. He could see that one Zodiac had just been lowered and that the last of boats was getting ready to be lifted off the deck.

Where was Crawford? Murphy wondered impatiently. He should have given the signal by now. They could only go so slow before they reached the ship and without the distraction, they would be caught immediately. "Damn it Doug, where are you?"

Suddenly there was a flash of light and a split second later the loud crack of gun going off. Murphy could tell it was one of the muskets and not a mercenary weapon.

But that wasn't the signal. What was going on? What was Doug doing? Murphy wanted to scream out loud. But then again, what if it wasn't Doug?

Murphy's stomach turned as he remembered that Thing One had escaped. What if he had found Doug? What if he had defied Hoku's orders not to harm them and had killed him instead because Doug had shot him? If he did, then there would be no signal and the natives wouldn't know what to do. He had drilled into their heads not to do anything until they heard the signal.

He looked up and saw that the first boat just beginning to pull away from the ship. Time was running out. Think Murphy, think!

Then he heard it.

A lone, single blast of a horn wailed, piercing the silent night. Murphy smiled to himself. "Way to go, Doug!" he said quietly, then spoke out loud. "Get ready to give it full throttle, Kai."

Suddenly they were surrounded by a symphony of sound as every member of the tribe blew into their conch horns as long and loud as they could. A second later the darkness was pierced. Light streamed from the jungle as the natives all broke open their pots, each of which had a burning torch inside. The effect was spectacular as the jungle surrounding the ship seemed to explode in light and sound. The icing on the cake came when Crawford and his men all fired their muskets.

"Now!" Murphy shouted.

Kai opened up the throttle on their boat and everyone started shouting out wildly that they were all under attack. Just then, the rattle of the machine gun tapped out a short steady beat. At first, the women's aim was off; rounds splashed into the water or ricocheted from the hull.

After the first few bursts, they managed to hit the boat that was just pulling away from the ship. Several men were hit and the rest jumped over the side as the boat sped away with no one at the controls. Kai just missed a collision with it, barely steering their boat out of the way as the *Flying Dutchman* went speeding by.

The pandemonium of light and sound was glorious.

Then men on deck were shooting wildly into the jungle, not realizing the natives with the torches had disappeared moments after they had broken the pots. The crane had another Zodiac hovering about three feet off the deck when everything had started. It now started swinging wildly like an out of control pendulum, knocking over men and equipment, adding to the chaos.

Murphy could see that Parker was the one running the crane and he knew that the crewman was an expert at handling it; he was taking advantage of the situation by slinging the boat across the deck to cause a little mayhem of his own. Some of the mercenaries were also coming to that same conclusion and were pointing their weapons at him ready to fire, but before they could, another burst of machine gun fire raked the ship, scattering them. Murphy saw Parker dive out of the cab of the crane and disappear.

Confusion reigned on the deck of the *Pacific Searcher*. Everyone was too busy fighting the unseen enemy to pay them any attention as their hijacked Zodiac pulled alongside, which was just what Murphy was hoping for.

He had thought long and hard about this moment, about when he would set foot back on board the ship and what he would have to do. This wasn't a bar brawl and wasn't a game; everyone here was playing for keeps. He knew that if someone were invading his home or threatening a loved one, he could take a life, but could he simply point his gun at someone and just pull the trigger?

He wasn't a soldier, trained to kill, but after much soul searching he realized that the answer was, yes. He was not pulling the trigger to save the world; he had to make the reason smaller, more personal. He wasn't fighting for a great cause, but to save his shipmates, get justice for the death of the captain, and perhaps most important of all, to save Sarah. Those were the reason why he could step onto the ship and start shooting if he had to.

Murphy grabbed a line and pulled himself up on deck. He quickly made the boat fast and reached down and started helping the natives out.

"Hey, what are you doing?" Murphy heard a shout behind him. He turned his head and slowly brought up his rifle. The moment of truth had come sooner rather than later.

He turned and looked at the man; he had a hard, lean face and cold eyes but there was no look of recognition.

Good, Murphy thought. "I've got prisoners for Hoku. Get over here and help me with them."

The man hesitated for a moment and Murphy couldn't tell if he was suspicious or just didn't want to get caught out in the open.

"Now!" Murphy shouted again.

The man decided it was better to obey than to question and came rushing over. Murphy stood on one side while the man stood on the other and together they helped the natives and the fake guards out of the boat.

As they were getting out, everyone kept their heads down so the man couldn't get a clear view of their faces. Kai was the last one in the boat.

As he reached up and took the man's hand, Kai looked the mercenary straight in the eyes.

Kai held his gaze for a moment until the man suddenly recognized him, which was what he was waiting for. A slight smile curled Kai's lips as he suddenly yanked the man down into the boat and in one easy motion spun him around and rammed his head into the side of the ship. The mercenary's body went limp and Kai let it slip quietly into the water.

Kai reached up and Murphy grabbed his hand and pulled him onboard. "He was not friendly to our people," Kai remarked.

"Remind me not to get on your bad side," Murphy replied.

The native just looked at him, not quite understanding what he meant.

"Never mind. Come on, we've got to get below and free the rest of the crew."

Just then, another volley of machine gun fire slammed into the ship, hitting a few of the mercenaries and sending several more diving into the water.

"Besides, we might be safer below deck than on it," he said only half-jokingly. Murphy had briefed everyone on the layout of the ship and they all knew exactly where the crew's quarters were, and where the small arms locker was. The plan was to use the ploy of escorting the native prisoners as long as they could, then fight their way through if they had to.

The searchlight, which was mounted on a platform on the mast above the superstructure swung to the left, following the tracers, and swept toward the hilltop where the machine gun nest was situated. All the men on deck concentrated their fire there, laying down a withering barrage.

"We must destroy that light," Kai shouted.

"I know, but we have to wait." Murphy replied.

"Wait for what? We must go now."

Murphy shook his head. "I'm sorry, Kai but if we make our move now, they'll just mow us down. I know it's hard, but we have to be patient for just a moment longer."

Suddenly it became quiet as the gunfire stopped; the mercenaries had emptied all their clips. Just then Murphy heard a single shot ring out. He could tell that it was one of the muskets but it was different; louder, more powerful. There was a flash of light, then sparks flew everywhere as the spotlight blew up.

"Perfect timing, Doug. Hell of a shot too." Murphy patted Kai on the back. "Now we go."

With everyone's attention on the exploding spotlight, Murphy leaned around the corner of the stern deckhouse and began firing. He hit two men who were on the main deck, then ducked back behind the corner so they couldn't see where the gunfire was coming from.

He turned back around to tell Kai to go around to the other side but he was nowhere to be seen. Where had he gone? Murphy wondered angrily; he had told Kai to stay with him.

Murphy was just leaning around the corner again when he heard a noise above him. He looked up just in time to get out of the way of a falling body. He stared at the body in surprise then swung up his gun.

Kai was leaning over the edge and smiling. "I am better with this," he said, holding up his knife with one hand, "than this," he said, holding up the rifle with the other.

Murphy just nodded. "I'm going to work my way up to the bridge. Go below and help the others find the crew. But be careful, you're dressed like a bad guy and my crew doesn't know you. If you get in trouble, tell them I sent you."

Kai nodded then disappeared. Murphy made his way over to the starboard side of the ship and inched his way along the stern deckhouse, working toward the bow and the bridge. There were fewer men on this side of the ship and Murphy used the distraction of one of the native musket volleys to club one of the mercenaries with the butt of his rifle.

Murphy was now faced with a choice: should he work his way up to the bridge though the inside passages where he would have a better chance of getting there undetected, or simply sprint up the two flights of stairs on the outside and rush the bridge?

Time versus speed, stealth versus surprise. What should he do?

"The hell with it," he said. He turned the corner to go up the ladder, and came face-to-face with one of the mercenaries.

"Sorry." Murphy said, quickly recovering. He nodded to the man then as nonchalantly as he could moved to step around him. He was almost past him when out of the corner of his eye he saw a flash of recognition on the man's face: the mercenary knew who he was.

Murphy spun around and tried to hit him with the butt of his rifle, but they were too close and he only succeeded in shoving him against the bulkhead. The mercenary threw a quick left punch with his free hand that snapped Murphy's head back and split his lip, but did no real damage.

"I don't have time for this," Murphy growled. He reared back and head butted his adversary in the face. He was rewarded with an instant headache, but also, more importantly, with the sound of snapping bone and cartilage; he had broken the man's nose. With his opponent reeling from the pain, Murphy grabbed him by his collar and heaved him over the railing.

Murphy dashed up the stairs two at a time, and rushed onto the bridge deck. He crouched down and quickly made his way to the starboard flying bridge and stole a quick peek. Hoku, Sarah, and one other guard were the only ones there.

Murphy took several deep breaths, then flung open the door and charged in. The guard immediately tried to draw his pistol but Murphy was quicker as he fired two rounds into the man's chest. Hoku immediately raised his arms in a signal of surrender.

Murphy locked the door behind him and rushed over and locked the other two doors, making sure to keep his rifle trained on Hoku. He then went over and checked the man lying on the floor. He saw blood pooling beneath his body, and realized the man hadn't been wearing a vest.

"Welcome Mr. Murphy, we've been expecting you," Hoku said, almost cheerfully.

"Couldn't you come up with something a little more original than that?" Murphy asked.

"Thank God you're here," Sarah said as she stood up and ran over and gave him a big hug.

Murphy kept the gun leveled at Hoku. "Tie him up," he said to her.

"You'd better do it," Sarah said, shaking her head. "You always could tie knots better than me. Give me the rifle and I'll keep an eye on him."

Murphy nodded then handed Sarah the rifle. Sarah took a step back and Hoku immediately drew the gun from his holster. "Sarah..." Murphy started to warn her but stopped in midsentence when he saw that instead of aiming the gun at Hoku, she was handing it over to him.

"Sarah?"

Hoku bellowed with laughter as Murphy stood dumbfounded, watching Sarah casually walk back and sit down at her workstation.

"Don't act so surprised Dallas," Sarah said, "I got to thinking that I was willing to help for nothing. Save the planet, but who was going to save me? Hoku is right; it's all about motivation. How's a seven figure paycheck for motivation? But I need your help."

"My help, why?"

"Doug was very clever, both in how he deceived Hoku, and how he got into the L.E.M. program. But Doug's not the only one who knows his way around a keyboard. And while you didn't realize it, you had the second set of confirmation codes needed to access the file all this time."

"What are you talking about Sarah? Like I told Hoku earlier, I don't have any codes."

Sarah smiled. "You see, that's the beauty of it. You have the codes but just don't realize it. That is part of the built in security system for an event like this. You have the failsafe set and would only be told about it in case of an emergency."

"Okay, even if what you say is true, why would I want to help you? You betrayed us all, *twice*. You got the captain killed, and now you expect me to just say, 'sure, no problem'?"

"Think about it Dallas. We'll be set for life! We can do anything we want, anytime. Hoku is not some wacko terrorist who wants to blow up the world; he's out to make a buck just like everyone else. You know I'm right Dallas, the two of us could be so happy together. I can get my castle and you can be my knight in shining armor again." She smiled. "Not to mention having your own killer man cave.

"You just think about it while I start the sequence for accessing the L.E.M. file. She turned from him and started typing on the keyboard. "Again, because of security protocols, we will be accessing the release codes through another program. You might want to go to Doug's station and start working. Just punch in your password and start working on the *Kobayashi Maru* file."

"*Kobayashi Maru?*" Murphy said, with a puzzled look.

"Pretty clever huh?" She replied with a wink.

Murphy offered no resistance as she got up and led him over to Crawford's work station and sat him down. She returned to her station while Murphy just sat there like the proverbial bump on a log. He heard Hoku in the background, rambling on, either threating him or trying to convince him that it was in his best interest to cooperate, but he wasn't listening. He was too busy trying to process everything that Sarah had said.

Was she really doing this?

"Dallas!" He heard his name being shouted.

"Stay with me here," Sarah said, "I can't do this alone. You're going to have to trust me on this one, Dallas."

He wanted to believe; he wanted to trust Sarah and to believe that this would all have a happy ending but he just wasn't sure. He didn't know if he had the faith.

Right or wrong, he started typing.

Hoku became transfixed as he watched Murphy typing, slowly realizing that his goal was finally within his grasp, that all the planning and hard work was paying off. Mesmerized, he slowly got up and absent mindedly placed his gun on the arm of the chair.

Murphy was typing faster now, his fingers moving with purpose. Hoku was standing behind him, staring intensely at the screen. Neither he nor Murphy noticed Sarah as she moved.

"Stop, Dallas!"

Both men turned to find Sarah standing behind them, holding Hoku's gun.

"Move," Sarah said, looking at Hoku, flipping the barrel of the gun off to the side. "I just want to make sure you don't get hurt when I blow his head off." She was talking to Murphy, but her eyes never left Hoku.

"What are you doing Sarah?" Murphy asked, looking very confused.

"I'm going to kill him," she replied in a cold monotone. "I could have killed you earlier," she said staring coldly at him, "and trust me, it was all I could do not to."

"Well then why didn't you then if you had the chance?" Hoku said, sarcastically, taunting her.

Because I had to wait until you brought the ship back here so we could recapture it."

"Don't do this Sarah," Murphy pleaded. "He's not worth it. You'll regret it for the rest of your life."

She smiled hollowly. "No I won't. He took everything from me. I trusted him and believed in his cause only to find out that it was all a lie and I was just being used. He made me betray my friends, the trust you had in me and it led to the death of Captain Yates, and *that* is something that I will regret for the rest of my life, not shooing this scum bag."

"I had so hoped that you would have made the right decision," Hoku said as he slowly shook his head. "But I can see that you still have misguided loyalties. Such a pity."

"Pity this," Sarah said as she pointed the gun at Hoku's chest and pulled the trigger.

The silence was deafening.

Instead of smoke and the smell of gunpowder, it was laughter that filled the room. Hoku wagged his head at Sarah's look of utter dismay as he reached into his pocket and pulled out another gun. "I had hoped you had really joined us but I had to be sure, so I left the gun on the chair."

"You mean this was a test?" Sarah said bitterly.

Hoku smirked. "I left the gun to see what your true intentions were, and yes, it was a test and I'm afraid you failed."

Murphy watched the exchange going on between Hoku and Sarah and he couldn't tell if she was more upset that she got caught or that he was testing her. He slowly inched his way to the side, hoping that the distraction would be enough that he could jump Hoku. It wasn't.

"That's far enough Dallas," Hoku said as he pointed the gun at him. "Unlike yours," he said looking back at Sarah, "this one is loaded."

Hoku stepped up and took the gun out of Sarah's hand then sat back down in his chair. "Do I really need to demonstrate my intentions again Dallas?" He pointed the gun at Sarah. "Now finish typing in the codes."

"Okay, okay," Murphy stared at the screen for a moment then slowly moved his hands to the keyboard. He touched the keys then quickly pulled his hands back.

"Quit stalling," Hoku said impatiently as Murphy heard the unmistakable sound of the pistol being cocked.

Murphy took a deep breath and typed in the last code sequence. Then he turned around and looked at Hoku.

"All you have to do is hit the 'enter' key," he said as he slowly stood, "I just can't do it, so be my guest." He took two steps back and waited.

Hoku looked at Murphy for a moment then a smile spread across his face. He stepped down from the chair and stood in front of the computer, a look of triumph filling his face. Then he reached down and hit the 'enter' key.

The screen went blank for a moment, then it was replaced with a star field and the theme music from the original *Star Trek* began to play. The Starship *Enterprise* came into view and fired a photon torpedo straight at the screen. In the lower left hand corner of the screen there was a digital counter that started at five and went backwards. As the counter reached zero, the torpedo exploded. A brilliant, white flash filled the display, and then it went blank.

Hoku stared at the screen in disbelief, not knowing what to think. Suddenly they heard a rumbling deep within the ship and then what sounded like a series of circuit breakers being tripped.

The entire ship was thrust into darkness.

"You tricked me!" Hoku shouted out angrily.

Murphy was just about to lunge at Hoku, but the other man seemed to read his mind. "Don't," he ordered, "or after I kill you, Sarah will be next."

Murphy clenched his fists in frustration then took a step back, but his gaze never left Hoku's. Even in the dark he could see Hoku's angry, icy stare, rage burning in his eyes at being tricked. Murphy took a small measure of satisfaction at Hoku's frustration, but that was erased by what the man did next.

Hoku started to laugh.

It started out as a few chuckles, but grew in intensity and soon turned into full belly laughs verging on hysteria. Even though it was dark, Murphy and Sarah both looked at each other to see if either knew why Hoku was laughing.

"What's so funny?" Murphy asked.

"I'm sorry. It's just that the irony here is beyond words. You see, in your botched attempt to stop me, the only thing that you managed to do is insure my success. You've sealed your own fate and now there is no way to stop me." Hoku again burst into laughter.

"What are you talking about?"

"I came back to get the rest of the codes because I wanted to have the virus completely uploaded into the mainframe before the end of the maintenance cycle. That way it would go completely undetected. But after this," Hoku replied, waving his arms around the darkened room, "I suddenly realized I don't need the codes. I may not be able to download it directly, but the virus is still in the system nonetheless, thanks to you and your friend.

"When the maintenance cycle is over, the virus will simply be uploaded along with all the other waiting data that's been stored until the computer was up and running again. And now that you've destroyed the electrical system of the ship, there's no way you can warn them about it or stop it. You may have won the battle, but you've lost the war."

Murphy was stunned at the implications of Hoku's words. Had they just shot themselves in the foot, doing more harm than good or was Hoku just stalling, trying to buy time?

He felt the news as if it were a physical blow. He had felt like this only one other time in his life, the day Sarah had told him that she wanted a divorce.

He felt like collapsing in despair, but something caught his eye, a flash of movement, a shadow moving in behind Hoku. Murphy tried not to stare and looked away as quickly as he could. He wasn't sure if Hoku could see the expression in his eyes in the dark room but he didn't want to take the chance and alert him.

"Good evening Mr. Crawford," Hoku said, "you move quietly for a big man, but now quietly enough." Hoku quickly spun around and brought up the gun.

The flash was blinding and the gun's report was ear-shattering. Sarah screamed as a body crumpled to the floor.

CHAPTER FORTY THREE

"I also move pretty darn fast too," Crawford said, standing over the dead body of Hoku.

"Doug!" Murphy and Sarah shouted in unison and both rushed forward to hug their friend.

"How did you get in here?" Murphy asked. "I locked the doors."

Crawford smiled and held up a set of keys, "I'm a bridge officer, remember?"

"I take it that since you're here, we won?"

"The battle is pretty much over. A few of Hoku's men escaped into the jungle but Kai and his warriors are tracking them down, so I expect they'll be in captivity very soon, and the rest of the mercenaries are either dead or being locked up in the cargo hold even as we speak."

"Did you hear what Hoku said?" Murphy asked. "Is he right? Is the virus already in the computer now? Did we go through all this for nothing?"

"It depends; he's essentially right if you didn't transmit the AA code before you fried everything."

"AA code? What are you talking about? I don't understand, I don't even know what that is," Sarah replied defensively.

"An AA code, Address Alert Code, is a code that alerts the mainframe that there's a potential threat from an IP address and it puts everything sent from that IP into a spam folder to be looked at on an offline computer to determine whether there's a threat or not."

"Great, just great!" Sarah said, and threw her hands up in bitter frustration. "We fried the radio so there's no way to warn anybody so that means we went through all of this for nothing. That's it then, we're screwed."

Murphy shook his head, "I refuse to have come this far only to be defeated. There has to be something we can do."

"Nice thought," Sarah said, "but you heard Doug. We didn't upload the AA code, there's nothing we can do."

"Is there still time to upload the AA code?" Murphy asked.

"Aren't you listening," Sarah said, frustrated. "All the electronics are fried; we have no way to transmit it, and even if we did, we're too far south. We'd have to travel north like Hoku did in order to be within range of the satellite. We're dead in the water, both figuratively and literally."

Murphy ignored her. "If there *was* a way to transmit the code, could we?"

Crawford thought for a moment then slowly nodded. "We'd have to upload the alert so the techs would see it before the end of the maintenance cycle."

"Which would be...?"

"Which would be tonight." Crawford looked at his watch. "At about six o'clock our time."

"What if we used the radio in the chopper?" Murphy asked. "It wasn't affected by the ship's meltdown."

Crawford shook his head. "Like Sarah said, we're too far south for the satellite link up, and besides, the radio doesn't have the range."

"So we fly the chopper north until it *is* in range."

"The chopper's radio's power output is too low. The signal strength is too weak for the satellite to pick it up."

"But if it was strong enough, how far north would we have to go before we'd be in range?" Murphy asked.

Crawford shook his head again and shrugged. "It's hard to say. Four, maybe five hundred miles."

Sarah looked at Murphy. "Well, can it fly that far?" she asked, her tone still guarded.

"You leave that part up to me; you two techno geeks need to come up with a way to boost the radio's power output."

Sarah shook her head. "You're serious aren't you? You know this is a crazy idea, right?"

Murphy raised his hands and swept them around the room. "No crazier than all of this."

Sarah nodded reluctantly. "I guess I can't argue with that. So how much time do we have?"

Crawford looked at his watch again and did some quick mental calculations. "Considering the distance involved to get within satellite range, the speed of the chopper and the timing of the satellite's orbits, we have four, maybe five hours tops to prep the chopper before it has to be in the air."

Now it was Murphy's turn to look at his watch. "That doesn't give us much time then, does it?" He clapped his hands together like he was coming out of a football huddle.

"So let's get moving then, people!"

The next several hours were a flurry of activity, with everyone focused on the helicopter, tending to the machine like workers bees attending to their queen.

With fifteen minutes to take-off, Murphy tightened the last bolt and stood back admiring his handy work when he was joined by Crawford.

"Okay," Murphy said, "everything is all set on my end. As you can see, I jury-rigged two auxiliary fuel tanks on the inside of the struts where they meet the pontoons. I'm hoping they'll give us another 150 miles or so."

He walked over and opened the cockpit door and looked in. "Okay, explain to me how this thing that you and Sarah built works." He looked at his watch. "Give me the short version; I gotta be going."

"You don't have the time to learn how it works and we don't have the time to stand here and argue. I'm going with you to work the controls."

Both men turned to see Sarah walking up wearing a green flight suit and carrying a pack over her shoulder. "This Frankenstein monster of circuits Doug and I created here is not some plug-and-play

DVD player. You won't be able fly and operate it at the same time, so the sooner you accept that I have to go with you, the sooner we can get out of here. Besides, don't you remember what the chief said about arguing with me?"

Murphy turned to Crawford for help, but his friend just held up his hands. "Hey, I've seen that look before, and I'm not foolish enough to even try to change her mind...are you?"

Murphy sighed in resignation. Crawford was right. When Sarah had that look, there was no point in arguing, besides, she was right. "Get in," he grunted. He knew she had to go, but he didn't have to like it, but deep down inside he was glad she was going.

"I rigged up a portable generator to one of the secondary short range radios that we had in storage for parts." Crawford said. "The signal is pretty weak, but I should be able to stay in contact with you for at least a little while."

Murphy nodded in approval. "Good. It'll be nice to know you'll be there if we need you."

Murphy threw the ignition switch on the Hughes/MD500 that had been specially fitted with pontoons for marine use. The 420 hp Allison engine roared to life, and the 13-foot rotor blades started spinning. Quickly the whoosh, whoosh, whoosh of the rotating airfoils turned into a deafening roar as the blades swept hurricane force winds across the deck of the ship.

Crawford gave them a thumbs-up then motioned that he was going up to the bridge.

"Can you hear me?" Crawford asked a moment later.

"Five by five, Doug." The helicopter whined as Murphy increased to full power. They lifted off the deck a few inches then fell back down, bouncing like a basketball on the rubber pontoons.

"She's heavy. The extra fuel and all the equipment you guys installed is really weighing her down," Murphy said over the headset. "I'm going to have to redline her to get off the deck."

The engine whined even louder as Murphy pushed the struggling helicopter to its limit. The chopper slowly climbed and at two hundred feet, Murphy turned the tail around and pointed the nose out to sea.

"Okay Doug, we're on our way. I'll keep you posted."

"Roger that, and good luck."

Murphy worked the controls of the struggling aircraft with all the skills and deftness of a brain surgeon and the touch of a magician. With agonizing slowness, they reached five thousand feet where Murphy leveled the aircraft out. With a visible sigh of relief, he relaxed his grip on the controls.

"Okay, what kind of techno magic did you and Doug come up with?"

"Doug wanted to boost the range of the signal while I wanted to increase the power strength of the signal."

"Range versus power?"

Sarah nodded. "He argued that the most important thing we needed was to extended range while I said that that didn't matter if the signal was too weak for the satellite to lock onto it and upload the data."

"Why not do both?"

"Because we didn't have time. We only had enough time to install one set of components, not two. However, we compromised as best we could. I managed to increase the signal strength by fifty percent while increasing the range by about twenty percent."

"Doesn't sound like a bad compromise. How long until we're within transmission range?"

"It'll be about an hour or so until we're at the outer limits, two to three for optimum range. Speaking of range," she said, pointing out the front windshield, "those clouds don't look too friendly."

In front of them, a massive bank of clouds was moving down from the north, quickly consuming the surrounding blue sky. They weren't a swirling mass of clouds like a hurricane or tornado, but moved as one solid unit, like a giant slab of concrete moving across the sky. The clouds were dark and menacing, heavy with wind and rain. A single bolt of lightning slashed across the front like a warning signal telling them to turn around and go back.

"No, they don't look very friendly do they?" Murphy said. "But we don't have the fuel or the time to fly around them and they reach too high to go above them. You'd better stow everything the best you can, we're in for bumpy flight."

Sarah quickly secured everything and they flew for about half an hour, passing the time in idle conversation. A few times the helicopter bounced through pockets of turbulence, like a car running over a rough road, but nothing worse than either of them had experienced during a regular commercial airline flight.

Without warning, rain splattered against the windshield like it was being fired from a shotgun. The assault was so sudden and forceful that Sarah let out an involuntary yelp and Murphy jerked the controls, bouncing the helicopter, adding all the more to the confusion. Murphy quickly recovered but the helicopter continued to shake as the storm began to flex its muscles. Another shaft of lighting flashed across the front of the chopper, giving them one last warning.

The rain was now slapping against the canopy in waves, like breakers pounding a shore. The wind also joined in the fray, pummeling the flying machine from every direction.

"How much longer until we're within range?" Murphy shouted over the drone of the engine and howling of the storm.

"About an hour or so till optimum range," Sarah shouted back.

"We don't have an hour. Start transmitting now!"

After a few minutes of fidgeting with the controls, she flipped the last switch and a series of five green lights in a row blinked on then off with the first light flickering intermittently like the dots and dashes of someone sending Morse code.

"Okay flyboy, it's up to you to keep us in the air long enough for the signal to get through." Sarah said. "See those five lights? They're just like the bars on your cell phone, the more bars you have, the greater the signal strength and the better chance we have of reaching the satellite."

By now, the first light was burning steadily with the second light flashing intermittently and the third sporadic but very weak. Sarah fiddled with the controls and the second light turned to a steady glow.

Suddenly a blinding, brilliantly bright flash of light flooded the cockpit of the helicopter and it started to spin out of control. They had been struck by lightning.

"Dallas!"

"It's okay, I got it," he lied. He could see panic beginning to fill Sarah's eyes but to her credit she hadn't given into it yet. "Your lights are out," he shouted, pointing to the transmitter. He knew the system was probably fried from the lightning strike but he knew he had to give her something to concentrate on or else panic would tear her to pieces. "See if you can get that thing turned back on."

Sarah nodded and eagerly concentrated on her equipment.

The helicopter bounced up and down and twisted like a mechanical bull in a country western bar. Between struggling with the controls, he managed to stop the spinning and turn off the alarms.

"Dallas!" He heard her shout his name again, only this time her voice was filled with even more panic than before. "Fire! We're on fire!"

Murphy looked down through the window at his feet and saw that there were flames on the pontoon and that they were following a tiny trickle of gas that was leaking from the external fuel tank. Even though the tanks were nearly empty, he knew that if the flames reached them, the explosion would be enough to either bring them down or completely blow them out of the sky.

"Hang on!"

The helicopter started spinning again, only this time Murphy was doing it on purpose. He was trying to put out the flames, which shouldn't have been too difficult considering how hard it was raining and how fast the wind was blowing. But the flames stubbornly refused to go out.

The helicopter had rubberized fabric pontoons that were lighter and stronger than their aluminum counterparts and the flames had worked their way into the inner lining so the wind and rain were having no effect on the smoldering fire; it would be only a matter of time before the flames reached the fuel tank.

"Come over here," Murphy shouted.

Sarah saw the look on Murphy's face and she didn't like what she saw. "You're not thinking what I think you're thinking are you? I can't fly this thing."

"You know me far too well, and yes, you can. You have to!"

"I can't!"

"Yes you can! If you don't we'll both be dead in less than five minutes. I need you to slide under me so I will be sitting on your lap. As soon as I tell you to, I want you to grab the cyclic here and hold it as steady as you can."

"The what?"

"The cyclic, the control stick here in the middle."

Sarah reluctantly slid over and tucked herself under Murphy as he awkwardly tried to raise himself up and fly the helicopter at the same time.

"Have you gained weight?" Sarah said in a faint attempt at nervous humor as Murphy settled down onto her lap.

"Very funny. Now reach over with your right hand and grab the stick."

When he was sure she had a good grip, he slowly let go so she could get a feel for it. The chopper wobbled a little but she controlled it remarkably well.

"Good job. Now reach over with your left hand and grab the collective, the control here on the left side of the seat. It takes two hands to fly a helicopter so you need to keep it as level as possible so I can kick the tank off and get back in, okay?"

"You're crazy, you know that, right?" Sarah said.

Murphy put his hand on the door handle then turned back to her. "Yeah, but that's why you married me in the first place isn't it? Now keep it as level and steady as you can."

"Yes it was," she whispered under her breath.

Murphy tightened his grip on the handle then opened the door. Instantly the wind caught the door and flung it open, yanking him halfway out and then as if it were spring loaded, another gust slammed the door shut, shoving him back into the cockpit. He crashed into Sarah, sending her flying to the other side of the canopy.

Immediately the helicopter started spinning and losing altitude fast. The door hit Murphy in the head when it slammed shut and he lay dazed and crumpled, lying halfway in the seat and halfway on the floor. He blinked hard trying to bring things back into focus, but with alarms blaring and the helicopter spinning like a top, he was fighting a losing battle.

He caught a glimpse of Sarah and saw terror filled eyes, but she pulled herself together. Fear was replaced with determination as she struggled to reach over and grab him.

With her help, he managed to get back into his seat and the whirling dervish slowed to a stop as he regained control. A quick glance at the altimeter showed they had lost nearly four thousand feet in their out-of-control plunge.

"Are you okay?" He asked.

"Just peachy," she said as she plopped back down into her seat. She looked at him and then pointed. "The question is, are *you* okay?"

Murphy gave her a funny look then turned around and looked at the side of the canopy where she was pointing. The window in the door was shattered and looked like a giant spider web where his head had slammed into it. "Wow, and I don't even have a headache," he paused then quickly continued, "and no comment about my hard head either."

Murphy looked down and saw the smoldering flames were just inches from the connector valve. "Hurry. We have to try this again." Sarah scooted over and took the controls again and Murphy braced himself as he grabbed the door handle once more. This time he barely cracked it open. When it didn't fly open and yank him into space, he opened it a little more and put his left foot down on top of the pontoon.

Murphy was immediately soaked to the bone the second he stepped out and Sarah didn't fare much better as the wind propelled the rain into the cockpit. She started to shiver and shake from the cold but managed to keep the helicopter level. Murphy gave her one last nod then lowered his other foot onto the pontoon and carefully inched his way forward, just enough for his left foot to reach the fuel tank.

He reared his leg up and brought it down hard on the tank. Pain shot through his leg from the impact but the tank didn't budge.

"Hurry up!" Sarah shouted between chattering teeth. "I'm freezing and I can't hold it steady much longer."

Murphy didn't answer as he concentrated on the tank. He could see small wisps of smoke escaping from the pontoon.

Just as he raised his leg to strike again, a gust of wind flooded through the open door, filling the cockpit like a parachute. The blast was so powerful that it sent Sarah reeling for a second time back across the cockpit, to end up plastered against the far door. She looked up and screamed when she saw the other canopy door had slammed shut and didn't see Murphy standing on the pontoon anymore.

CHAPTER FORTY FOUR

The helicopter started to lurch and spin out of control as another set of alarms started going off. Trembling from cold and fear, she jumped back into the pilot's seat and grappled with the controls, struggling to keep the stricken helicopter in the air while frantically looking for Murphy.

When the wind had caught the helicopter, it threw Murphy off balance and he slipped on the wet pontoon which probably saved his life as his fingers would have been severed by the force of the slamming door. His right knee smashed into the fuel tank and pain instantly sliced through his body. The tank held just long enough for him to grab hold of the landing strut before it gave way and tore off. It dangled for a moment, held only by the rubber fuel line. The wind grabbed the tank and tossed it around like it was a piece of paper, slamming it painfully into his leg several more times.

Finally the hose broke and the tank fell away into the abyss. Murphy wanted to sigh with relief that the tank was gone, but he didn't have time. When the tank fell, so did he as he was standing on it. He kept his grip on the strut but was slammed into the steel support.

The reprieve was short lived; he could feel his hands beginning to slip on the rain-soaked strut. The wind was tugging at him as he swung his legs wildly, trying to get them onto the pontoon for support.

He managed to land his right heel on top of the pontoon and he started to pull himself up, but as he did, his heel tore through the pontoon. He looked down with confusion and dismay as a large puff of smoke billowed out from where his foot was. His dismay quickly changed to horror as a flash of flame erupted from the side of the pontoon.

The fire had been smoldering inside the float and had eaten away at the rubberized lining. As his foot broke through, the sudden rush of air and leaking fuel ignited the smoldering embers. In a panic, Murphy starting thrashing wildly, trying to pull his foot out but his heel was caught on the melting side of the pontoon. A tongue of fire shot up out of the hole like a charmed snake and struck at his pant leg. As wet as his pants were from the rain, they easily ignited, being soaked in the high-octane fuel.

Frantically he struggled to pull himself the rest of the way up. Even now, he could feel the heat on his leg but there was nothing he could do. With his last ounce of strength, Murphy pulled himself up onto the float and twisted his foot enough to pop it out of the hole. He hooked one arm around the top of the landing strut and reached down with the other to beat out the flames.

He lay there for a moment, gasping for breath then pushed against the wind and rain and inched his way up to the door. He reached up with his right hand to grab the door but his fingers were just a few tantalizing inches short of the handle. Holding on to the strut, he carefully tucked his knees under him as he prepared to leap for the handle.

Just as he was about to jump, the helicopter jerked to one side and propelled him forward. He easily grabbed the handle but in the process, his face smashed into the door.

Sarah let out a startled scream as she heard the loud smack and saw Murphy's face pressed against the glass. "Get in here!" She shouted and waved him in.

Murphy managed to get the door open, and Sarah hauled him into his seat as she scooted back into hers. Murphy collapsed into the seat and clutched the controls.

As his strength began to return, he noticed the alarm buzzers going off again and quickly scanned the instruments. "This is not good."

"What?"

"When the door was open, the amount of rain that came in was tremendous and now it's worked its way into the instruments and they're beginning to short out. Can you raise Doug?"

Sarah shook her head. "No, the bolt of lightning shorted out the radio. We stopped

transmitting right after it hit."

"Okay, I think that we...." Just then several small sparks shot out of the top instrument panel and half the lights started flickering on and off and another set of alarms added to the now growing symphony.

"Not good, not good. We're going down, and fast. Break out the life raft under your seat and hang on tight."

"Why do we need a life raft?" Sarah questioned. "This thing's got pontoons."

"It's got *one* pontoon! There's a huge hole in the left float. As soon as we hit the water, we'll start to sink. The right one might keep us up long enough to inflate the raft and jump off." Murphy continued to talk while the helicopter spiraled down and Sarah wasted no time in digging out the raft.

"I want your door open before we hit the water. As soon as we touch down, I want you out the door and pulling the inflator cord on the raft. When we hit, the rotor blades will still be turning and when they hit the water they'll throw spray everywhere and make such a racket that you'll think all hell is breaking loose. Ignore it, just get out and get that raft inflated. My side will sink first so I'll be right behind you."

"Dallas..." Sarah said quietly then tapered off.

Murphy looked at her. The six years they'd know each other and the three years they were married passed by in just moments, all the joy, pain, regrets and hopes; the good times and the bad. All the emotions that they had ever shared together seemed to be captured in that single tick-tock moment of time.

"I know," he replied softly. The moment was shattered as they broke through the clouds at a mere five hundred feet above the angry sea beneath them. The waves were covered in white foam as the wind ripped across the surface.

The swells were short and choppy and thankfully not very high. Unless things got dramatically worse, they would be able to ride out the storm in the raft without too much trouble...*if* they didn't get worse.

The helicopter was spiraling down in a tight circle now. It was dizzying but Murphy still had a little control over it. But at a hundred feet, the tail rotor went out and they started spinning wildly. "I've lost it!" Murphy shouted, "hang on!"

The helicopter crashed hard, nose down on the left side. Dazed, Sarah had to take a moment to realize what had happened and where they were. By the time she started to reach for the door handle, she could feel the cold water swirling around her feet.

Instantly she panicked and started clawing at the door, trying to find the handle. By the time she found it and pushed the door open, the water was up to her waist. Frantically she shoved the heavy raft up and out like it was a box of Kleenex.

The helicopter was lying on its side now and she stood on the pontoon and pulled the cord, inflating the raft. Just as she was stepping in, she realized that Murphy wasn't standing beside her. She was just about to step back into the cockpit to search for him when a wave slammed into the helicopter. She fell forward onto the canopy, then bounced off and fell into the water. She heard a loud crack as the helicopter snapped in half and suddenly sank like a rock.

Because it sank so fast and she was so close, the suction started to pull her down with it. She didn't even have time to scream before her head went under water. Sarah kicked with all her might but she could still feel herself being dragged farther and farther underwater. She was just about to give up all hope when she felt a strong hand grab hold of her wrist and yank her up. The force of the jerk nearly pulled her arm out of her socket but she didn't care. At least she was going up now instead of down.

Sarah breached the surface gasping for air. She was so happy to see Murphy and to be alive, she threw her arms around him in a tight hug and nearly drowned him before he could fight her off.

"Come on, let's get in the raft," he said between gulps of air. Murphy grabbed for the trailing rope and started pulling the raft to them. Totally exhausted, the pair barely managed to haul themselves into the raft and seal the flap before they both collapsed.

Murphy slowly opened his eyes to find his world had turned orange. Thinking he was having some sort of dream he blinked several times but the blue sky he remembered just wasn't there. Slowly he became aware of a weight pressing against his chest. He started to look down and for the first time he realized that his head was tilted back. As he brought his head down, his surroundings became clear. When he opened his eyes, he had been staring at the side of the raft, just inches from his face.

He looked down to see Sarah lying on his chest. Her gentle and rhythmic breathing was comforting. Then he also noticed something else; it was quiet and calm. The storm had passed. He tried not to wake her but she stirred as he moved.

"Good morning Sunshine," he said as she opened one eye. She looked up lazily at him and smiled, then shot up like someone had taken a cattle prod to her.

"The helicopter, storm, lighting..."

"It's okay, it's okay, we made it, we're safe."

Sarah took a moment to clear her head. "Does Doug know where we are?"

"He knows our general location from our last contact, but that was two hours before we went down," Murphy replied, his voice trailing off.

"And?"

"And... by general location I mean about a two hundred mile radius which gives them about 40,000 square mile to search in and find an eight foot orange raft and I don't know if we're in the shipping lanes or not.."

"I sure wish you could lie better."

"We'll be okay, we've got a little food and water and we can add to it by catching any rainwater and maybe snag ourselves a fish or two." Murphy chuckled a little. "You said we never had time to talk to each other. Looks like we'll have plenty of time now."

Sarah just looked at him for a moment, then reached over and hit him on the arm. But then she smiled then gave him a little kiss. "Sometimes you're such a dork."

He enjoyed the attention for a few seconds, then clapped his hands together. "Okay, let's see what we've got to work with here."

The excitement of just being alive soon wore off. Checking their supplies, they had enough, if rationed properly, to last them for about nine days; longer if they got rainwater and caught some fish.

The sea was a flat piece of glass, leaving no trace of the maelstrom they had survived. Now their biggest enemy was not the elements but boredom. Gradually the conversation died down and sleeping was the only reprieve.

Life fell into a routine of fishing during the day and stargazing at night. By the end of the third day, as he was drifting off to sleep, Murphy decided that he would rather be here with Sarah the way they were than be anywhere else in the world without her.

"G'day mate."

What a strange dream to be having, Murphy thought. He'd never dreamed with people talking with an accent before.

"Might we be of some assistance?" he heard the voice say.

He didn't want to wake up right now, he wanted to sleep. "Go away," Murphy murmured under his breath as he shifted slightly still holding Sarah as she slept.

Suddenly there was a blast so loud and long Murphy thought the world had ended and it was Judgment Day. He sprang up, nearly throwing Sarah to the other side of the raft as he spun around. He looked up and saw the face of a man with blond hair, in his late twenties, smiling from ear to ear.

"You Yanks sure do love your sleep," the man said. "I'm Tyler Watson of the *White Albatross*. Do you need any help?"

Albatross...Albatross? Murphy thought; then it dawned on him. "You're the research vessel from the University of Sydney, right?" Murphy asked, fully awake now.

"That's us, mate!"

"Dallas, what the..." Sarah said as she stuck her head out the flap. She stopped in mid-sentence when she saw the ship alongside.

"Are we ever glad to see you," Murphy said, "I'm Dallas Murphy and this..."

"Yes, Ms. Price from the *Pacific Searcher*," Watson interrupted. "We arrived at the island two days ago and they told us everything that had happened and asked if we could go looking for you."

"Did we get through?" Murphy asked.

"Don't know. We lost part of our main radio antenna to the storm a few days back, so long range communications is down. Once we get back to Shangri-La, we'll see if we can borrow some parts from your ship and get the radio back up and check in with Sydney."

"Shangri-La?" Sarah asked.

Watson smiled. "Yeah, that's the name we gave to the island where you two came from."

Murphy smiled. "It does fit doesn't it?"

CHAPTER FORTY FIVE

Two days later they were back at the island, seated in front of a roaring fire. The islanders were throwing a celebration feast as a way of thanking Murphy and the others for saving them.

"So Captain..." Murphy said to Watson, "were you able to get through to Sydney yet?"

Watson put down his drink which was in an old ceramic mug. "Just got through. Sydney relayed all the information to your headquarters and they said your message got through and they were able to isolate the virus before it could cause any real damage."

"Well, we can't thank you enough," Murphy said as he looked at Sarah and Crawford then raised his glass to Watson's in a toast.

"Here, here," Crawford and Sarah replied as they all raised their cups. The feast continued with everyone eating and laughing and getting to know the real natives of the island.

As the celebration began to wind down, Sarah noticed that Murphy was quiet and she went over to him. "What's wrong, Dallas?"

"I don't know, maybe this really was Shangri-La."

"What do you mean?"

"Look at this place. The first banquet we had here, the food was just as good and exotic looking but this time instead of grass skirts and leather armor, the native have on Nike tennis shoes, Hawaiian shirts and walking short. Maybe this was Paradise Lost."

"Wow, since when did you become such a philosopher?"

Murphy chuckled. "Being in a tiny raft in the middle of the ocean tends to humble a man and make him think about things, you know?" He paused for a moment then picked up his plate. It had a design different from the ones that Hoku had used earlier, but it still looked like an original from Diablo Oscuro's collection.

"I can't believe the lengths Hoku went to con us. He even knew I was a history buff and was fascinated by the pirate Diablo Oscuro."

"He had to. With the stakes as high as they were, they had to do their research and get everything right down to the smallest detail. They had to know what lures to use to make you bite. Who could have guessed that the treasure was really here?"

"Speaking of lures," Crawford said as he came up and sat down beside them, "while you two were out on your little joy flight, I had a chance to look at the pendants that you gave me from Kekao. Remember how you said that the ones that Kekao gave us actually attracted the panther and the ones the natives had were a repellant and how you switched them when the cat attacked?"

Murphy nodded, "Yes."

Crawford smiled, "I hate to tell you this, old buddy, but you switched the wrong one."

Murphy looked puzzled. "What are you talking about?"

"You gave Kekao the repellant one and kept the one that attracted the cat."

Murphy looked stunned. "But the cat...it attacked Kekao, not me..."

Sarah smiled. "Fate protects fools, little children, and sailors named Murphy."

"Speaking of fate," Murphy said, "What happened to you? Why were you so late with the attack signal?"

"There almost was no signal," Crawford said as he rubbed his jaw. Thing One found me and Ru and I tried to stop him by hitting his fist with my face. Ru managed to fire the musket point blank at Thing One. The flash blinded him and I was able to club him over the head and knock him out."

Murphy nodded in approval. "Good job."

"Miss Price, Mr. Murphy, Mr. Crawford," Watson said as he came walking up, "my crew and I will be heading back to the ship now and we'll be sailing with the morning tide back to Sydney. As you know, we suffered some damage in the storm and your company is willing to make a very generous donation towards the repairs to our ship if we can get you back to civilization as quickly as possible. Would you care to come back to the ship with us now or in the morning?"

Sarah looked up and smiled at the Australian. "Thank you, that's very kind of you, but I think I will stay here a bit longer with my husband."

"Very well. We'll see you back at the ship then. Good night."

"*Husband?* Did you say *husband?*" Murphy asked, too much in shock to smile at the idea.

Sarah smiled and took Murphy's hand. "Being in a tiny raft in the middle of the ocean tends to humble a woman and make her think about things, you know?"

"Wow, I don't know what to say."

"Shut up and don't say anything. Just enjoy the evening."

Murphy nodded and put his arm around her and it felt good as she nestled closer. Right now he really was in Shangri-La.

After a few minutes of enjoying the music and staring at the flames dancing in the fire pit, he popped the last piece of fruit into his mouth and looked at his plate again. What a magnificent fake he thought.

"You know, I really wish we could have brought back some of Diablo Oscuro's treasure," Murphy commented.

"What, you want to be rich?"

"No; well yes, the money would be nice, I could really get you that castle you've always wanted, but I was thinking more along the lines of just proving that he was not just a legend and that he really did exist and to finally answer some of the questions about what really happened to him and all his treasure."

"Yeah, but I think it really is all for the best that the treasure is buried in the mountain and remains there," Sarah said. "You know that if word got out about the treasure, everybody and his brother would descend upon this island like a swarm of locusts and devour it, forever ruining these people's lives."

Murphy nodded, "I guess you're right. Still…"

A native girl in her late teens wearing a pink tank top under a white, opened button shirt came up with a plate and offered them some more fruit. As she set the plate down, she noticed him admiring it.

"Do you like the plate, Mr. Murphy? You can take some with you if you like. We have plenty more."

"Thanks, no. The people who took over your island brought a lot with them, huh?"

"Oh, no sir, these are our plates, we have lots of them."

Stunned, he looked at Sarah then back at the girl. "You do? You have more of these?"

"Oh yes," she beamed.

He looked at Sarah again, then asked the girl. "What else do you have?" his mind beginning to race.

"In the back of the cave where you rescued us, there are many crates and boxes and a lot of very heavy chests. Would you like to see?"

THE END

Continue on for a sample of

Arctic Fire

a thriller by Paul Byers

CHAPTER FIVE

Pike throttled back and a brought the *Yankee Clipper* down to 8,000 feet and set the auto-pilot. He reached under his seat and grabbed a sandwich. His stomach was still a little queasy from the dogfight but he was hungry none the less. The roast beef was a little dry so he reached back under and grabbed a fruit drink pouch. He would have preferred a cold bottle of water or tall glass of milk, or better yet, a frosty mug of root beer, but none of those traveled well in his cramped cockpit.

With steely-eyed determination he took off the little straw and prepared to *try* and poke it through the tiny serving hole. He could pilot a fighter jet, decipher blueprints that would drive DaVinci mad and balance his checkbook at the end of the month, yet there were two things in life he couldn't do: figure out what made women tick, and how to put the straw in a juice pouch without spilling it all over himself. After four failed attempts, which were two more than he usually tried, he reached into the shoulder pocket of his flight suit and pulled out a small Swiss Army Knife.

This was one of the more unusual of the Swiss knives; this one didn't have all the gizmos and gadgets: it actually had a blade that he could use. He'd learned from years of experience and dozens of dry cleaning bills just how to open one of these things without getting juice all over himself. He flipped out the blade, then carefully grabbed the top of the pouch with his left hand. With the skill of a surgeon, he inserted the blade into the pouch and began cutting.

The tab was removed and surgery was almost complete; all he had to do now was insert the straw, and enjoy. Just as he was putting in the straw, the *Clipper* hit a pocket of rough air and bounced up and down harder than a Model T Ford on a washboard road. As he bounced, he accidentally squeezed the pouch, sending the straw shooting out like a missile and juice gushing out like a geyser. Some of the juice hit the top of the canopy then started "raining" down in tiny droplets while more splattered on his flight suit, but the majority of it landed in his lap. Pike looked down and shook his head, hoping it would dry before he had to land and refuel. No amount of explaining would curb the snickers and laughs he would get as he climbed out of the cockpit if his suit were still wet. He ate his sandwich and downed what was left of the juice.

There were advantages to having your own private jet to fly in, but there were also disadvantages too, one being boredom. He hadn't quite figured out how to get a stewardess on board yet. He began tuning the radio to see if he could find anything interesting to listen to and help pass the time. He passed over two country western stations, one song was about getting out of prison and the other was about a dog and an old pickup truck. Next, he scanned across a soft rock station that almost put him to sleep on the spot.

Suddenly something up ahead caught his eye, so he decided to drop down and take a look. He leveled off at 5000 feet and tipped his wing down as he did a fly over. There were two high school busses parked on the side of the road with four cars pulled in behind them. Several men were standing around the front of the lead bus while the drivers were working on changing a flat tire. Cheerleaders, football players and students were milling around the busses, cell phones in hand, no doubt relaying their harrowing plight to friends and families.

Pike brought the *Clipper* around for another pass, only this time he came in low and fast. He skimmed over the desert floor at about 500 feet and pushed the airspeed up to 400 knots. Every eye on the ground was watching as he roared by. Pike smiled to himself; this was one of those times when it was good to have your own jet. A couple of the football players raised their helmets and cheered as he went by while several of the cheerleaders shook their pompoms and did a quick cheer. As he streaked by the two drivers gave him a wave and he returned it with a quick salute and waggle of his wings. He smiled as he did a quick snap roll and then pulled up and out. Tom Cruise, eat your heart out.

The small adrenaline rush soon faded and he was back to channel surfing again. He found two rock stations, one classical, a talk show talking about the economy, what else? With nothing he really wanted to listen to, he was about to turn the radio off when the last station caught his ear.

"Breaking news. Police have just reported that the US Bank in Logandale has been robbed at gunpoint. One bank guard has been killed and another teller has also been shot and is in critical condition. Nevada Highway Patrol reports that the suspects are driving a dark green, late model Dodge Charger, and they are in a high-speed pursuit heading north on Highway 93. Suspects are armed and considered extremely dangerous. Anyone traveling north or south bound on Highway 93 between Ash Springs and Las Vegas should use extreme caution."

Pike frowned as an uneasy feeling crept into the cockpit with him. He had all the latest GPS navigational equipment but sometimes plain, good old-fashioned paper maps worked best. He unfolded one and quickly checked his location against his GPS, then turned the *Clipper* south and followed the road, hoping all the while that he was wrong. A few minutes later his worst fears were confirmed. In the distance he saw a trail of flashing lights following about a mile behind a dark sedan moving faster than a bat out of hell. They were on a collision course, heading straight for the stranded school busses. These criminals were desperate men who had already killed, Pike shuddered to think what would happen if they got their hands on a bus full of hostages.

There were only a few minutes before they would reach the kids; he had to do something, but what? If he were in his car, he would have hit the steering wheel out of frustration, since there was no wheel; he did the next best thing and slammed his fist against the side of his canopy. He pulled back up to 5000 feet and swung back to the north, towards the buses. Time was running out, and he still didn't have any ideas of what he was going to do and he could only hit his canopy so many times. What could he do? It's not like he could dive down and strafe the bad guys...or could he?

Suddenly, the seed of a wild thought was sown. He knew he should have stopped and torn it out by the roots, but instead, he watered it with desperation and a plan soon began to flourish. Quickly he found the busses and surveyed the surrounding area. The vehicles were behind a small outcropping at the top of a slight rise. Pike banked hard around and saw the suspects coming up over a small hill. Soon they would drop down into a large, shallow draw. It was perfect.

He would probably lose his pilot's license for this but he couldn't stand by and do nothing. He pushed the throttle forward nearly to the stops and brought the *Yankee Clipper* out wide and flew down the middle of the draw, heading straight for the bandits' car. He concentrated as he flew down the draw, keeping a careful eye on the altimeter and air speed indicator as he put the plane in a shallow dive. For a moment he had visions of himself as William Holden in the movie *Bridges at Toko-Ri* or as the young Luke Skywalker as he focused on lining up on the car. He swore that if he heard the words... "Use the Force Luke," he was bailing out. The *Clipper* quickly gained speed and reached 600 mph in a matter of seconds. He was down to 2500 feet and still descending, still picking up speed.

The bank robbers had widened the distance between themselves and their pursuers to nearly a mile and a half now; timing would be everything. Pike continued to dive and was at 1500 feet and pushing 725 mph, just a little lower, just a little faster. At a half-mile out, he pushed the throttle to the stops and nudged the stick forward.

His hands were sweating and he could feel his heart racing, pounding out a beat that any punk-rock band would have trouble keeping up with. His mouth was dryer than the sands of the Nevada desert below and forget about even trying to describe how his stomach felt. Was this what it was like to go into real combat? Playing tag with the F-15s earlier had been fun and exciting, but nothing was really at stake, no lives to be saved or lost, only pride and egos, but this was different. Here, now, there was a very real threat, with the very real possibility of lives being lost, not only to the kids if they were taken hostage by the murderers, but to himself. One wrong move, one mistake at this speed and altitude and he wouldn't even have time to say "Oh crap" before he would plow into the desert floor.

Just before he reached the car, Pike took one last deep breath and leveled out at 500 feet and watched as his air speed reached 767 mph. That's when it happened.